CASSIE SWINDON

The Never Hour

Copyright 2024 by Cassie Swindon

All rights reserved.

No part of this book may be reproduced in any form or by any electronic or mechanical means, including information storage and retrieval systems, without written permission from the author, except for the use of brief quotations in a book review.

ISBN paperback: 9798334312791

Cover Design by: BZN Studio Design

Binding Design by: Liz Heaven of Raven Pages Design

Interior Formatting by: Jennifer Laslie

Editing by Kristen Breanne

This work is fiction. Names, characters, places, and incidents either are the product of the author's imagination or are used fictitiously. Any resemblance to actual persons, living or dead, businesses, companies, cities, or events is entirely fictional

Dedicated to:

The young at heart

ALSO BY CASSIE SWINDON

The Linked Trilogy

Scorched

Severed

Shattered

The Golden Chains Trilogy

Break the Stone

Hunt the Storm

Stop the Clock

The Fairy Tale Flip Series

The Wicked Blue

The Phantom Ink

(The Never Hour)

Upcoming

Of Witches & Men Series

Of Poison & Pumpkins

Of Venom & Vineyards

Of Toxins & Teacups

*please note that prequel short stories are available at

www.cassieswindon.com as teasers*

Acknowledgments

Thank you to so many who show your support to myself and other Indie authors. You're making our dreams come true.

To my production team, thank you! I have an awesome group of editors, proofreaders, designers, artists, and formatters who make this story a reality. Without you, it'd only be a document on my computer. Please check my website at www.cassieswindon.com for a list of all the professionals and how to contact them.

I truly appreciate all the readers who have visited me at author events, shown enthusiasm as an ARC reader, sent me encouraging messages, and even those of you who create your own amazing content inspired by my characters. You make the grueling work worthwhile.

Lastly, there are six main people I fully rely on to maintain my sanity as a creator. Matt, Kyella, Bryson, Aubree, Anna, and Amy Bo. Thank you for everything. You know what you did. (Okay, I'll include you too, Jordi...my grumpy, fluffy helper.)

PROLOGUE

2 Years Ago

Some people are fractured in the most delicate of places. Not me. I'm solid as a tree, thriving and full of life without a care in the world. Speaking of trees, a dozen orange trees with leafy canopies stand proudly in the night before me like guards protecting a castle, or in this case, my favorite bar, Walk the Plank. Ibrahim, the owner, must've planted the oranges for a specialty cocktail this summer.

I shimmy off the last rung of the building's escape ladder and readjust my flowy skirt. The crescent moon blows me a kiss of good luck since tonight's agenda is different than usual. For five years I've visited Kensington once a month for whimsical adventures, people-watching, shopping, and hookups. But this time, I'm not allowed to play. Quite annoying, honestly.

I squint into the window to see if the Venetress has

already arrived. Sure enough, the sorceress sits at a dark booth, reading behind vintage glasses. It's surprising no one is staring at a woman holding a thick novel at midnight, especially with no alcohol ordered. Hopefully, she'll give me the answers I'm seeking.

I'm overwhelmed by the scent of oranges as I walk inside. Maybe the aroma will be forever trapped in the air conditioning vents. In fact, my hair will most likely smell of oranges when I return home.

I check out the dance floor, where the music has seduced fewer women than usual. Probably because the poor DJ isn't playing any songs released after the Fifth Leopard Year. I laugh to myself as one girl spanks another and then accidentally spills liquid all over the floor. I don't envy the poor bartender who'll have to clean the mess. In fact, I can't remember the last time I mopped or wiped anything in my home. Maybe the sprites do my chores? Who cares? Responsibility tastes of poison anyway.

Under the dim lights, I catch sight of a man already walking over to the mess, towel in hand. He catches my gaze and does a doubletake, pinning me with dark brown eyes. I guess he's a new hire. I give the guy a little smile and a nod. He stops in place. And just stares. Goddess Above, he's intimidating. Impatiently, I wait for any type of normal reply, but he gives absolutely none.

I glance behind me, wondering if the man is looking at someone else who just walked in. Nope. In the doorway, only the trees' leaves flutter in the night breeze.

"Piper." The Venetress calls my name from her table and waves me down.

I should walk directly to Zoanne since I have less than an hour to ask her my questions. For some reason, my heels are stuck in place. Little flutters twist in my stomach in that strange, unreliable way.

"Piper?" Zoanne calls again. "I'm over here."

I ignore her and drink in the intensity of the man's energy. What in the Abyss is going on? Why is he staring? One of the dancers bumps into him and then presses a hand against his broad chest. Smiling up at him, she's obviously saying something flirtatious and ridiculous, even though I can't hear it over the music. While her lips move close to his ear, his eyes are still lasered onto mine.

What an odd duck. Maybe he's daydreaming? I wouldn't blame him. Dreams are my favorite place to live. I shake my head and walk over to Zoanne in the booth.

"Hey, sorry about that," I say and place my baseball hat on the table. Most people wouldn't wear a skirt and cap together, but most people also don't talk to sprites and mermaids daily.

"No problem. I know you said you only have an hour, so do you have the payment?"

"Yes, but first, guess what I'm thinking, Zo."

A fake smile quirks her lips and she tilts her head to the side. "Um, I go by Zoanne."

"You're no fun. Fine, here's your payment."

I slide a pouch that holds a rare valuable powder

under the table into her hands. "Do not tell anyone about this."

Zoanne nods as she grasps the bundle and slips it into her bag. "Okay, what do you need to know?"

"Does it help if I give any background information first?" I tap my fingers on the table and glance at the clock.

"My gifts aren't pure science, but yes, if you give me some basic knowledge, it'll make the pieces of the puzzle fit more clearly. And you can only ask two questions, so phrase them specifically."

I try to concentrate on what exactly to ask but that same bartender is burning a hole in the back of my head. Who is he? When did he start working here? Why is he staring at me?

Focus, Piper. "Okay, so, you know I live in Neveraj," I whisper, "And you know its life source is Pixie dust."

She nods, her purple eyes wide. "What's it like there?"

"Imagine the warm suns on your skin and sand under your fingernails. The gritty texture also coats your knees as you dig a hole. Wiggling inside, you find that the hole leads to a tunnel. Crawling is the only way to get through to the other side," I pause, trying to read her expression. "Have you ever seen a tunnel made of silk? Or a cake made of sapphires? I have. Neveraj is where stars collide against your fingertips without consequence and rivers of golden dust run down the mountainside. I've seen things you wouldn't believe and heard impossible stories from creatures that shouldn't exist."

Her eyebrows scrunch tight. "I don't...I don't believe you."

"I don't expect any adult to believe me. Well, sometimes I can get off topic, where was I? Oh, in Neveraj, death and illness are rare, but a willow tree died three weeks ago." I cringe at my words. "This wasn't a normal death."

"What do you mean?"

"Shadows...they...overtook the willow. I stumbled across it while flying. One day it was living and happy, thriving. The next time I saw it, the tree was gray, shriveled with a substance swirling over it. The sprites already named the disease RavenSoul. It's spreading. And the tree next to the willow also started to decompose. Last week, I gathered all the sprites and asked them to heal the trees with Pixie. They tried but couldn't." I squint when headlights from a hoverboard pass the window. "So, my first question is..."

"This is it?" Zoanne steeples her fingers together. "You're ready?"

I watch her eyes turn scarlet as I ask, "Why can't the sprites replenish the Pixie?"

Her eyes roll to the back of her head so only the whites show. I clear my throat, unsure how long it will take. Her lips move silently, sharply in the jerky movements of harsh consonants. Then Zoanne's hands slam on the table. I bounce in my seat. Her long fingernails scrape the wooden table in strange patterns and symbols before she gasps and her eyes shoot open, completely scarlet.

"The only safe, natural way to gather raw Pixie is collecting from the Pixie Falls," she says in a ghostly voice that's not hers. "Only raw Pixie can defeat the shadows."

"That's what the sprites are supposed to do? Collect Pixie from the Falls and pour it on RavenSoul?"

Shoot. That was two questions. I've already screwed myself.

"Raw Pixie...magical orbs." Zoanne shudders so violently that I have to lean forward to hold her shoulders still. "Three challenges will be offered to collect orbs. The first challenge gives the prize of the smallest orb, the second challenge awards another, and the third challenge gifts the champion with the largest orb," she screeches as if in pain and ghost-white foam begins to pour from her mouth. "Each contender must complete the challenges in order. They can't return to the beginning until all three are finish—" A strangled choking sound erupts from her throat.

"Zoanne?" I hold her cheeks with both hands and watch her possessed eyes. "Zoanne, wake up."

Her body goes slack and flops to the side. No! This isn't fair. I don't know how to deal with emergencies, nor do I want to. I could flag down someone who might be prepared. I should run. My heart slams in my chest. Shaking, I dig in her purse to find the Pixie I had paid her with. I unzip the container and coat her lips, her cheeks, and her throat with it, leaving extra just in case.

"Come on, come on. Please work."

She lays unconscious on the booth seat, her chest

rising and falling slowly. With her black hair falling mop-like around her, I can't see her face.

"Zoanne?" I shake her, then sprinkle a little Pixie on her neck, then sit and wait. Crack my knuckles.

Eventually, when I'm about to leave, she mumbles weakly and puts a hand to her head. "Oooh, that one was rough,"

When she sits up, the air is torn from my lungs. She's clearly ten years younger. Golden shimmer paints all the body parts I smothered with Pixie, but her features radiate youth.

Her wrinkles have disappeared, featuring someone barely of age to be allowed into this bar. Should I tell her how potent it was? Will she live longer now? Pixie is only supposed to freeze aging, not reverse it. Maybe it works differently on her because she's a Venetress.

"Got all your answers?" she asks quietly, fatigue probably settling in her bones.

Almost. I didn't ask where RavenSoul originated and why it's here. Her gaze rises to something above my shoulder.

Without turning, I can feel the new man's energy fixated on me.

CHAPTER ONE

Piper

2 Years Later

Only a fool considers their future. Tomorrow is just a theory, a day that will never arrive. Why bother with a word like *forever*, when it'll never come? Never—such a strange concept. Yet one Never Hour is all I have, a magical opening between home and the rest of the world.

I sit at the bar in Walk the Plank, which holds the familiar scent of citrus, also splashed into my cocktail. Deadly moonlight slants through all the paned windows, from the high ceilings down to the clock that ticks away much too quickly. I've had a love-hate relationship with all clocks and pocket watches since I put my life on pause.

Because here in Kensington, on this side of The Window, time chases after me. Only fifty-five minutes remain until my opportunity closes. I should be accustomed to the rush at this point, yet distraction is inevitable. The same three reminders, as always, are listed on a crumpled paper in my pocket in case I get distracted. I pull it out and read it to myself again.

1. Get intel about Holland Jameson
2. Seduce a contender to bring home
3. Annoy the Abyss out of Wyshawn

Because a little fun doesn't hurt anyone.

A bartender places both hands on the countertop. "How do you like the Starboard Daiquiri, Piper?"

"Ibrahim!" I jump. "Sweetie, you came out of nowhere."

"I've been standing in front of you for five minutes," the bar owner says with a smile. "You're always daydreaming."

I lean over the counter and wrap him in a half-hug. The strings hanging from my hoodie dip a little into my drink, but oh well. "You know I'd love another drink, old man."

"Old man? Wow, I'm not even forty."

"Well, I've been twenty-nine for a few years," I tease, though he doesn't know I'm telling the truth.

"Well, Wyshawn's around your age, isn't he? Have you ever noticed that he only cuts those fruit stars for you?" His gaze flickers behind me to acknowledge a presence I've already felt. I unsuccessfully try to shake off the tingling of my nerves. Wyshawn is so close I can smell his cologne. I don't dare turn around. "So, what's new, Piper? It's been a while," Ibrahim says.

"Oh, you know me, just stealing another person, like usual..."

Ibrahim laughs. "Always joking around. We need to keep you around to keep things fun."

"Hey, man..." The deep voice that haunts my dreams murmurs. "What did those girls order?"

Wyshawn is about to join us. Quickly, I drop my chin and yank my hood further over my messy hair. It's too hot for this outfit, but I never plan ahead. Maybe he won't recognize me if I freeze and stay silent. Plus, eavesdropping has always been one of my favorite pastimes, even if spying isn't on my list of things to accomplish tonight. My list. Shit, I have to concentrate. Focus, Piper.

"The redhead got the Canary Coconut Punch," Ibrahim responds, "and the rest would all like the Rusty Anchor Margarita."

Wyshawn grunts something under his breath, then says, "I'm working a double shift Wednesday, so don't come in, boss-man."

"Wait, isn't that your day at the center?" Ibrahim's

voice drops quiet. "I've been waiting on your insider scoop about the Pixie rumors. Hear anything yet?"

My knee jerks up. It smacks underneath the bar. Pixie powder? Here? How? When?

"Pixie isn't real." Wyshawn's chuckle rumbles deep within me. "And I only volunteer."

"You'll ask around about Pixie when you're there next though, right?" Ibrahim asks.

Wyshawn sighs. "I dunno."

"But just imagine…a world with an anti-aging drug. That'll change everything."

Pixie can't ever cross through The Window again. I made that mistake only once before. It's concerning that rumors are circulating. Who would have access to it?

Delicious chords of a banjo from across the room distract me. From the stool, I scope out the bar, searching for someone from out of town. In the open-concept room, everyone is visible in one sweep. In a booth, two guys sword-fight each other with straws. They're too young to take, probably a decade shy of my twenty-nine.

A beautiful woman struts by. I scan her head to toe. Nope, she's wearing a wedding ring.

The sorority girls huddled near the graffiti wall are way too trashed to consider taking one home. I need to find a mark balanced between coherent and easily persuadable.

Next to me, the older gentleman technically could work, but he looks a bit depressed. Since I'm stuck with whoever I choose for weeks, I need to at least tolerate their company. Plus, since playing *'adult'* games is preferable, I'd want someone to flirt with at least. Nothing serious would result from my shenanigans of course. Relationships are never an option since I can only afford feelings on a budget. My dream Partner lives within books, crafted from fictional characters. They're all I need. Especially since a make-believe Partner can't disappoint me. Another great reason I live far from society.

Maybe this will be one of the nights I don't find a contender at all. Ugh. I wish upon a star that someone would walk in like a miracle, someone who has the potential to beat all three challenges. I'm tired of all my choices failing month after month. At some point, a competitor has to win the prize necessary to save my home. Recently, the shadows have been growing too quickly, infesting more wildlife daily. If I don't find a way to restore the Pixie supply, I won't have a home for long.

I glance around once more, hoping I missed a traveling businessman.

Instead, I meet eyes with the only downside to this bar—a sulking, six-foot brick wall who is mixing drinks behind the counter—Wyshawn S. Darl. Softly, he hums to himself, low and deep, like a storm rolling in. He's got some nerve to glare at me so intensely. I match his stare while sipping my fruity cocktail, letting the pineapple taste wash over my tongue. As usual, Wyshawn created another delicious drink, decorated with his signature, cut out in the shape of a star. I'll never admit to him how much I love the unique touch.

The banjo player misses a note. I follow a hearty

laugh to the stage and notice a man dressed in Ozaron fashion, bellowing the lyrics completely out of tune. It doesn't look like he lives locally. It's my one strict rule; don't take a local to Neveraj. Goddess above, he's completely boisterous, so vibrant, and proud. Perfect. I've found my mark.

"Aren't you hot in a hoodie?" Wyshawn asks. "You can stop hiding under there."

I drop the hood, refusing to let my cheeks flush this time. His eyes, darker than the deepest corner of Cannibal's Cave, hold secrets, ones I never wish to know. Well, maybe I'd be satisfied with just one.

From Wyshawn's dark brown complexion, others might assume he's from Runlose, but I happen to know he was born and raised here in Kensington, not that I remember anything else personal about him. Swallowing my nerves, I slide my fingertips over the spot where my dagger is sheathed on my upper thigh. It's not that Wyshawn is dangerous. He just always has this uncanny way of making a shiver scrape up my spine.

"On the prowl again?" Wyshawn's voice should be illegal. Its smooth texture glides through my core like liquid chocolate. No one should sound that delicious.

I finish my cocktail and return his glare. A flicker of something new shines in his eyes, a challenge. That can't be right. Wyshawn is the epitome of boring predictability, flat stability, responsibility, and all other 'adulting' characteristics. He's a man who lacks enthusiasm, creativity, or passion, and who has somehow lost his inner childhood dreams. Those traits terrify me, so I've chosen to keep my distance in case they're contagious.

Even the way he currently wipes the bartop in the same pattern as always proves his rigidity. It's hypnotic though, his big hands rhythmically moving back and forth, left to right, with the perfect amount of pressure applied to not create streaks. Back and forth like a goddess-damned disgusting art form.

"Why were you hiding?" He flips the bar towel over his shoulder. "Tired of Venus already?" He points to the dance floor. "I saw you with that chic last month."

I clear my throat. I'm not discussing my make-out sessions with Wyshawn, of all people. How is it that he happened to be here the same night I was last time? And the time before that? And come to think of it, each and every visit I've made to Walk the Plank.

His studious expression adds to my annoyance. His only saving grace is how much he cares for his parents, the one thing we have in common. I've happened to overhear how he pays for his mom's long-term care at the local senior center. The poor woman has lost half her memory and she's not yet fifty-five years old. Devastating. If doctors somehow got a handful of my Pixie, his mom's life could drastically change.

"It's rare to see you so quiet," he says.

I want to ask Wyshawn a hundred questions about his earlier conversation with Ibrahim. Well, I would, if he were literally anyone else on this planet.

"I guessed your middle name since last month," I say, purposefully changing the subject. "I already ruled out

Wyshawn Scrupulous Darl and Wyshawn Scathing Darl. So how about Wyshawn Scornful Darl?"

He always takes way too long to answer, often deciding to simply stare at me and stay silent, to infuriate me no doubt. For some reason, I wait on pins and needles anyway.

"Not Scornful? Darn. Well, anyways, I need your help with something," I say casually and slide a ripped picture of Holland over the sticky counter.

To this, his brows rise. "Who's this?"

"Have you heard of Holland Jameson?"

"Nope." He leans closer, both forearms resting on the bar. I hate that I get a whiff of his cologne. In this humidity, the scent is hard to describe, but I would bathe in it. Not because it's Wyshawn's but because it happens to be scrumptious. Does he put it on before or after dressing?

I shake away the intrusive thoughts of him standing naked in front of a mirror. Maybe the man doesn't even have a home and lives in the closet of this bar. I'm only able to learn personal information about him by eavesdropping despite knowing Wyshawn for two whole years. Well, kind of. Technically I've known him for twenty-four separate hours. One hour a month for two years. He's a practical stranger. A close-minded, stubborn, insensitive gnome who smells good every once in a while. Since I'm so selfless, I can endure little doses of Wyshawn for the greater good of learning about Pixie.

"If you give me any leads on Holland, I'll give you four bars of gold," I tell him.

His jaw drops and he glances around the bar.

"I'm not joking. I need to find her. Do you want me to write it down? Holland, H-O-L-L—"

"I know how to spell. I got it, Jade."

Goddess, I love his nickname for me. This little habit started last year when he pointed out that I'm always wearing something green. The reminder makes me glance down at my current pine-shaded hoodie. I refuse to acknowledge he may be right.

"Yeah, I'll ask around..." He pauses. "...*if* you tell me why you only come here at midnight every thirteenth."

Shit. Hopefully, no one else has been as observant of the pattern. I don't dare look away first.

"Didn't think I'd notice?" The corner of his lip twitches and I hold my breath, wondering if I'll be the first soul to witness Wyshawn's smile. Would it be as devastating as I imagine? "Hold on. You look pissed." He lays his hand softly on mine. "Did this Holland character hurt you in any way?"

A sudden zing shoots up my arm. Holy shit. I sweep my hand out from under his. His head tilts to the side and he opens his mouth to say something but closes it again. Why did that feel so weird? Wait...was that the first time he's ever touched me? I think it was. How is that possible after two years?

"Well, this has been exhilarating," I say over the loud music, "but I have a date to seduce."

Wyshawn's mouth tightens sharper than a whip. "Grow up, already," he mumbles, then turns towards the alcohol bottles.

"I'll grow up the day you learn how to have fun."

Hopping to my feet, I scoot behind women in crop tops and miniskirts, briefly checking each hand for a prosthetic. If Holland Jameson tries to trick me with a disguise, that's one thing she can't easily hide. Maybe she'll stop running one day and face me properly—thief to thief.

I walk by the dancers as they tower over me. How any woman deals with being over five feet tall will always amaze me. As I glide across the room, my hand dips into each oversized pocket and I swipe anything I touch. A string of black pearls. A new Taj device. I don't need one since home doesn't have cell service, but what's the fun in wasting my skill? Maybe Tank will enjoy taking it apart and rebuilding it.

As the current song fades, I stop directly in front of my new target. The stranger's thick hair, dyed dark blue, is tied into a low knot at the base of his neck. I should be figuring out what motivates him, but the only thing I can focus on is Wyshawn's heated gaze scorching into my back. Is it just my imagination? If I turned, would he truly be staring me down? Never mind, I need to focus.

"Your singing was epic," I say to the man in such a fake sweet voice it makes me want to gag. I have to crane my neck high to meet his gaze. "Can I steal you a drink?"

He grins. "Steal?"

"Of course. What's the point of living without fun?"

"I like you." He sets down his empty glass and holds out his hand.

My eyes drop to his watch instead, so similar to the

one my dads both wore. It'll go great with my collection. When I hold out my hand, he kisses the back of my knuckles. I feel nothing. All I consider is the obligation to convince him to come home with me. Only thirty minutes remain until The Window closes and I won't get stuck on this side of it again. After making that mistake once, I'll never do it again. Tank wouldn't ever let me hear the end of it.

"Did you hear me?" the man asks, concern written in his expression.

"Huh?" I slide closer. "I'm sorry. What did you say?"

He smirks and grips my waist tighter. "I'm Cade. You?"

"Piper. You from around here?"

"Nope, it's actually my first time along the coast."

"Great. Single?"

"As single as they come," he says with a smile neither serpent nor sunshine, but something in between.

"I think you're exactly who I've been looking for."

"Oh, is that so?" Cade tilts his head to the side, amused. "And how do I meet your requirements?"

"Well, you still have to answer my next three questions perfectly to pass."

"Sure." His eyebrows wiggle a bit. "Me first. Truth or dare?"

Our sides brush against each other and I don't hate it but there's no spark. Cade is attractive enough with his perfect jawline. I bet his mom was a model and his dad was an orthodontist. Yet, it's hard to trust myself. I've always been cursed with the naivety to find beauty wherever I go. Even Wyshawn has called me out on having rose-colored glasses.

Wait. Why am I thinking of Wyshawn? Sure, he has this exciting job working at a lively bar, but only because he needs money. Other than that single asset going for him, he's too reserved, too orderly. And it drives me insane.

"Dare," I reply easily.

"Yup, we're gonna have fun. I dare you to kiss me."

I rise onto my tiptoes, but still have a long way to climb. He meets me the rest of the way but hovers just over my mouth, giving me full control.

"Not yet," I whisper.

Cade's laugh is a little puff of air that pops against my lips. "Fair enough. Now what are your questions?"

"Would you rather eat a chair in one sitting or get a tattoo that covers the bottom of your foot?"

"Oh, you're into torture. Good to know. Alright, I'm going with the tattoo so I can brag about it to all my buddies," he says with a smirk.

"Number two, if you could go anywhere right now where would it be?" I ask.

"Runlose Music Festival," Cade says. "My favorite band is playing."

"Last. What do you most regret?"

He pauses, searches my face, then smiles again. "Not meeting you earlier."

"Perfect, let's go."

He slides an arm around my waist. "How about that booth? The music is too loud here."

I look to where he's pointing, but it's too far from any exit. This can't be a long sit-down conversation. It's time to wrap this up. "I have a better idea." I stand on my tiptoes to whisper in his ear but he's still too tall, so I pull his shoulder down. "There's a shooting star show tonight," I lie. "Let's go to the roof."

I lead him to the door marked 'Rooftop,' but before we cross the threshold a hand slices out in front of me.

"Uh, dude. I've got it thanks," Cade says to whoever stopped our momentum.

"Not him." That voice. Wyshawn's specific deep baritone slips between the crevices of my mind, marking its territory. I whip my head up to meet his face. For the first time since I've known him, there's wildfire lighting up Wyshawn's eyes.

"Not. Him," he repeats sternly.

"Um, excuse me?" I try to move Wyshawn's hand out of the way, but it stays solid as an iron gate. "You work here, right?" I pretend to be an idiot. "I think someone needs another drink over at the bar, sir."

"They can wait," Wyshawn practically growls. "Piper, please. Not him." Wyshawn doesn't take his eyes off mine.

I don't have enough time to pick someone else. Cade is probably harmless. And if not, after I take him through The Window, I'll have a clan of sprites to protect me.

"Do you know this guy?" Cade protectively shifts me closer to his chest.

I bite my bottom lip as I keep my eyes locked on

Wyshawn's while responding to Cade. "No, maybe he's a new bouncer."

A traitorous part of me feels guilty when Wyshawn's brows pinch together. I'm about to push him aside when a thunderous boom crashes outside.

CHAPTER TWO

Wyshawn

Technically it's not my job to check on the ruckus outside. Yet I would if Piper's intoxicating scent of mint wasn't coiled around my throat like tendrils, suffocating me in ironic bliss. On any other night, I'd break up the fight in the alley, but Piper needs to see reason first, even if she smells like pleasure.

Sometimes I wonder if she has bewitched me. She has a constant glint in her eyes that could only be described as mischievous. I run a quick scan over her body. Of course, her hoodie is green. Green is either her power amplifier or security blanket. Maybe she has seductive magic that is stored in all her green outfits. It fuckin' sucks that she only sees me as a friend. I could tolerate watching her leave with any other decent lucky bastard. What she does with her time and her body is unfortunately none of my business—yet. But *this* guy? Nope. He's always making shady deals with pirates.

"Let us through," Piper says, and I let her push my arm down.

Her movements remind me of a bird, quick and sharp, meant to fly. Knowing she'll hate me for it, I step between her and the door leading to the roof.

"Why don't you live a little?" She tries to spike her words with venom, but I bet anything that brushes her lips tastes like cheesecake.

Her cat-like eyes laser into mine and I savor their emerald gleam, the color of new growth. After she leaves, I'll have to wait another month to see her sprinkled freckles and her dimpled cheek that cast a spell over me. For some reason, her adorable pointed nose has always reminded me of the famous painting in Lacordia's biggest art museum. The piece called 'Freedom' is a strange blend of a young girl and an old woman combined. At certain angles, the viewer sees an image of a child, but in the blink of an eye, the portrait will depict a grandma in her last moments.

Now her gaze stays locked on mine. All I want to do is run my hand through her blonde hair, which often has a feather or leaves spurting out of it.

I check the clock, only twenty-five minutes until she

will leave. Again. Even though it tortures me to see her drag different Partners with her, at least I can keep the creepers away from her.

"Please, move." Piper gently pushes against my chest.

"We have rules. No one is allowed on the roof," I mumble to her.

She looks at me through dark thick lashes and then crosses her arms. She's more magic than woman. "I'd love to see the stars," she says innocently.

"Hey, man, just let us up. It's not a big deal," the guy chimes in, full of arrogance and entitlement, a real piece of work. I know his brand-name button-up shirt doesn't impress her. She's never cared about wealth with her past selections. Sure, it's obvious he goes to the gym, but she's also previously picked people who fit a bean-pole tech-genius stereotype.

It irritates me to no end that she doesn't have a specific type. How am I supposed to analyze her interests if there's no consistency? I've seen Piper take home a woman with pink braids, other Brothers, a curvy woman with hearing aids, the loud types, the wild, the short, the tall, she tries them all. Well, all except for me—not that I'd want her to. Fuck it. Yes, I want her to. I need her to.

I scan the guy she chose again. At my height of six feet, with the same build, we'd be an even match if he threw a punch.

She blows out a big sigh and runs her small hand through her tousled short blonde hair. "Fine, you win. We'll stay downstairs."

I check her thigh to make sure she's carrying her

blade. If this asshole tries anything, she better use it on him. I move like a snail back to the bar, my sneakers squeaking against the sticky floor. Some regulars try to flag me down, but I move slowly with half my attention still on Piper. She stays by the rooftop exit door and lets the jackass wedge her between his body and the wall.

"Hey, Wy," my manager, Ibrahim, calls out above the music. "Wanna...drinking with us?...meeting Venus... Cracked Diamond."

I only catch parts of his question since my head is pounding at the sight of Piper being trapped by this man. I hear her laugh and it sends a shot of toxicity through my veins.

"No, man," I say to Ibrahim while keeping my eyes on Piper. "I need to wake early to fix my cousin's window. She doesn't have anyone else to help her."

"...the gentleman." His brief chuckle gets drowned out by the blender for a bit. "Though, I bet you...won't spend a minute longer there than you need to," he shouts over the music.

I'm not *that* antisocial.

"I meant...another inspecting gig?" He continues to rattle on.

Ugh, I hate that job.

"...offer you full time?"

One of my other jobs as a contract health inspector at restaurants and bars provides extra money to help out my parents. I had nearly quit before hearing rumors that the Pixie dealer meets at bars. If Pixie is real, it could save Mum's memory. With its ability to stop aging, her Early

Onset Memory Loss (or EOML) might slow or stop altogether.

Ibrahim's laugh jolts me out of my plan. "One of these days I'm going to force you to take a day off, man." He shakes his head, smiling. "You'll work yourself to death. When was the last time you did anything for yourself?"

Another loud crash comes from outside, but I'm not leaving Piper alone with that creep. Ibrahim jumps over the counter like the athlete he is and stomps out the front. The band playing on stage misses a few notes. I'm not a musician, but I have an uncanny knack for noticing small details that get ignored by others, which is why the small change in the corner of my eye makes my mind implode. That shithead's hand is running over Piper's ass.

I refuse to be the controlling alpha, the guy who doesn't trust a woman's power, but I have to focus to loosen my clenched jaw.

"Hey! Can I get whatever drink has that adorable little pineapple star like that one?" a customer asks, pointing to Piper's leftover glass.

"No."

"You'd make it for a captain of the sea though, right?"

With tense muscles, I check his outfit, realizing it's Captain Schmee, a pirate who Ibrahim has banned countless times. Fuck.

Heart rate doubling, I take a step to the left to block any view of Piper. At least she's somewhat hidden in the shadows. Her date is harmless compared to Schmee.

"What can I get you?" I grab the closest glass, which will definitely not have the pineapple star I've only ever cut for one person.

"Whatever has rum," Schmee says.

The music screeches to a stop, one instrument at a time. Another four men walk in, all wearing Captain Schmee's famous colors, black and blue. One of them rips the accordion from the musician and stomps on it with his boots. I cringe but don't move an inch while most of the customers scatter out the side doors or open windows.

"You own this joint?" one pirate yells at me as he marches over.

"No."

"Well, who does?"

"Don't see him."

The pirate rushes the bar and reaches across, grabbing my shirt with one hand. "Then tell me where he is."

I play out a dozen scenarios in my mind. Crack the bottle of rum over the counter and slit his wrist with it. Duck below the bar and open the hatch to the escape tunnel. Flip off all the lights. Slam his hand in the blender until his bones crunch and split. But I can't do any of them. Because of her. I can't risk a scene or a fight with Piper close by.

"If I knew, I'd tell ya, man. But this might work out better. He's a damn asshole. Here, let me open the register for ya and take whatever. He deserves it." I slowly move toward the piles of cash, but only because it's where we also store our lasers. If I'm quick enough I can shoot him straight between the eyes and fry his brains.

"We're not after any coin." Schmee raises his own laser to my temple.

Shit. I raise both hands.

"We're here for the Pixie."

They must be joking.

"Ibrahim?" I shout into the near-empty room.

The pirates laugh and move forward into a semi-circle around me. The only thing that stands between me and them is the bar. I have tons of shit back here I can chuck at them. I eye a knife we use to chop lemons.

"Don't think about it, Mr. Darl."

My name on Schmee's tongue paralyzes me. My whole body shuts down.

"That's right. We know who you are. I've been keeping an ear out. You're the one who shows up at every single bar on this coast." He shines the laser light onto my skin so I can feel its heat, but doesn't push the activation button...yet. "What have you been doing at Lady Corsette's, huh? It wouldn't happen to be dealing Pixie, would it?"

"Uh..."

"Look, mates, he doesn't even know how to lie," one laughs, then throws his dagger at a dart board across the room.

I swear under my breath. It landed only feet from where I last saw Piper standing. Has he spotted her?

"And that's not the only place you've been," another

chimes in. "Someone made a deal at Blindman's Bluff last night. Who do you think that could've been? We have your face on the security camera footage."

Schmee moves the laser lower until it shoots light onto my collarbone. As if in slow motion I watch his finger flip the switch. Scorching pain seers into my skin as he quickly draws a line of heat across my shoulder. My eyes water from the agony. My body sways. There's no need to glance down when I can smell the burnt flesh right under my nose. Black spots appear in my vision. I focus on slowing my breathing. Easing my heart rate. Loosening my muscles again. How do I get out of here?

"Rethink that answer, Darl," Schmee growls. "Who dealt Pixie at Blindman's?"

His finger twitches again and I brace myself for the torture when a scuffling sound comes from my side. Someone launches towards me. Before I know it, Piper is standing on the bar, like a badass. Ballsy move. Reckless but gutsy. The pirate's laser zeroes in on her thigh instead of my head.

"It was me," she says, staring them all down like a huntress ready to strike. "I used his name. I've been dealing Pixie for months."

"Get down," I roar at her and reach to swing her down. "She's lying. It was me."

Schmee grabs her first. "Tie them up."

CHAPTER
THREE

Piper

These filthy pirates stink like pesky foxes who rolled in mud for simple shits and giggles. At the opposite end of the rope line, two pirates pat down the first prisoner. There are only five others before they get to me. I turn away and keep my head down. Rough hemp from the rope digs into both wrists that are tied behind my back. Each time I try to loosen the knot, it goes taut around my chest and arms too. Even though I'm starting to sweat under this stupid hoodie, at least the layer protects my skin. Poor Wyshawn is wearing short sleeves so welts are already forming on his skin from when he's tried to wiggle free. Unfortunately, he's tied so close to me that our hips collide.

"Did it get hotter in here?" I whisper.

"You're worried about the heat? We might die in the next two minutes," Wyshawn says while unsuccessfully wrestling against the rope, quite comically I might add.

Nothing scares me. If one day I die from a mudslide avalanche or while trying to outrun a jaguar, at least I'd go while doing something fun.

"We need a plan to get out of here." His gaze darts to the nearest window.

"Everything will be fine."

"Then why are you wincing?" Wyshawn whispers.

"Be quiet, will you?"

He doesn't know that my charm bracelet has a tiny knife hanging from it. Nor does he know that I'm carefully sawing away at the rope at a painful angle. Back and forth. Right and left. With each saw the rope rips against my skin. Goddess, this hurts.

I check the clock once more. Only fifteen minutes until The Window closes. The best-case scenario is I manage to escape, then still have to steal food and find shelter for a month until I can return home.

At the door, Captain Schmee stands guard, arms crossed over his chest. Two lasers hang from his belt loop.

"We have to find it before Jameson does..." one of the pirates grumbles.

I stifle my gasp and lean towards their conversation,

a thousand questions rushing me at once. Could they be talking about Holland Jameson? Has that no-good con artist finally returned?

The pirates move on to their second prisoner. If I break free, I may have just enough time to cut Wyshawn loose too.

"Hey!" I kick his shin slightly, making sure it won't bruise. "Why did they say your name before? The pirates were clearly looking for someone named '*Darl*.'"

"I'm surprised you even know my last name," Wyshawn mumbles low.

My chest tightens. We may not ever see eye-to-eye, but of course I know Wyshawn's last name, and that he rides a Jetonia27 hoverboard and has never owned a pet. And that his two younger sisters, Jeniqua and Mikali idolize him. I've heard enough information to know his Mum, Georgia, is the one with early onset memory loss, and Maram is the one who gave birth to him thirty-one years ago on October fifth of Falcon Year. The details that form Wyshawn fill a useless drawer in my mind—how he dislikes jaywalkers, how he hates when customers at the bar call his long, black hairstyle anything other than micro-dreads. And don't get me started on how the only shows he watches are detective mysteries. Oh, plus, he hates any and all bugs. If I held a spider in my palm, he'd most likely run to Ozaron—without breaking a sweat, I might add.

"Piper, I made a plan," he interrupts my thoughts. "I'll pretend to faint. One of them will rush over, and when he leans over, I'll head-butt his skull."

Next to him, Cade snorts. "That won't work, dude. Just give them the Pixie."

The pirates move closer. My heart rate doubles. We're running out of time.

"They know your name, dude." Cade's tone is the sharp edge of a sword. "Cooperate and it'll all be over."

"Yup. We have proof that you've been to clubs all over the coast." A pirate holds his Taj device that shows a picture of Wyshawn at another bar. A giant neon sign in the background flashes: 'The Cracked Diamond.'

"It's for a different job," Wyshawn says quietly, searching my face. "I'm a health inspector too."

I'm not sure why he's looking at me for validation. His confession doesn't surprise me in the least. It makes sense that Wyshawn has another job as he's trying to support his parents.

"Nice cover," Cade snarls. "I can't believe I'm tied up on my vacation."

I bite my lip as I keep sawing the rope thinner and thinner behind my back. It's almost cut through. My shoulders hitch with each swipe. Just a few slices. I clench my teeth and tear the last fragments apart.

I'm free! Thank Luna Almighty!

Immediately, my shoulders loosen and the sensation returns to my fingertips as a tingling heat. The pirates move on to Cade, patting him down from top to bottom. Pretending I'm still bound behind my back, I start sawing Wyshawn's knot. I don't have to look at his face to feel his energy shift when he realizes what I'm doing. His fingertips stop clawing at the rope and his body goes as still as a statue. It's as if our minds merge into one for a moment. My hands tremble from the rush of adrenaline, making my blade accidentally knick his skin, but he doesn't even flinch.

"Sorry," I whisper when a trickle of warm stickiness spreads over my wrist.

"Keep going."

This is taking too long. I'm about to ask the pirates a question as a distraction when Wyshawn speaks first. "Did you know we once found treasure?"

The second pirate stops frisking Cade. "You did? Where?"

I swallow and take a steady breath like I do before starting all of my stories. "Well, there so happens to be a town on the coastline named Reflier with streets made purely of coins and only coins," I begin, speaking softly so the pirates have to focus to hear. I saw at Wyshawn's rope so damn slowly and continue. "Every adult glues their hard-earned money to the ground at the end of each week. Little by little their road grows longer, stretching to the next town. Their beliefs trap them in fear because, long ago, when a woman stepped across the threshold, she never returned. Her grandchildren still plan to find her, with the coin road leading the way."

"You sound like a child. That's not real!" the pirate hisses and throws up his hands.

"Of course it is, I've been there," I say, just as my knife springs Wyshawn's wrists free.

Wyshawn bursts forward. He slams the pirate into

the brick wall. His skull smacks with a loud thud. The pirate crumples to the floor.

"The fuck?" Schmee yells from the front door, charging at us.

I lunge for a large knife by the lemons. Belly flat against the bartop, I stretch. Can't reach. Stretch my arms farther. Glasses and bottles of alcohol topple around me and shatter as I finally grab it.

Painful grunts, whacks, and thunks all blend behind me in chaos. The shouts tear at my eardrums. Focus, Piper.

When I look up, Schmee points a laser at me. "You!"

I duck. The weapon burns one of his own pirates. Staying low, I rush to Cade. Slice him free. He punches another pirate in the face. Something bangs. No time.

"Hurry! Run!" Wyshawn grabs my wrist and pulls me towards the closest door.

It squeals in protest as he thrusts it open. Cade pushes me aside, and my shoulder rams into the stairwell wall. He darts ahead first. Asshole.

I climb the stairs, sneakers skidding on the slippery surface. Breathing heavy.

"Faster!" Wyshawn booms behind me.

Up. Up. Faster. My footsteps echo against the walls. My legs burn. Check behind me. No one.

"Wyshawn??" I run back down. "You damn, insufferable..." Panting. "Ridiculous man..." Can't breathe. "It's not time to play the hero."

At the bottom, he's trying to keep the door pulled shut on his own. Every muscle in his arms swells tight.

Loud hammering pounds on the other side, then Schmee's voice explodes. "Give me the Pixie!"

"Come on!" I gesture for Wyshawn to follow, knowing he won't.

His face twists as he screams, "Goooooooo!"

Stupid, stubborn man. I tear my charm bracelet off. Wrap it around a metal hook and then loop it around the doorknob to lock it shut.

"Wyshawn! Please!" I wrestle his hands off the door and tug him away.

He meets my eyes, fear claiming his expression like a sprite near iron.

Together, we bolt up the stairs. Left foot. Right foot. Chest tight. Rumbling beats strike against the door and echo in the stairwell. Loud hollers hunt our every move. We make it to the second floor. Third floor. Fourth floor. Panting, my quads flare in protest at the top.

I thrust open the rooftop door and stumble into the warm night to see Cade checking the fire escape ladder. Nearby campfire fumes waft through the air. Wyshawn flings the door shut and pushes his back against it, not even a little out of breath. I bend over, both hands braced on my knees as I suck in a deep breath.

"What do we do?" Wyshawn's wild gaze glances around the empty roof. He runs one hand down his face.

I look to the sky to calm my racing heart. Even my precious stars cry out for us to hurry. I stare at the colossal forest looming behind the bar. I'm one of the few humans with the knowledge of the magical dome protecting it, disguising it. The rest of Lacordia knows it as J. Roger National Park, its alias. To Wyshawn it looks like thousands of majestic trees stabbing the sky, but what actually hides there is something else—something magical.

"We need a plan," Wyshawn yells, sweat seeping through the V of his t-shirt.

"Why plan when we can fly?" I say, whizzing towards my backpack.

Near the edge, Cade messes with the fire escape ladder, which is broken, and also pointless, given the pirates waiting on the street.

"We're going to Neveraj," I say, knowing nothing will go wrong once we're there.

"How about a *real* plan," Wyshawn says with an unnecessary sting to his tone.

"I know what I'm doing."

Except, I've never tried to fly while carrying two people. A bolt of red light from a laser shoots up from street level and burns a leaf off a nearby branch. Cade yelps and spins away from the edge.

"Having fun yet?" I ask, feeling the smile rise on my cheeks as I dig through my bag for my wingsuit.

"How will we get away?" Cade's voice wavers, like he's in shock.

"Fly, of course."

"Fly?" Wyshawn's voice cracks. "How?"

Finally, I find what I'm looking for and pull out my wingsuit. It's mostly black, except for the wings. The green and gold silk of those can't be adequately described with words.

"What in the Abyss is that?" Wyshawn steps toward me and I ignore the magnet pull of his energy.

I whip off my hoodie faster than the pirates pounding below. I quickly step into the wingsuit. The spandex outfit fits over my yoga pants and tanktop like a one-piece bathing suit. Unable to contain myself, I lock eyes with Wyshawn and watch his expression as I push the button to release the wings. His jaw drops like a Hornbill as my wings spread wide.

I'm used to jumping off high ledges, but holding this much weight brings a new element of danger that makes it that much more exciting.

"Come here!" I step close to the edge of the building at my typical launch spot, toes dangling over the side. Pure ecstasy.

"Piper, wait!" Wyshawn sucks in a breath, both arms outstretched towards me.

It's a bit unfortunate that I've never had the chance to explain to Wyshawn what we're about to do. It might make this next part a whole lot easier. There was never a reason to tell him since rule number one has and always will be: don't bring a local to Neveraj, but if I leave him here then Schmee and his crew will either torture or kill him.

"We're going to jump off the roof?" Cade pumps a fist in the air. "Bring it on! Where are the other suits?"

"This is the only one. Hold onto this strap. It's kind of like hang-gliding." I click a latch onto his pants belt loop, then do the same to Wyshawn's.

His eyes widen. "You're going to carry me?"

"No," I pull them both closer to my hips. "I'm going to hold both of you."

"Piper." Wyshawn's voice shakes, and he tilts his head to the stars. "Let's think this through. I– I can't do this."

Any second now the pirates will find a way to the roof. Worse, any minute The Window will close.

"You have to. All it takes is faith and trust," I say.

"No, you don't understand." His throat bobs. "I'm afraid of heights."

"You can be scared and brave at the same time." I take his hand and show him where to hold onto the strap.

"Are you aiming for that tree?" He nods across into the forest beyond.

"Sure." I lie, then reposition Cade's hand on my suit. "Maybe you should both close your eyes."

"Why?" they say at the same time.

I squint into the darkness, searching for the shimmering gold specks of The Window's perimeter. There are only about a dozen left. If we're too heavy and drop too fast, we'll miss it.

"Piper." Wyshawn's whole body begins to shake, "I can't do this."

I pull him a little further over the edge, the front halves of our feet hanging off. Another red beam fires, scorching a branch until it is sliced in half. The whole thing plummets to the earth and breaks in half on the forest floor with a crashing *thud*.

"On the count of three, I need you to jump as hard and as far as you can, got it?"

"Got it!" Cade whoops excitedly.

Wyshawn shakes his head. "No, I don't—"

"One..." I tighten my grip around Wyshawn's waist.

A few of the golden specks framing The Window fade out. No, not yet!

From the stairwell, male voices clamber. Louder.

"Two..."

"Piper, p-please..." Wyshawn stutters.

"Three!"

I leap off the rooftop edge. Right away the suit pulls tight against my body. My wingspan is so long that we should soar. Normally a feeling of weightlessness consumes me. Not this time. Something isn't right. We're dropping too fast. Too soon. We're not going to make it. I can't think. We're too heavy. This can't be happening. No time. My hands reach up instinctively. With one last look at Cade, I quickly grasp the latch connecting his hip to mine and unclip it. He drops through the air like a boulder.

"Fuuuuuuuuuuck!" Cade screams as he falls. Falls. Falls.

I swallow sour vomit down my throat. With only two glittering specks remaining, Wyshawn Darling and I dive through The Window into Neveraj.

CHAPTER
FOUR

Wyshawn

Where in the fuckin' Abyss are we?
In one breath, the scent changes to wet soil. Misty wind whips my face as we dip through the darkness like a diving eagle. It feels like I'm falling into a dreamscape but with terror lining the edges. Where are we? Did I hit my head? The moon drips with scarlet secrets, glowing on a type of tree I've never seen before. There's no way this plant lives in J. Roger Park. Ahead, little lights flicker on and off—fireflies—which don't live in Kensington.

"Welcome to Neveraj," Piper says, her voice peppered with the impossible.

Yes, this must be a reality game because she wears sublime wings, longer than an albatross'. They range from a lime shade to sage to a mossy green and blend in perfectly with the landscape below.

I've purposefully avoided looking down until now. Please land. Please, please. We're going to crash. I'm going to die. The ground hypnotizes me; all I can do is stare at my impending death site. Which is where?

Jungle is the only word that fits the scenery that has devoured us. Thriving and untamed, the trees have the pulsating energy of a living, breathing soul. The abundance of thick flora is so rich it belongs in a painting. Even at this late hour, birds of all shapes trill and cackle. Piper calls back to them, or am I hallucinating everything?

I glance over, trying to decipher the look of joy plastered on her face. Is she delusional? Am I? Did she slip me a drug and now we're riding a high together? Wait, where's that second guy?

We swerve lower. A warning flares in my gut but I simply hold onto Piper tighter. I've never been this close to her, never felt her heartbeat on my skin. I'm torn; half of me wants to savor this moment, and the other half is about to pass out.

Ahead, branches jut towards us like spikes, but she dodges them all.

"Weeee!" Piper squeals.

No, no, no. Please land. Land on the damned ground.

The ground! With the fluidity of a hawk, she eases onto a long branch, folding her wings at the perfect moment. As she flutters to a soft stop, I stumble and almost topple over the other side. Thank goddess I'm still connected to her wingsuit.

After a few clicks of a button, her wings disappear into her back. For my sanity, I ignore the spandex suit and the way it hugs her curves. She strips the suit off one limb at a time, revealing her black yoga pants and a green tanktop. Green. That woman is always wearing something green. Is her underwear green? Don't think about that. Stop picturing it.

Once we're no longer connected, I immediately grasp the trunk and clench my eyes shut. I grip the bark so tightly that it digs into my arms. Take a deep breath. It'll be okay. I can climb down one branch at a time, then we can go home.

"Well, that was a first," Piper sounds giddy. "You've earned your wings, Starling."

"Starling?" I peel one eye open, disturbed by her lack of awareness that I'm about to have a panic attack thirty feet in the air.

"Yeah, your middle name starts with an 'S,' so that's probably it. The only other 'S' birds that came to mind were snowy owl and swan but I wouldn't want to be offensive, given that—" She gestures to my face.

"That I'm black."

"I was going to say a natural singer," she says, skimming her fingertips against my throat. I can't lie—her touch sends a pleasant shiver up my spine.

"So, you went with a bird of song? What about one of logic and structure?" I ask.

She laughs, a little sound that zings through my veins, then says, "Well, you sing beautifully."

"I don't sing."

"Okaaaaay," she says sarcastically. "You definitely *never* sing or hum behind the bar on the nights you're in a good mood."

I pause, wondering when I had ever hummed anything in front of her. Sure, when I'm relaxed at home while cooking or with my parents I may sing sometimes, but never in front of others in public.

Suddenly, an unsettling scream bleeds through the night air. Piper shifts closer to me on the branch. "We need to get lower," she whispers, "You should stick close. Predators live out there, hiding amongst the trees. We don't want to wake them."

My hands cramp but there's no chance I can pry my fingers from the trunk.

"If you ever let a Tilsdoon corner you, it'll be the last thing you see." She starts her descent as if it's nothing more than hopping on a playground.

"Has a creature ever attacked you?"

"I'm here, aren't I?" Her bubbly voice fills me with comfort for only a moment.

"Where exactly is *here*?"

"I already told you. Neveraj. And you're welcome for saving your life, by the way."

The jungle hisses, holding creatures I don't want to

meet in the dark, more deadly than the pirates back at Walk the Plank. I may be seeing things, but I swear, these trees lean toward our conversation as if eavesdropping. I bet they keep secrets better than the potion seller on Main Street.

With each passing second, Piper moves lower. I have no choice but to follow her or I'll live in this tree for the rest of my days.

"Great, so we'll walk back?"

"Nope. Not until the next Never Hour."

"Are you making things up as you go?"

"Of course. Aren't we all?"

"This isn't funny. I need information, Jade."

She sighs. "Time is different here, but when the stars align, in about a month, The Window will reopen and I'll take you home. In the meantime, just relax."

I'm floored. A month? There's no way I can wait that long. *This isn't real. Wake up.* My alarm must've been silenced. Mum and Mother are expecting me to visit the geriatric center this morning, I can't be late. There hasn't been a single instance where I haven't shown. I wouldn't dare worry them when they already have enough to deal with.

When I open my eyes, my blanket will be on the floor like always, and the clock on my microwave will read 6:22. I shake my head for good measure, then slowly peel my eyes open again.

Endless green still surrounds me in a dome of plant life. Right and left. Ahead and behind. I swear the trees are watching me, betting on my next move. Once my feet hit the ground, the breeze carries the scent of ripened blackberries to me.

"We need to find a way home *now*," I say as I jog to Piper on shaky legs. Even the dirt underfoot groans like a living being.

"No can do."

"Wait, Piper, I have questions."

She smirks, then sidesteps me. "I thought you might say that, so here's a story."

"I don't want a story."

"Everyone loves a story." Piper jumps atop a seesawing log. "So...there are a set number of trees on this planet, no more or less than the exact amount that exists. Some are magical trees, which only live in one location."

"What does this have to do with anything?"

"Ssh," Piper waves my words away into the breeze and hops off the log like a careless child. "As the legend says, a fisherman from centuries ago named Jordi McForty's life ambition was to find the legendary magical trees. He had heard of them from merfolk myths passed down through generations. But one day, while fishing for his son's dinner, Jordi lost his legs in a boating accident. Depressed, he abandoned his dream to find the trees and focused on raising his son. When old age caught him in time's endless game of tag, Jordi passed the story to his son. Overcome with awe, the son sold their home and bought two tickets to Lacordia. Arriving in the city of Kensington, he pulled his father on a wagon for miles until they reached the forest that looms behind the bar." Piper hops into a mud puddle and squishes her shoes around. With each pivot the mud sloshes and schlucks against her sneakers. "Patience is like ice, Starling, so listen. Jordi McForty recognized the glowing trees from the legend. The son pushed the wagon through the threshold. Jordi disappeared into the dome. No wagon and no father. The son smiled and followed, unaware that they had the story all wrong." Piper goes quiet, and of course, I lean in to hear the rest. Randomly, she flings out both her arms and spins like a helicopter. "Don't you simply adore the taste of promised rain?"

All I can do is shake my head. A thousand comments lie on the tip of my tongue followed by several questions catapulting in my mind like cannonballs. Instead of voicing them, I'm transfixed by her complete glee. She looks like someone who won the lottery, while at a carnival, experiencing her first kiss, while coated in golden moonlight. She's like a glorious Venetress enchanting me.

"Um, Piper. I can't stay here."

Instead of a reply, disembodied, harsh whispers rise out of the nearby stream. I squat down to inspect the lush plants and exotic flowers that could be poisonous for all I know.

"Come on, Starling. Crocodile Creek isn't a place to linger." Piper giggles next to me, the sound like sprinkles on a cake.

The little rushing river bubbles with something just under the surface. I step back but am too curious to leave. The bubbles grow larger, multiplying. My hand juts out to keep Piper away. Slowly, rings ripple and I hold my breath, waiting for the monster to attack. A little green nose pokes above the surface, two nostrils sniffing the air. Piper pushes past my arm like I'm made of tape begging to be ripped. "Epoch! You little demon. I thought I saw you in the orchids. Okay, it's my turn," she laughs. "Count to ten and close your eyes." Then Piper lunges behind a tree without any explanation.

I glance ahead into the shadowed trees and then back at the water. A small, lizard-type animal scurries to the bank and waddles over a rock. Its long, green snout stays open, like it has a lockjaw, revealing a set of dagger-sharp fangs. It doesn't even give me a second look. The animal chases after Piper with its scaly tail wagging.

Hold up. Is she playing a game with a gecko? Or is it a chameleon? This is ridiculous. I need to go home. Yet the only person with answers just ran away.

Damn Piper. She's so unfocused, irresponsible, and clearly immature. I rub my temples to loosen the built-up tension. On the flip side, she's so spontaneous, brave, fierce, and energized—a fireball coiled into such a small form.

I follow the slithering river down the slope of footprints in the mud. Massive leaves crunch underfoot, each one a shape that's difficult to explain, a shape that doesn't fit my vocabulary. I don't quite shout her name into the darkness between the trees. It carries a vow of deadly ambush. My feet sink slightly into the soft ground, and I swear a bud opens into a fully bloomed flower in front of my eyes. No. It's a trick of the light. Nothing can grow that fast.

"Piper, this isn't funny."

"Isn't funny," a low voice mocks from the gloom.

I flinch, then check behind me. No one's there. I wipe my clammy hands on my pants. Should I hide? Or turn back? Every sound is intensified, from the ghostly wind to the eerie midnight birdsongs. Keeping my back along each tree, I rub against the bark so nothing can sneak up from behind. Take one step at a time. My breath bursts in and out. Piper will be right ahead, waiting, probably ready to make a joke about how long it took me to find her. If only I had a damn flashlight. My Taj! I pull the device from my pocket and hover my finger over the flashlight button. No signal. Useless.

Something wraps around my ankles. I gasp and kick. Vines twist around my legs, curling, tightening. I scream and grab at them with my hands. It whistles in eagerness. Impossible. Plants don't speak. They don't think.

"Get off me!" I swat and tear.

A swooshing sound rushes past my ears, ending in a loud *thwack*. The vines fall loose and a small hand tangles into mine.

"Wyshawn, let's go," Piper chirps, "My friends are waiting for you."

The moonlight finds a way through the canopy above and illuminates her cheeks. "Piper, I want to go home." I grip her hand tightly.

"It's time to play another game, Starling." She grins.

"Guess what Lillian looks like. Wait, no, guess Tank's favorite food. Wait, I have a better one, guess Epoch's best hiding spot."

Something in me snaps. I lift her chin, more roughly than I had planned. The trusting way she looks up at me through her long lashes breaks a piece of my sanity. "Take me home," I demand. "Now."

"Can't. The Window to Kensington only opens on the thirteenth of each month," she says, carefree, then leads me through the winding trees. "Like I said, I'll track the stars and let you know when it's time. It could be days or weeks since time is a fickle monster. Once the time between thirteenths took five months to pass on this side of The Window."

"I can't be stuck here."

"A little fun won't kill you. Think of it as a vacation."

"If we're truly here, in this jungle, then why isn't it humid and sweltering?"

"Who uses the word sweltering?" She raises a brow in question.

I wait until she's ready to give me a serious answer, which may be never, since it's Piper after all.

She finally sighs. "If anything doesn't follow natural laws here then just blame it on magic. Easy enough."

"You don't want to know the real answers?"

"Why bother?"

She's my best chance at surviving the night so I march along, trying to create a decent plan. There must be a way to get home. Mum and Mother count on me. I can't just disappear. What will happen to all my jobs?

Who will pay my bills? Exhaustion anchors my steps into the mud. What time is it anyway? How long have we been zigzagging around lethal barbs and toxic flowers? The moon hasn't shifted in the cloudless sky even a bit. At least the temperature made an impeccable choice, not a degree over or under seventy. As a master of my thermostat, I'd obviously know the difference.

I yawn. It's got to be past two a.m. by now. Piper looks back at me, snorting through a laugh. Her face is rosy from the trek and a playful pinch teases the corner of her mouth like a wicked kiss.

"Come on, Starling, we're almost there."

Little balls of golden glitter flitter and float. When I squint, they resemble the fireflies I saw earlier. At least when I finally wake from this disaster, I'll have a memory of her giving me a nickname I like. As well as the X-rated imagery of skinning that spandex wingsuit off her curves. I hit my toe and stagger over a hidden log. She catches me mid-fall, well, she accepts my body weight as I fall onto her. We land in the dirt, positioning me on top of her.

On.

Top.

Of.

Piper.

Fuck. My hands press into the ground on both sides of her head. Her cucumber-green eyes beam into my soul, twinkling with mischief. For a few violent breaths, I can't move, can't breathe. My heart spasms under my ribs. I've thought about this position with her thousands of times. Slowly, she wiggles her hand free, reaches up, and runs a finger over my bottom lip.

"Like what you see?" she asks, her cheeks flushing, her gaze exploring, dipping to my chest.

My dick is hard in an instant. Can't let her notice. There's no time for this. I gulp. I'm about to roll off, but she arches her back and wraps her legs up around my waist. Damn it all. Damn her.

"Jade," my voice sounds strained, strangled, out of control, "you better know what you're doing."

"Look up," she whispers, amusement lining every syllable.

"What?"

"Look. Up." She nods, watching my face intently.

So, I do. My jaw falls open and I fix on the sight above, where a crooked sign reads: 'The Hidden Gem.'

A fantastical treehouse is perched high, more tree than home. Purely made of magic, for what else could have created such a fortress? It steals my breath. Making the worst decision of my life, one I'll always regret, I roll off Piper and stand. I tip my neck back, not taking my eyes off the castle in the trees. Planks, maybe from a shipwreck, form the walls. It looks like a child's fort on steroids, with fish netting draped over one side, plus feathers and fur decorating the details. Little windows, crooked and small, wrapped in ivy, open to the inside.

Intricate carvings scrape out the exterior of the planks, showing images of birds in the wood. From cranes to hummingbirds to pelicans, dozens are drawn by an artist's hand. Piper may be the bird expert, but at least I know a few species. Thousands of words are etched in endless lines, but I can't read any of them from here.

"I knew you'd like it!" She bounces around me.

In any other circumstance, my attention would be on her face, the smile that lights my darkness. Yet, I can't steal my eyes from the treehouse. Goosebumps slide along the back of my neck. For the first time since she jumped off the rooftop, I feel fully aware and more energized than ever. I wish Mum and Mother were here to see how many varieties of green can paint one place, all distinctly different from each other, yet blending like watercolors on canvas.

How did someone build this? How long did it take? What's inside? Is someone up there? Will it collapse if I climb? Why do I want to explore it when I'm afraid of heights? I rub a hand down my stubbled jaw. Maybe a few minutes of discomfort is worth the risk, to gain answers.

Ahead, Piper stands at the base of one of the trees with the lizard creature balancing on her shoulder. She hovers her hand near the trunk. I realize there's a doorknob when she twists it slowly.

With a sly smirk, she asks, "Are you ready for a tour of my home?"

CHAPTER
FIVE

Piper

We wind up the narrow, spiral wooden staircase within the tree trunk. I never should've brought Wyshawn home. I broke my one and only rule. Every safety net I've weaved could tear apart if he blabs. But because Cade, '*stayed behind,*' I need Wyshawn. I can't wait a whole month to find a different contender for the challenges.

Once inside my treasure trove, I tug off my tanktop and throw it into a pile of dirty laundry, then collapse onto the worn-down couch. Maybe the other cushions still spring, but my special spot molds into an exact imprint of my ass. I hold out my arm for Epoch to skitter off to find his next meal. Instead of wiggling under the planks, he crawls across the floor to Wyshawn's boots and sits on his shoe.

"That's weird. He likes you," I say, then lean my head back on the pillow.

I'm ready to crash after the busy night, eager to close my eyes, even if it's only a few hours until the suns-rise, but Wyshawn's silence is filled with intense questions. Instead of meeting his weighted stare, I glance around the room, trying to view it from his eyes. I've never cared about other's opinions when I've brought strangers home. However, Wyshawn isn't a stranger. Suddenly, details I've never noticed stand out—in a bad way.

The sink overflows with teacups, my hook of green hats hanging on the wall is crooked and the jar full of dead bugs near Epoch's empty cage gives a doomsday vibe. Wyshawn's boots brush dirt away from the map that's painted onto my floor. It had never occurred to me to clean until Wyshawn. Reluctantly, I follow his gaze to the large cobwebs in the corners, then to the mile-high stack of journals on a counter, to the table of my most prized collection—clocks and watches of every shape, size, and color, among other stolen goods. My favorite clock sits in the middle, one that has symbols instead of numbers, like a puzzle begging to be solved.

Wyshawn seems in a daze by the wild plants that wrap around a pillar in one of the corners. He steps over the little stems bursting through the cracks of the planks, sprouting little buds. This man is usually the definition of calm, cool, and collected—so why are flowers sending him into a spiral?

"Now it makes sense why she always has leaves stuck to her clothes," he whispers.

At least his attention hasn't yet settled on the shadows curling near my bed—if a mattress on the floorboards constitutes a bed. These shadows that have been slowly overtaking Neveraj are why I've been forced to bring contenders here.

Wyshawn sways on his feet. "I can't believe this is happening to me," he mumbles, then finally faces me. "What happened to the other guy with the blue hair, your date?"

I flip my wrist casually. "He decided to stay back and try his luck with the pirates."

What Wyshawn doesn't know won't hurt him. Hopefully Cade survived his plummet to a road of cobblestones. It'd leave a mark though. Wait, didn't Wyshawn get injured?

I reach into the drawer of the small end table made of a tree trunk and grab antibiotic healing ointment, then toss it his way. He catches it and reads the label.

"Did we go through a portal?" Wyshawn asks while rubbing the medicine cream over his burn.

Ugh. His curiosity might create a problem. Wyshawn is the last person I want here. Someone who is too responsible won't bode well for me. How will this work? Usually, in the first few nights, if there's a connection, I'll sleep with my contender. It makes the following month so much more bearable if play is involved. This time is different. Sex is definitely not an option with Wyshawn. I won't have an easy release to take the edge off of sharing my space.

"No, it's not a portal. What you think is a park is actually Neveraj in disguise. Ever since the fisherman was swallowed by the trees, a boundary was formed. In Kensington, if anyone strolls to the edge of J. Roger Park, a magical spell makes them turn around and forget their reason for going that way. There's a protective dome over us right now, shielding us from the rest of the world."

"That's not possible."

Anything is possible, like how I've stayed twenty-nine for the last few years. He should be thanking me. Adulting is overrated and he won't age while he's here. My eyes shutter closed and another yawn cranks my mouth open wide as I say, "Sleep anywhere but my bed. I'll answer your questions in the morning."

I hear Wyshawn's swift shuffles move closer and then a thud sound. Groaning, I open my eyes to lock onto his, wide, confused, and a bit crazed. "No, Piper, I need answers. Now. How did we get here? I don't understand."

A cloud of golden specks fall atop Wyshawn's micro-dreads. He immediately closes his eyes and slumps to the floor at my feet. In sleep, his brows finally relax and the soft openness of his lips make me feel like I'm intruding on something private.

My best friend, Tank, whizzes out from behind Wyshawn with a giddy, up-to-no-good smile plastered on his tiny face.

'**Tank!**' I use gestures since sprites only

communicate with hand signals. '**That was epic! Thank you for putting him to sleep.**' I tip my fake cap to him.

As he flips and flits about, his boisterous energy is almost enough to convince the suns to rise early. '**Are we doing the regular plan?**' Tank signs with his tiny hands, no bigger than my fingernail.

'**No, this one will be different. He'll make things complicated,**' I sign.

If he weren't already airborne, Tank's gleeful bouncing would shoot him upward like a trampoline. '**Nothing is too hard for me, Pipe.**' His boyish smile is so contagious that I can't help but chuckle.

'**I know. I have complete faith in you. In the morning, I'll need your help convincing Wyshawn to complete the challenges. I don't think he'll believe the truth.**'

Tank floats in front of my face, waiting for his next directive, but my eyes weigh too heavily to fight sleep any longer. I rest my head on the back of the couch and start naming constellations until life and time fade away entirely.

I know it's a dream from the ethereal glow of the sky. And that I'm voluntarily standing at the opening of Cannibal's Cave— the one place I'd never visit alone. Beams of light spear out of the cave in a way that defies physics. Every thought screams at me to wake up, to snap out of it, but I'm entranced. I've never crossed the threshold of the cave before, ever since Dad and Father warned me of the shadows born within its darkness.

Dad's mangled cry seeps out from the depths, followed by Father's painful wail. I take a step forward, then pause. Once upon a time, I would risk everything, sprint blindly into any opposition to free them. I'm not the same girl I used to be. Two streaks of light dart out of the cave's mouth. I expect a river of blood to dribble down the stalagmites' sharp fang and puddle at my feet. Feet. What a silly word. Feet. I stare at my feet. Stuck in the dirt. Can't move forward to help the men who raised me. Can't run from the danger.

"Dad!" I scream, but no sound comes out. "Father!"

Shadows creep from the cave-like tentacles. Gray and black fog forms into the parents I've lost, but their shapes are all wrong. Dad's nose is cut cold, his eyes calculating instead of soft and warm. And Father's hands are covered in scars and claws instead of blue nail polish tipping each finger.

I can't help. I can't fight. And I can't watch them be taken again. It's better to avoid it all.

I glance between the two floating monstrosities imitating my family. Then turn away.

Wind whips at my face, throwing a blast of leaves and dirt like bullets. I wince and cover my face. When I open my eyes, Dad and Father have vanished, but RavenSoul *remains.*

I awake to the bitter scent of coffee and the sweet scent of camu camu fruit. The same parrots, cotingas, and toucans scrabble outside my east-facing window as usual. I'm about to throw a pillow at them when the sound of glassware clanking together makes me bolt upright. My eyes zip open. Hands grip the dagger strapped to my thigh.

In the kitchen, a man stands shirtless at the counter, with a sculpted back draped in long locks. My heart rate doubles until memories of last night blend together. It's just Wyshawn. My shoulders ease against the couch cushion as I watch him tinker with a knife. Each little slice makes his back muscles flex, and I don't quite mind the view. Maybe I'll make one more rule— Wyshawn can never wear a shirt again.

The thought is arousing yet despicable. An uptight guy like him has no business being in the jungle. He's like a meticulous hawk who hunts little bugs like they're bits of information to be devoured. No, that's a terrible metaphor; he hates bugs.

Epoch appears and settles on my lap. His species is called a Cuvier's Dwarf Caiman, better known as the smallest living crocodile. It's never been determined whether he was born in Neveraj or on the other side, but his Venetress-hunting skills have been helpful in the past.

None of the challenges would be needed if I could steal back the Pixie that Holland stole from my parents. Holland's stash would be a whole lot simpler if I could only find her.

"I know you're awake," Wyshawn says calmly over his shoulder.

Good, he's not as wired or freaked out this morning. Maybe he'll finally thank me for giving him a once-in-a-lifetime experience full of adventure.

Thunk thunk goes his knife on the cutting board. Bulge bulge goes his bicep. Delicious. No, he's not a toy like the others. I can't get distracted this time.

"I'm not awake," I reply, yawning, then scan the room in the morning light. Filthy. Hmm, why am I even noticing?

Wyshawn grunts and begins chopping harder, faster.

Wait, is that attitude I'm detecting? Anger? At me? I saved his damn life. Twice.

"I bet you'll want to shower," I say as I strip off my pants. "It's—"

"Outside, I already found it."

"Oh, good." Something feels off, but I ignore it, a skill I've mastered.

Walking across the room in my sports bra and underwear, I stop at the kitchen sink. In my peripheral vision, I can see Wyshawn's chest now too. His back might be cut lean and strong, but his front impossibly outshines his rear. When he shifts his hair to hang over his chest, I have to force myself to look away. I've heard he's a runner, but wasn't expecting him to be this fit.

"I hate clothes too," I say as I splash water from the sink over my shoulders, hair, and neck.

Water drips. Drips. Drips to the floor. He stills. Turns only his head. He scans me up and down with so much heat behind his gaze that I could ignite like a phoenix. His throat bobs and I'm immediately turned on at the sight. What the Abyss is going on with me? I don't usually get so horny first thing in the morning. Hhm, I've also never seen Wyshawn in daylight. Maybe he's different than his midnight-grumpiness I've grown accustomed to.

"You're making a mess," he growls when his eyes land on a puddle on the floor.

Or maybe he's always moody with a stick up his ass.

"It's a treehouse," I say, holding my arms out wide. "What do you think happens when it rains?"

He chops the fruit harder than a beaver gnaws on wood. Thunk. Thunk.

"I wouldn't know, would I?" he mumbles. "Since you've taken me to a foreign land and are keeping me completely in the dark. It's not like you warned me of the sinkhole down the hill or that there are wild monkeys who like to chase."

I raise a hand to my mouth, trying to stifle the laughter. "Did you try to escape, my Starling? Did you run away this morning, thinking you'd find home?"

His chopping stops and he turns toward me fully this time. "Don't. Laugh. Piper." He points the knife at me. "*You* did this. *You* brought me here. So *you* will explain what's going on. Starting from the beginning. Why do you only visit Walk the Plank once a month? Why do you take a date every time, then return alone? Is this some kind of sex operation? Because I don't want any part of it."

Goddess, he looks good when his chest rises and falls that fast. He notices his raised knife and places it on the counter. I move closer, faking confidence, and run a finger up his bare chest. "You say you don't want any sexcapades...yet you stand shirtless in my kitchen."

He huffs and bites his bottom lip. Interesting. Another new Wyshawn expression to catalog.

"Don't worry, Tank and I will explain everything," I say.

"Who's Tank?"

"Your worst nightmare," I say. "Now put on a shirt."

"Why?"

"Because I said so."

"But why?" he asks.

"Why do you always have to ask a million questions?"

"Why do you always avoid the answers?"

I peek around his side to see what he's preparing for breakfast. The display on the two plates is a bouquet of flavors and colors. Camu camu lies next to expertly sliced passion fruit, sprinkled with berries and bacaba. Crescents of seductive aguaje frame cupuacu chunks, making my mouth water. And of course, pineapples in the shape of stars finish the look, his signature. I reach for my favorite.

He gently slaps my hand away. "None for you."

"What?"

"I'll share one piece for each question you answer."

I nudge him a bit. Apparently, stone walls don't move. Suddenly, all that matters is beating him in this game and grabbing a piece of fruit. I've always been nimble, like a gymnast. Not all athletes have to be large and heavy to be efficient.

I move quickly. Fake-out to the left. I try to swerve around his broad stance, but he's too wide. Blocks me. Hooks his arm around my waist like I'm a child. I grapple for purchase in the air. Useless short arms. If he even considers thinking this is funny, I might do a little stabby stab with that knife on the counter.

"Wyshawn! For Ulsa's sake, just give me a bite."

"Not until you," he starts, but I punch him in the stomach, "... cooperate." The word explodes in a half-grunt.

A little humming sound whirls from outside. I grin, knowing my savior and bestie for life is about to lay the hammer down. Despite how tiny sprites are, they're incredibly strong. From behind Wyshawn, Tank lifts a piece of pineapple, tosses it in the air and I catch it in my mouth.

"Hey!" Wyshawn spins around. "Woah, holy shit, what is that?"

'**Excuse me?**' Tank signs. '**I'm a *he*, not a *that*.**'

"That's Tank. He's a timber sprite. Ever since I moved here, he has chosen to live with me instead of his clan. Don't you love his camo outfit?"

Wyshawn drops his head into both hands. "I wanted this to all be a nightmare, but I've tasted the best damn oranges of my life, seen tropical birds, and smelled something indescribable in the breeze. Do you swear you didn't drug me?"

When he slowly lifts his head and I study his face,

guilt tickles at my heart for just a moment. Maybe I do owe him a little explanation after he collected that fruit and prepared breakfast. Unless he poisoned it first.

"Fine," I say, leaning against the opposing counter. "What do you want to know?"

"Thank goddess." His gaze settles on my bare legs.

"Eyes up here, Starling."

His jaw ticks. "You said a magic window only opens on the thirteenth of every month. Does that window connect this place to Kensington?"

"Yes."

"And we...flew...through that window last night."

"Yes."

"Which means the other times you've visited Walk the Plank, you've brought those past dates here with you."

"Yes."

He frowns and his eyes jump to my bed. Thankfully RavenSoul snuck away in the night.

It's best to keep my answers short. He doesn't need to know that I selectively choose the persuadable or drunk customers at his bar in hopes they wouldn't remember as much of the journey through The Window. Or that I always pick foreigners who have less of a chance to return to Kensington. I refuse to tell him that those I've returned to their life don't know when The Window opens again or how to spot its exact location or that we have Pixie powder that stops aging. He already knows twice as much as anyone.

"Why trick people?" Wyshawn mirrors me by crossing his arms.

"For the challenges." I tilt my head, wondering if he'll also do the same. "Well, a deal is a deal. I gave you three answers. I think you owe me three bites."

Glaring, he slowly reaches behind himself and grips one of the plates. He holds it out as a peace offering in front of us. I grab more than three right before he lifts it out of reach.

"Tell me about these challenges." His brows knit together in a way that makes me want to smooth them out, just to see if he'll allow it.

"I need someone to defeat three challenges."

"Explain."

"You're so bossy." I nibble one of the fruit pieces and savor the juice rolling over my tongue.

"Piper, damn it. Please explain."

I sigh and lift three fingers. "The first challenge symbolizes the past, the second for the present, and the last represents possible futures. The scenarios are different for each person so there's no way to know what to expect. I can't prepare you in any way or help you through them. For each challenge you complete, I'll let you pick gold as payment or whatever you want from my treasure."

"Why?"

"Because you deserve a little reward for hard work. I'm not a monster. Skies Above, you are a pessimist."

He leans closer. "I meant, *why* do you need these challenges completed."

I glance at Tank and sign, '**How much should I tell him?**'

'**As little as possible,**' he replies with his hands. '**Definitely don't tell him about Pixie.**'

"What do Tank's movements mean?" Wyshawn points between us, gaze flickering back and forth.

"He signs to speak. Tank just reminded me to tell you that once you start the first challenge, you have to finish in order...first, second, then third. Once you fail, you're done with that one but you can still move on to the next."

"You're acting as if I've agreed to help in these challenges."

"You're not the least bit interested?"

"No, I just want to go home, which apparently, I can't do for a month, or possibly five, which doesn't make sense." He throws both hands in the air. "Once I've gathered enough food, I'm going on a hike to find another way to Kensington."

"There's no other exit. Don't you want money to take care of your moms?"

He freezes. "How do you know about them?"

"I'm not an idiot, Wyshawn, I pay attention. Listen, the gold I'll give you could let you quit one of your jobs, so you have time to visit your parents."

He's about to argue, but his mouth closes tight.

"See, it's a perfect situation. You're stuck here anyways, so might as well win some prizes, right?"

"How about I just steal your gold instead? Sounds a bit easier."

"And when has Wyshawn Darl ever chosen the immoral way?"

Epoch scurries over the counter by Wyshawn's back and jumps onto his forearm. The man doesn't flinch. "What is this animal?"

"Think of him as a baby croc," I say, smiling, and reach out to offer Epoch my hand. He usually jumps right on but instead cozies up against Wyshawn's skin. Strange.

Wyshawn drops his head back and stares at the ceiling. "Piper, listen, I want to believe you, but your story doesn't make sense. Why are there challenges at all? What do you get out of this? The way you're explaining this sounds like you abduct innocent travelers from their lives, throw them into a secret land with strange rules, and then give them money after an undetermined amount of time. This doesn't add up, you're leaving out details."

"Sure, it makes sense. It's a little something called fun. It's a game. Don't you like playing?"

"No."

'**Figures**,' Tank signs from behind his head and I stifle a laugh.

"Let me get this straight." Wyshawn blows out a big puff of air and meets my eyes again. Goddess they're such a gorgeous dark color. When I'm looking into his eyes it's like into the unknown. He continues. "You expect me to believe that you simply want to watch random strangers go through obstacles for your amusement?"

"You're not a stranger."

"You don't know anything about me, Jade."

My patience is running thin with all his accusations. I step forward and point a finger towards his stupidly perfect chest. "I know that monsters creep between cracks, whether it be between the flesh of a paper cut, or the keys of a piano, or the sliver of time between when you're awake to falling unconscious on your pillow. Many of the monsters wish to bury themselves as deep as possible inside these crevices."

"What in the Abyss does that mean?"

"It's a story, Wyshawn. Use your damn imagination. Stories are what make our hearts keep beating, our lives worth living. Humans and sprites and merfolk alike all crave stories through any form of art. Whether it's paintings or song lyrics or a book or a conversation with a stranger. It's the one thread that connects us, the link between our cultures—the desperation to feel by listening to stories with texture. All you talk about is statistics, boring numbers, and blah blah blah."

He steps forward this time, decreasing the space between us. "Imagination doesn't work in the *real* world."

I throw both hands in the air. "Are you kidding me?"

"Why are you upset?"

"What do you mean, why am I upset? Isn't it obvious?"

"I wouldn't be asking if it were," he says.

This close, his coconut scent washes over me. Damn

it, the man stole my soap. Which I could lick off his pecs. Focus, Piper. Focus.

I stomp forward and we're only inches apart. "This *place* is my real world. It's my home. Just because it doesn't mean something to you, doesn't mean it's worthless."

"We'll talk about this later." He surrenders and tromps out of the kitchen. "So, where am I staying during this captivity?"

"Here. I'm kind enough to share my home." I laugh to myself. "I bet you're thinking we need a bathroom schedule or meal plan to survive."

"Of course we do. A system needs to be set or it'll be chaos." He gestures around the treehouse. "I'll clean this up, but once I organize, you need to keep things in order."

"It's MY house."

"Yes, but am I your guest or prisoner?" He squats by my bookshelf and begins reorganizing.

I don't think I've ever rolled my eyes so fiercely before. "Okay, fine, as long as you don't nag when you find the occasional mess."

"You have books from every genre."

"And your point is?"

"I only read autobiographies," he says under his breath.

"You can't be serious."

"Don't you have one type of story you gravitate towards? It's reliable that way, predictable."

"I need to discover all the worlds, not just one."

He gazes at me and I momentarily forget why I've never taken him home before until he rudely asks, "Then why have you lived here for so long? In one place?"

Silence. He glares. I glare better and longer. I'll win this thing between us because I win at every game.

A knock on my tree door below comes from outside. "Shit, one of my Lost Ones is here."

CHAPTER SIX

Wyshawn

Goddess, I adore Piper way too much. She reminds me of a fairy who leaves cupcakes and sprinkles in her wake, even if a little deviousness laces her edges. The way she pours her stories into the universe, trusting the stars to catch her words inspires me to be more than what I've settled into. Yet there's no chance I'll ever tell her that because I'm practically the only eligible single soul in this universe she has never flirted with. She's probably oblivious to how I feel about her. Would she have brought me here if we weren't under pirate attack?

As she frolics down the spiral stairs to answer the door, I peek out one of the windows. The heights don't bother me as intensely since I'm not attached to a pair of death wings. Below, the front porch—a scuffed patch of dirt—is empty. Only wild trees, arching into yoga poses, bend around the front entrance. I have to admit that this Neveraj place is oozing with otherworldly charisma. Not once before today would I have considered nature to have a soul.

So many descriptions come to mind, but none fully encompass the scene. Slippery, damp, oppressive. This jungle is a predator itself. And wetness is an understatement. The very air is wet. All the foliage is dense with piles of fallen vegetation, mostly banana stalks. It sounds like everything is alive, a noisy symphony of birds and frogs and crickets. The sky boasts its elaborate robin blue shade with a parade of puffy clouds. I have the sense that the dense lush jungle vibrates because of its intriguing secrets. Pops of red, orange, and yellow bloom over there where I collected fruit this morning. I can hear splashes of an animal in what I assume is a stream hidden by vegetation. Hopefully it's not a giant panther. Beautiful birds chirp atop the roof of mossy green. I bet my so-called 'bird expert' would know their names. A slight breeze caresses my cheek, sending the hammock attached to the ceiling swinging back and forth, back and forth.

I can't believe Piper actually lives in this enchanting tree. Out of obligation, I have to hate it here since, number one, there are so many bugs, and number two, I can't return home to help my moms. What would they think of me sleeping in a treehouse last night?

Perusing the interior of Piper's home sends shockwaves of energy through my blood. The main room is as chaotic as Piper herself. A hook of green hats tilts, many about to spill. If they do fall, it won't make much difference, since clothes litter the floor, presumably both clean and dirty, from yoga pants to sports bras, to sneakers. Which reminds me of this morning when I awoke to a fresh set of clothes next to me, exactly my size. What I'm most fascinated by is the wooden dining table covered in random trinkets, clocks, jewelry, and any object small enough to fit inside a pocket or palm. I scan the contents, some valuable, others not. Where did she get all these? Why does she keep them? Then my eyes land on at least fifteen duplicates of a familiar pen with Walk the Plank's logo on the side. I swipe it quickly and hold it up to my eyes.

"Why is she collecting these?" I ask the empty room. Well, not completely empty since Epoch is keeping me company, staring at me from atop a journal. Who has a reptile as a pet? Sure, I love cats and dogs, but a lizard?

The realization crashes down that Piper's lifestyle may be my reality for the next month. I should be furious at her for putting me in this position, but it's terribly difficult to stay angry at someone who saved my life. Twice.

At least she has a functioning kitchen. If I ever did have the chance to quit all my jobs and start over, I'd go to school to become a chef. Piper was right that I'd be able to quit being a health inspector if I had more money. I glance around the treehouse, slowly this time. Where would she keep a stash of hidden gold? Not that I'd ever steal it, but I'm also definitely not participating in challenges. No, thank you, not interested. They don't make sense anyways. How can obstacles be created from my past and future when Piper doesn't know my history? At this point, I'm sure she's not a Venetress.

The tiny sprite, dressed in camo, zooms by my face. Tank is about the size of my hand, which makes his sword smaller than a toothpick. Maybe I should ask him about Pixie, but I must play my cards right. Until I stepped foot in Neveraj, I'd never truly believed Pixie was real. Now, I'm not so sure. Every time Tank has interacted with Piper, using gestures and body language to communicate, his exuberance exceeds any joy my younger sisters ever showed as children. But when he streaks past me again, he shoots me a threatening snarl. What did I do to offend him? I act like I didn't see his glare and tie my hair at the base of my neck with a string lying on Piper's table of goodies.

Soft chatter comes from downstairs. Two female voices. While Piper is distracted, this is the perfect time to form a plan to return home. I've already vetoed the idea of aimlessly wandering around the jungle alone again. It'd be delusional to expect to survive when I'm completely uneducated about this terrain and don't have supplies. Now that I've seen how vast it is, I'm not arrogant enough to believe I can conquer the wild. Quiet sounds creak as Piper climbs the spiral stairs again, someone following in her wake. I reach for the white shirt that had appeared this morning and throw it on quickly.

"Wyshawn, meet my other best friend, Lillian. She's a type of Terra Nymph," Piper says enthusiastically.

I stumble at the sight of Piper's friend. There's no way to describe this new creature, other than a human-shaped tree. Her skin is gritty and textured with flecks of bark and bugs. She smiles at me, and I know I'm staring too long.

"You must be the bartender I've heard so much about." Lillian, tall and slender, stretches out one arm.

Unsure what to do, I glance at Piper, who nods. Gently, I shake the twig sticking out of Lillian with my hand, careful not to snap it in half.

"Hey. Sorry if I'm being rude. I've never heard of Terra Nymphs."

"Don't worry about it." Lillian's voice is lower than a typical female register and sounds a bit dusty as she speaks. "Plus, I'm the rude one." She tracks dirt over the wooden planks as she moves towards the window. "Because I warned Piper not to bring you here."

If Lillian didn't already control every ounce of my attention, she surely does now. "Warn her? What do you mean?"

Piper waves in the air, like it's no big deal, and answers for her. "Lillian reads messages that the rain leaves in the soil. Every month before I cross through The Window she has one terrible premonition or another. Don't worry about it." When she finishes it takes all my effort not to drop my gaze to her cunning mouth.

"What was the message?"

Fascinated, I watch Lillian shed bits of dirt with each movement and wonder how the mess doesn't drive Piper insane.

"The one who fights with a youthful charm will strengthen the shadow and bring us harm."

"Um...okay." I scratch my stubble along my cheek. "What does that mean?"

"I bet you're a nice guy, but you'll only bring trouble." Lillian slowly trudges towards me. "I'm aware you can't leave until the next Never Hour, but it was a mistake in coming here." She holds out a small acorn and drops it in my hand. "Keep this. It'll grant a wish for you when need it. You only get one, so use it wisely."

Unbelieving, I roll the filthy acorn in my hand. "Uh, thanks," I say, then pocket the acorn out of respect and head back to the table of knickknacks.

The women chatter about a garden nearby and I hear the word RavenSoul used as a name. I try not to listen to their hushed back and forth and focus on gathering supplies to create a signal for my Taj. Since I don't have any service out here to contact Mum and Mother, I may as well try to fix that problem first.

Epoch slithers along the table while I grab some rusty tools. Part of me wants to interrupt their conversation and ask Piper the story related to each object she has collected. What do they mean to her? She may be a messy, scrappy princess but she does things with purpose. Why do these random objects have significance? It's probably best that I don't ask. Instead, I should focus on escaping Neveraj.

Using the little dwarli from the table, I twist two ejoks together for the first step of a satellite panel. After a lull in their whispers, I look up and see Piper watching me and my hands at work. I swear she's about to tell me to be careful, so I ease on how tightly I screw the pieces. Her shoulders immediately relax.

"So, she told you about the challenges?" Lillian's mud forms a glub trail behind her as she tromps closer.

I bend down and squint at the ejoks. "I'm not competing."

"Why not?" Lillian's eyes widen. "We've all done them. Not only are they fun, but you learn a bit about yourself too."

I stop my tinkering for a second and glance at Piper. "*You've* done the challenges?"

She clears her throat and moves to the window where red birds squawk on the sill. "Yeah, I've finished two."

"Not the third?"

"There's no point thinking about the future," she says over her shoulder, and my lips long to taste the sweet bird tattoo on her skin. "All we need is the present moment."

"You're scared," Lillian spurts, not rudely but with the heaviness of a repeated debate between them.

"Am not."

"Hey, Jade," I interrupt, with a strange need to

protect her from Lillian's accusations. "What type of bird is your tattoo?"

"A Resplendent Quetzal."

"Why did you choose that one?"

"It's for my dads. They always called me their precious one. The nymphs view the quetzal as the goddess of the air and as a symbol of goodness and light."

I'm in shock at how accurately the symbol represents my Piper. She whirls around again with a wide smile planted on her face. "Let me tell you a story, Wyshawn. I can't quite tidy my mind or my drawers for that matter. They're both often overflowing with the most dramatic stories. In fact, the map of my mind is like a mysterious maze with thoughts of flying distracting me at every turn."

A warmth spreads through my chest at her ramblings. "Sure, I could use some entertainment while I work on this."

"What are you making?"

"A way to contact my family with my Taj."

"It won't work." Piper skips to my side confidently, then lays her hand on mine. "It'd be a better use of your time to try a challenge."

I move my hand out from under hers and sync two metals together. "Go on. Tell me your story."

"If you were told that inside a room laid three buckets, each full of a different treasure, but also cursed, which would you pick? The left bucket would be overflowing with gold, but you'd only be able to speak in lies. The middle bucket would have an endless supply of food pouring out, but you'd never be able to see a family member again. And the last bucket would let you steal someone else's wish. Which would you pick?"

"This doesn't sound like a story." My gaze is hypnotized by her bright, eager, green eyes.

"Of course it is, but first you need to answer."

"I'd pick none. I wouldn't participate."

"That means you'd sit on the bench of your own life, watching it pass you by."

"No, it means I'm not willing to risk something valuable to me." My words come out more harshly than intended because I want Piper to understand. "Truth, family, and selflessness are all important. The prize doesn't outweigh the negatives."

"Spoken like someone who thinks things through," Lillian says, nodding. "I'm rooting for you, but you shouldn't be here."

"Let me finish my story." Piper throws up her arms. "My dads would have picked the gold, which would've meant they only lie." She sighs. "They're a unique pair. When they told me how to find Neveraj, through riddles and puzzles, it took me a long time to decode their message. Their clues led me here. This home is my everything because they wanted me here."

I set my tools down and stretch my wrists. "Is this story literal or metaphorical?"

Piper huffs, followed by a giant frown. I never want to be the reason for her frustration, but it seems to happen more often than not. "It doesn't matter anymore." Her voice drops, making me wonder if they both died. If she's about my age, then they couldn't have died much older than sixty.

"They're far away." Piper drops her gaze and crosses her arms over her chest. "May as well be past the second star on the left."

I'm about to comment that it's in the middle of the morning with no stars in sight, but I don't want to change the subject. I also don't want to just stand here when my body is urging me to hold her in my arms and comfort her. No one full of such life should have to suffer. Piper deserves the suns' eternal light because that's the vibe she reflects onto the world.

"Father loved to knit when he had the time but barely ever finished a project. And Dad was a bird enthusiast, taught me everything I know."

"I understand the difficulty of losing a parent," I admit.

She steps closer, her head tilted. "But your moms both live in Kensington."

Without any clue how she knows that, I nod. "Yeah, but Mum has EOML. Half the time her mind is lost in a fog. Sometimes I want to shake her and scream to rattle her memories back into place."

I stand in silence, staring down at my bare feet. Unsure of how long I wait for a reply, for her to tell me how wrong I am for such a thought, I simply stand and stare. A cockroach skitters to my left and even though I despise bugs, I stay still. Something about this moment, in our living breathing present, tells me not to react, not to move. All I do is breathe. Until Piper's hand grazes my arm.

"We're here now. Not in a memory. What's in front of us is the only thing that can matter, right?" she asks.

"That's not how it works for me."

"Okay, fine. Will you humor me, though?" Determined, she squeezes my hand gently. "If put in a position to choose between three options, could you do it? If you were truly forced to pick, which option would it be? The gold, the food, or the wish?"

"The wish," I exhale, hyper-focused on her touch. "Because I'd simply ask the wish's owner what they originally wanted and ask for that."

"I need you, Starling. My wish is for you to try the challenges."

All I'd ever wanted was to make Piper happy. Now that I have the opportunity I'm going to ruin my only shot.

"No," I say softly. "I'd need more information first. I don't run into the unknown blindly. I don't jump off roofs or forget my past and ignore the future. I'm not like you."

A flash of images from long ago resurface. The soft delicate hands of Mum holding me tight when my sisters were both sick. "I have to stay smart and make safe choices for my family. I don't have the luxury to play around. My mum needs me."

"What are mothers like?" Piper asks, her eyes watering with unshed tears.

"They're...well, they're not all the same. Mine are the

soft breeze that brushes your skin in autumn, the laughs I know by heart, the voices in my head that uplift me when unsure, the ones who call me at my lunch breaks, the scent of yams cooking, the hand that held mine when I was small.

"Mother loves scrapbooking and crafts. Once I brought her to an art festival and lost track of her. Couldn't find her for hours." I chuckle at the memory. "Mum used to be a librarian. She was known around town for wearing a different pair of glasses daily. I'm pretty sure she has over three hundred pairs. The thing is, she doesn't even need them. Her eyesight is fine."

Surprised that my eyes are closed, I open them. A tear trickles down Piper's cheek. It's been a while since I've seen a woman cry and the last person I want to hurt is her.

"I'm sorry I took you from your moms," she says.

"Would you have left me in Kensington if I had asked you to?"

She pauses briefly and then replies, "No."

If anyone else responded that way, I'd probably be irritated, but Piper has an endearing way of doing things. She's had to survive without her family for who-knows-how-long. A part of me wants to forgive her, let her know it's not a problem, and I'll figure out a solution. But if there's any chance of creating a relationship with her in the future, it can't start on a lie.

"I'm still mad at you."

Her eyes dip to the collection of bar pens I lined up neatly in a row. "I know."

"Why do you have these?" I ask. "They're each worth a cent or less."

"They were yours." A soft smile rises at the corner of her mouth which makes me break.

A beat passes, then two, as we hold eye contact for far too long. "Hypothetically, if I were to complete the challenges," I start, "I need to know why they're so important."

She sucks in a deep breath, catches Lillian's eye across the room, then says, "For the Pixie."

I hold my breath. If Pixie really stops aging, it's the only thing I'd consider stealing.

Piper pulls a little leather pouch out of her backpack. Slowly, she dumps the contents into her palm. A small, clear sphere sits in her hand filled with gold sand. "Neveraj is...sick. This land's energy source is Pixie and it's being stolen."

"Can I see some?"

Her eyes narrow a bit as she slowly hands the pouch over. I hold it up to my eyes, hoping to witness magic, but it simply looks like pretty, glittery sand.

"You'll believe, just wait. The only safe way to gather new, raw Pixie is with an orb. We'd dip it in the Pixie Falls and fill the orb with dust. And the only way to obtain these orbs is by winning them as prizes after challenges. The first challenge gives the smallest orb, the second challenge awards a medium-sized orb, and the third challenge would give us the largest orb. Then we take the orbs to the Falls to fill them with Pixie."

I try to process all the rules. "Who else knows about

Pixie being real?" I ask, unsure if I will ever fully believe it has magic.

"The Lost Ones, my dads and their ex-business partner, Holland. And now you. But someone has been dealing it at the bars in Kensington. My dads are...gone... so it's got to be Holland. Of course, once the gossip of an anti-aging drug spread, the pirates have been swarming all of Lacordia's coast."

"How do you know the land is sick?" I ask.

"The sprites and nymphs live, eat, and breathe Pixie. They can feel the strength fading." Piper exchanges a knowing glance with Lillian again then says, "If I don't find a way to replenish what's been taken, the land won't provide for me anymore. I won't be able to live here anymore."

I pause, hearing all the ways she's explaining that it'll affect *her* and not the natives like Lillian or Tank. Carefully, I pose my next question, hoping she's already considered it. "If this is the case, then the sprites and nymphs would be in danger too, right?"

"Yeah, that too."

"Take me to the first challenge site," I say.

Piper's eyes brighten again, this time because of me.

CHAPTER SEVEN

Piper

The morning breeze dances through the windows and kisses my neck. I should hang nets since Wyshawn hates bugs so much. I doubt he'd enjoy waking up to a grasshopper on his face. Actually, that would be quite entertaining. I can imagine his manly squeal now. Across the room, Wyshawn realigns my collection of pens, so they're all perfectly parallel. What would he do if I messed them into a nonsensical pile again? A smile creeps up at the thought. I'm not sure why I ever kept those pens. Sure, I write in my journals, but there are other better-quality ones I've stolen sticking out of a cracked coffee mug. Wyshawn studies the pens like his life depends on it and I wonder what he's thinking.

Will he always despise me for taking him away from his moms? It must be nice to have a supportive family who lives locally. Something I'll never experience.

Tank lands on the plate of fruit and gives me a look like he's reading my mind. I sign to him to be nicer to Wyshawn. Apparently, even a one-pound sprite can act jealous without reason. He replies with a sassy remark that isn't worth my time. What's gotten into him? Both my best friends woke up on the wrong side of the bed this morning. I have half a mind to shun Lillian from my Hidden Gem for the next month. How dare she tell Wyshawn that premonition? I can hear her voice repeating it in my head, *'The one who fights with a youthful charm will strengthen the shadow and bring us harm.'* I may believe in some crazy shit, but nothing is fated in this world. Plus, the future doesn't even matter.

At least Lillian was the one knocking on our door and not a Lost One like I had expected. Felix, Kyle, and Zheo are nothing but trouble. They all refused to return to their prior life once they learned that Neveraj provides for them. In the years I've lived here, not once have I had to earn an income, buy clothes, hunt for food, or pay a mortgage. All of life's annoying inconveniences that come along with adulting don't exist in Neveraj, which is why I need to keep RavenSoul away from my home.

I pluck a new hat from my hook. Today I wear the dark green cowgirl hat with emerald jewels bedazzling the rim. The aroma of incoming rain wafts stronger with each passing second, so I'll need more suitable clothes. It would be highly delightful to strip in front of Wyshawn and memorize his shocked response, but I feel a little guilty putting him through so much already. I grab a clean, black v-neck shirt and camo cargo pants. I step behind the little barrier folding screen and change my outfit. Taking a look in the cracked mirror, I nod my hat to the little lady who looks mighty ready for an epic adventure.

"Are you gonna admire yourself all day or what?" Lillian asks from the kitchen.

She'll never care about the fit of an outfit, since Terra Nymphs don't wear clothes.

"Are you going with us?" I holler back.

"No, I'll only slow you down."

Turning, I check out my ass in the mirror. If I'm stuck with Wyshawn in the jungle all day, I may as well give him something to look at. Is he an ass or boob man? I don't have much in the chest region to flaunt. Though other dates never complained. Maybe I'll take the long path today, near Skull Rock where the Lost Ones live. It'd be interesting to see how Wyshawn responds to my exes living nearby. Not that I care what Wyshawn thinks about.

When I step out into the main room, Wyshawn glances up from his tinkering project. He may as well surrender. His phone won't work here, no matter what type of satellite he tries to invent. His gaze roams from my sneakers up my outfit and lands just short of my eyes. Is he staring at my lips?

A tingling sensation flings up my spine and gives me a quick jitter. I step past him. "Ready?"

"Sure." He wipes his dirty hands on the pants Neveraj provided for him this morning.

They fit him perfectly. He hasn't asked where they came from yet. Does he expect they're a pair from an ex? Perhaps he wouldn't be surprised if we ran into Felix or Kyle later.

"Walk or fly?" I'd rather not have our bodies forced so close again, so I shouldn't have given him a choice. "By the way, we'll get wet today. It'll storm soon."

Wyshawn shakes his head, gaze flickering to the window. "The sky is clear and light blue."

A few beats pass between us, and I can tell the instant he realizes I may know what I'm talking about. He's the type who prepares and who carries an umbrella even if the sky is bright with suns-shine. The seriousness on his face is comical as he silently debates his options—dealing with his fear of heights or walking while drenched.

"It's your terrain," he says softly. "You know what you're doing, so I'll do what you think is best."

"Even if my choice is soaring above the trees with the chance of falling?"

He gulps. "Yes."

I take a step forward. "Even if it means crossing a creek of crocodiles?"

He bites his bottom lip, and it's weird that I even notice. "Yes."

Again, I lessen the space between us. "Why?"

"Because I said I'd help you."

Epoch munches on the fruit in the background making slobbery, slurping, and sucking sounds. It's quite distracting, but I don't dare break eye contact with Wyshawn first. Why does everything with him rise to a level ten of intensity? Even my stupid heartbeat is racing too fast.

"Okay, we're walking. You're too heavy to fly attached to me. Next time, you'll use the spare wingsuit." I attach my dagger to my thigh and sign to Tank. '**You coming?**'

He nods and zips out the window to meet us downstairs. Epoch skitters off the plate and crawls down the leg of the table. I already know he'll wiggle up my pant leg and tuck himself into my pocket. There's no time to waste, so I grab my pack full of essentials and am about to swing it on when Wyshawn slides it off my arm and onto his back.

I glare until he lowers his chin, daring me to argue. "I'll allow it," I say.

"You're welcome," he grumbles.

Once we're down on muddy terrain, it's clear that the temperature has dropped. Leaves chase and play with each other at my heels. Behind me, twigs crunch under

Wyshawn's heavy stomps. He must weigh over two hundred pounds with his height and physique. Any predator will hear us marching from a mile away.

"Can you walk a bit louder?" I glance over my shoulder.

He has to duck under a branch I easily walked under without bending.

"Tell me about Holland," he says.

"You want the boring version or the fun version?" I hop over a log.

"The detailed version."

I avoid an ant hill and point down to warn him. "Okay, so Holland and my dads were best friends, a team of thieves. Well, more like con artists. The three of them could make anyone believe that unicorns existed."

"Do they?" He accelerates the pace to walk next to me instead of behind me.

"Maybe. I'll tell you a quick story and you decide. When a girl named Lucinda Lane wanted to mix a love potion she needed three items: the hair of a unicorn, a perfectly shaped walnut shell, and a secret from the one she loves. It's a tricky, ironic thing that the spell calls for a secret. If someone asked you for a secret, would you give it to them? What secret would it be? In any case, Lucinda Lane spent three nights hunting a unicorn. She skipped many days of school and when her professor asked if anything was wrong at home, she only looked up at him with the lovesick eyes of a seventeen-year-old. The teacher knew she had a little crush on him but was truly worried about all her absences.

"Anyways, after setting many elaborate traps she finally caught the unicorn, killed it, and plucked extra hair just in case. The walnut shell was much more difficult because even though she collected thousands, none were close to a perfect bowl shape.

"Collecting the secret was next. She followed Mr. Turner one night after the school day ended, through the cold alleyways until he stopped before a door. Before knocking, Mr. Turner glanced behind him, not catching sight of lovesick Lucinda hiding in the shadows. When the homeowner opened it from the other side, and light poured out, Lucinda couldn't look away from the two men kissing in the doorway. She threw her potion bottle on the street, letting it shatter into pieces, and ran away in tears."

"Uh, I'm supposed to know whether unicorns exist from that story?" Wyshawn's look of bewilderment might be considered cute by others. I hold in a laugh. "Um, so back to what you want to know. Holland and my dads tricked Captain Schmee and stole a bunch of his gold. His crew chased them to the roof of Walk the Plank, go figure."

"Sounds familiar," Wyshawn says, steadying me by my waist when I slip.

My skin ignites under my shirt where he touches me. He clears his throat and gestures for me to continue.

"Well, when the trio was cornered on the roof, they decided to try and jump to the nearest branch in J. Roger Park. All three of them jumped and flew through The Window together by accident."

"How convenient."

"Yeah, so fast forward a few years after they discovered Pixie powder. Holland eventually betrayed my dads by turning them in to the authorities with proof that they conned people out of money."

"Why?"

"Probably to keep more Pixie and gold to herself. I didn't have the chance to ask when I was called at boarding school to be told both my dads were going to trial."

"Wait, I thought your dads died?"

"No. Prison."

He shakes his head in obvious confusion. "How long ago was this?"

At this question, I have to think. Time often slips away from my grasp. I've been twenty-nine for years while living in Neveraj. Before that, I had spent years searching for The Window with the terrible clues my dads gave me. And before that, I can barely remember.

"I think I was around seventeen years old?"

"What did you do? Did you live with your biological mom?" Wyshawn swats at a fly swarming his ears.

"No, she was never in my life and died a while ago. And I never had one home, since my dads needed to be on the run constantly. The few things we did own, like our hoverboards, the state repossessed."

"That's a rough way to be forced to grow up." Wyshawn's pace slows and I turn to face him.

I toss him a smirk to lighten the mood. "Who ever said I've grown up?"

The first raindrop splatters on my shoulder, warm and excited. In my pocket, Epoch must sense the air charged with impending lightning in the distance because he curls into a tight ball. I tap my pocket gently to comfort him.

"You're looking for revenge, Jade?"

His sweet nickname for me does something to my insides. There's a spot in the middle of my stomach, deep, right in the center under my belly button, that coils tight. I don't respond. I want Wyshawn to believe I'm a good person.

"For now, I just need her Pixie stash. I don't care about the money or justice."

"Don't you want her to suffer in a cell after what she did to your dads?"

The drizzle accelerates to a soft rain, and I do my best not to glance at Wyshawn's shirt sticking to his chest. Surprisingly, he seems comfortable as he avoids thorn bushes and holes.

"Whether or not Holland betrayed them, my dads *did* commit crimes. I love them and miss them, but they deserve the time they were given." I shrug and jump over another log, warped and unsafe to step on.

Wyshawn follows my steps, trusting, and letting me guide him through the unknown. The faith he's put in me is quite...sexy to be honest. Not himself as a person, just the fact that he's not second-guessing every move I make. Felix and Kyle had always wanted to take the lead. Typical men.

"Have you searched for Holland in Neveraj?" Wyshawn asks.

"Yes, endlessly." I crack a dead branch in half and toss it out of the way. "I doubt she stayed here since she enjoys a life of conning so much. Her tricks out in the world would be more satisfying than hiding."

The sky drops needles of rain in bursts, but the high canopy of leaves blocks the downfall. I hunch my shoulders, colder than usual for a summer storm.

"I've been visiting *Walk the Plank* for two reasons, to hear gossip if Holland has returned, because once she runs out of her stash, I bet she'll try to visit Neveraj again. That's where I'll catch her."

"And the other reason?"

The breeze stills and the temperature drops again, strangely. A weird warning clamps in my gut. I stop in my place. Look to the left. The right.

"Piper?"

"Ssh!" I put one finger to my lips.

Ahead, the trees sway slowly despite the lack of breeze. Rhythmic pitter-patter sounds splash in puddles. No twigs snap. No leaves crunch. It's not an animal, but I can feel a toxic energy all the same. That's when I see it. Slow shadows reach around the trunk of a tree with smoky fingers beckoning me to follow. RavenSoul. When raindrops slice through it, a hissing sound meets my ears, like oils hitting a frying pan. I back up a step, accidentally pushing myself against Wyshawn's chest.

"Piper? What's wrong?" He cups both my elbows in his warm hands. "What do you see?"

My chest tightens. He doesn't see RavenSoul taunting us? He doesn't see the thick gray mass lengthening over the weeds and wildflowers? The shadows grow higher, blocking the trees. A cruel cold makes my skin start to shiver. I retreat further. Never have I feared something enough to run. Yet, everything in my body is screaming at me to go. Leave.

RavenSoul extends from the base of a tree, rolling towards me like a fatal fog. All breath is trapped inside. A scream trapped in my chest. I stumble to the side. Wyshawn reaches out to catch me, but we both spill down a slope. We roll. Fast. A smack to my head. My arm hits something hard. Ram to the knees. Somersault. Flip. Roll. Scratches sliced open on my skin. Pain.

"Piper!"

We're a tangle of limbs and banging skulls. Over and under each other. Flip and roll. Down the hill. I flail my arms blindly. Grasp at anything. Finally, I thud to a stop against Wyshawn's chest, upside-down. He's panting, cradling my leg in his arms. My sneaker by his ear.

"Ow!" I take note of my body. Gently rotate my ankles and wrists. I pat my stomach with trembling hands. Nothing's broken but bruises will cover my body tomorrow. And I'll need antibiotics for all these scrapes.

"Shit! You okay?" Wyshawn helps me sit upright.

The second he readjusts, something swoops around us. Pushes us close together again.

In a single breath, we're lifted into the air. My scream rips through the jungle. My body jerks to an abrupt stop. When I can breathe again, I blink everything into focus.

Twenty feet below, on the ground, my green hat fills with rainwater like a bucket. Wyshawn and I dangle inside a giant rope trap. Together. I'm entirely straddling him, my crotch wedged against his. My legs hang through the holes of the netting.

"Well…fuck…" He squeezes his eyes shut.

CHAPTER
EIGHT

Wyshawn

My cock stiffens immediately as she wiggles on my crotch. Damn it. How am I supposed to control myself when the one woman I've fantasized about naked for the past two years is straddling me? Her scent radiates an intoxicating vanilla and mint. Why me? What did I do to deserve this torture? If she were interested in me even the slightest, then I'd see how this might play out, but Piper has chosen others repeatedly when I've been an available option since day one. Piper shifts, trying to lift herself off me, which only makes it worse.

"Did you just moan?" she asks me, then freezes in place, one eyebrow raised. Liquid beads of rain slide down the side of her face and I want to fuckin' lick them from her skin.

"No." I lean to readjust, but the rope cradling us presses against my backpack, caging me against her chest.

"Yes, you moaned again," she says, a smile forming. "You sound like a dying cow."

"Do not."

This unfortunate situation can be fixed. I check the angles of our interlocked bodies. Instead of calculating the best maneuver towards freedom, I thank the Sols Above that she's wearing pants instead of a skirt. Does she prefer cotton or silk lingerie? Has she ever thought of me when touching herself? My dick twitches again.

"Damn, Wyshawn." She bites her lip., "Has it been a while since your last *tussle*?"

I almost choke. "Tussle? Really?"

"What word would you rather me use? Lay? Intercourse? Mating? Yeah, I'll use that one. When was your last mating event, Mr. Darl?"

"Can we not talk about this right now?"

"My last time was three weeks ago. In fact, Kyle never left Neveraj. If you keep pressing yourself against me like that, I may have to go hunt him down tonight."

Her ex lives here? Fantastic. "Piper, please. I'm begging you to sit still."

Instead, she intentionally grinds her groin against

mine, making us swing back and forth a bit. Laughing, she says, "I'm just having a bit of fun. Don't all guys like fun?"

"No," I say, clenching my molars until they're about to crack.

I can't tolerate one more second. I reach out. I should ask her permission first, I really should. Instead, I quickly grab her waist and lift her straight up. Her thighs appear in my line of sight first, then her knees. With a squeal, she's dangling above my head, flapping her arms, which makes more rain splatter onto my head.

"Hey! Put me down!"

I lift her behind my head and place her so she's wedged between my backpack and the rope. Her physical closeness is still too overwhelming. We need to get out of this trap ASAP.

"Give me your dagger," I say, reaching behind me.

"No thanks."

There's a scratching sound, and even though I can't turn to see, the gentle swaying proves she's trying to cut us free. Of course she takes matters into her own hands. It's one of the many traits I admire about her. This adventurous, confident side has always been evident, but I've never had to see her react in life-or-death situations. Though she's an assertive, quick thinker, this twenty-foot drop could kill us if she doesn't plan.

"Wait, let's think this through first."

"Nah, I got this." Her voice sounds amused as she continues to hack. It sucks that I know by her pitch what mood she's in. Her whimsical smile has been imprinted on my mind for too long. "This is the second time I've freed you from rope, Starling. Do you have a bondage fetish?"

"That's not funny."

"Of course it is. I'm hilarious, admit it."

"You may be *something* but a comedian doesn't come to mind."

Epoch's little webbed feet tickle my shoulder as he climbs over and down my chest. Scritch scratch goes her blade. Drip drop goes the rain on my head. At least my dick has calmed himself. All I have to do is not think of Piper on my lap for the rest of eternity.

"Tell me about this ex of yours," I say, hoping that'll make me go ultra soft.

"Jealous much?"

"Never mind."

"Oh, no, no, no. Aren't you the master of curiosity, after all? I'll answer."

For the first time, I risk looking down. All at once, the browns and greens surrounding us spin in and out of focus. My hands get clammy, and I can feel myself starting to sweat. We're going to fall.

"I can't stay up here," I say, hearing the slight tremor in my voice. "I need to get down."

"Ssh, Wyshawn. Close your eyes and focus on my voice." Her teasing tone shifts to comforting.

I do as she says and shut them, letting the darkness and sound of birds wash over me.

"Do you ever feel as if you carry the weight of fear, day after day?" she begins. "That you're being pushed into the ground from the heavy load riding on your back so all you want is to rip it off, but at the same time, you're afraid to let go? You're afraid to see what's possible without that burden suffocating you?"

"Uh...I..."

"Never mind. Forget I said that. I'll tell you a story."

I don't want to ignore what she mentioned, but maybe she's not ready to say more.

"So, have I ever told you how awesome your hair is? In Coendriel, hair has power. Long hair like yours can be a river of strength, but it's all about intention. Blonde hair, when weaved together, can braid visions of good dreams. A nest of a bun on the top of one's head has the potential to protect from enemies. And don't even get me started on curls. Bouncy ringlets contain energy in each spring, but be warned, if you don't believe, your hair will be a mat of useless strands that can't hold an ounce of starlight."

The *scratch-scratch* of the rope sawing still makes my knuckles clench the rope tighter, but my heart rate has slowed from the sound of her lullaby voice.

"What about my hair? What story does it tell?"

"What story do you want it to tell?"

A snap. Then we drop a bit. Another snap. I clutch the rope tighter.

"Whoops! You may want to brace yourseeeeeeee—"

The bottom of the trap gives out.

We drop.

We're going to die. She's going to die. I won't let her die.

Air whooshes against my face. Piper slams into me. She's screaming. I wrap one arm around her waist and ball her into my chest. I land on my side. Hard as a rock. Pain crashes into my arm. Black spots briefly overtake my vision. Piper huffs out a shocked breath. My body acts like a tortoise shell protecting her until wild arms slap against my chest. Did I hurt her?

"Piper?" I release her from the bubble of my frame cocooning her and panic at the sight of her face.

She's gaping at me, mouth open wide like she's trying to suck in a breath and can't. Her eyes are like saucers and watering. Piper flaps her hands in a frenzy and then clutches her throat.

"I'm here." I kneel next to her, trying to remember CPR but unsure when to start. She's conscious, able to move, and alert. "It's okay, Piper. I think you got the wind knocked out of you. It's okay, try to think of something that calms you."

I seize her thrashing hands in mine and hold them tight. "Look in my eyes. It'll be okay," I intentionally speak slowly. "It's almost over. You're having a spasm in your diaphragm. This happened to my sister once. Jeniqua played soccer in high school and got smacked so hard that she fell and landed straight on her back. Scared the Abyss out of me. I was down on the field before the ref even noticed. Good girl, there you go, slow everything down. Relax. Good girl."

Finally, her features soften, and she releases the death grip on my hands. "Thank you," she says in a strained voice, then visibly swallows.

All my thoughts jumble into a mess of relief that it wasn't more serious. I'm not a doctor. I had no clue if she'd be okay. What if a bug got wedged in her windpipe? What if her rib had torn a hole into her lung?

"You're cut a bit." Piper points to my knee where crimson dribbles down into the soil.

"I...are *you* okay?" I ask but she's already snatching the cowgirl hat from the mud.

Only those who know what to look for would detect the hesitancy in her eyes, but she masks it so well with a rich smile. "Yup, come on, my moaning cow, we're almost to the lagoon."

Half of my body betrays the other with a laugh. "Will you answer more of my questions on the way?"

"Follow me. The rain is about to stop, but you still need to watch for sinkholes."

"Fabulous."

I sludge through the mud behind her in silence. Why does she keep looking to our left? There aren't any new bird sounds in that direction. Is she lost?

My gaze drops to her ass then I shake my head. No, there's no use thinking about touching her when it'll never happen again. Plus, she basically announced to the jungle that she has a date tonight. I'll have to make the most of my time alone in The Hidden Gem while she's at his place. Images of a man's hands on her stomach, outlining her ribs, tickling her breasts...

Stop it! Stop thinking about her. What matters? Pixie. Yes, maybe I can find the stash when she's riding another dude in ecstasy.

Tank dashes in front of me like a poisonous dart and circles around my ears. It'd be offensive to swat him like an insect, but I also doubt that all sprites are this rude.

"Sinkhole." Piper points to the left to what looks like a puddle of mud, like all the others. "Only step where I step."

"Thanks," I mumble, feeling a bit in a daze. "So, I've been thinking about something."

"Aren't you always?"

"If your dads found The Window by accident, did you learn why it was created? Who made a bridge between Kensington and Neveraj and why?"

"You're thinking of it all wrong. The Window has always been in existence, just like magic. For the sprites and nymphs, it represents a sacred rite of passage. The voyage is necessary for these natives because when they choose to travel through The Window and back, it stops their aging," Piper says, picking up a long walking stick. She pokes at the mud puddles ahead.

"Tank decided to stay twenty-five, so on that birthday, he jumped through. His body has appeared to be age twenty-five ever since. And Lillian chose to travel through when she turned thirty-three. Once adult sprites and nymphs complete their passage, they're free to come and go on the thirteenth. Some creatures travel the world and as long as they have enough Pixie stored with them, they won't age. If their stash is depleted, they begin to age again and need to return home to stop it. The three challenges are for them to earn extra Pixie for trips abroad. If they want to travel far, they'd have more Pixie stored to keep them sustained."

"You've done the first two challenges," I say, stepping only where her sneakers leave prints. "What was it like?"

"Well, everyone's challenges are different. So far it seems like each challenge gives the contender three choices. When I did the first one, about my past, I was given the choice of either confronting my dads about their career or staying locked in a dark box for an undetermined amount of time or trying to stop so-called bad guys from taking our home." She tilts her head to the side. "They felt like nightmares, where I knew I wasn't awake, but could control the outcome."

"Which one did you choose?"

"Guess," she says just as a whip of breeze moves a longer chunk of hair over her forehead. I want to brush it out of her eyes just so I have a better lock on the emerald greens that defy reality.

I consider her question. She wouldn't choose to be locked in a cage. The dark might not be a fear of hers specifically, but no sane human would pick that when the length of time is unknown. Secondly, children often want roots established and are worried about their foundation being swept out from under them. Security must mean a good deal to her, more than I had expected. Lastly, telling her parents she wanted them to quit conning might be nerve-wracking but at least it was with someone she loved instead of facing a villain.

"Your dads," I say.

Piper's nose scrunches to form an expression I haven't seen on her often. She waves the walking stick through the low tree branches, making gold powder mizzle into her hair. Goddess, she's gorgeous. It's not just the curve of her hips and the fullness of her lips or the sharpness of her cheekbones. Her beauty is radiated through the challenge ever-present in her actions.

"Why are you looking at me like that?" she asks.

"There's a crocodile between your breasts."

Piper glances down where Epoch's green nose pokes down. "Oh yeah, he likes the space between Miss Coffer and Miss Doubloon."

"You named your boobs?"

Despite the small distance separating us, Piper points at me like her finger is a dagger. "Wyshawn Stickler Darl! You, sir, just smiled!"

"That's not my middle name." I tuck my lips back into a straight line where they belong. "You're imagining things again. I'm soaked and bruised and sore. Can we just get there already?"

This time, I lead the way, not caring if I sink into a mud hole so large that it swallows me whole. Because that would be better than her toying with me. I can't tolerate a flirtatious Piper, not when she has plans to sleep with that Kyle guy soon. I may be able to extinguish problems at work faster than others and run a half marathon in under one hour and forty minutes and sit by my Mum who doesn't recognize me some days, but I'm only human. I'll never be strong enough to be okay thinking about Piper with another Partner.

Ahead, the tall trees shift to different shapes. I wonder how many are nymphs, listening to our conversation and tracking our movements.

"There it is," Piper whispers behind me, "Mermaid's Cove."

A massive leaf, bigger than my head, blocks our view. When I lift it out of the way, I actually gasp. The mud blends into sand full of seashells, which leads to crystal water inside a lagoon. Little promises of suns beam onto the water, making it sparkle like diamonds before the clouds' envy covers the light again. I can't believe how clear the water is. Seaweed dances in the shallows, where brightly colored exotic fish dip and race.

Piper's energy magnetizes me forward and the scent of saltwater wafts through the breeze.

"Is that a stingray?"

"If you think stingrays are amazing, wait till a mermaid swims up."

I've heard of the new sea witch, Axton, and his bride, Eribelle, but I haven't met a merfolk before. All my childhood, the stories of Nerida have always been that—simply stories.

Piper whips off her black shirt and tosses it onto a log. I stare at the cleavage filling out her sports bra. Hey, I'm not going to complain. Then her shoes go flopping off, spread out in the sand.

"Come on, Starling!" she shouts over her shoulder as she splashes into the shallows. "The water is warm after the rain!" she yells with more joy than a kid at an amusement park. "Let's go cliff diving!"

Her bird tattoo on her shoulder blade will be the end of me. Like the Quetzal, she's made of magic, meant to fly through this life; and I'm meant to watch from the ground to catch her if she ever falls.

CHAPTER
NINE

Piper

The scent of saltwater blows in my face. I run into the shallows, splashing water up my back, until the resistance makes me stumble forward. Laughing, I dip underwater but keep my eyes closed. No matter how much I love swimming, the salt still stings unpleasantly. Epoch drops out of my pocket and tickles my legs underwater. My little croc loves to swim more than I love to fly. This lagoon is such a refreshing change from a life within the trees. Don't get me wrong, I love The Hidden Gem and hiking in the jungle, but on my worst days, Mermaid Cove is where I visit to revitalize. Instead of the palette of green hues that I'm used to, cyan and navy shades engulf us completely. Even the blue macaw's azure feathers are brighter here. He squawks a welcome song from a higher branch, watching me float on my back. The suns peek out to warm my face only momentarily before gray clouds capture them again.

"Come on, Wyshawn!" I yell to where he stands on the sand, arms crossed. "I'll race you."

He shakes his head slowly, but I swear a slight curl turns up the edge of his mouth. Behind him Tank hovers, glaring at the back of Wyshawn's head. I'll need to have a talk with him later. No one deserves such pure animosity.

"Fine, I'll cliff jump by myself!" I wade towards the rock wall. I'm hyperaware of my slippery grip on the rockface since the storm didn't do me any favors.

"Be careful, Piper!" Wyshawn warns.

The wall has decided to be vexing today after all. Arms shaking, I struggle to hold my weight with just my fingertips clinging onto tiny ledges. Epoch encourages me with tiny growls as if he's working just as hard.

"Hey, Wyshawn. Did you know that the word slippery has a birth story?"

"Quit talking and pay attention to your feet. No, don't plant it there, go up a little, yeah, right there."

"I'll tell you the story of slipperiness," I grunt while pulling myself higher.

"Is that a word?"

"It is now."

"So, as you know, during first dates, all young couples can choose to be slippery. Anybody, with their Partner, can morph into shapeless liquid with the ability to glide through any crack, as long as they're holding the hand of the other. Imagine oozing between rocks and filling the inside of a cave like goo. Once, a young man who let go of his boyfriend's hand suffered for the next eighty years, oiling into sleek, unnatural shapes. Until one night, he woke to complete darkness, but with the feeling of a familiar hand in his. Gone were his nightmares of slipping and sliding through vessels alone. Because he had wished for it all to finally end, that darkness and nothingness with his lover was better than being alone."

My breaths come short and quick and I barely make it to the peak of the rock wall. At the top, I raise both hands to the thunderclouds and twirl in ecstasy. Pelicans swoop in the distance then rise again with fish in their bills. It's strange how the ocean strokes the edge of my self-control. What I'd give to parasail over the wild waves! I sigh. It's never been determined how far the borders of Neveraj reach.

"Piper, get away from the edge!" Wyshawn shouts from directly below, as he treads water at the base of the cliff wall.

"I'm only twenty feet high, it's fine." I wink at Tank, who has finally come to his senses and is ready for fun.

"If you fall wrong, you'll get all scratched up," Wyshawn hollers again.

"Well, I guess I should get a running leap then!"

"No, I didn't mean—"

I hear his frustrated groan below. Ten steps should be enough, as long as I don't slip on any wet rocks. "One," I say while patting Epoch in my pants pocket to prepare him for the launch.

"Piper, no, just climb down."

'**Two**!' Tank signs happily.

"Three!" I sprint. Rocks hard under my bare feet. Leap. Soar. The thrill of flying tastes like golden gumdrops and sounds like velvet words caressing my ears. Air whooshes past my face as I drop drop drop. Splash into the water. I purposefully stay underwater a bit longer than I should, to see how Wyshawn will react. With each passing second his muffled voice becomes more and more frantic. Such a worry-wart.

I break the surface and wipe the water from my face. "Your turn."

"Are you crazy?" He swims closer, concern etched into those dark brown eyes. "You could've hit your head."

"I'm fine."

"Piper, save me from stress and use your brain once in a while."

"Excuse me?"

"Never mind," he grumbles. "Can we please go ashore now?"

Twigs snap on the beach, so I glance towards the backpack. A shadow emerges from the trees. This time, thankfully, it's not RavenSoul. A familiar silhouette jumps straight to my backpack.

"Hey! Don't even think about it, Kyle!"

He stops in his tracks and raises both hands in surrender. "I was only going to take the sandwiches."

I won't ever let myself regret my sexual choices. Pleasure is pleasure. Plus, I'm twenty-nine—give or take a few years—I can play without feeling guilty if it's mutual. Though, of all my Partners I've slept with, I sincerely hate how Kyle disarms me so quickly with his smile.

"No, the sandwiches are for us. Go back to your skeletons." I wave an arm at him like I'm shooing away a dog.

"Us?" He steps closer, reminding me of the way he used to tease me first, circling me in before pouncing. "Oh, I see you have another toy. Good luck, man. You'll need it with this one."

Wyshawn is by my side before I can even respond. To Kyle, his stance may look relaxed and in control, but I can see the tick in Wyshawn's jaw. Behind his back, his hands clench into fists. Interesting. I never guessed the uptight rule follower would throw a punch.

"I guess I'll have to complete the challenge on an empty stomach," Kyle says with another wicked smile, while unnecessarily stripping off his wet shirt. "No biggie, I've done it before. You gonna stay and watch me win again, Piper?"

"I can feel you rolling your eyes," Wyshawn whispers next to me. "How do you want me to respond?"

Taken by surprise that a man would wait, think things through, and consider what I want first, I gawk at Wyshawn's stern face. I swear, I've never used the term flabbergasted before, but in this moment I think it's appropriate. I'm utterly flabbergasted.

"Let's watch Kyle compete. If he wins, we can steal his orb."

"Piper Jade Pan, stealing is wrong!" Wyshawn pretends to sound outraged, but there's a hint of pride in his tone.

"Stealing is what I do best." I reach for Wyshawn's hand to guide him out of the lagoon, but he flinches and pulls away. "What in the Abyss was *that* for?"

"What?" Wyshawn's tone tries to act unaware but guilt is written across his forehead.

"Nothing. Come on, the best view to watch is over here," I whisper, hurrying through the water.

"So, you already made it through the future challenge?" I ask Kyle.

"Yup, time to start over." Kyle runs a hand over his buzz cut. It's obvious from how the tan lines formed where his brown hair should be.

'**Is that allowed?**' I sign to Tank, who has been opening the bag of sandwiches.

Tank nods. I had never considered that once a contender beats all three challenges they could start over from the beginning. It makes sense for the nymphs and sprites, but no human I've brought here has ever gotten that far. Until Kyle.

"Well, show us how a pro does it then," I say

gesturing to the now-empty lagoon. Taking a seat on a boulder by our pack, I pat the neighboring rock for Wyshawn.

He glances back and forth between the rock and Kyle, who's stretching on the sand like an absolute lunatic. If he encounters the same obstacles as last time, he probably won't need any physical strength or endurance. Come to think of it, now I'm intrigued whether the challenge will give him three new selections.

"Front row tickets. Don't be shy," I say, tapping the rock again.

Slowly, Wyshawn tromps over to me, water dripping down his whole body. A strange wish overcomes me that he would be shirtless too. Not that I'd compare the two. Kyle is a man of arrogance and action, someone who would ride a bull, take ten shots in a row, or mask as an undercover spy in Captain Schmee's crew just to see if he could survive. On the other hand, Wyshawn probably prefers to curl up on a well-worn couch to read a book during a thunderstorm. Speaking of, a slight drizzle begins to fall again. There's no point in trying to cover my hair since I'm already soaked to the bone. A little more rain won't make any difference.

On the next boulder, Wyshawn sits on the edge, as far from me as possible, tense and hyper-alert. He clears his throat, and his beautiful frown deepens into a scowl. That severe intensity almost makes me laugh but I won't make a jab at him with Kyle so close, at risk of overhearing.

"Alright, start the show." I clap slowly but neither Tank nor Wyshawn joins me.

Per custom, Kyle kneels and holds both palms out and up, vulnerable. When he closes his eyes, I take the moment to appreciate the curves of his chest. He's definitely been climbing taller trees since we were last together.

"I call to this land so dear," he starts, "to risk for the prize of an orb. Show me the challenges I do fear. I give my blood that you'll absorb."

"Blood?" Wyshawn's gaze whips to mine. "What does he mean by blood?"

"Wait and see."

It'd be a cool effect if the sky always darkened before a challenge like it does now. Maybe I'll let Wyshawn believe it's part of the energy, the magic. His focus is fixated on the lagoon as bubbles erupt from Below. They grow larger until the tips of three silver cutlasses rise from the water. Their perfect sheen reminds me of a shock of lightning, quite appropriate for the upcoming weather.

Tank flies in front of my face. '**We should get back home. There's no point in watching this doofus perform.**'

'**I always have a plan, Tank, trust me.**'

'**And you used to always include *me* in your plans too**,' he signs, then zooms off into the jungle alone, leaving me behind.

My heart drops a bit at his abrupt departure. I know over time friendships evolve, but I would have never expected him to turn cold against me.

"Wait, are those..." Wyshawn begins, leaning forward. "Are those swords?"

I shush him and stand, too excited to sit patiently. From the first weapon, a burst of silver light shoots into the air from its sharp tip. Within the light is a scene, playing like a film—Kyle being rejected by a woman when he's on one knee with a ring in his hand. Okay, so his first past fear is the same as last time. The second cutlass shows a scene of his father dying—also a repeat. A few extra beats linger. Thunder crashes faintly and the rolling boom lasts as long as it takes for the third cutlass to toss out a new scene. He's in a fistfight with someone, losing terribly. That isn't the same fear as before. How can someone's feelings about their past change?

Kyle steps toward the third cutlass, his fear of losing a fight. When did that brawl happen? How old was he? Why did it replace the past fear? He grabs the hilt and without hesitation, slices a gash along his forearm. Blood drips from the blade but never hits the water.

Crimson liquid, thicker than the rain, grows larger and larger, morphing from a shapeless mass into the form of a man who stands in front of Kyle. None of his features are recognizable, only the ruby blob of a human, with fists raised and knees bent, ready to throw a jab at any moment. If Kyle hesitates too long, it could cost him his life. I may not have been completely upfront with Wyshawn about all the rules of the challenges. There is no guarantee to survive any of the three.

Lightning splits the sky.

"Exquisite," I whisper and step closer, greedy for Kyle's battle.

Red lunges first, striking with a punch. It's as if crimson ink splatters across Kyle's cheek. I wring my hands together, eager for Kyle to win. The sooner he's done, the faster I can steal his orb.

Kyle's punch slaps Red's gut. Blow after blow. Thunder cracks. The men huff and grunt. Jab. Cross. Hook. Uppercut. That looks painful. Red dodges. Kyle swings. Red arches out of the way. My heartbeat is out of my body.

"Come on, Kyle!" I cheer.

Rain beats down, hammering the water. I have to create a shield over my eyes to see them.

"Piper, let's leave." Wyshawn's voice is drowned out as if coming from another world. "This is getting out of hand. I don't want you to get hurt," he says.

No way. I wouldn't leave this show even if he begged. Kyle needs to beat Red. He needs to face his fear of losing. He needs to...wait. I squint at the fighting duo. Kyle hits the guy's face three times in a row. Each time the whack-whack-whack echoes across all of Neveraj. Damn it. If Kyle's fear is losing, he can't win this. He has to overcome his past pain and purposefully surrender to be awarded the orb.

"Kyle!" I scream but there's no way he can hear me over the torrent of rain and thunder. I jump to Wyshawn and grab his shoulders to face me. "He has to lose!"

"What?"

Out of the corner of my eye, the color red explodes

like fireworks, but it's not over. They swipe at each other. Bash. Slap. Hit. It'll never end. They're too evenly matched—same speed, same strength, same technique, same build. It's as if…is Kyle fighting himself?

"Wyshawn," I yell, throat scratching, and still he leans down so his ear is close to my mouth. "He won't get an orb if he wins the fight. Kyle *has* to lose."

"I…understand?" Half his words are erased by the fierce wind. "…you want?"

This time I place my lips against the shell of his ear, skin on skin. It sends a wash of womanly sensations all through me. "Kyle has to lose!"

Wyshawn nods. Before I know it, he lifts me. Sets me on the rock. His eyes lasered onto mine. "Don't get off this rock, Piper."

I open my mouth to question him, but he runs toward Kyle. Thunder booms again. I jump off the rock faster than a Crested Coua.

Shit. I don't know what will happen if he enters Kyle's challenge. If only Tank were here to ask. I rush forward, ready to pull Wyshawn back, but he's too damned fast.

"Stop!" I scream, water flooding my voice. "Wyshawn! No! Get out!"

Wyshawn catapults into the madness. Clenched fists raised. All of a sudden, we're all in unprecedented territory.

"What the?" Kyle hurls a punch.

Wyshawn blocks. Slips out of the way. Slides to Kyle's right. Rams a punch straight into his temple. Kyle falls into the sand. Unconscious. Knocked out. That was fuckin' fast. Well, Kyle can't win now, but my Starling is now facing someone else's fear—a fighter made of blood and crimson tears.

I watch Wyshawn. Maybe I'll have to reconsider a few things. That is, if he survives the next five minutes.

CHAPTER TEN

Wyshawn

I need to keep this monster away from Piper. It's a deranged creature made of nightmares, completely disturbed. I cringe at the coppery scent of blood mixed with the rainfall pouring over us in sheets. Hopefully, Piper will shield herself behind a tree. Kyle lies still at my feet, breathing, but unmoving. The creature doesn't have eyes, but I can feel him glaring. He hasn't attacked yet. It's as if he's waiting for something—like he knows something I don't.

I move into his personal space, all my muscles tight and ready. Planting my feet in a solid stance, I raise my fists again. He moves to the left, I mirror him. He had hit with precise punches earlier. If I keep him on the offensive, he might tire faster.

"Act calm," I whisper to myself, rain dribbling over my lips.

He dives forward, fist flying fast. I dip to my knees. Keep my eye on the target, and swerve behind him. He jumps, about to tackle, when the loudest thunder I've ever heard roars over the lagoon. It ripples through the sky, followed by lightning streak after lightning streak. I pitch into the shallows from pure shock. Even the monster cowers. It's as if the storm is our audience, furious at me for joining their fight. Another bolt flashes like a golden vein through the dark sky and pierces through the center of the monster's chest.

"Holy fuck!" I tumble flat onto my stomach in the water, only my head above the surface.

I look all around, where cherry droplets of blood are suspended above the lagoon, frozen in time.

A shrill voice comes from the beach. "Wyshawn!"

She comes over to me. Piper's face has gone ashen white as she helps me rise to my feet. Both soaked, our breaths bursting in and out.

"Wh-what the Sols just happened?" She's shaking uncontrollably and flinches at the next, smaller clap of thunder. She grabs on to my arm so hard I'm unsure whether she's aware of it.

"Let's get out of here," I say.

Piper stares at me, but it's as if she's transfixed. I think she's rooted to the spot, so I crouch, ready to carry her over my shoulder, when another arrow of lightning stabs the sand. Quickly, I shove Piper behind me, holding her steady with one hand. The murderous rain yields a little so that I don't have to shield my eyes anymore. When I see what appears ahead in the sand, I wish that I could've been oblivious for a few more moments. Three massive swords are rising from the sand, each with a demonic energy I'd rather not explore. My heart beats frantically against my ribs. My chest tightens. I know they're for me. Deep in my gut, there's no questioning that I have involuntarily entered the challenge by inserting myself into Kyle's.

The rain weakens more, letting me clearly see the silver light that flows out of the first sword. Within the magical hue, thousands and thousands of bugs crawl over a child's prone body. Cockroaches enter through the nostrils. Spiders crawl into a partially opened mouth and beetles creep into the ear canals. I shudder and take a step back, bumping into Piper.

"Go home," I demand and push her gently away.

The second sword funnels light depicting a new scene. On the rooftop of a skyscraper, a boy wobbles on the edge of the building, arms out wide, hovering between stability and plummeting hundreds of feet below. I gulp. These are two of my worst childhood fears that have plagued me. What kind of sick, twisted game is this?

The third sword channels the last glow of silver light, showing a summary of my third fear. My elementary school principal criticizes my error in her office. She transforms into a boss reprimanding me for a mistake at my job, then an ex-girlfriend shouting condescendingly about how much I damaged our relationship. Inaccuracies and oversights—being at fault—my third fear.

I'm about to take a step forward to pick the second option, the heights, the least traumatizing, when all three swords rise of their own accord and point straight at me. Is the game malfunctioning? This didn't happen to Kyle. I don't risk asking Piper, not wanting to alert the sentient weapons to her location.

They float in my direction, hovering over the water. I take a step in reverse, but it only goads them on faster. I have no weapon. I'm not fast enough to outswim them. Would they chase me through the lagoon anyways? They hurtle towards me. All I can do is cover my face with my arms and squeeze my eyes shut.

A sharp pain thrashes through my skin. Twice. Three times. But then it stops. Silence. Not even the pitter-patter of the remaining raindrops landing in the water at my shins. No more booming thunder. Not a bird makes a peep. It feels like my breathing has ceased. Slowly, I open my eyes, expecting the swords to be an inch from my face, ready to strike me down. They're gone. Instead, there is a view more terrifying than I could imagine when all fears merge into one nightmare.

I'm at the top of a skyscraper, higher than all the surrounding buildings, but instead of facing the street below, I'm facing the rooftop. A massive, gray shape, formed of thousands of bugs towers over me. It holds a rope in its hand, with the other end tied around my waist. Centipedes slither out of the creature's hand and across the rope, inching towards my body. My hands are cuffed behind my back so I can't swat them away as they near.

"Stop!" I scream, fueled by terror, and shake my head wildly. I can't run. I can't curl into a ball on the ground. I can't shield myself. My pulse races and the sound of my heartbeat thrashes in my ears. It's as if the world is closing in on me. "Please! Don't!"

The monster opens its mouth wide, and dozens of tarantulas wriggle and writhe down its face, towards the rope connecting us. There's a lump in my throat when I try to scream again. No sound comes out. My legs are shaking but if they give out, I might fall off the damn roof. I dare to look over the edge to see how far the drop is. Dizzy. About to start hyperventilating. Her voice rips through my mind.

"You can do this, Starling. It's not real!"

She's still here, supporting me. Is she right? Piper completed this challenge once. How did she ever face fears like this?

"You messed up," the bug monster hisses at me and takes a little step forward.

The rope slackens, making my body tip over the edge further.

"I'm sorry," I whimper, my voice not sounding familiar. "Don't drop me."

"But you broke the rules. You didn't pay attention and for that, you will suffer." The insects grow larger with each insult. "How can we ever depend on you now? Your laziness is to blame for this disaster! There's no coming back from this mistake and it's all on you!"

"No!" I squeeze my eyes shut as the bugs slink from the rope onto my stomach.

"You'll never be able to set this right!" the monster bellows and I hear more squirming sounds.

A feathery sensation tingles my chest in the worst possible way. That's when I know the first bug has crawled under my shirt. Its legs are on my skin. I thrash against the rope, trying to shake them off.

"We no longer need you," the finality of the monster's tone makes my eyes fly open in horror.

Piper's muffled voice is shouting again. I use all my energy to focus on her words. "It's not real, Starling. Not real."

"Not real," I manage to spit out. "You're not real."

The horrendous creature frowns and then explodes. Bugs attack me from every angle. The rope drops. And in a shocked gasp, I fall backward off the roof. Plunge to my demise. This is the end.

I open my eyes to a pair of juniper green irises that sparkle.

"Are you okay?" Piper says, colliding on top of my flat body in a choking hug. "You're alive! That was the first time anyone has faced three fears in the same challenge." She speaks so quickly that I can barely process her words. "In fact, no one has ever battled two at the same time. I checked with the closest tree nymph."

"When did you have time to do that?"

"You were up there for hours! Can you believe it?" She laughs in a bubbly way. "You're famous with the nymphs now, Wyshawn!"

"Piper?" I croak out, my voice hoarse.

Her animated smile radiating relief is worth the torture I just endured. "Yes?"

"Can you roll off me, please?"

"Oh!" She realizes she's straddling me—again—and flops off. Piper stretches her back like a satisfied cat and then helps me stand with such fluidity that I'm in awe. Or maybe I'm in denial of being alive.

I scan my body for injuries. No bug bites mark my skin. There are three scars from where the swords all took my blood as payment. Wait, the scratches are already healed, and Kyle isn't laying in the sand where I had knocked him out. He either left or a mermaid ate him.

I clear my throat and face Piper. "So, um, did I win the prize?"

"Definitely not. I'm not sure if you beat any of them actually."

Did Piper witness the whole challenge? Why did all three fears attack me simultaneously? Without the prize in hand, my body feels like an anchor, sinking lower and lower.

"I need food," I say as I immediately collapse where the sand meets the water.

"Oh! Yes, I have snacks."

Rustling sounds come from behind me, followed by

Piper cursing. Maybe Kyle had stolen our sandwiches after all.

"I'll find you berries, hold on."

I'm pretty sure my body is in shock, so I simply let it unwind. The storm is long gone and the suns are daring to peek out from behind the clouds. I realize that I don't need their warmth, that my clothes are completely dry.

"You must be tired. You battled for hours." A scratchy voice of a nymph comes from my side. "We would like to congratulate you, Wyshawn Darl of Kensington, Lacordia. You have accomplished a feat no one else has."

I suck in a deep breath. "I didn't win an orb."

"I know," says the nymph, "but I meant interfering with another's challenge. That was noble of you to help, even if it was for the wrong reason."

At this, I turn towards her. "Wrong reason?"

"You knew Piper would steal Kyle's orb if he won, correct?"

"Oh, right. Well, I'd do anything for…I'd help… sometimes Piper needs…"

"Love can be a tricky thing, can't it?"

I pause and think of what to say. "I wouldn't know. I've never been in love. I think you misunderstand."

"Do I?"

We stare at each other for far too long…until Piper's soft footsteps skip out from the jungle.

"Do you like blueberries or strawberries better?" Piper says, sitting next to me in the sand.

"I'm so hungry, I could eat *you* right now."

Her eyes widen but she doesn't say a word. We're

quite a pair, covered in crusted mud and bruises. I gobble all her berries, ravenous for more. The nymph silently tromps away, her roots leading her back towards the jungle.

"Did you know that in the sixth jaguar year, there was a haunted mermaid?" Piper's story-telling voice is smoother than a lullaby. "She believed she had met the love of her life at a lavish party under a whimsical full moon. She tried to find him after it ended but had no luck. The next morning, she described the merman to her sisters, who all denied his existence. For the rest of her years, she searched for a portal to an alternate universe that she believed held her Partner. Opportunities came and went, and life swept by decade after decade, until she was moments from her eternal crossover. With her sisters by her side, holding her hand, somberly waiting for her departure, the mermaid spotted a glimpse of her merman in a tunnel of light. When her sisters asked why she was smiling when death called her name, the mermaid whispered, '*I didn't need to search did I? You were by my side the whole time,*'" Piper finishes.

I catch myself leaning in, wanting more, but clear my throat and ask, "Is that truth or fiction?"

"There can be truth in fiction." Piper smiles, erasing the haunting story from existence. "News has spread quickly of your heroics." She nudges my side. "Aqua is on her way. She's the leader of the merfolk."

"Why is she coming?"

"Hey, Wyshawn, you've got a little something, right here," Piper changes the subject and points to her teeth.

I'm picking a piece of blueberry peel from between my own teeth when ahead, the water ripples slightly. My heart rate speeds in fear that the swords are rising again. There's no way I want to go through that again. Would the second challenge be as difficult? But instead of swords, wet brown hair rises from the water, followed by a porcelain white face. The poetic beauty of the mermaid is not comprehensible. With features like no human artist could draw, she encompasses the enigma of an enchantress. As quickly as my body went into fight mode, I submit to relaxation again.

"Miss Piper Pan, we've heard about your new Partner," Aqua says in a melodic voice.

Out of the corner of my eyes, Piper's cheeks flush red. "He's not my...um, I heard you want to talk to us?"

"Yes, to you both." Aqua fixes her violet gaze on me. "First to Mr. Wyshawn S. Darl. You don't belong here. I'd like to offer to escort you from Neveraj. I hope Piper has explained to you that The Window she brought you through won't open again until the next Never Hour. However, we merfolk have another Window under the sea. We'd like to offer a ride underwater so you can go home early. We have a plant you'd swallow to let you breathe underwater until you reach the other side."

"Leave?" Piper's hand finds my leg.

If I leave now, Mum and Mother won't have to spend time worrying about me and the anxiety-provoking unknowns of this land will no longer be an issue. Maybe Piper will give me gold for finishing a challenge, and I could go back to a better life than before—one less job to burden my time.

Piper's lips hang partially open as she reads my face. If I stay, I can learn more about a dangerous yet magical world that many humans will never experience. I'd have extra time with Piper and still have the chance to steal Pixie to help Mum.

"Wyshawn?" Aqua snaps me out of my trance. "We need a decision."

"I appreciate your offer, but I promised Piper I'd teach her how to cook."

Aqua nods without judgment and turns to Piper. "We're leaving. RavenSoul is too strong. It's causing chaos under the surface. Wildlife is dying. We're no longer safe."

"But Aqua! You can't just leave. What about all our fun times? Our games?"

"Games?. It's 'bout time you grow up." Aqua's brows furrow deeply. "Time to move on."

"No." Piper's voice wavers.

"There's no changing our mind," Aqua sighs. "Actually, I came to ask you to leave too. Consider staying on the other side of the Window in the future."

Piper bows her head and mumbles, "I don't believe in the future."

"Very well. Mr. Darl, perhaps I'll see you in a harbor another day. Goodbye, Piper."

Aqua splashes a little as she dives into the water and disappears into the depths. I listen to the ebbs and flows of my breath. A mermaid in the flesh. Who has another way out. Had.

"I don't think I agreed to learn how to cook," Piper says quietly.

I don't have the energy to joke right now. "Hey, Piper? What's RavenSoul?"

"I'll tell you back at home." Piper stands and grabs the backpack.

I try to get up but sway on my feet. Now that everything has calmed, black spots blind my vision. In my state, she'll be lucky if my legs don't give out. There's no chance I'll be able to hike all the way to The Hidden Gem.

"Piper?"

"What?"

She must've heard the desperation in my voice because she's by my side when I slump towards the ground and everything goes dark.

CHAPTER
ELEVEN

Piper

Wyshawn has slept for four days. Four whole days which is unusual after a challenge so I've been watching him like a hawk.

From the kitchen, I glance over at him sprawled like a starfish on top of my bed, in only his underwear. I've been tempted to peek but kept my manners. It's a good thing Tank had come back to help me haul him home or he would still be asleep at Mermaid's Lagoon. Believe me, those tiny sprites can easily haul two-hundred pounds.

And don't get me started on those damn mermaids. I can't believe Aqua and her clan left. They'll come back, of course they will. Neveraj is as much their home as mine. No one would choose to leave, especially because I don't believe what she said about RavenSoul spreading under water.

With my blade, I cut off part of the codfish Epoch had caught for dinner, unsure what part is edible. Why learn to cook when my dads made my meals, then this land provided me with sustenance? I wipe off my dagger and insert it back into the sheath. If only my weapon could battle a shadow. How am I supposed to beat RavenSoul? Wyshawn wasn't even close to winning his first orb, but that's no surprise since he had to face three fears at once. Not quite fair if you ask me.

I remember my first challenge as clear as a Skeleton Flower. My hands had been clammy, but I didn't let my nerves show since Tank was watching. Like always, I had three fears to choose from: confronting my dads about their career, staying locked in a dark box, or trying to stop collectors from taking our home. Wyshawn had been correct that I chose my dads. No matter how terrifying it'd be to speak against them, they'll always be my safe space.

A bright parrot caws outside the window. It hovers on the other side of the netting I hung to keep bugs away. I sing a little tune back, smiling at our little game. This angle doesn't show the sky, but I know the suns-set waits just over the bend. Epoch skitters across the counter and chomps at the air savagely, trying to devour the parrot.

"Epoch! That wasn't nice. It just wanted to put on a show."

He turns in a circle twice and then lays atop one of my hats. I light a match and start a small fire to cook this codfish. Seven months ago, I had overheard Wyshawn tell his coworker that he loved codfish and planned to order it on his date the next night. Did he ever go on that date? Does he have a girlfriend waiting at home, wondering why he hasn't returned? How has this possibility not crossed my mind yet? It's not like I'd be jealous.

My gaze falls to his peaceful, sleeping face again. What kind of women would attract him? Probably a lawyer, someone who has their life compacted so well that it fits in the designer suitcase she carries to and from the office. No. Two uptight people in the same apartment might cause too much friction. He's probably dating a teacher, someone super sweet, a people-pleaser who his moms both adore. Georgia and Maram must already be picturing the grandbabies and the gifts to spoil them with. His girlfriend, probably named Sheila, doesn't steal pens from bars but will buy custom pens for their future children, with their names engraved on the side, all starting with the same letter—Silas, Sonja, and Steven.

I wonder if Sheila knows of Wyshawn's intense fear of bugs, heights, and failure. Her favorite color is probably bright pink, and she has already decorated their shared living space with floral wall paper. Wyshawn agrees because it makes her happy.

It feels like a bone inside me snaps. Are there such things as chest-bones? My hand automatically rises and presses between my breasts. Obviously, I have ribs that encage a vital heart, but this sensation feels deeper. Are there ways to crack a bone that lives deep, like within one's soul? Maybe it's a muscle spasm. Yeah, a muscle that surrounds my lungs must be convulsing from the adrenaline of...nothing...I've done nothing but sit around for four days.

"Breathe, Piper," I say aloud, slowing my breath and watching Wyshawn's chest rise and fall like I'm hypnotized.

Up and down. He's so broad and built. Does Sheila lay near him, curled close to his side, when they sleep, or does he like space to manspread? The sight of him now in the starfish shape of a mighty X might be the answer, each hand apart in opposite corners, each foot the tip of a triangle. I could keep him here, to prevent him from kissing Sheila again. No rule says I must show him where The Window leads back to Kensington.

Grabbing a spatula, I flip the fish, hoping the scent of his favorite meal arouses him. It's not like I've neglected him or anything. For days, I've played nurse by sprinkling water down his throat, adjusting his pillows, and reading him a book bedside. It's been fun role-playing, temporarily that is. I can't see myself ever taking care of someone like this again.

"Wyshawn!" I yell to see if he'll snap out of it.

No response.

Since Tank keeps flying off to Sol-knows-where, I've only had Lillian as company. I swear if she burdens me with one more premonition, I'm going to throw a mud pie at her. Her visions aren't real, there's no point in considering that they may happen.

My bowl of mushrooms tips over the counter, shattering into pieces against the wooden planks. Epoch pokes his little adorable head out from underneath.

"I thought you were taking a nap, little one?" I say, brushing most of the shards through the gaps between the planks.

He opens his mouth wide and lets out a tiny ferocious growl that would scare an ant.

When Neveraj doesn't magically sweep away my mess, as usual, I motion to Epoch, "Well, help me clean it up. Crocs have four feet. I only have two."

He stomps his two front webbed feet and sits in place, refusing my command.

"Fine, then it's not my fault if you step on broken glass later. I can live with it if you can."

Epoch's snout raises, sniffing the air. I mimic him and inhale smoke. "Oh, shit!"

The codfish is completely and fully on fire. Copper flames crackle and grow. I fan my hands in the air. If my Hidden Gem ignites, I'll have nowhere to sleep, nowhere to live, no home. Nothing.

"Damn it, Piper!" Wyshawn's groggy voice rumbles behind me, just before I'm shoved to the side.

He throws my only heavy blanket onto the fire, smothering the flame immediately.

"Are you trying to get yourself killed?" With one hand leaning on the counter, in a slight bend, weak and unsteady, Wyshawn breathes heavily. Still bent strangely, he groans and holds a hand to his stomach. What if he has internal bleeding from the challenge? Would he have survived this long?

"I was cooking you dinner," I spit out. "You're welcome."

"You were about to burn the jungle down. Haven't you learned anything about safety? One would think that to live in the jungle, you'd have gained something called survival skills," he says in a tone that bothers me more than it should.

I may not be a genius, but I'm not an idiot. I've built hundreds of fires in my kitchen to make s'mores and this is the first and only one to explode. It's not my fault he enjoys a weird type of fish that erupts into chaos. I return his glare. If the man doesn't think I'm competent enough to cook one dinner, then he doesn't need my help with whatever is wrong with his stomach. He can figure out his medical issues for himself. This nurse game is terrible, and I quit. No more coddling a six-foot giant, regardless of how seriously he may be injured, sick, or in need. It's always been me against the world anyway, so staying in that comfort zone is my best bet.

Epoch will still eat the fish, but he should suffer a little too for not cleaning his broken glass. I use tongs to toss the burnt fish out the window, destroying the bug-net in the process. Epoch scampers after it, out the window, and down the side of the treehouse.

"What was that net for?" Wyshawn's voice is softer as he points where half the bug-net has fallen loose.

I mumble and stomp toward my changing area. There's no chance I'll admit to designing a net that was supposed to make him more comfortable.

"Piper, hey, come on, look at me." He catches my arm, not letting me pass. "Hey, I'm sorry. The fire scared me and I...you need to be more careful."

"What I don't need is you telling me what to do." I twist his hand off me, but he winces and doubles over again.

"Aah!"

"It's okay, easy. Sit down," I say, letting him lean against me as we stagger to the couch.

"My stomach."

The way his face is scrunched so tight makes me wonder why I never captured a doctor to keep on Neveraj. She'd do me a lot more good than having someone like Kyle, Zheo, or Felix.

When I lower Wyshawn onto the couch, even though he's falling apart, I'm hyperaware of his skin against mine, and that all he has on is snug briefs. The sight of how much space it takes up, when soft, is a bit distracting, to say the least. I've been with my fair share of men and women, with an array of body types. Yet, I must admit, even if just to myself, that Wyshawn's entirety from head to toe is sexier than any other human on this forsaken planet.

And Sheila has seen all of him. Oh, Sheila, Sheila, has he pounded you into the headboard until you've begged for him to explode inside you? Ugh, picturing him on top of another woman feels like being swallowed by Cannibal's Cave.

"I think you were right," he says.

"What?" I blink, focusing on his dark eyes. "Right about what?"

"I think I'm just hungry. Really, really famished. Thanks for cooking for me, Piper. That was thoughtful of you, but do you happen to have anything ready now, like a protein bar or fruit?"

Nuts fall from the rooftop, between the cracks in the ceiling, showering us like hail. Wyshawn's face is comically shocked.

"Neveraj usually provides for us. If you need clothes, shelter, an escape route, medicine…oh, I guess I won't ever need a doctor then."

"What?" The curiosity lining his expression reminds me of a pleasant time in my past, a time I don't let myself ponder often.

"Nothing," I say, shaking my head.

As he starts to eat the nuts, fresh clothes appear from the floorboards. This time, it's jeans with a button-up shirt in pickle green. He notices it at the same time I do, and his gaze rockets over to my assortment of green hats.

"I think you should wear the shamrock visor to match that," I say.

His soft smile is the healing potion I've needed to

make the bone-splitting ache in my chest disappear. "Only if you wear the olive fedora," he says.

Tank flies in through the window. Overhearing our conversation, he magics both hats onto our heads and I can't help but laugh at how ridiculous Wyshawn looks. In all the nights I've visited *Walk the Plank*, he's never worn green.

"Wait, do you know where my old pants are? The ones I was wearing before you stripped me."

"I didn't strip you," I say quickly. "I could've, but I didn't."

He eases into the first long pant leg. "Did you want to?"

"I...no...why do you need the old pair?"

"The acorn Lillian gave me is in the pocket. It's not like I believe it'll grant a wish, but just in case..."

"You mean that one?" I point to my table of shenanigans, where his acorn sits next to a line of broken pocket watches.

When Wyshawn snatches the acorn, his other hand brushes against the pens I stole. "You never explained why you *really* collect these."

"Ask Sheila," I mumble, grabbing nuts for myself and stuffing my cheeks so there's no chance to say anything else on the subject.

"Who?"

"Yo imaginawy gifwund," I jumble between bites.

"I caught the first half of that." Wyshawn, unfortunately, rolls up the sleeve of his button-up, all the way to his elbows, in a way that makes me stop breathing. "My imaginary what?"

"Giwlfwiend."

"My girlfriend?"

"Sheila." I sigh and put all my energy into looking out the window.

"Oh, right, *that* Sheila." His penetrating gaze burns a hole in my cheek but I'm the game master. I can outlast this man in any situation.

"So, can we talk about it?" he asks quietly.

"No, I know Sheila's taller than me and hangs towels after she uses them and draws cartoons on sticky notes then leaves them around the apartment for you to find. On Sundays, she takes tea in the west gardens. Her hobbies include croquet, and riding atop her finest steed, Mister Huffalump. You make sure you don't have any obligations when Sheila attends the croquet club, just so you can see her smile in action." I stretch my jaw to stop my molars from clenching. "I know she buys you professional-grade cutlery and roasting pans and a cheese slicer and—"

"I'm gonna stop you right there." He munches another nut casually, as if he's entirely entertained by my rambling. "Why do you think Shenna—"

"Sheila," I correct.

"Right, why do you think Sheila would buy me cutlery and roasting pans?"

"For your dream job as a chef. She'd know exactly what you like and—"

His amused smile fades. "Jade…"

"Yes, Starling?"

"I haven't told anyone I want to be a chef. Not a soul."

I hop, jump, and skip over his confession like it doesn't matter and wonder how someone can be so goal driven. I've never had a dream of who or what I'd want to become later in life. The fact that he probably has steps laid out and planned is a bit too neurotic for me to even contemplate. I'll never understand people who have a list to guide them when it'd be better to not worry.

"What I meant..." Wyshawn begins, clearing his throat, "...is can we talk about my challenge? Was any of that real?"

"Once upon a time, in a house of glass lived an old man who didn't know the difference between his nightmares and reality." I pause to see if he's listening. When Wyshawn leans closer, I continue. "The town's children would venture to the glass house, dare one another to break one of the glass walls. The bravest child, usually the freckled girl, would knock against the glass with her fingertips. On the other side, the man would do a variety of things: sometimes peer back at her as if staring into the eyes of his granddaughter, other times he was caught swinging from his indoor trapeze bar to make her laugh, others he would be kneeling on the expensive carpet, arms outstretched high while screaming an unknown language. The children never knew if he assumed their encounters were reality or one of his nightmares because one day, he simply was not there."

"Piper, I love your stories, but sometimes you use them as a crutch to avoid my questions. I need to know how to win the next time."

"Tell me something, is achievement the only thing that's important to you?" I snap, knowing he doesn't deserve my sour mood. I want Wyshawn to cherish my stories, to relish in them, and beg for more.

He pauses, battling my intensity with his own, and says, "Achievement is better than always sitting back to enjoy the ride. At least, that's what Sheila always says." A flicker of a smirk rises on his face, absolutely infuriating me.

"Yeah, Sheila *would* say that."

I head towards the door. Since he's awake now, there's no need to pretend like I care if he's alive. The oranges and pinks that cut the sky need me to tell their secrets to, so I start towards the nearest hill. What's even better are the stars that will follow, for they're the only ones who know my heart.

"Piper, you also avoided my other question," Wyshawn says from the window, his top half hanging out. "What is this netting for?"

"To tie you up in my dungeon."

CHAPTER
TWELVE

Wyshawn

Unsettling whispers sneak through the wind, chilling my bones. Three vicious days have passed in silence since Piper snapped at me. It's been as quiet as death since she continually leaves the treehouse to practice flying. I've passed the time by going on informative runs through the jungle, cooking Piper meals, gathering flowers into a bouquet for her counter, and rehanging the netting over the windows—the ones I know she made for my benefit. Also, in order to survive, I've gotten into the habit of rubbing one out each time she's away on her flights.

Thankfully, I haven't been caught with a fistful of my dick by Lillian or Tank yet, and I don't want that to change, so I stand at the window on the lookout, only halfway concentrating on the snakes slithering below. The other half of my mind is imagining Piper naked, her smooth cream skin glowing in the light, the playful smile on her lips. How many fingers does she like twirling inside her? My cock is so hard it's near painful. I picture her teasing me, bending over purposefully to give me a front-row view of her ass. I stroke myself faster, wishing this vision was real. She'd be close enough that I'd only need to take one step forward until my tip rubbed against her entrance. Tension builds tight, ready to snap. What would her moan sound like? Would her voice sound different when she called out my name?

Fuck!

Without control, I come instantly. My orgasm shocks through me, almost making my legs buckle. Once my breathing settles, I quickly yank up my pants and lean my forehead against the wall. No other woman has destroyed me in this way. It's only been three hours since the last time I've beaten myself off with thoughts of Piper touching me. She's addicting, maddening, intoxicating. Will this never end? Piper Pan will be the death of me.

In this downtime, Lillian has taught me the names of trees and which plants are poisonous. What I haven't learned is how to beat the second challenge, what to expect, and if there is any way to collect Pixie other than by an orb. Apparently, there isn't even a rule about when

I can compete, as long as I give blood and recite the sinister invocation. I've memorized it in case Piper isn't with me when I sneak off to find the location. I haven't been able to ask her to show me where to go since she won't give me the time of day.

I'm not even sure why she's furious with me—because I asked her to stay on task instead of telling me another story? Because I want information to win? Or because I joked about my pretend ex-girlfriend? Piper's flamed cheeks were pretty adorable when she was rambling about Sheila. It's absurd that I'd want anyone else. Sure, I haven't told Piper how I feel, but she should know by the way I look at her, fix her pocket watches, and sit as close as possible on the couch.

I know she doesn't trust me yet, especially since she hasn't even told me the full story about her past. Yesterday when she was out flying, I found letters from her dads, dated a year ago with a return address from the roughest prison in Lacordia.

The scent of mint wafts through the breeze, letting me know Piper is about to land from her evening flight. I peek out the window, the one framed with strangled tree limbs fighting for their space, just in time to witness Piper gliding between high branches, angled straight towards her landing spot. Goddess, the wingsuit fits her so snugly that it should be illegal. Every curve teases me with its outline. A swoosh sounds as the massive wings change shape and fold right before she lands in a run. Well-practiced, she slows, fluidly and effortlessly.

The air zaps with heated energy when she realizes

I'm watching, yet she refuses to look my way. Soft ruffling sounds come next which I've deducted from her patterns mean that she's folding the wingsuit into her backpack and doesn't plan on taking another flight today.

When she walks in and drops her backpack to the floor, I can't tolerate her horrid pout any longer, and I finally speak for the first time in three days. "Good afternoon."

Her eyes narrow, full of venom. "Do you care about me at *all*?"

"That's the first thing you decide to say after three days? Piper, look around! I'm showing you that I care."

"I don't need you to clean or fix my stuff or make me food."

"Tell me what you need, and I'll give it to you."

Holy Luna, she's so damned adorable when she sticks her hip out like that, I can't stay mad. Her foot taps against the decomposing wooden planks, making them creak.

"Support my passions. What exactly did you say, the other day? Oh yeah, '*I use my stories as a crutch.*' If you don't want to hear my stories, stay somewhere else."

From here I can see her eyes water. Shit, don't cry. Please, don't cry.

"Piper, I'm sorry I said that." I soften my tone. "It was dismissive."

Her shoulders loosen and her hands drop to her sides, limp. "Thank you," she says quietly.

"But that doesn't mean I'm going to stop doing the other things. You might not need someone to help you, but I want to. I *like* cooking for you."

"Why?" She places the closest hat onto her head, a beanie of seafoam green.

"Cooking is action-based. I'm getting a task checked off the list."

Piper tilts her head to the side, exposing her long neck, skin that I want to taste, a view that tortures me. In an instant. a spark seems to ignite in her mind. "Okay, I'll make a deal. For every meal you cook, I'll tell you a story."

"Every single meal? How can you even think of that many stories?"

"Since I'm usually flying during lunch, we probably have less than twenty dinners left together."

Frustrated, I run a hand over my new, short beard. The island had provided a razor, but Piper seems to like the look.

Anyways, she's right. We don't know for sure how much time we have left stuck together and I'd been stupidly wasting my time in a silent-treatment game. If I can't win a challenge or steal Pixie, then a change of focus is needed. What if Piper could be convinced to live in Kensington? After Aqua's warning, it would be irresponsible to not prioritize Piper's safety long-term.

I start dinner by pulling chicken out of her magical freezer box, waiting for her to protest. Thankfully, she doesn't but watches my movements like an eagle. It's times like these when Piper puts so much direct attention on me, that it's difficult to consider that she doesn't feel the same chemistry.

"So? How was your flight, Jade?"

My nickname for her does the trick. Finally, she lets out a giant exhale and sinks into her favorite spot on the couch. Those poofy cushions swallow her whole.

"RavenSoul is worsening."

My hands stop chopping the chicken. I don't dare move, not wanting to spook her. Information is how I function. I'd drink liquid fire if she's willing to tell me anything more about Neveraj or Pixie.

"It's the shadow monster," Piper says, then readjusts so she's lying on a mound of her green clothes. "I can't figure out where it's coming from, or why it's spreading, but everything it comes in contact with dies."

Time feels like it's slowing down. How have I let this happen? I set the knife down with all my remaining restraint. "Piper. *Don't* tell me you've been putting yourself in harm's way and searching for it alone."

Epoch skitters across the countertop and snatches a bit of raw chicken in his mouth, like a little demon, then scampers away before I can catch him.

Piper rubs her temples. "I'm trying to find its origin. That could help me figure out why it started."

"You haven't touched it, right?" There's a brutal hum pulsing under my skin, a warning.

"It could never catch me if it tried."

My gaze darts to the window, then to the cracks between the planks that form her home. A shadow isn't solid, it could sweep through here at any time. "Piper! This isn't a joke. You could've gotten hurt out there, and I'd...please promise me you won't go alone next time."

She sits up quickly, eyebrows raised. "You're volunteering to fly with me next time?"

"Yes."

"Fantastic! I've been waiting to trial out the second wingsuit. Tomorrow?"

Slowly, I lift the knife and continue to chop the chicken. The fatty pieces get pushed to one side of the board while the quality meat stays in the center. It feels a bit gruesome and morbid to cook this after being surrounded by such an array of birds recently. Words repeat in my mind: corpse, skeleton, our mouths being its casket. I swear the inky eyes of the jungle watch me prepare our meal.

"Wyshawn, answer me. Will you fly with me tomorrow?"

"If you show me where the second challenge is."

On her makeshift stove, little flames roar to life when I start a fire. Within minutes, Tank, Lillian, and Epoch will all appear, like usual, ready for the meal they can smell.

"I can show you using my floor map, right now...you know, in case RavenSoul eats me and you have no other resources."

The knife falls to the floor. I put both hands on the counter, bracing myself. "For the love of Luna, don't joke about your safety. I can handle a lot but not that."

"Geez, *someone* is frazzled and needs to get laid," she whispers.

Tingles cover my body at the thought of stripping her bare, laying her down, and cupping her ass. No, I don't want a one-night stand. I've always been the guy to over-commit, and that won't change in this world.

In the middle of her home, light hugs the creaking, wooden floorboards that show an image of a treehouse, labeled Hidden Gem. "Can you see the whole map from there?"

I peek over the counter to confirm my view, then nod while I continue cooking.

"Skull Rock is home of the Lost Ones—Kyle, Zheo, and Felix."

"Zheo and Felix? More of your exes."

"Jealous, Starling?"

I give her a look.

"Mermaid Lagoon is over there, by the ocean. Here's the Hanging Devil, oh and Marooner's Rock is so fun, I should take you some time," she says excitedly.

"What's that dark blob scratched out?"

"Cannibal's Cave. I won't be going there." She doesn't meet my gaze. "And here is Eagles' Peak."

"Those look like rope bridges above a canyon."

"That's right, but you'll overcome your fear of heights by then."

"And why can't *you* do the second challenge?" I ask, wondering how far the canyon drops.

"I've already done it. My only option is to do the third

challenge next, the one set in the future, but I'm not interested."

Once the chicken starts sizzling, I flip it over to heat the other side. The top is a perfect golden brown and tender to the touch. "Then tell me what the challenge was like for you. Maybe it'll help me win."

Piper leaps from Eagles' Peak on the map to something called Sprite Hangout, then looks up through her long, dark eyelashes. Does she know how that expression wrecks me?

"I had three choices, one bridge leading me to each option. The first fear was to torture Tank, the second was to burn The Hidden Gem to the ground, and the third was to leave through The Window for good. As you now know, when in the simulation it feels real, and all the fears attack. It may sound easy, but all three options felt impossible."

"Which did you choose?"

"I'd never hurt a friend. Never. And as long as I can stay in Neveraj, I'd be okay building another home. I burned the treehouse to the ground. I've only felt comparable pain one other time in my life."

"When your dads...left?"

She goes quiet and turns her back to me so I can't see her face. "Unlike me, their friend *did* choose to hurt them. That wretched woman. I don't like talking about what she did." Piper puts both hands on her lips and stares out the window. "When I return you to Walk the Plank, I bet more news will have spread about Pixie since the pirates were investigating it."

I scoop the chicken onto four bamboo plates. A long yawn stretches from behind me as Lillian trumbles across the room, her roots dragging. With each step, another leaf falls like a feather, slow and graceful. Does a nymph grieve their lost parts?

After her, Tank zips to and fro like he's on a sugar rush. He hovers over his plate and chomps into the chicken without utensils. It doesn't matter that he's the size of my hand, Tank will eat just as much as me. He signs something with his hands to Piper while chewing. She nods and signs back. I want to ask what they're saying, but is it rude to interrupt their conversation? They go back and forth, as if bickering, but also excited about the topic.

"The Lost Ones will hear about this idea," Lillian interjects. "You may as well invite them too."

"Nah, parties are better without them." Piper wipes her mouth with a napkin after clearing her plate. "Wyshawn, will you go on a date with me?"

The food gets lodged in my throat. I try to suck in air. Nothing. Blocked. I hold my hands to my throat.

"You're choking!" Piper jumps in front of me and punches my stomach so hard that the food flies out and lands on her floor in a chunky little pile.

Epoch immediately crawls over and licks it up.

"Here, drink water," Piper says as she hands over a glass. "Luna Above, I didn't think you'd be so appalled at the idea of a night out with me."

"You're asking me out?" I try to settle my racing heart.

"Just for funzies. Tank is throwing a party to celebrate your win after the second challenge. And you'll be my date." She twirls once on her toes, then settles back into her chair. "We'll dress up, and the sprites will create music, the nymphs will dance and you can cook something to share. It'll be amazing. We usually have parties at the Hanging Devil. Oh, you'll love it! Tank is amazing at decorating."

"We don't know that I'll win yet."

"Do you plan to lose?"

"No."

Lillian is always the last one done eating. At a snail's pace, she licks her plate clean with a rough, long tongue of bark. Afterwards, the island magically whisks our dishes away and they're cleaned in an instant, then returned to their designated area. I realize Piper isn't forced to live as a slob if her home will magically tidy for her; she simply chooses to tornado her clothes everywhere, like an art form. What used to be annoying I now view as endearing. She lives purposefully in chaos. The Hidden Gem wouldn't be the same without her quirky habits.

Tank nods and flies outside. Half the time he's around, it feels like he's holding a heavy secret he refuses to unload. There's something suspicious about that little guy. At the table, Lillian falls asleep, like she has the last few nights, her branches slowly tilting towards the floor.

Per routine, Piper also claims her spot on the couch. Journal in hand, she scratches Sol-knows-what on the paper. I've been tempted to read her entries while she's been out flying every day but decided against it.

"What do you write about?" I plop next to her on the couch.

"Want me to read you yesterday's entry?" She glances up with hesitancy in her gaze. "Of course, you do. I'm a great narrator. Buckle in, Starling."

"Do your worst." I gesture for her to start. There's a chance I've been smiling a lot more since I landed in Neveraj.

"Bitter revenge is a poisonous taste," she begins. "A hunger claimed a young Venetress's heart. Unable to overcome her rage and grief, a teenager named Kavianne cursed her older sister. Thorns possessed the unfortunate woman's body, poking out of her skin from wrists to ankles. Kavianne didn't give her sister the answer of how to break the curse and watched her suffer, observing her through years of torture without offering a helping hand. In the end, Kavianne never expected that her sister had already forgiven her, and still loved her, despite the rash impulsivity she had exploded with in that moment of weakness."

"That's...dark," I say, "Is that a character you made up?"

"Not this one." She slaps her journal closed. "You haven't heard about Mora? The Venetress who lives near Villeneuve in Ozaron? She was cursed with thorns by her own sister."

I must be staring at her strangely because she laughs,

the sound tastes like brownie batter, thick and full of everything I want.

"Man, you must've been living under a rock," she says while tossing her journal next to the others.

"I work a lot."

"Well, you won't be working for the next few weeks. Enjoy the time off."

The hours pass by in a single breath under a blood sky. She tells me story after story, half I save to memory but half were layered in so much detail that they'll never see the light of day again. With each new character, new plot, and new setting, she scoots closer on the couch. As the suns disappear and the night welcomes the moon, she sheds off clothing items getting more comfortable. First goes one sock, lost for eternity in the couch crevices. The second sock, obviously not matching the first, falls to its death onto the floor and sinks between the wooden planks to the jungle below. During one of her thriller stories, she gets goosebumps and her nipples harden under her bra. She's not the least bit aware and I use every ounce of effort to keep my gaze on her eyes. If sitting silently the whole night will give me this gift of her sharing her passion, I'll gladly forego rest. When her enthusiasm eventually slows and she sits back, quiet, the vibe evolves into something new. Goddess, she's my personal drug, laced in seductive dreams.

"Let's try something different after you win the second challenge," Piper says softly.

"Different?" Alarms and sirens go off in my head. "Why?"

Her smile rips my self-control to shreds. "After you win the orb I'll share the bed."

My heart stops beating as I study her face. It's a dare, a test. She can't mean sex, just an innocent sleep next to each other. Maybe her heart will open to the idea of us cuddling together, that she might want me the way I desperately thirst for her.

CHAPTER
THIRTEEN

Piper

We couldn't fly out the next day or the day after that. Thunderstorms had a different plan for us, trapping Wyshawn and me in The Hidden Gem in epic torture. I had forgotten to mention before that each time it rains, the land collects a thousand balloons, all lost to their owner. Withered and half-deflated, they create an umbrella of sorts over my treehouse to keep us mostly dry.

Every time a new unique feature of Neveraj presents itself, Wyshawn has tried to explain it away with rationale and science. He and his explanations have been quite entertaining. What sucks me in most is his willingness to go outside his comfort zone. Like last night, he even chopped branches above my bed because he knows I like to fall asleep while star gazing. And don't get me started on the way he faced his fear by capturing fireflies in jars outside the window just for my viewing pleasure. Every meal he's cooked for me has been flavored with passion and dedication. When I journal, he gives me space. When I pace from my wound-up-nerves due to lack of flying, he distracts me by asking about my collection of stolen trinkets. This damned man knows what I need when I need it. I hate it. Hate him. Hatred is my only option because the other feeling is inconceivable.

I've spent years alone daydreaming about the qualities of a near-perfect Partner, not that I'd ever want a real relationship. It just so happens that Wyshawn Starling Darl checks off far too many of them. The person I'd share my soul with has always been one made of fiction, a Neverbody, a non-starter, an impossibility. Then enter Wyshawn. This is a real problem.

I don't want to be attracted to Wyshawn. I'm done with disappointments and heartbreak. When my dads were taken, it hit too hard. I refuse to become attached again, so this lust will resolve on its own eventually. Plus, if I get too horny, three Lost Ones are willing to please.

Harsh suns-light slants through the ceiling as we suit up for our flight. I purposefully avoid looking at Wyshawn in all spandex, stretching over his lean muscles, tall frame, and broad shoulders. Hopefully his long hair won't get caught in the wings. That could lead to an unfortunate beheading.

"You look absolutely thrilled," I tease as he fiddles with the straps nervously.

He mumbles something under his breath, keeping his head bowed, then asks, "So, what's the plan?"

"No plan. We fly and search for shadows."

"If you let me in on your ideas, I could help make a route, track where we've been, and chart the best options. We need details and facts to focus on your observations. Little steps like this could save time."

"Time isn't something I believe in."

His head snaps up and a shocked, bewildered, but amused look claims his face. "You...don't believe in time? How is that possible?"

"Do you believe in an underworld?"

"Uh, no."

"How is that possible?" I ask.

"Touché." He scrubs a hand down his face and shakes his head. "Let's get this over with."

"See, you're thrilled. I told you."

"Sheila would never make me do this."

I slap his shoulder, making him laugh harder than I've ever heard. The sound sends butterflies fluttering through my stomach. Bad sign. I don't need any frickin' butterflies. I nod for him to follow me, which he does. After removing one of the bug nets, we scale out a window onto a long tree branch.

"Don't look down. Follow my moves."

We climb higher and higher. I pray to mighty Luna

Above that he remembers all the training I gave him yesterday about aero dynamics. Who am I kidding? It's Wyshawn, he probably has my lecture stored in different files of his mind, labeled with unique fonts.

"You're doing great!" I say, feeling uncomfy using such encouraging words. I'm the girl with an edge, the one with a blade attached to my hip, not a cheerleader.

"Tell me a story, or just talk, anything will help." His voice trembles below me. When I check, his arms are shaking. "Please?"

"A weightless Weaven was born, made of only air. A wisp she was, as light as a breath, as heavy as an empty cloud. Her face, the shape of a changing moment, her eyes the color of nothing. Weaven was adored by all, hated by none. She only ever wanted to find her mother. This dream never turned into reality, since her mother died at childbirth. When the time came, the wind Goddess proclaimed that all beasts of the sky would be Weaven's mother."

We're already at the highest branch thick enough to hold us—a great launching spot. He's at my side, hip against hip, with a slight sheen of sweat glistening on his forehead. What would he do if I pinned him against the tree trunk and trailed my fingertip down his neck?

"You're so—" he says with his usual stoic face.

"Impractical?" I interrupt, not wanting to hear the insult from his lips. "Frustrating? Flippant? Impulsive?"

"I was going to say creative, imaginative, and free."

His words knock the breath from my lungs. Free. I've never considered that word, yet it fits so well. Free as a bird soaring through the skies. I can't let him know how much that means to me. I turn away from him, push the button on my suit, spread my wings, and leap.

Wind kisses my cheeks as I hoot and holler into the sky.

"Piper!"

"Jump! Come on!"

I hear him groan but know he'll follow. My heart sings as the wings glide perfectly through the air. There's no chance I can contain my smile and a squeal bursts from my mouth. Suns-shine radiates through my body and a gleeful drumming pounds in my chest. After two days cooped up at home, this rush of adrenaline is like an intoxicating drug. Luckily for Wyshawn, there aren't as many trees on this path. The further we go, the more spread out they become, until the jungle stops abruptly, a line on the earth, and opens to a valley.

I should slow down and check on him, but the liberating sensation is too overwhelming. My body feels infused with a sparkling glow that surges through my veins. Every green below sharpens to separate shades—parakeet to turacos to glistening tanagers. The sound is a constant familiar swish of wind whipping by my face. A few shadow shapes blanket the deep valley, but they're only mirroring the clouds above. No RavenSoul here. I turn to the right and dip lower. Maybe it's snaking between the long grass. A slash of crimson contrasts against the endless emerald sea and I squint. It's moving quickly. No red animals come to mind that are native to this valley. When I swoop lower, two black silhouettes sandwich the red. Ah, my Lost Ones are on an adventure again. Maybe they could benefit from a story or two.

Something soft swipes against my collarbone, light as a feather. Then a wiggle comes next.

"Epoch! You could've suffocated in there. You know not to burrow in my suit."

Unable to grab him with my hands on my landing lever, I hope he holds on for dear life. In a minute, the Lost Ones below will hear us, so we may as well have fun. I readjust my angle to plummet straight toward Kyle, Zheo, and Felix. Their surprised hollers brighten my spirits even more. Arms swing at me as they duck out of the way. I barely miss one and swoop back up. Dive again, like an eagle ready to capture its prey. Kyle's deep yell makes me snort out loud.

"Piper! Stop it! You'll scare her to pieces!" Kyle shouts.

Her? Who?

Kyle and Felix are with a young unfamiliar woman. How is she here? Who is she?

"Who is that?"

Oh, I had forgotten about Wyshawn. Still flying, his landing looks as smooth as barbed wire. If I had known earlier that we'd run into the Lost Ones, I never would've invited Wyshawn. He shouldn't have to face Kyle again. I land gracefully next to them, my sneakers hitting the dry dirt. The long grass flitters up to my knees, but since I'm wearing my typical long yoga pants they don't tickle my skin.

The summer breeze blows the newcomer's shoulder-length brown hair slightly, but I can barely register her other facial features when her hollow eyes stare back at me, eerily vacant. Her ivory lace blouse needs a wash. It's covered by a thin, cardinal-red cardigan meant for fashion and doesn't make any sense for this weather. She wears black laced high-heeled boots that cover her shins and end just below the knee, also not belonging in Neveraj.

"Where did you come from?" I ask.

Her devious smile curves up to points sharper than the tip of a hook. "The second star on the left."

I stumble backward, trip on something, and land flat on my ass. "What did you just say?"

"Piper!" Wyshawn roars. "Don't ever do that again! You left me!"

I scramble to my feet, shushing him, while Kyle and Felix bend over in laughter. Our little circle becomes a tornado of chaos. Epoch jumps off my shoulder and lands on the woman. He bites her neck and she screams. A whole murder of crows flies out of the nearest tree.

Wyshawn's face is contorted with rage and fear while my exes are both highly entertained by the scene. I watch Epoch, suspicious since he is a trained Venetress hunter. Slowly, I back up and touch Wyshawn's chest.

"I'm sorry," I whisper to him without taking my eyes off the woman. "Let's go home."

"No, there's no chance I'm flying again! How am I supposed to trust you, Piper?"

Kyle's face has turned the shade of a cherry while choking on his laughter. He's never been a natural at reading the energy of others, otherwise he'd be as still as a statue due to the tension.

"Wyshawn!" I hiss under my breath. "You can be mad all you want, but we need to leave. Now."

His accusations finally stop short. Wyshawn's eyes rise towards the others and it's as if he's registering them for the first time, which is odd given how well he typically notices his surroundings. His throat bobs and he nods to me slowly. I wonder if he realizes that his arm is cast out as a barrier between me and them. Without a word, I lace his fingers with mine and pull him away from the others. I march as fast as possible to match his long strides. He flattens the tall grass with his heavy stomps. I can feel the Venetress' attention on the back of my head but refuse to turn around until we're far enough away. It's not that I fear spellcasters in general, but there shouldn't be one here.

"You don't want to meet Holly?" Kyle bellows out.

That name snakes up my spine. Holly? As in *Holland*? A sour taste invades my mouth. It takes concentration to keep walking, to act like her name doesn't affect me, to move Wyshawn to safety. Goddess, I'm such an idiot. He'd be safer in The Hidden Gem, cooking and cleaning like he loves. Instead, selfishly, I dragged him on a hunt for shadows. Then, like a moron, I abandoned him during our flight and left him to his own devices in the air. Plus, I exposed him to a possible threat. Even if I would have let myself enjoy his company, this man deserves a better friend than me.

"Piper, tell me what's wrong." Wyshawn continues

to walk next to me, but his voice is softer. "How can I help?"

I want to bury myself. After everything I just put him through, he has forgiven me so easily? Seriously? I should've begged the mermaids to take him through their Window when given the chance. That way he'd be secure at home, not having to worry about the deadly threats here.

"Piper!" He squeezes my hand. "Stop running. They're not chasing us. What do you need?"

"I need you to go away!" I rip my hand from his. His mouth opens and I know what he'll say before it comes out. I muster the courage to lie to his face. "I know you don't understand. I should've told you this from the beginning, but I was trying to be nice. I don't want you in my home, Wyshawn. I never have. And I don't want to share my space or my stuff or waste my breath telling you stories."

"Jade ..." He takes a small step forward, but I hold up both hands.

"You need to find somewhere else to live. I'm assuming you've memorized the map on my floor. The magic will guide me to you right before the Never Hour, don't worry. Until then, I don't want to see you. Can you understand that?"

Human emotion is an interesting concept. Only minutes ago I was riding a high of elation in the sky. Now, at the sight of his expression, it feels like an anchor has been struck through my chest. This—this moment right here is why I don't want to deal with life on the other side, why I'm content living alone, why there's no significant future for me. Real life, choosing to live, is only full of pain and misery.

For the last few days, I've let Wyshawn distract me from what matters while playing a fake life of make-believe. I need to focus on finding Pixie, healing Neveraj, and defeating RavenSoul. Sending Wyshawn away will benefit us both. He'll be away from the Lost Ones, and I'll be free of his chains.

"You want me to leave," he says—not a question.

"I want...yes. I'll find you in a few weeks."

He bites his lip, studies my face, then closes his eyes. When he opens them, a stone wall has replaced the deep dark cavern that used to beckon me inside. It doesn't matter. I've always been afraid of the unknown.

"Tell Lillian I'll need a raincheck," he says coolly, then turns his back as the jungle swallows him whole.

CHAPTER FOURTEEN

Wyshawn

A few weeks my ass. I'll complete the next challenge tonight. Piper can try to push me away all she wants, but it won't work. There's no chance I'll be flying, so I tear off the tight wingsuit, feeling free again. I have half a mind to chuck it into the weeds so I never have to fly again, but Piper wouldn't appreciate that.

The intense afternoon suns makes me sweat beads as I hike toward Eagles' Peak. I remember the map of Neveraj like I know my favorite recipe. I may not have a plan, and these trees may be stalking my moves, and shadows might creep behind each trunk, but I can pretend everything is fine.

Something spooked Piper when we ran into her exes. We must've flown decently far from The Hidden Gem because the air is quieter here. No breeze teases the long grass, and the unrelenting suns aren't hidden behind a canopy of branches. Here, in this prairie, I'm as exposed as a rodent to a soaring eagle. A flood of sunshine drowns the meadow in an uncomfortable way and all the familiar sounds are gone. There's no rushing river water gushing down the slope. Even the greens have shifted to shades of brown, tan, beige, wheat, and cream. Since no clouds block the suns, it's easy to mark which way is north. Step by step, I march towards the second challenge. The lack of bird songs chills my bones. The word vulnerable keeps popping into my mind as a warning.

Finally, I hit the landmark of crossbones and skulls carved into two boulders. From here on out, the hike is straight uphill. Rocks and pebbles skitter underfoot. Twice, I fall to my knees but catch myself, hands out so my palms bear the brunt of the scrapes. A few solitary trees scatter the scene, carrying fresh forbidden fruit. Lillian had taught me this kind is poisonous. I wouldn't eat one anyway if my life depended on it, since they're all rotten and full of crawling beetles.

A path develops from a worn trail. The longer I follow it, the more I gag on the smell of sulfide. The odor must be my imagination, or a trick of this land, because raw sewage, burning flesh, and corpse flowers combined couldn't create such a hideous stench. I hasten my pace since the air itself tastes sour and leaves a bad residue in my mouth.

Someone whispers my name behind me, but when I turn only the long grasses stare back.

"Piper?" My heart rate speeds at the thought that maybe she returned to me.

Silence.

"Kyle?"

"Tank?"

I trudge up the hill, legs screaming. This would be an ideal time for the distraction of an original Piper story. In our time together, she's had this uncanny knack of bringing out my softer gentler side. Never have I considered others' emotions as much as hers. Piper easily imagines how the world could be a better place and that mentality rubs off on me. She could make such a difference in Kensington if she applied herself to any passion. Why does she hide her life away here as a voluntary outcast? If she gave us a chance, maybe she'd see more of me than all seriousness and structure and I'd learn more about why she is always searching for endless fun.

I take a break from hiking, bending over at the waist, out of breath. With both hands on my knees, I stare down at the dirt. Dozens of ants crawl over my boots so I shake them off. Disgusting. Another foul stench chokes my lungs, like rotten food mixed with skunk spray. I try to breathe through my mouth and create a shield over my eyes to find Eagles' Peak faster. There it is, under the streaking suns-rays. A massive rope bridge is attached to a cliff's edge. Halfway, it breaks off in three directions. Didn't Piper say each challenge has three choices?

I jog through the tall grass, flattening it along the way. If any threats are following me, I've given them an easy trail. Oh well. At the entrance to the bridge, I peer over the side and immediately go dizzy. Why does it have to be so high? Shaking, I drop to my knees and lay flat on my stomach. There's no chance I can do this. In the rancid breeze, the bridge teeters back and forth, creaking slowly. *Creak. Creak. Creak.*

Nope, can't do it. I'll just have to find Piper and beg for her to let me borrow Pixie. She must understand how much Mum needs it. Though, wouldn't a million humans benefit? What makes me and my family special? If Piper shares, she'd have an obligation to donate to everyone. I groan, knowing I have to win it myself.

A fluttering sensation feathers against my neck. I'm about to slap whatever bug is trying to bite me, but a flash of gold blinds me. "Tank?" I ask when the sprite hovers above the dirt at my nose. "What are you doing here?"

He gestures wildly for me to stand up. On wobbly legs, I rise. Somehow, this view feels even worse than when I was balancing on the edge of a skyscraper in the first challenge. Maybe because this one is real. If I fall, I die.

Tank flies towards my zipper and points to my dick, with a stern look. He hasn't caught me jacking off while

Piper's away, has he? Is that why her best friend tracked me out here instead of returning home—to judge me?

Again, he points, but this time darts into my pocket.

"What the?" I jump as his body squirms in my pants. "Get out!"

Tank exits, holding an acorn that's half his size.

"Lillian's gift?" I ask, forgetting that I had brought it with me "What do you want me to do with this?"

Tank zooms around my head, his wings buzzing softly each time he changes directions.

"I don't understand. I'm sorry." I restore the acorn to my pocket and take a deep breath.

The longer I wait to start the challenge, the worse my panic will paralyze me. It's now or never. My left foot jiggles the wooden plank and both hands clutch the rough rope so tightly I'll be sore tomorrow. At a snail's pace, I linger on each slab, praying to the Sols that it doesn't crack. Turning back looks just as terrifying as continuing forward so I keep my eyes on the spot where it breaks into three options. Ten more steps.

Tank hovers in front of my face, flying backward. He gestures for me to move forward, forward, keep going.

"I can," I whisper, voice croaky. Eight more steps.

Tank may have despised me since day one, but he's the one here, encouraging me.

"I got this." My palms burn from scratching against the rope.

Five steps remain. The bridge shakes. Three more. I hold my breath. Take a giant step to land on the steady board in the middle, gated off with a sturdier fence around its border. Unable to control myself, I glance below and take in the giant pillars supporting this section from far below.

Where is the ground? All I can see is gray and I can viscerally smell sweat and vomit.

Not wanting to breathe in this acidic taste a moment longer, I squint ahead as my three options appear in the suns-beams. The first shows a hovering outline of a rectangle of sparkling specks glittering and shining. It disappears, then flashes back into view, then disappears again. I shrug, not even knowing what that represents. The challenge is supposed to show a current fear, but I don't know what this rectangle means. My second option starts to form, a pile of golden powder. I assume it's Pixie dust, but before I can examine it, it evaporates. Again, it forms, in abundance, then vanishes in a blink. I need Pixie desperately, and if it is gone, I'm screwed. I glimpse the third bridge, still empty. Raising my hand over my eyes so I'm no longer blinded, I see a silhouette of a body, first snake-green sneakers, then petite legs. When I see the waist, it's obvious the projection mirrors Piper. Her back is to me and she begins to walk away, across the bridge to the far side.

"Wait!"

I take a step after her, then remember I need to choose between a random rectangle, a pile of Pixie, or Piper. Which do I want more? Pixie could help Mum, but there's no guarantee how long it'll delay her memory loss. What if I bring Pixie home but the powder doesn't make any difference? Piper, on the other hand, could be my entire life, my whole future, the reason for becoming a better man. Before I can choose, the end of the first bridge snaps off its hook and falls into the canyon below, taking the rectangle with it.

"That's never happened before!" a female voice shouts out. "Hurry up!"

Who was that? I glance around. Across the canyon, Lillian watches me in horror, all her limbs flailing towards me, like she's wanting to remove me from the challenge. Another deathly croak reminds me to move. I lunge towards Piper on the third bridge and sprint across the shaky beams. It wasn't made for this speed and rocks violently. Next to us the second bridge snaps and the pile of Pixie drops into the Abyss too.

"Move!" I don't know if illusions can hear or follow directions, but she doesn't react.

When I reach Piper's back, I lift her into my arms, surprised that she has weight and feels real. A look of complete shock overwhelms her face when she meets my gaze. Big emerald eyes, confused and so realistic, widen fully.

"Wyshawn?" Her voice sounds real.

Her body shakes in fear like a human. Fuck. Is this actually happening?

My legs push harder. The rope ahead frays. It tears. Then loosens. We drop a bit. Piper screams and curls into my chest. I hold her tighter. Run faster, need to get to the safe side. My chest burns. Then it snaps. Falls.

"Noo!!" I throw Piper with all my might to the other side.

As I plummet, her body lands on the grass.

My hands claw for purchase. Pain slices up my arms. Along my sides. My head hits something hard, then my hip. I grab. Grope. Squeeze a branch. Out of breath. I pull myself up little by little. It's more difficult than damn pull-ups. Pebbles and soil come loose from the rock on the cliff wall and skitter down my body.

"Wyshawn!"

I glance up, checking to see how far I fell. Over the edge, the top of Piper's blonde hair glistens in the sunslight.

"Hold on, I'll come get you!" she hollers and a few rocks tumble into my hair.

"No!" I can barely talk between agonizing grunts. "Stay there!"

Slowly, painfully, I haul myself branch by branch to the top and scrape my stomach over the edge onto the grass. Panting, I immediately crawl away from the cliffside. Flat on my back, I'm expecting her to hand me water from her backpack or skim her finger down my bloodied arms.

Nothing.

Sore, exhausted, sweaty, and still breathing heavy, I sit up. She's gone. Was it all part of the game? Or did she leave me again?

I flop to my back again and stare at the bright cobalt sky to calm my racing heart. In and out. Settle down. I'm safe and Piper isn't in danger. It's over. I sit up again and wipe dirt off my clothes, then rub my arms where bruises will form tomorrow.

"Well, that happened," I speak to no one.

Next to me, the ground cracks a little. My body goes on alert, but I'm too tired to roll away. At first, I think a flower is sprouting in hyperspeed until a clear sphere protrudes from the soil. It hovers above my hand, empty and beckoning me. Is this a trick? Wait, it's the orb, my prize for winning. I beat a challenge without knowing the logistics. Is it because I survived or because I picked the correct option?

Tank flies over and lands on top of it, blocking me from touching the orb.

"Hey! That's mine."

He gestures wildly with his hands and I have no way of understanding until a female voice speaks behind me. I startle and whirl around to see Lillian watching me.

She starts interpreting. "Tank wants to make a deal."

"What kind of deal?"

"You can take the orb, but he also needs you to do a favor. Take this Starlight," Lillian says as Tank holds out a vial of a liquid golden syrup. "When you leave at The Never Hour make sure to go through The Window before Piper. When you pass through, pour this Starlight in the air."

"That's it?" I ask.

Tank nods.

"Why?"

"It'll seal shut. No one goes in or out again," Lillian explains.

"So, you're going to trap Piper? Give her no choice

but to stay?" I ask, anger filling my words. "She will be caged."

"It's not caging her," Lillian interprets, this time hesitantly, pausing uncomfortably. "You'd be doing her a...favor."

I snort and cross my arms, not liking any part of this plan. "Enlighten me."

"Piper hates going to Kensington. She's gone out of necessity but always comes home complaining about the people and how much she wishes she could stay home."

"She hates Kensington?" Instead of interacting with Tank, I ask Lillian this time. "Is this true?"

Tank cuts off Lillian from whatever she was about to say, so she continues to interpret, "Yeah. There's a bartender there she always goes on and on about; how he's infuriating and uptight and boring and drives her insane."

"She said that?" My hopes fall in an instant.

I stare at the liquid Starlight in the vial that's bigger than Tank himself. There are too many unanswered questions. Maybe she should stay here, but I need to talk to her about this first. For now, I'll agree to pacify Tank and let him believe I'm on board.

His eyes narrow and he gestures again.

"I don't want to say *that*," Lillian says, shooting him a look.

He signs again, this time a longer conversation goes on between them. Finally, Lillian translates, "Tank says... if you don't agree, then he will tell Piper her Dads broke out of prison months ago and haven't tried to reach out to her. It'll break her spirit. Do you want Piper to hurt?"

I swallow and crack my knuckles, then glance between the vial and the orb—two containers holding two magical particles that could change my life. I know what I need to do.

CHAPTER
FIFTEEN

Piper

I lean against my kitchen table, trying to catch my breath. Moments ago, my body had jolted through some crazy, impossible ultra dimension, that took me to the bridge at Eagle's Peak. I was just there, in Wyshawn's arms, and now I'm back home. What the Abyss? My whole body is shaking wildly. I need something to ground me.

"Tank?" My voice shakes as I glance around my empty home. "Lillian?"

Only the familiar bird cries reply, as if nothing insane happened. Maybe I'm dehydrated or sleep-deprived.

Stumbling into the kitchen, my hip crashes against the counter as I fumble for a protein bar and shove half of it into my mouth. My heart still hammers. Was I dreaming or did the magic of Neveraj transport me to Wyshawn? If so, why?

I tilt my neck up and open my mouth like a baby bird. Fresh water from the leaves pours into my mouth in a perfect stream. Still, I can't shake the feeling that I need to be where Wyshawn is, that he's in danger, and that I'm too late. I stuff my body into my wingsuit in record time and jump out my window. The sound of my wings flapping usually soothes me, but instead of gliding serendipitously, I push harder into the oncoming wind. Hundreds of questions rush through my mind, which is strange because when I fly, I usually don't have a single thought.

I duck under a branch. Slide between two trunks. Strain against the wind that's doing its best to keep me away. Ahead, Eagle's Peak glows under the afternoon suns, but I can't see Wyshawn. That's when all three bridges come into view, each collapsed into the canyon. My heart races.

"No!" I speed up, urging my wings to pump faster.

How could the bridges break? Lillian once told me they'd survived horrendous storms for centuries. A strange compulsion overtakes my senses, screaming at me that I need to fly faster. I've never felt such a pressing, grave energy looming over me before. It's as if death stalks me behind the clouds, about to chase me through the sky. On instinct, I turn around to check if I'm being followed. Sure enough, RavenSoul hunts me in a mass of swirling gray fog that opens its jaw and bares its fangs. I dip out of the way right before a tentacle of shadow tries to clutch my ankle. Below, Wyshawn comes into view, near the cliffside edge. Both Tank and Lillian sandwich him.

"Wyshawn!" I scream.

He turns fast, his eyes widening. Coldness creeps closer as RavenSoul chases. I swear my foot is touching ice.

"Wyshawn! Run!"

He tilts his head in question. Why is he confused? Doesn't he see the murderous shadow figure lurching after me, wanting to devour us all? He waves with one arm, or maybe he's blocking the suns' rays. The deadly chill travels to my knee. For the first time, whispers ooze out of the possessed RavenSoul. I hear my fathers' names on repeat. 'Brax and Davien,' it hisses again and again. 'Brax and Davien.'

Maybe it violated my mind and I'm losing my sanity, but I refuse to let it damage Wyshawn's consciousness too. He's too good to be traumatized like me. If he's not going to run, then I'll have to fly him out of here. I brace my shoulders for the incoming weight, swoop down, and grab Wyshawn under his armpits.

"Woah!" He flails for a moment before I latch his belt loop into my suit. It's not safe, but better than nothing.

"Hold on here," I yell.

"Piper, slow down!" He grabs the handlebar.

We fly at such an awkward angle that I know we'll

have to touch down before arriving back at The Hidden Gem.

"I can't! It'll hurt you!"

"What will?" Wyshawn scans the treetops below. "I don't see anything."

If we weren't in an emergency, I'd applaud him for facing his fear by staring directly down instead of clenching his eyes shut.

"Behind us!" I yell into the wind.

"There's nothing there, Piper. Can we land? Please?"

I wiggle my foot, realizing it's no longer freezing. Did we scare the shadows away somehow? Did RavenSoul change its mind? Reluctantly, I slow down and check behind us. He's right. No shadows.

Wyshawn's breath is hot against my neck, making a shiver slip up my spine. "You okay?" he asks as his gaze pierces through my armor. "I guess you forgive me, then?"

Forgive *him*? I'm the one that needs to apologize. I pushed him away before explaining why I panicked about Holland. I had lied and was cruel to him. Obviously, I don't want him to live somewhere else, but how do I explain that Holland is here with the Lost Ones if I don't have clear answers myself?

The scent of grapefruit informs me that we've arrived at the Hanging Devil. A cluster of emotions are playing dodgeball in my chest, attempting to burst from my body, but I need to wait until we land to sort them out. I focus on our favorite party spot where the epic vine swing and hammocks sway in the breeze and where the bamboo slide curls out of a tall tree. Next to it, the rock-climbing wall towers tall, though it has always taken second place compared to my favorite: the trampoline pit crafted from nature. I doubt Wyshawn will want to try any of them. At the moment, I don't feel like playing games either.

We dip lower and I'm ready to take in my wings for the landing when Wyshawn's soft voice blows in my ear, "I'm sorry, Piper. Please know that."

He's sorry? What an endearing imbecile. My feet thud onto the ground, one, two, three, four, until we come to a stop. Quickly, I unstrap Wyshawn and he loses his balance. Instead of supporting him, I shove his chest. Apparently, not hard enough, because he barely moves.

"Don't scare me!" I yell, feeling heat rise to my cheeks.

His jaw drops open and he raises both hands.

"You almost died!" I storm closer and push Wyshawn again, this time his back casually bumps against the trunk behind him. "I was trusting you to stay safe and the second we're apart, you almost get yourself killed!"

I need to punch something, kick a tree down, or scream at the top of my lungs. Instead, a lake of tears has the audacity to pool in my eyes.

"Piper..." Wyshawn starts, his voice soft, his eyes too tender.

"You aren't supposed to need me to rescue you!" I scream, my throat already sore and scratchy. "How could you!?"

I'm inches from his chest and want to bury my face in

his shirt. This horrible, wretched, vulnerable feeling is eating me alive from the inside. Why does it feel like something is scraping out my innards into a hollow cave at the same time as warm suns-shine fills the cavity? I hate this.

"I hate you!" I scream.

"I don't think so, Jade," he says so clearly, full of such raw emotion that a tear slides down my cheek.

With both hands, I yank his neck down and crash our lips together. He tastes like a Sunday rainstorm and feels like my favorite pillow. Wyshawn groans into my mouth, my name on his breath like a prayer. His ravenous tongue slips against mine with expertise. I moan, unable to control myself. Damn, the tongue on this man. It's as if he has longed to kiss me for a lifetime.

If this will be our one and only kiss, I'll take everything he has to give me. Flames ignite within and I cling to him, letting him lift me off the ground. His arms, strong and sturdy, aggressively pin my back against a tree. His hands wrap around my waist, squeezing tightly. We clash together like two titans battling for victory. I claw at his back.

"Fuck," he whispers against my neck, licking a trail of kisses to my ear.

When he nibbles my sweet spot, I gasp, then feel his cock throb to life under my ass. What would it feel like against me? Inside me? Heat boils my skin from head to toe. A starved, fresh wave of desperation makes me crave more of him. He's too far away, too separated from my body. I need him everywhere at once—even if only to show him how much he infuriates me. I've never been so sensitive to someone's touch before. His wandering hands send me into a dizzying spiral with each torturous caress.

"My Starling," I whisper onto his lips.

He sucks in a famished breath, sending arousal racing through me so intensely that black spots mark my vision for a few seconds. Wyshawn's fingertips run under my shirt, over my stomach, soft as a butterfly. The tickling sensation makes my muscles coil and my fingers dig into his back.

"Piper..." He barely whispers my name before I kiss him again and again. "Jade...baby ..." he says, out of breath. "... slow down..." Another kiss to my collarbone. "I'm not going anywhere."

Reality smacks into me like a tidal wave hitting the beach. Of course he's going somewhere. He's leaving. Wyshawn will return home in a couple of weeks. What's my number one rule? Don't bring a local to Neveraj. I want to savor his thick lips for the next minute, hour, week, but I end our kiss and separate our bodies.

"Piper?" He runs a hand down his beard and studies me intently for a beat too long.

"Let's treat your wounds," I say nodding to his scratches.

I gather the best flowers and berries in sight for healing and mush them together to create a paste between my fingertips. Gently, I slab the blueish cream over the bloodied scrapes that are visible. If a hurricane of hormones weren't rushing through my veins, I'd tell him to take his shirt off to address any on his chest too.

In another world, I'd make him a picnic date, but instead of food, we'd taste each other's bodies on a soft blanket by a waterfall, exploring slowly. I'd gift him one of my favorite collectibles from over the years, one that reminds me of him. Maybe I'd ask to meet his moms, but that is all futuristic planning. There's no point in sharing hopes and dreams with someone or being willing to endure potential hardships when I'm not capable of any committed relationship. If I weren't Piper Pan of Neveraj, the girl who refuses to grow up, I'd nuzzle myself against this man while falling asleep. I'd embrace Wyshawn each morning like he was my only adventure worth exploring.

The impossibilities remind me of a story I once wrote.

"Some say the mythical blanket of flowers is real, especially Miss Adelaide Bloom," I start and his lips close, knowing I'm about to say more. "Because she made it herself. She coaxed hundreds of love flowers from her garden to grow. With painstaking preciseness, she plucked petal after petal, stitching their edges together until a blanket the size of a house was formed. The most impressive quality wasn't its size or the carefulness it took to create, or that the petals stayed as fresh as the day they were plucked, but that Adelaide lived inside the house herself and built an entire family and legacy from her passion and creation."

"That's a beautiful story, but don't you think we need

to talk about what just happened?" Wyshawn says, his voice low and husky.

"Hold on, you've got cuts from when you fell at Eagle's Pass."

"Don't change the subject." His brows tighten. "Wait, how do you know I fell at the bridge?"

I hold his dark gaze, waiting for him to clarify. Does he not remember holding me in his arms? Or throwing me into the grass so I wouldn't fall over the cliff too?

Wyshawn takes a step back. "No, you weren't there. You couldn't have been. I thought—I thought you were an illusion, a play on magic." Shocked and flustered, he leans against the tree. "Piper, you could've died."

I gulp. He thought I was a mirage and still risked his life for mine. Every bit of me wants to smooth the worries out of his clenched jaw, but he's not mine to comfort and never will be. "Well, *you* almost let RavenSoul kill you."

He shakes his head. "I believe you saw something, Piper, but maybe it was the magic of this place. I definitely didn't see any shadows. Plus, you're the one who cast me away." His finger is pointed at me like a dagger aimed at my heart. "You said you didn't want me around, that I hold you back and am a liability you didn't volunteer for. There must've always been a reason you stay locked up, hidden in Neveraj and I'm starting to understand why. You're scared. You pushed me away. Why won't you rely on me? I'm here, Jade. I'm here for you."

I lunge towards him again, heart thumping, body

zinging with an untamed urgency I've never experienced. When our lips touch again, he starts to kiss me with the same intensity as the first time, then pulls away before I can settle into him.

"Wait," he says, voice feral. "I will not be like your other Lost Ones." Holding both my elbows in his hands, he gently tucks me on one side of the tree trunk, leaving me alone.

Deep in my gut, I'm positive he won't abandon me like I did him. I collect myself, while he mutters nonsense to himself. With shaky hands, I strip out of the spandex wingsuit and flatten down my clothes.

On the other side of the trunk, he paces, running a hand over the back of his neck. He stops. Pivots. Cracks his knuckles. He looks up to the canopy of leaves and branches that block out the direct suns and mumbles something. His hand dips into his pocket and for the first time, I notice the small, spherical shape. He won the orb. Whatever happened on the bridge during his challenge was a success. Half of my body reacts, ready to steal it from him, while the other half stares at his full lips. For a few minutes, they belonged to me. I was the only woman he considered, the only one he wanted.

"Don't worry, you were much better than Sheila," he says.

Is that a suppressed smirk? I grab a handful of wet soil and fling it at his pants. "You terrible..." I throw another palm of dirt. "...no good...rotten..."

Wyshawn laughs.

The sound is like liquid cracking down the middle.

My heart can't take his smile in its truest form. This appallingly independent, atrociously trustworthy, horribly practical man is destroying me from the inside out. How am I supposed to live a life of bliss after that kiss, knowing I'll never experience it again?

Once he takes his hands in mine to stop the ferocious dirt war, he says, "Piper, please tell me what scared you earlier. And don't worry, I won't kiss you again. I can see the sheer horror written all over your face. I don't know what came over me, but it's done. No more."

There are no words. He's apologizing again. For *my* mistake. No, those kisses weren't a mistake, just a weakness in the moment. I don't regret them, but he's right, it can't happen again. Nothing will ever happen between us anyway. Still, his promise cuts deep all the same.

"The person with Kyle and Felix wasn't the third Lost One," I say, dropping my hands from his. "Somehow, they brought someone new through The Window. I'm not sure how long she's been here."

"So, you freaked out because they brought a *woman*?" He speaks slowly, calculating his words. "Jealous that they're spending time with her?"

Whatever obstacles are coming next, I'll need an ally for them. Even if Wyshawn can't see RavenSoul, two of us are stronger than one. "They said her name is Holly."

"Wait, do you think that was *the* Holland Jameson? The one you've been searching for?"

"She didn't have a prosthetic hand..."

"Then it's not her. There's nothing to worry about."

"But there's something off about her either way."

"Okay, then," Wyshawn says, nodding. "What's the plan?"

'**It's time to celebrate**," Tank flies between us and signs, '**for Wyshawn's victory! Don't worry, Piper, I brought your party hat.**'

CHAPTER SIXTEEN

Wyshawn

Tank drops an olive-colored beret on Piper's wind-blown hair. I'm still in a bit of shock that my hands were tangled in her hair only minutes ago. The hat dips crookedly over one of her eyes and I hold my breath for a moment.

Piper kissed me. Twice.

The only woman for me had voluntarily wrapped her legs around me like she'd lock onto my waist for eternity. There was absolutely no holding back on her end. Did I say something to turn her on? After years of imagining what it'd be like, the reality outdid all my fantasies. Fuck.

Me. What am I supposed to do when all I can focus on is her lips? The moron that I am, I told her it'd never happen again. Liar. I'm such a liar, not to mention a complete mess.

She has destroyed me for all future women, yet I'm probably just a silly game to her. Ever since she flew into my life like a rare bird—full of motion and cheer, I've put her on a pedestal. Now that I've gotten to know more layers of her, she's fallen from grace, but I want her even more. Crave her.

I don't want to attend a party. I would rather spend time talking to Piper about her feelings. The suns slowly start their goodbye routine, dipping lower in the sky. Tank zips from tree to tree using magic of sorts to string lights and décor for his party. It feels foolish to celebrate when we should hike straight to Pixie Falls, but all my ideas are put on hold when Piper begs me for one night of fun, to '*forget her worries*.'

I sit next to a mushroom—not just any mushroom since it's over four feet tall—and I try to open the prize orb. There's no opening or latch option to collect Pixie powder. So I guess she made the right call in staying here for the evening until I open it.

For the first time since I've arrived in Neveraj, Piper has created a plan that we might pull off—inviting Holland to the party. Maybe my knack for organization and prepping is rubbing off on her a little. Lillian has been tasked with spreading the word about our party among the nymphs. If it spreads far enough into the jungle, the Lost Ones will show up, hopefully with Holly.

"What's up with these mushrooms?" I trail my finger down the smooth, slippery curve of one near my shoe.

"It's where the dragons live," Piper calls across the clearing as she pulls weeds to create a dance area for the sprites, who according to Tank are all dressing like it's a masquerade.

"You're joking, right?" I pull my hand away quickly and scoot further from the plant. "Dragons can't fit in there."

Piper shrugs then bends over to pull another weed; of course, her fine ass is plump and exactly at eye level. I'd help her with the task, but my cock is too stiff. The memory of her smirking at me when she felt me pulsing against her makes me question whether she'd mind at all if I walked towards her with an enormous hard-on, but my moms have raised me to be respectful, so I won't be approaching her until my body can calm down.

A sprite flutters into the glade, a flamingo painted on her face and pink feathers sticking out of her crown. Her tiny hands hold dozens of white flowers, probably heavier than her body weight. Without an introduction, she drapes them over high branches, where they hang like whimsical curtains. More sprites wave their hands, and an arched trellis appears out of thin air, wrapped in thorns and bubblegum roses. The scene already looks like something from a fairy tale.

Fresh mint fills my lungs and I turn to see Piper, her potent gaze watching my reaction to the sprites. She sits next to me on the grass, hip to hip, and I'm both completely relaxed while extremely tense. How is that possible? She puts me on edge while making me feel like I'm home.

"Epoch wanted to be a dragon once." Piper reaches around her waist and pulls him out of a crossbody bag that had been camouflaged against her sporty tanktop. "Didn't you, baby boy?" She kisses his long snout, making him yawn awake.

The croc's long, thin tongue pokes out and he chomps at the air, still half asleep. Once his eyes fully open, he skitters down Piper's abdomen and crawls under a mushroom.

"Dragons are born from seeds: flax, sesame, pumpkin, chia, and even sunflower seeds. They're the creatures who chose not to grow into a plant or vegetable, but wanted to sprout wings and fly to see the world."

I can't take my eyes off her. I need Piper's endless playfulness and wit in my life like I need oxygen. "Is this one of your stories or fact?"

"Who says my stories aren't written from truths?"

"Go on then," I say, leaning back against a boulder, "tell me more about these dragons."

From who-knows-where, picnic baskets fly towards the clearing, followed by blankets, all orchestrated by a sprite waving his arms around like a madman. A soft melody trickles from the jungle, but the origin of the instrument sounds foreign, like the whistle of an acacia.

"Dragons mate for life," Piper continues, and I can feel her stare on my cheek. I refuse to look her way because if I do, all my self-control will be shattered. I'll kiss her in an instant when I see the excited glow of her emerald eyes each time she tells her stories.

"Dragons not only choose to become what they are but also spend years waiting for their soulmate. When found, no force in nature could separate the couple. Some humans have tried, because dragon scales are worth more than gold, more than secrets or immortality."

"What could be more valuable than eternal life?"

"Peace. To live a life without fear, even if it's a mortal one." She clears her throat. "At least that's what the stories say."

I send a prayer to the holy Sols setting in the sky that she won't freak out. Hesitantly, I slide my hand under hers and wrap her fingers between mine. A little sigh slips out of her soft lips—ones I've tasted—lips that will haunt me until my dying day. In this moment, I wish to be a damned dragon and beg her to choose me.

"Wyshawn..." She squeezes my hand once, then pulls her hand away. "I have no future to give you...or anyone."

Her words are a laser beam burning my skin. I could fight for her by listing all the reasons why she's wrong and make a stand for our potential, but I want her to choose me, not to be convinced. In silence, we watch the sprites decorate as vases fly into the glade and bouquets bunch together without a touch.

When soft purples are the only color left painting the sky, I gather the courage to ask, "What happens if a dragon doesn't want the one who pursues her? Does he keep trying? Does he live a life alone?"

This time, I do turn to face her. The setting suns cast a golden glow on her skin, illuminating her spirit. One day, maybe a decade down the road, Piper will finally let another dragon adore her, cherish her, and love her. Until then, I'll be who she needs. If this fierce woman only asks me for one thing during my time here, I'll gladly agree, then back away and give her space.

"We can go to Pixie Falls first thing in the morning." She avoids my questions. "Thanks so much for winning the orb for me. You don't understand how much I appreciate that, Wyshawn."

Fuck.

How have I not realized that she *has* asked something of me already? Pixie. She needs dust to restore her home. And this whole time I've been planning to steal it. Damn. I hang my head low.

"Did I ever tell you why this place is so important to me?" She tickles the bottom of a mushroom. "My dads deserve their sentence behind bars, but no one should be betrayed by their teammate. The day their sentence started, when I had to say goodbye, is when they slipped me the riddled map. I still remember the last words Father spoke to me. '*Find Neveraj, sweetie. If you stay there until we get out, we won't miss your life. Time is different there. Follow these clues.*' At first, I thought it was a lost cause, but then Tank helped me.

"What I'm trying to tell you is, I haven't aged in years. Sure, time has passed, but I'm the exact same as when I first came here."

"Piper—"

"Let me finish. I can't move forward, Wyshawn, even if I wanted to. I'll stay here, at this age, as long as it takes until my dads return. They've been through enough from Holland betraying them. The least I can do is gift them back the time they missed, ya know? Give them a restart button."

I make sure she's fully listening before I say, "You've still changed and learned while here. If you live here for thirty more years, your face may not have added a new wrinkle and your blood pressure might stay youthful and your joints might not creak, but you'll still grow from experiences. The Piper-in-thirty-years may look the same as you do now, but she won't be the same person. Just like you're not the same as when I met you two years ago."

She shakes her head.

"There's no stopping life. Your dads will be grateful that you tried so hard, but after a while they'll see the truth—you are not the same Piper as before and they were crazy to expect you to wait for them, to put everything on pause."

"No, no, no," Piper says, jumping to her feet. "I haven't grown. Not at all. I still don't make my bed or have a job or pay taxes. I don't know how to cook, or do my laundry or...you're wrong. Admit you're wrong!"

A rustling sound comes from the jungle, followed by crunching leaves and then thudding footsteps. Out from the trees, emerges four people– two women, two men. Kyle, who I recognize from the first challenge, leads with the others trailing in a parade. The woman in all red must be Holly, she sticks out like a fire truck in a tub of vanilla yogurt.

"We're here!" one man shouts. His shaved head is covered in tattoos, and I wonder if he's Felix or Zheo.

Did Piper date him? Did she kiss him? Sleep with him? An image of him thrusting into her attacks my front lobe so I stare at the sprites' lights to block it out.

"And we brought alcohol!" the magenta-haired woman who isn't Holly holds a bottle in each hand.

Did those hands run a pathway from Piper's belly button down to her—ugh, I can't do this. My hands turn clammy at the thought.

"Hey, Zheo, it's been a while," Piper says and grabs a bottle of liquor from the woman's hand.

Well, that answers my question. The tattooed guy must be Felix. He wears a solid black, loose shirt over tight pants that fit his slender frame. When I scan down his body, I notice the top of his hands are also covered in tattoos. I've never cared to get any body art since they'd barely be noticeable on my dark skin. I glance to the other Lost Ones, the outcasts of this world, who had formed an alliance once upon a time. Kyle, their apparent leader, stands with both hands on his hips, claiming as much space as possible. The sprites all keep their distance from him. Is he dangerous or simply unpleasant? Zheo mingles with the nymphs, and gestures to the sprites in a manner that seems fluent. Her pure laugh might've caught my attention long ago before Piper.

At the center of the clearing, surrounded by sprites,

presumed-Holly sways with ease. Her crimson dress swooshes hypnotically at her knees. This can't be the Holland Jameson that Piper described. Yes, Pixie dust has powers, but it can't *reverse* aging, could it? This woman can't be older than my thirty years. Will Piper be relieved that she doesn't have to deal with a threat or disappointed that she still hasn't found the one responsible for upending her dads' lives?

"Come here," Holly says in a sing-song voice and curls her finger at me. "Dance with me."

My first instinct is to say no, but maybe if she trusts me, I can learn more about this newcomer. Against all my instincts, I rise and join her to dance. Nearby, the others are taking turns drinking gulps from the liquor, but I need to stay sober for Piper's sake. Holly holds out both hands with a warm welcoming smile. Her long black wavy hair falls naturally down her back in a way I may have once considered attractive.

"You're barely moving," she chuckles. "Move your hips a little."

I let her touch me, hyperaware of Piper's attention on us. "What's your name?" I ask, trying to keep my voice light.

"Holly."

"I've met a bunch of Holly's as a bartender. Last name?"

"I don't think last names matter here, like a few other things." Her gaze drops to my beltline.

"Such as?" I try to loosen my strained voice, so she doesn't catch on to how uncomfortable I am.

"Rules for one thing, social norms, monogamy. I've gotta admit, between you, Kyle, and Felix, a woman could be satisfied for years, as long as you stay this fit," she adds. Her hand wraps around my bicep. "You plan on exercising, right?"

I pinch my lips together, forcibly rein in my frustration before it damages her openness towards me.

"You're still so stiff, honey, relax and feel the music." She closes her eyes and tilts her head towards the bruised sky as it settles into a dark navy gloom.

Her sideways smirk doesn't comfort me in the least. I can't help but notice one strap of her dress slips off her shoulder. A gentleman would let her know, but the last thing I want to do is continue this conversation.

"Thanks for the dance." I turn towards Piper, ready to apologize for Holly touching me but she's not paying attention as I had expected. Instead, her back is turned, laughing at Kyle's joke without a care in the world about who I'm touching.

Had I imagined the chemistry between us or does she flirt with everyone? Kyle's hand wraps around her waist and pulls her closer. I wish there was a door to slam or a log to kick in half. It'd be nice to punch the man straight in the jaw or see him suffer, even if not caused by me.

I walk behind her and lean over her shoulder, careful not to get too close, "Hey, Piper, I'm going to head out. I'll see you in the morning."

Her whole body sways and falls against my chest. She doesn't stop when our bodies meet, but staggers fully into me. I catch her as she fumbles the bottle in her hand. It crashes into the weeds and shatters to pieces.

"Piper?" I lift her to her feet and pay closer attention to her expression.

She raises a hand to her head, both eyes narrow and unfocused. "Oh, my head hurts."

"What happened?" I crouch down to check her eyes more closely, both bloodshot and glossy. "You've barely had anything to drink."

"It hurts," Piper repeats, her gaze clouding over with a slack expression on her face. "My head."

With one hand I bring her into my chest and curl her in close. "What did you do?" I boom to Kyle.

He raises both hands in the air and backs a step away. "I didn't do anything, man."

"Kyle's right." Holly joins our circle and tilts her head at Piper. "You can blame me. Your little girlfriend here just drank a strong-ass poison called Baneberox. Don't worry, I'll give her the antidote after you give me your orb."

"You poisoned her?! What's wrong with you?"

"Give me the orb."

My mind races, searching for a different solution. No time. I thrust my hand into my pocket and place it in Holly's palm. "Here! Now give it to me!"

"Not so fast." Holly eyes the orb like she's staring at a lottery ticket. "Tell me how to find the Pixie Falls."

Piper's eyes shutter closed and her body goes limp.

"Piper! Wake up!" I tap her cheeks lightly while holding her full weight in one arm. "Her lips are turning blue, come on!" The sound of my heartbeat thrashes in my ears.

"Where are the Falls, Darl?" Holly hisses, all façade washed away.

"I don't know. I've never been there."

Holly circles us, and I'm completely at her mercy as she says, "Then she'll die in the next five minutes."

I clench my eyes shut and imagine the painted floor map of Neveraj. Concentrating doesn't come easy when my pulse is racing and Piper's life is on the line. The location of Marooner's Rock and Cannibal's Cave are clear as well as Mermaid Lagoon. I follow the imaginary path to The Hidden Gem and to our current location at Hanging Devil and over to Eagle's Peak. If Pixie Falls acts like a waterfall, it'd have to start from a higher altitude near a cliff or mountainside. Or tracing back Crocodile Creek, heading north, would probably lead to the base of the falls. However, that river is made of water, not golden dust.

"It's next to Memory Hideout up north," I say quickly, hoping she doesn't hear the lie in my voice. "Off the trail, there's a bunch of green bandanas tied around trees to show the way. Follow their path."

She throws a vial at my free hand. "Make sure she drinks it all."

Miraculously, I catch it without dropping Piper and unplug the cork with my teeth. As the Lost Souls jog away, I tip the vial into Piper's parted lips. The entire jungle holds its breath.

"Come on, babe," I lift her neck a little, so she doesn't choke, and pour the rest in. "Drink."

My breathing comes quick and shallow as I wait for her to stir.

"Tank, can you help her with your magic?" I ask, hearing my voice come out high and strange.

He shakes his head and lands on Piper's shoulder, then stomps his tiny feet against her. She barely moves.

Why did I take my eyes off her? I feel as if I'm being smothered. This can't happen. She was fine five minutes ago. Because of my stupidity, Piper's going to die. I'll lose her before she was ever mine. A caterpillar crawls over her arm. In a wicked heartbeat, Tank slashes his sword through the bug's body. Gold blood spills out of the insect onto Piper's skin. Her skin shimmers in golden glitter and it stretches over her neck, covering her face. Suddenly, Piper coughs, sucking in air, chest rising and falling fast.

"Hey, I'm here, it's okay," I say, inspecting her eyes.

Her hand goes to her throat and then rubs down her stomach. "Wh-what happened?" Trembling, Piper rests her head and blinks up at me.

A lightness flows through me, soft and feathery. I'm so grateful she's safe that I can't unscramble my thoughts. How could Holly resort to such drastic measures? What if the group returns after learning my directions to the Falls were fake? I let out a quiet exhale and flop down next to her. The stars shimmer above, radiantly, reminding me how insignificant I am in this world.

"Well…I bet Sheila knows not to drink poison," I say.

Her attempted laughter comes out wilted and broken. She asks, "Poison? No wonder it tasted like your coconut cocktail."

"Hey, you love that drink." I sigh, watching her face. "Are you okay?"

"Yeah, I think so."

For the first time, I have no plan. How am I supposed to keep Piper happy and safe at the same time? There's no right answer, no easy way forward. We're also running out of time. Once I return home, I may never see Piper again. That thought alone makes all my muscles tense.

Suddenly, a high-pitched scream wails from the jungle.

"What the?" Piper wobbles to her feet and stumbles toward the sound before I can stop her. "That sounds like Lillian."

I follow because what else can I possibly do? Ahead, a large cluster of nymphs run in chaos.

"RavenSoul!" one yells.

"The shadows got her," another yells while dragging long roots in its wake.

Piper stops in her tracks right in front of me and I almost slam into her back but catch myself just in time. Ahead, Lillian twists in agony, with gray shadows curling all around her trunk.

"The one who fights…youthful charm…" she says in an eerie voice, "…strengthens the shadow…bring us harm."

Deadly shadows grow larger and overtake her quickly. Within moments, Lillian's screams go silent and agony rips across her face.

"What the fuck is that?" I ask, pointing at the shadow.

CHAPTER
SEVENTEEN

Piper

I need to save Lillian, but I'm frozen in place. Can't breathe. Where's Wyshawn? He'll always help me. The whole clearing erupts into chaos. A nymph spears a sharp branch into a sprite. He bleeds gold liquid onto Lillian, healing her until the shadows disappear, and slowly, she awakens. The glade is a flurry of madness as the sprites counter-attack the nymphs, hacking away at their bark in revenge.

"Over here!" A strong hand pulls me down behind a boulder, where I find myself tucked between the rock and Wyshawn's chest.

His sweaty scent mixed with coffee beans is oddly comforting in comparison to the wild beating of his heart against my ear. It's as if he knows my instinctive desire to join in on the fight. I'm unsure which side I'd support since Tank and Lillian are both my best friends, two species who have always lived in harmony. Until RavenSoul.

I curl my head further under Wyshawn's chin in hopes of blocking out the excruciating screams and howls. This fight goes against the nature of our world.

"It's RavenSoul," I tell Wyshawn, "The shadows that were in Lillian have corrupted my friends. This isn't like them. I have to help."

Wyshawn grips me tighter, not allowing me to leave. In a strange way, I'm a bit grateful. The responsibility of stopping a battle shouldn't rest on my shoulders. They can take care of their own problems. The cacophony on the other side of the boulder eventually quiets. For a while, it's only our breathing in and out that I can hear. Even the surrounding nocturnal birds hold in their songs.

"I think the sprites left," he whispers against my temple. That soft breath brings a tingle over my body.

Slowly, and ever so quietly, I stand and check over the rock. The decorations resemble a scene from a massacre, red ribbon bleeding out of the soil, popped balloons littered as choking hazards for animals, and streamers torn and shredded. They all surround the massive corpse of one nymph and a tiny dead sprite by its side. Healed, Lillian towers over her savior, tears falling down her leafy cheeks.

"My brother," Lillian cries, dropping to her knees. "Nooooo!"

I lean back against Wyshawn's solid chest. "We should leave. This is too much."

He holds me steady and takes a step towards the gut-churning wailing, which moves me forward with him. No, I don't want to deal with this. I don't want to face death or pain. Neveraj is supposed to be fun and games, laughter and parties, jokes and stories—not this.

When we're directly next to the bodies, Wyshawn caging me with his arms, Lillian meets my eyes. "He saved me. Just like when we were kids, he always put me first."

How did I not know my best friend had a brother? Am I that self-centered?

"When RavenSoul overtook my body," Lillian drops her head, "I felt so cold, so tired, so defeated, like it sucked out my will to live and any love I felt for others." She rubs a branch over his fallen body. "Right when the shadows touched me, I could feel myself spiraling towards a vortex of the in-between."

I gulp. "How can we..." I clear my throat. "What do you..."

"What do you need? We can help," Wyshawn clarifies for me.

"Let's sing to our loved one." Lillian's voice cracks as Tank joins her side, defeated and full of sorrow.

"You didn't leave," I say and glance towards Tank's cousin split in two on the ground.

Tank shakes his head and signs they he wants to bury his cousin. After I translate to Wyshawn, he moves to a place where the moon shines and begins to dig a hole, on his hands and knees. It won't have to be deep since Tank's cousin is about five pounds and six inches tall.

Lillian begins singing in a language I've never heard and soon Wyshawn hums along respectfully. His deep voice vibrates through my bones, calming my nerves.

How are we supposed to move forward from this? I don't want to deal with two opposing sides. Sprites and nymphs have never fought before.

Across the clearing, Wyshawn lays the sprite into the grave and Tank covers his cousin's body. I'd rather eat a thousand starfish than join them. Dealing with grief isn't on my resume. If I hide behind the boulder, maybe they won't see me. Tank can rely on his sprite friends for his loss because I have no experience with helping anyone through a rough time.

A bat swoops low, then flaps away, urging me to follow him into the night. If only I had my wingsuit I could flee. When the stars shine brighter and higher in the sky, Lillian and Tank leave in different directions, both holding the weight of the world on their sagging shoulders.

Wyshawn's footsteps head straight to my hiding spot. I should've known he'd be hyperaware of my location. Dirty and sweaty, he crouches next to me and gently pulls my head to rest against the side of his arm. I suck in a deep breath and allow myself a moment of comfort.

In one night, I've enticed Holland to a party, managed to be poisoned, lost our orb—the only chance at collecting raw Pixie, and watched both my friends lose a family member. Exhaustion overtakes my whole body, head to toe. I wouldn't be able to hunt Holland even if I wanted.

"Did you tell her the location of the Pixie Falls?" I ask Wyshawn.

"What?" He rubs a hand down his tired face.

"Right before I passed out, I remember she asked where Pixie Falls was."

"No." He shakes his head, clearly defeated. "The way I see it, we have two choices; track the group and steal the orb back, or go do the third challenge. If you want the challenge, then I'll just need an hour of sleep first."

His eyes fall shut and he rests his long, black locks against the rock, neck craned back. The exposed lump in his throat makes him look so vulnerable to attack, yet he trusts me enough to watch over him as he rests his eyes.

"Or a third option. We go home and pretend like the last few hours never happened. It's easier. And more pleasant."

"You mean give up?" Wyshawn leans back a bit so he can see my face. "Doesn't sound like the fiery Jade I know."

I lean into the moonlight so he can clearly see my expression, so he fully understands what kind of person I am. "We can play strip-truth-or-dare. I wasn't done with that kiss."

I'm a sucker for a good distraction from all the confusing emotions that life thrusts at me. I've rarely regretted getting under an attractive man or woman, and there's no point in starting new habits with Wyshawn. Sex with him would definitely take my mind off tonight's murders.

In a heartbeat, I straddle Wyshawn and realize I can be wrong once in a while because I instantly regret this choice. The disappointment that washes over his face is too much to register.

"What's that look for? You deserve *thank you sex* for saving my life…twice."

"Piper, stop it," he growls and flings me off his lap faster than a falcon swerves. Quickly, he stands and brushes dirt off his pants, not that it changes much. We're both filthy. "Don't do that again." Wyshawn glares, eyes dark and serious. "I'm not a fuckboy, so don't treat me like shit, Piper. I care about you." His voice is so deep it sends a shiver up my spine. I hold my ground as he takes a step closer and continues. "I've always cared for you and probably always will, but there's no chance in Luna I'll let you screw me and then push me away." His voice grows louder, making a desire deep within my gut pulse with need. "If you give yourself to me, I want all of you, the past, present, and yes, the future. I want your stories and your fears, your nightmares and your dreams, and everything in between. If you can't give that to me, and if you don't want the same of me, then Don't. Fuckin'. Start." His jaw is so clenched that I want to rub his muscles smooth. "Understand?"

My body is flushed and flooded with something I can't name. I gulp and nod. He's right. Wyshawn deserves better than this.

I reach into my crossbody where Epoch is thankfully nestled, blissfully unaware of the funerals and bad moods. Under his scaly tail, I dig for one of my favorite collectibles, a mini snow globe. About the size of the orb, it shows a scene I'll never witness, snowflakes falling on a happy full family. I have no idea how long my dads will remain in prison. I snatched this globe for a specific purpose. It can video call anyone, even in this world. Since modern technology doesn't work in Neveraj, I've saved the globe since it's been my only connection to the other side of The Window. Long ago, I had searched for it, hoping I could contact my dads but the prison walls have been impenetrable, immune to its powers.

"I have something for you," I say softly and hold the snow globe out to Wyshawn.

He shakes it and watches the snow fall, then raises one eyebrow in question. "Uh, is this your way of apologizing?"

"Yeah, hold it in your palm, and imagine those tiny people in the snow as someone you most want to speak with. You have to really want it, or it won't work."

Wyshawn's forehead scrunches and he brings the snow globe to eye level. I hold my breath, expecting the swirling snow to clear and show one of his moms.

"Maybe say her name? If she answers she'll be looking into her Taj."

"Maram," he sounds like a man out of options, someone who has bared his soul and has been left hung to dry.

Which I guess is true. He said he cares about me. His confession gives me gooseflesh. He said he'll always care about me. For some reason, he wants all of me as I am. And he hopes I want him just as much. An impossible ask. I never should've brought him here.

A face appears in the globe, fuzzy at first, then with delicate details of a black woman, somewhere between fifty and sixty. She shares features with Wyshawn, but in a feminine version, so I assume she's the biological mother.

"Shawnie?" Maram squints. "Are you on vacation? I've never seen a constellation like that."

His attention darts to the sky for a second. I focus on my favorite star, the second one from the left, and make a nonsensical wish—for Wyshawn to one day find what he's looking for. I can't be the person he described earlier, but someone else out there waits for his kind soul.

"How far did you travel, sugah?" Maram laughs. "I've been saying for years that you deserve a break. I'm so glad that stubborn brain of yours finally saw reason and used your savings for something other than us ol' ladies."

"How's Mum?" he says with such a dire need to hear good news that my heart spasms in my chest.

"Oh, she's...she's about the same, sugah. Though, the doctors say she doesn't qualify for the experimental study we applied for."

He cringes and I can tell he's trying to hide his frustration. "That's okay, it was only a backup. I'll be home soon with a solution. Keep working on the memory book her therapist taught you, okay? And stick to the routines, don't make any major changes, and—"

"Shawnie, I got this handled. Enjoy your time...oh! Who is that? She's gorgeous. Hi there, miss, did he meet you before the trip? I'm expecting so since my baby boy doesn't date casually, but you probably know that by now. If you two are traveling together, why haven't I met you yet? What's your name?"

Wyshawn glances to me, his jaw hanging open, speechless. "Uh, Mother, this is Pipe—"

"I'm his tour guide for the day, ma'am. It's nice to meet you but our time is running short."

His jaw clenches tight and he releases a sigh before breaking eye contact with me. "Mother, I'm sorry I didn't call you last week or visit at the usual time."

She waves him off. "Goddess Above, life doesn't always have to follow a strict protocol. I'm a big girl and can handle myself when my boy needs a break. Now, shoo, go enjoy yourself or I won't let you visit."

Her face disappears from the snow globe. "Wait!" Wyshawn grips it tighter and brings it to his nose. "Come back. I'll get Pixie and it'll save Mum. Everything will be okay."

I swipe it from his grasp, placing it back in my purse. "It's done. She can't hear you."

He leans one hip against the boulder and buries his face in one hand. A stifled sob erupts from his throat, and I practically leap back. Wyshawn needs someone who knows how to comfort him, who has experience in relationships.

I haven't seen a grown man cry since Father left the courthouse in cuffs. Carefully, I slide towards Wyshawn and pull him into a hug. It feels absolutely ridiculous attempting to hold someone twice my weight. He leans on me anyhow. One arm around my back.

"Mum is the one who sang me to sleep, who volunteered to chaperone recess to keep an eye on the bullies, drove me to track practice, and taught me how to shave. She beat me in the hardest board games invented and now she can't even remember my name!"

"Oh, Wyshawn." I bury my face in his chest.

He squeezes me tighter until I'm fully wrapped in his scent, his muscles, his soul. Never in my life have I felt so lacking. He's trusting me to hold him up, to be his teammate, and give him what he needs? What if he needs Pixie more than I do? What if this land is dying to send a message that it's time to share Pixie?

I rub his back softly and ask, "Did you know everyone in Cretala is given a snow globe on their thirteenth birthday? Since their country is claimed by icebergs and blizzards, their globes are called 'mist globes.' When they shake it, a cloudy fog blankets the scene."

"Are you inventing this as you go?" Wyshawn sniffs softly and raises his shoulder to wipe his nose dry.

"Don't interrupt me," I tease and glance at the party wreckage. Wyshawn needs rest, to sleep in a real bed tonight, not among slaughtered cupcakes and a carnage of bouquets. "Mist globes are unique and hand-made by the famous artist family that lives in their castle. For generations, their children's children have learned the trade of creating the most beautiful minuscule scenes to fit inside the fragile glass globes." I pause and imagine what that type of workshop would look like—probably something close to a sprite village since they'd need such small hands to complete the detailed finishing touches.

"Go on."

"Well, I've never been to Cretala, but I once saw a mist globe and I've been looking for something as memorable and unique ever since. Sure, thievery is in my blood, but it means more when there's a specific item to search for."

"Did you ever find it?"

"No," I chuckle softly. "I created the story, little Starling. There are no such things as mist globes."

"I mean, did you ever find something memorable and unique?"

I gaze up at his face, outlined by the moonlight. "Yeah, I have."

CHAPTER EIGHTEEN

Wyshawn

Usually the scent of rainfall soothes me. Splatters plink against the protective shield above The Hidden Gem. I'm surprised all of Neveraj hasn't flooded by now. I lay on Piper's couch and listen to the plop plop plop. No matter how many times she offers to share her bed with me, I continue to sleep on the old couch.

The last few days here with Piper have been torture. Neither Lillian nor Tank have returned since the fight. Their absence has made Piper shut down entirely. Guilt has plagued me since that night in the glade. No one deserves such a tragic ending. If I had believed Piper's claims about RavenSoul, I could've done something to prevent the attack on Lillian. If I had learned sprite sign language faster, I could've convinced them not to charge her brother.

Thousands of questions still bombard my mind. Where did Holly get poison? And why does she need Pixie so desperately that she'd risk murdering Piper? We've been lucky with the crappy weather recently, giving Piper time to recover. Ever since she drank the Baneberox, she's been dizzy and light-headed. How can I ease her tension? Even now, she's mumbling in her sleep.

It's taken me a while to determine the best 'thank you' gift—a new journal for her stories. Piper deserves something special after sharing the snow globe's magic with me. Seeing Mother again refreshed my energy and sharpened my mind with a plan. When the rainstorms stop, I'll attempt the third challenge. Maybe I won't have to choose between Mum and Piper. There must be a way to split the Pixie into two piles.

From across the room, I fluff the pillows and clothes that smell like Piper. Earlier, she'd been calling out to her dads during nightmares. I consider waking her when she starts tossing and turning again...until a new name crosses her lips.

"Wyshawn," she whispers.

My entire world inverts. Was that a moan? Piper lies on her stomach, head turned to the side so I can see her face. Her eyes are still closed, smooth and calm, but her fist tightens the bedsheet into a ball.

"Slower," she whispers. "Wy...shawn."

I'm about to lose my mind when her ass lifts, forming a hill under the blanket. My cock jerks to attention faster than a whip. Holy shit. Is she dreaming of me? I watch her hips slowly rise and fall in a phantom wave. I use every ounce of self-control not to stroke my dick when she moans again. Then her brows tighten into a scrunch, breaking my restraint. It's not like I'm going to touch her or anything. I sweep a hand under my shorts and pump once. Damn.

Hungry, I want to kiss her collarbones, her breasts, anything she likes, to make her moan again. I want her gripping the sheets because of me pulsing inside her, stretching her out. I want her gasp in my mouth and to satisfy this deep ache for her in my core.

Each time her ass perks back a little, I thrust into my hand in the same rhythm. Goddess Above, I want to tease circles with my tongue on her throat and thread my hands through her silky hair. Piper moans again, a little louder, and this time her hand disappears under the blanket. Fuck. She's touching herself. My erection is so hard it feels ready to snap.

Everything goes quiet and her body stills. I freeze. Did she wake up? Would she hate me in the morning if she knew I watched her? I hold my breath.

"Wyshawn?" Her voice is crackly, rough from sleep, but not a whisper. "Come here."

I don't dare move. My heart hammers behind my ribs. When the blankets rustle and she pushes off her elbows, eyes open, I know I've been caught. A tiny, sleepy smirk tickles the corner of her lip.

"Come here," she says again, alert and aware.

The only thing I'm capable of doing is breathing. Can't talk. Can't even remove my hand from my dick.

"Wyshawn, I need release." Piper yawns and tilts her head to the side. She repositions so I can see the perky points of her nipples through the thin fabric of her pistachio green tanktop. I'm about to die. "Starling," she continues, tucking a loose strand of her blonde hair behind her ear. "I'll do something for you too."

"Please." My voice cracks, splitting like my heart is severing down its middle.

Her half smile grows and she lazily crawls off her bed, across the floor. She moves in slow motion. Maybe I'm the one dreaming now. Her top hangs loose in a low scoop so this time I can fully see down her shirt, both breasts hanging, swinging slightly as she moves closer. One hand. One knee. Second hand, second knee. My chest burns from anticipation, but I have to clarify to her what I meant.

"I mean..." I spit out, breath ragged. "Please, *don't* touch me," I say, knowing I sound like I'm choking. "If we—if I do this, it's just for you."

At my knees, she nods in understanding and sits on her heels. Then my angel bites her bottom lip. Just shoot me dead. I'm completely gone. Even if she never reciprocates my feelings, I don't see any possible way I could want another woman as badly as I pine for Piper. Not allowing her to touch me will be the ultimate torment. But I must have boundaries. There's no chance I'll regret pleasing her; I'll only wish I had more. If this little slice of her is the most vulnerable moment she'll ever give me, I want to memorize every sound, each facial expression.

"I want you to touch me. Everywhere," Piper whispers and steadies her hands on the floor behind her so her hips push forward. The planks below her creak.

Still kneeling on her heels, she leans back so the thin tanktop drapes over her flat stomach. The lower she leans back, it rises higher on her legs and slowly reveals her upper thighs and the pale flesh I long to nip. Flexible as an acrobat, she lowers completely onto the floor, legs pinned under her. Her emerald eyes darken to match the tone of a midnight serenade. I can't look away. She has me hypnotized until slowly, her knees separate, revealing the V of her body. No panties. I'm broken. My cock pushes against my pants, demanding freedom.

Carefully, while my pulse is racing wildly, I lower off the couch. The roughness of the wooden planks below my knees grounds me in the fact that this is reality. Piper wants me to touch her. She wants my hands on her. I'd be a fool to turn her down.

I position over her and my hair cascades over my face. Taking in her pure willingness, I shiver with desire. Lit by the moon, she's never been more gorgeous, more soft. Each of her curves rolls naturally in valleys and peaks. My hands itch to explore. My cock throbs painfully. Warmth floods my veins and I have to grit my molars to stay focused.

"Are you sure?" I ask, sucking in her intoxicating minty scent.

She nods, looking bashful for the first time.

"What are your rules?"

"You're the one with rules, Starling. Just make me feel good."

Fine. I'll have to make the rules. No kissing. Don't let her touch me.

"Keep your hands on the floor the whole time, or I'll stop," I demand.

Doing as I say, Piper repositions her legs so they're spread out flat under me. "Yes, sir," Piper says, licking her lip. The sight snaps my reserve like a clipped rubber band.

I've never looked into someone's eyes this long. It's as if we're both terrified that if we blink or turn away, the moment will vanish. Slowly, I skim my fingertip down her throat, over her shoulder, and shift her spaghetti strap off so it falls around her arm. She shudders and her chest rises and falls a little faster. I swear her gaze deepens, trying to dig out my essence with one look. I do the same movement on the other side, sliding her other tanktop strap down her arm. Following my command, she doesn't move her hands an inch. So I lean down, bite the strap, and pull it with my teeth past her elbow, forearm, wrist, and fingertips, leaving a brush of my lips down the path.

Piper lets out a little sigh, which provokes an intense fluttering deep in my stomach to curl into a tight knot.

My cock pleads for her, pushing against my pants so tight that I let out an animalistic groan.

"Are you okay?" Her head snaps up, hair off the floor, and her mouth parts. Her eyes dip to my crotch, concerned. "I meant it, Wyshawn. Let me—"

"No, Jade..." I squeeze my eyes closed for a moment and concentrate on an ice bucket. Yes, dipping myself into an ice bath. "Promise me, you'll keep your hands right there."

She visibly gulps, then rests her head back against the floor. "Okay, but this is taking too long, you're killing me."

"You asked for it."

Knowing it's the first time, and probably the only time I'll see her naked, I slowly bewitch the rest of her tanktop down her body. First, her breasts pop free, exposed nipples already hard. Holy Luna, she's gorgeous. I trail a finger around each mound, desperate to kiss them. I swear my lips are tingling to taste.

"No kissing," I growl, half-grunt.

"What?" She's already breathing heavier from my fingertip barely doing anything. If this light touch around her breasts is all it takes to arouse her, then my job won't be difficult. "You said you'd..." Her back arches. "...oooh, more."

My fingers rub, tweak, stroke, squeeze. Soft at first. Next, I pinch hard, then do nothing at all so she can feel the soft night breeze caress her exposed upper half. Piper's breathing grows faster, and her eyes continually dart to my lips. Unable to hold back any longer, I tug the rest of her tanktop down her stomach, past her thighs and knees, then ankles, memorizing each inch the whole way.

Bare below me, Piper's skin flushes from her chest to her cheeks.

"Stunning," I whisper against her skin, not allowing my lips to touch.

My confession coaxes a surprisingly content moan from her. I've barely gotten started. My hand slides up and down her stomach gently and leisurely, like a slow swing of a rocking chair. Her breathing turns louder, torturing me with anticipation. Thankfully, mercifully, she hasn't moved her hands from her side; they're plastered against the floor. That doesn't mean they're relaxed though. Each finger is pressed and flexed, pushing against the wooden planks.

"Wyshawn...please," Piper pants, this time her eyes are closed tight, and her grip on the floorboards becomes more intense.

"Look at me, Jade."

Exactly when her eyes open, I finally touch her clit. Her hips jolt suddenly, so I take my other hand to pin her down. I skate my fingertips along her inner upper thigh and draw in a swirling motion. Slight pressure. Back and forth. Soft and tantalizing.

At this point, my cock might not survive the night. It's going to explode. I have no choice but to rock my hips in the air, wishing I had purchase.

"Oh...oh!" she cries. Her back arches higher, but I hold her down. "Damn it, Wyshawn, more!"

I move my hand to the other thigh to even out the sensation. She writhes against me in a maddening wave.

"You want more?"

She nods and I dip one finger inside her. Fuckin' Goddess. So slippery wet. Perfect for me. If I don't kiss her, I'll lose my mind. For her, I'll break every rule. I quiet her moans with my lips, my tongue. She kisses me with fierce intensity. This is our moment. There is no tomorrow, no other time, no before or after.

A fresh, heated ripple of need surges through my body. The hand bracing her hips moves to her clit. Working together, I stroke and circle. Massage and knead. I push in a second finger and she moans into my mouth. Her hips rise, angling for the best pressure.

"More," she prays to me between kisses. "One more."

I don't need to be told twice. I add a third finger. Carefully, little by little it joins the others. Then I bend them together as a unit, up and down. Damn. I twirl inside her in a circle. Her neck falls back and she screams a string of mindless obscenities. My forearm starts to cramp but I grit my teeth and twist my fingers faster. She's so tight.

"Close," she moans, arching, baring her throat to me.

Damn beautiful. Breathtaking. Her ass clenches. Her legs tighten and twitch. Her nails scrape against my legs. Then her whole body jerks still, taut, stiff. I've never seen her face so red. Is she holding her breath? Bit by bit, my Piper rides out the billowing swell of her orgasm, trembling. I'm completely ruined, addicted to this moment. Slowly, she unwinds, her body loosening, and she lets out a deep breath. Her release feels like a treasure and I smoothly pull out my fingers, soaked in her pleasure.

When she opens her bright eyes again, a peaceful lull paints her satisfied smile. "Wow."

Hovering over her, hyperaware of how badly I need to come while also conscious that abandoning her right now would be the worst mistake of my life, I stay still as a statue. She can decide what happens next. I've already broken the no-kissing rule, and all I can think about is breaking the other one.

"Are you sure you don't want—" she starts.

I gulp, and make sure my tongue says the right words. "I'm sure."

"Okay, well. Thank you for that," Piper squeaks out.

She blinks a few times, stretches, and then gathers her bunched tanktop by my knees. In complete shock, I simply watch her crawl back to her bed, curl into her blankets, and roll over.

What in the Sols just happened?

CHAPTER
NINETEEN

Piper

I t's hard to avoid Wyshawn's eye contact after last night. Goddess Above, I want to do that again and again. Even right now would be great.

I let the cushion of daylight form a wedge between us. We stand at the opening of the ominous Cannibal's Cave, boots covered in muck after hiking the uneven, treacherous terrain. Well, Wyshawn stands tall and ready, as I pretend to be fine, lying to myself. Everything will be okay. Last time, the idea of entering the caves terrified me to the point of paralysis. I can do this.

Wyshawn wraps his arm around my waist to guide

me. I refuse to think about the fact that I trust him to keep me safe or that I know he's already offered me more than the mind-blowing orgasm he gave me last night, or that I want more of him too.

Under dawn's soft light, I hear the call of the golden-headed Manakin competing with the Caracara for who can sing the most boisterous song. A Ramphastos flies above our heads and lands on a low branch. Its beady eyes try to warn me about something. Unfortunately, I don't speak bird yet. What an amazing talent that would be. All wildlife had been hiding during the unrelenting downpour, so it's nice to hear their tweets and trills again.

"So, the third challenge is in there?" Wyshawn keeps his hand on my waist.

If it were anyone else, I'd complain about how much he's touched me in the last few hours, or nag him that he's been basically magnetized to my body, but it's honestly quite comforting when I'm about to face the unknown darkness of the cave. I consider what my three biggest fears of the future might be, but dozens come to mind: feeling caged, being alone, living life without my dads, any change in general, the unknown. Nothing about tomorrow is a certainty. What if the cave swallows me whole and I never exit? What if the tunnel casts me out of Neveraj somehow? What if it steals the air from my lungs and I have no way of screaming out for help? What if...a thousand what ifs.

"You don't know what's in there?" Wyshawn asks, leaning towards the mouth of the cave.

"Nope."

"Alright," he sighs deeply, in that husky way I love. "If I'm not out in three hours, go home and don't come back for me."

I chuckle softly and step around him. "No, darling Starling. I'm doing the challenge."

His eyes widen. "I thought you refused. You said this challenge is pointless?"

"I did, yeah. I used to think that."

"Not anymore?" Hope sparks in his dark eyes. Hope that I'll one day crush if given the chance.

"Pixie is disappearing and RavenSoul grows stronger," I say, "Which means time won't remain stopped in Neveraj much longer. I may not want to think about the future, but that doesn't mean I can avoid it anymore."

"Do you think it'll let me join you?" he asks while taking my hand into his.

"May as well try. I'd rather not go alone."

"Sheila might find out about this date, though," he says, a smile playing on his lips, which makes a sizzling inferno soar through my body.

Sols Above, I adore him. Somehow, when I least expected it, Wyshawn managed to sneak his way into my heart. Focus, Piper. Now isn't the time to fantasize about him.

I nudge his side even though it doesn't affect his brick-wall stance. "I may have to fight Sheila when we get out."

Wyshawn thumbs my wrist, rubbing a small circle again and again. "What are you fighting her for?"

"A girl needs her secrets," I say with a wink, then walk toward the cave with fake confidence on trembling legs.

This could go terribly wrong. When Wyshawn entered Kyle's challenge, the obstacle went haywire. Here's to hoping that since I'm voluntarily inviting him with me, nothing will explode. Hand in hand, heart thumping chaotically, we march side by side into the darkness. The walls seem to close in around me as the light fades behind us. With each step, the air becomes colder and stiller. No breeze sweeps against my cheeks in here. At least the ground is solid, so I don't sink into mud. Still, I walk hesitantly, kicking pebbles ahead to hear them clatter and clank against the ground. My eyes have adjusted to the darkness, to form the outline of the walls, but there's no chance of telling when the ground might drop off into a hole. Bringing sprite light would've been a smart choice; I'd rather not plummet into a deep cavern and break my foot. Though, letting Wyshawn carry me in his arms sounds oddly cozy. Maybe I'll fake an injury tomorrow to test my theory. Tomorrow. Since when have I opened the door to contemplating the future?

"Hey, Jade, can you not squeeze my hand so tightly?" Wyshawn's voice echoes off the tunnel's walls. "My finger is about to snap in half."

"Oh, sorry," I say, relaxing my grip on his hand. My palms are sweaty, but I don't dare let go. "I wouldn't want to damage those fingers after you showed me what they're capable of."

"Jade...don't make me pin you against this wall."

We keep walking, but I won't let go of his hand. It's like he keeps me sane in this awful moment. "I'm scared, Wyshawn," I whisper.

"I'm scared too. Can you tell me a story?"

I try to swallow my fears. "Right now?"

"Yeah, it'll distract us," he says, from slightly ahead. I can tell he's walking in front of me, just in case.

"Okay, how about the story of The Land of Nothing? It's an island of volcanoes where fire-throwing humans, called Mystiers, live with flame-breathing monsters called Jugosaurs. They have a mystical cave under Mount Elidi full of vicious, glow-in-the-dark cat creatures who skitter around with fierce long claws. They eat anyone who—"

"Uh, Piper, that's probably the worst imagery right now," he says as he stumbles forward, tugging my hand a bit too hard.

"You okay?" I ask.

"Yeah, just tripped. Do you have a happier story?"

"Sure, this one is rumor though. I didn't write it. Have you heard of Axton, the sea nymph of Nerida?"

Wyshawn snorts. "I think I'd be as human as a hoverboard if I hadn't heard of him."

"Well, he was once wanted for treason and murder."

Suddenly, I bump into Wyshawn's back. I can barely see the outline of his face as he turns towards me. "Seriously? Murder?"

"He was framed for murdering Eribelle's best friend, Sampson, who died in a shipwreck." I start their story but get cut off when a whisper from the darkness curls up my spine to my ears. The voice hisses unnaturally, but I can't make out the words. "Did you hear that?" I ask, my heart beating frantically in my chest. This doesn't feel like my other whimsical adventures anymore.

"No," Wyshawn's thumb circles my wrist again. "Um, Piper, how do we know when the challenge begins? We've been walking for quite a long—"

His hand is ripped from mine as he's tugged downward. A blood-curdling scream rips from his throat. I drop to my knees and feel the ground shake.

"Wyshawn!" I grope the ground in front of me.

The floor has opened and leads down into a hole. "Wyshawn!" I scream so loud my throat burns. "Wyshawn?!"

No reply. My voice echoes against the walls again and again. How deep is the hole? What if the drop killed him? No, that's absurd. He'll be fine. He has to be. Once I finish the challenge, he'll pop out unharmed on the other side, waiting for me with his arms crossed and the stern line of his lips I've grown to adore.

But I can't force myself to stand, to move forward. How can I leave him here without knowing if he's safe? My breaths turn ragged. There's a ringing in my ears, followed by another whisper.

"*What if thissss is part of the challenge?*" it whispers in a voice similar to mine, layered with slime and puss.

I hug my knees to my chest, locking my hands together to shift into the smallest shape possible.

"What if the tesssst is whether you rissssssk the cave beyond or track into the depthsssss below without csssertainty you'll make it out alive?"

I squeeze my eyes shut and lower my forehead between my knees. "Stop talking!"

"What if your man is trapped in a masssssive sssspiderweb?" Its cackling makes my hair rise on end. *"You'd leave him there and sssssave yourssssself?"*

I cover my ears with both hands, then rock back and forth, humming the melody of the song Wyshawn sings when cooking for me.

"What if he landed in a pond full of carnivorousss fish? What if they sssssuck his sssskin off and crack his bones?"

"I'm not listening to you!" I cry out, clueless as to who might be speaking.

"What if your fathers are waiting for you on the other side of thisss tunnel, sssssweatheart?" It clicks its tongue one, two, three times. *"Didn't your besssstie tell you that they esssscaped monthssss ago?"*

"Shut up! You're lying," I whisper, but hear the tremor in my voice. "They would've found me by now."

"Go find out the truth, you ssssilly ssssscared girl. All you have to do is leave your love here."

Love?

I don't love Wyshawn. I won't allow myself to become attached that deeply. This voice can't be real; it's just my imagination, my inner child bursting free. I pry my eyes open and stare into the darkness. It's impossible to know which way is safe.

"*Ssssso, are you going to make a choicssse?*"

"No, get me out of here. End the challenge. I give up. I'm done."

Immediately, silky fabric wraps around my neck. I fall over to the side and shove a finger between the scarf and my throat. It pulls tighter, firm, fast, and secure. Strangled. So much pressure pushes against my throat. I gasp and kick at nothing. It compresses more, unyielding. Can't suck in air. Can't loosen it. Can't move. Can't breathe.

I'm dying in the darkness. Alone and afraid.

I wake to the sight of Wyshawn's gaze, crazed and worried. Gasping, I sit and clutch my throat, absent of any deadly ribbon.

"It's okay, it's over." He searches my face, his hands hovering over my neck where I still frantically grope. "Piper, stop, you'll scratch yourself." Wyshawn pulls my hands down and envelopes them in his.

"You fell," I say, sounding like a dying cat, then burst into tears.

They stream down my face, violent and salty, as if I haven't cried in years, which is probably true. I lean my forehead against Wyshawn's chest and let him hold my weight. Automatically, his hand rests against my back and he strokes with a long deep pressure along my spine.

"It's okay, I've got you," he says. "Let it out."

Around us, orchidaceae and bloomed passion flowers show off their beauty. We're still close to the cave, but thankfully I can't see the horrid entrance.

Snot runs out my nose, so I bury my head deeper into his shirt, sniffing in his scent, coffee-based from earlier this morning. "I'm sorry."

"It's okay, Sheila does my laundry."

I choke on a laugh and jab his rib with a finger.

"Hey! Not nice," he says with a smile that could heal my worst wounds. "Look at me, Jade. The cave called me your love."

"Impossible. You're too structured. And quiet."

He nods and wipes a tear from my cheek. "Go on."

"And you're too stuck on tradition." I clear my throat and the tears finally stop.

"And?" He gestures for more.

"You resist trying new things or looking for new ways to solve problems."

"It's like you've been paying attention a little."

"And you're too direct," I say, my heart calming and slowing a bit. "And honest to a fault. You can hurt others' feelings without even knowing it."

"Good, I need to be writing these down."

I sniff, wipe the dirt off my pants, and stand. "You can be insensitive or even cold when you get stuck in your own little world."

He rises next to me, the morning sun his backdrop. "Are you saying you want into my world?"

"I...wait...that's not what I meant."

I'm halfway turned away when he grabs my waist. Something about his touch feels so right, so genuine, like he fits. He twirls me towards his body, my favorite type of carnival ride, the ones that spin and I'm left holding my breath, until I'm suddenly jerked into reality. Staring up into his eyes, I know how much he wants to kiss me. Does he notice the same desire on my face? For the first time, I want to say 'no' for *his* benefit. Last night made it obvious that he cares more than I can ever reciprocate. It wouldn't be fair to lead him on. The way his gaze drowns me in intensity proves that I'm a treasure to him. For some obscene reason, Wyshawn views me differently than anyone else has. It's not my place to debate how wrong he is, or how much time he's wasting on me. The least I can do is prevent his inevitable heartbreak.

"Jade..." Wyshawn's deep voice floats from his mouth to my mid-section, gliding deep into the inappropriate places that have no business responding so quickly.

Wyshawn leans down, his lips ripe for the tasting. And damn has he tasted like pure divinity each time I've kissed him.

"Don't say it." I shake my head. "I can't."

Walking out of his embrace may be one of the hardest things I've done. That may not be saying much since I've had a life of luxury and ease—that is until my dads were incarcerated, and I was hunted by pirates. Then I was poisoned by someone who is likely a

Venetress, not to mention being chased down by a soul-sucking shadow. Huh, maybe my life hasn't been all candy and sugar. Sure, Neveraj has provided for me, but I've still had to deal with problems and find a way to save this land. I'm stronger than before. Better. Wiser.

The realization hits me like a tidal wave. Was Wyshawn right? Have I changed? If it's true, if I've actually grown, then my lingering fears are even more pathetic. Shouldn't I have conquered the third challenge by now?

"Let's try again. I want to go back in." I stomp down the muddy trail towards the cave.

"What?" Wyshawn jogs after me, his footsteps heavy and slow. "No way. Piper, listen to me. That cave is toxic. Plus, you told me the rules would make you start over again at the first challenge."

"Damn it, you're right. Effin Fuscous Flycatcher!"

"Excuse me?"

I sigh and rub my temples. "It's a bird, a brown one with a long tail and black bill," I say a little too sharply. "They tend to stay in undergrowth perches to catch bugs."

"Of course, I should've known." Wyshawn turns my chin towards him with one hand, and damn it if my panties don't get wet from that single, simple move. "I still have my chance at this challenge, remember. I'll go in, but only if you stay here."

"But—"

"Piper, please don't make me tie you to a tree. Don't test me, I'll do it."

"Fine, you go." I back up and his hand falls away. "Be the hero and get the orb, I'll stay here and be a pretty damsel."

His jaw clenches in frustration. He's trying not to get scrambled in another argument.

"Take my dagger," I say, unsheathing it from my thigh.

"No, keep it out and ready."

"You don't get your way twice, Mr. Darl. Either take the weapon or take me. One or the other."

"Okay, okay," Wyshawn says, snatching it from my hand. "Please stay here."

I lean against a tree and salute him. "Got it, captain."

Wyshawn disappears around the trees, his sloppy steps through the thick with muck grow quieter until there's only silence. High above, a group of monkeys holler and screech among the Oropendola flying between branches. By the suns' heat and position, I'd guess noon hasn't come yet, which means not much time has passed since the first time we were inside the cave.

Either Wyshawn's traits have rubbed off on me, or I am truly evolving, because I quickly make a four-step plan of how to help him. He hasn't let me down so I'm not going to wait on the outskirts while he faces his biggest fears alone. Once two minutes have ticked by, I push off the tree and follow his trail.

He should've known that I'd follow him.

CHAPTER TWENTY

Wyshawn

This time, the cave's interior looks entirely different than Piper's challenge, which seems impossible. For instance, it's not nearly as dark. Multiple *'To Do'* lists are scribbled on the walls in perfect, clear penmanship—my handwriting. The further I step towards the unknown, random signs appear, all showing different regulations like *'Do Not Enter'* and *'Employees Only'* to *'Speed Limit 45.'*

Then the voices start. Female, blended together. One stands out—not a voice I've heard before, yet I somehow know deep in my gut that it's the chef from a cooking class I've wanted to register for.

"*Turn your recipe in on time or you won't graduate; you'll be the shame of your family...How could you get this wrong?*" My gourmet meal is thrown into the trash..."*If you don't follow the specific ingredients, you won't ever meet the standards...You're not good enough...Follow the rules of the kitchen, Mr. Darl!...You don't want to be kicked out of the program, do you?*"

I blow out a series of short breaths to gain control of my torpedoing self-blame. Everything she says is true. I'm not talented enough to be a chef. Her criticism continues in the background until Mother's voice interjects. She's not speaking to me, but I somehow know this conversation will be had with my aunt in a few months:

"*We will only survive this if we maintain structure and routine...Georgia needs consistency as her memory fails... There won't be any time for games or the luxury of vacations when she can't remember which pills to take or how to find the ketchup...And don't get me started on insurance. I hate to ask Wyshawn and Jeniqua to contribute more money since insurance isn't covering enough for the facility.*"

I clutch Piper's dagger tighter to try and self-soothe. It feels like a rope is tied around my chest and pulling tighter. I need to help Mum and Mother faster. How do I get out of this cave? There's no way to decipher where the voices are coming from. I keep walking into the darkness, stones skittering as I kick them down the tunnel.

"*Wyshawn?*" Piper's voice presses out the others. I'm slightly shocked that there is any version of Piper in my future after she has made her lack of intentions perfectly clear.

"*Wyshawn?*" Her urgent, pleading voice sounds so clear as if it echoes off the cave's walls. What will future Piper say to add to the stack of worries accumulating? There's a soft clanging sound like metal. My gaze darts around. If only I had a flashlight.

"*You have to pick! Me or Georgia.*" Her voice fades in and out, muffled then lucid, cloudy then distinct again. How could she be so selfish as to force me to choose between her or Mum? "*Wyshawn!*" Piper's screeching voice blasts from behind me. "*Is it me or her?*"

I flinch and fidget with the dagger in my hands. Need to get out. Need to escape. Even in the darkness, a shadow crawls along the wall. Shapeless at first, it grows hands and long spindly fingers that point straight at me. I back up until my heels hit the stone. My heart races. Where are the exits? The shadow looms over me and reaches out, fingers curling into the shape of a hook.

Another scattering sound, like nails scratching along the stone, makes me jump.

"*You're wasting my life away by working so much, and for what?*" Piper's eerie voice squalls. "*It's not like you're investing any time in us...No! Instead, every hour goes towards your crazy mom who is losing her mind.*" When the cave turns bone-tinglingly silent, I want to crouch into a ball to hide, but Piper shouts again. "*Your mom is hopeless;*

it's time to forget about her and move on. Let's take a trip and finally have some fun."

"*WYSHAWN!*" The boom of Piper's voice shakes the cave and rocks tremble at my heels.

Danger lurks around every corner, so I raise the dagger in front of my face. Step by step, I inch my way forward. My heart slams harder. What if I'm going in the wrong direction?

"*Contribute more money! More Money! Money!*"

The shadow doubles in size. It's closer, fingers longer, claws stretching.

"*Won't graduate! Not good enough! Won't graduate!*"

An axe shape appears in the shadow's hands and is raised directly above my head.

"*Wasting my life!*"

"No!" I scream and the shadow freezes. "You're not real. This isn't real!" This time, I trust myself and close my eyes softly, then focus on my surroundings, what I can hear and smell and feel.

The hard stone presses against my back. Real. My shoes pivot against the hard ground. Real. I suck in a deep breath of thick muggy air into my lungs. Real. The light drip-drip of water falls in the distance. Real. My fears won't control me. I can become a chef if I want, whether I fail out of that program or not. Mum and Mother will find a way to pay for the facility with or without my help. Piper wouldn't ever make me choose. Plus, she doesn't envision a future with us anyway. All the voices were phantoms, figments of my imagination, latching onto my greatest concerns that cause panic.

Mint meets my nostrils and I inhale deeply. She's here. Slowly, still clutching the dagger, I open my eyes. No shadow monster lurks over me with a weapon of death. In its place, a large, glowing orb floats in the air.

"Wow, you did it," Piper says from the darkness.

"Are you real?" I say, and move closer to use the orb's light. "You're here?"

She chuckles in that easy way that makes me want to savor her laugh. "Yeah, lower your knife, big guy. I'm not going to attack."

I sheath her weapon in my belt loop. As Piper moves, her features come into focus. First, her kissable jawline, sharp and bold, then her soft skin, splattered with adorable freckles. Then those full lips that have already done damage to my heart. Her nose, small and pointy, brightens under the glow. Lastly, Piper's emerald gaze meets mine. The orb glitters gold, inches from her eyes.

Unsure if the pulsing energy between us is from the magic of the prize, or from my imagination as my heart continuously rams and pounds, I lean towards her. Her eyes drop to my lips for a beat, then back up, instantly ravenous. I don't care what hazards may prowl around the corner. I need to kiss her. Now. I know, with all my being, she wants the same. Right when our mouths are about to collide, Piper's hand gently pushes my chest back.

"No, we can't. While I was searching for you, I heard the voices of your challenge," she whispers, her heavy breath mixing with mine. "I refuse to be someone's fear—"

"Don't worry, Jade, it wasn't real," I say, bracing a hand behind her on the rough cave wall.

"...or someone's future."

"Right," I say, my voice sounding flat as I back up.

I'm unable to manage any other words. My arms drop, hanging slack at my sides. I don't need an elaboration. She probably wants to go straight to the Falls to fill the orb with Pixie. Heavy-footed, I trudge toward the speck of light in the distance. Suddenly, my movements lack any spark. Maybe I'm just tired from the challenge and need to rest. She's been my oxygen and I need a break from her all-consuming energy. Yeah, that's it. At the next opportunity, I'll find a place to nap that's not The Hidden Gem.

There are only so many times a man can survive rejection. I don't want to talk, but Piper apparently isn't clued in to my need. Once we reach the Falls, Piper won't need me anymore. She'll save Neveraj and I'll be twiddling my fingers until she returns me to Kensington. Why did I ever expect a different outcome when she warned me from day one that a relationship isn't an option? Never once has Piper shown me a sign that she'd want to commit.

"Want to hear a story while we walk?"

"Always."

"Birds are the most powerful animals in existence," she starts, oblivious to my internal struggle. "Their strength comes from freedom. They're not bound to a place, rather, they are at liberty to roam, flee, or leave at their will," she says in a strange tone, as if reminiscing.

"Once upon a time, there was a Jacamar, with its long sharp bill resting on a branch in this jungle. She was supposed to be on the lookout, above the stream, to warn her flock of any advancing predators. Instead, she lost focus and dashed after whirring dragonflies. She caught them with an audible snap of her bill and pounded each one on her perch before eating. Meanwhile, as the day turned progressively hotter, more animals trekked to the stream to cool off. Even a jaguar passed by without Jacamar noticing. Luckily enough, the cat didn't see our little friend but had his sights set on the rest of the group. Our innocent, naïve, selfish, useless Jacamar, with a full belly, heard the painful cries of her family too late. Below, feathers flew out of the jaguar's mouth. Terrified and alone, Jacamar started to sing and hop, pretending nothing had happened at all. She built a wall in her mind between what had just happened and what would happen, a separation that would never break."

This story had a different texture to it, a hint of metaphors more personal than her others. Several questions lingered on the tip of my tongue, but why bother asking when I only have days left with Piper? What's the point of getting to know someone better, opening up to them, when they don't want the same?

"I was supposed to be on lookout for my dads during their last heist," Piper volunteers, her voice a whisper trailing from behind. "They were using me as a ploy during a con involving a yacht dealer named Finley over in Coendriel." She pauses so long that I think she'll stop. "You'd think after all the years of games, I'd take my role seriously. Nope, when a new shiny toy presented itself, I selfishly left them high and dry. When the cops showed up, Holland showed proof of my dad's crimes, acting like a victim in the whole scheme." She lowers her voice so much that I slow my pace. "If I were there to warn them, maybe they never would've been arrested."

An honest confession doesn't sound like someone who wants to be closed off to a relationship or unwilling to trust someone with her deepest secrets. What can I possibly say to support her? Yes, she may be partially to blame for her fathers' misfortune, but that doesn't mean she needs to pause her life for their mistakes. Since she didn't receive jail time, she's been punishing herself, not allowing her life to move forward.

We arrive at the exit of the cave, where luscious plant life welcomes us with open arms. I step from a nightmare into a dream full of bird twitters and chitters. After living here for weeks, I still haven't learned the name of any bird species, which is unusual because I often grasp onto any new tidbit, storing information for a trivia night. Maybe I've also been holding back, not fully immersing myself in Neveraj, with the impending time bomb ticking down my days and hours in this beautiful land.

I turn around at a snail's pace. In broad daylight, the suns-rays kissing her skin, I clutch my chest at the sight of Piper's pleading, wide doe eyes, an expression I've never seen on her.

"Wyshawn, I do like you, but I don't have a future to give you. But I was thinking maybe could you accept the moments we have...right now...and take advantage of this time, right here?"

If Piper would allow me to take this Pixie to Mum first, maybe I can return every other month, half our lives in Neveraj and half in Kensington together. Relationships are all about compromise and negotiations, so if she's willing to try the now, then I won't press her about the later—yet.

"Yes, yes, of course," I say, unsure if I'm voluntarily jumping into a metaphorical pit of tarantulas. "We can do this your way, one day at a time."

"One *moment* at a time," she corrects, eyes still questioning me as I hold my arms out wide to crush her into a tight hug.

An overwhelming sensation of weightlessness makes me feel years younger. I want to swing from the branches with hope and bounce on my toes like a nervous teenager. Maybe there could be a thing between us after all.

"Did Sheila ever complain about your hugs?" Piper's sing-song voice has returned, and a bolt of fireworks has erupted in my chest.

"Sols Above, babe. You're the only one who fits in my arms." I reluctantly loosen my grip and kiss the top of her head.

Her eyes sparkle, bubbly and bright, and one hand slides up my stomach to my chest. This time it's not to push me away. "Kiss me, Wyshawn."

Our mouths mold together, with warm tenderness, then start to explore. She tastes of tangy lemonade, and I want to drink her. Piper clings to me with passion, like an obsession she's resisted for too long. This isn't a *'get it out of your system kiss'* or a *'you infuriate me'* kiss. With every sweep of her tongue and brush of her soft lips, it's clearly defined as an *'I hope for more'* kiss or an *'I want this'* kiss. We fit together so well. Why haven't we been doing this since the first second I laid eyes on her two years ago?

"Why does this"—she gasps against my mouth—"feel so good?"

"Mmmm," I pin her against the cliffside wall and press her against the moss.

My hands have a mind of their own, surveying every curve I can reach. The dips of her waist, the roundness of her ass in my palm, the divots of her spine. My fingers trail over, around, between every nook and cranny of her body as she moans and gasps against my touch. I'm hyperaware of her body's tiniest reactions and I need her to know how much she means to me. Nothing exists other than her—my Piper—my Jade.

Out of breath, she wiggles from my hold, laughing between panting sounds. "Wyshawn, that tickles."

My tongue continues to circle under her ear, what I'm expecting to be one of her sweet spots. She jerks in my arms a little like she's being shocked, and I never want to stop. The ground shifts beneath my boots. Strange. I'm about to reposition, to switch my weight onto my other leg when my body plummets. Piper screams. Mid-air, I grasp for her but don't feel anything. I fall fast. Land in something gooey and warm like thick pudding.

"It's okay!" Piper calls, but not from nearby. She's somewhere high above. "I'll make a ladder!"

I rub my shoulder and realize I'm in a giant hole. All around me, the ground moves, as I begin to sink.

CHAPTER
TWENTY-ONE

Piper

A massive mud sinkhole consumes Wyshawn. Already up to waist level, he doesn't have much time.

"Stop moving! It'll only take you faster!" I shout and search for the longest fallen branch on the jungle floor.

My boots kick leaves and twigs, parts of tattered nests, but nothing is long enough. There's no time to find anything else.

"What do I do?" His voice is laced with panic.

He lowers farther, mud level with his chest. I spin in a circle, looking for anything that will reach him. I frantically pat my pockets in hopes of a miracle. A small, round, hard bump reminds me of the one gift Lillian gave me years ago. Yes! I pull out the acorn and squeeze it in my clammy palm.

"I wish for Wyshawn's immediate safety," I say quickly, not taking my eyes off the hungry mud, now at his neck.

Wyshawn's eyes widen, and he starts to writhe again, accelerating his descent. "Help!" He glances beyond the trees, then looks to the sky. "Help!"

If this wish doesn't work, I...I can't even fathom my devastation. How could I take my morning flies again knowing Wyshawn isn't waiting for me with his half-smile and a homemade meal, thoughtfully prepared, hot and ready? How could I wear another hat, knowing he won't ever tease me again for them all being green? How could I look at my couch again with the memories of his body teasingly sprawled across the cushions, creating new indents next to mine?

For extra measure, I kiss the acorn and pray my plea again to the Goddesses Above. "I wish for Wyshawn's immediate safety."

I've been saving this acorn for a desperate moment and have survived without it for so long, casting it aside during lesser moments of need. Yet, Wyshawn has apparently shattered the version of who I used to be, the patterns I used to live by.

When the mud settles under his feet, hardening to dirt and lifts him like an elevator until he climbs out of the hole ungracefully. The way he tumbles onto the ground like a baby fawn would make me laugh in any other situation. I long to hug him and kiss him, but settle on helping by dragging him away from the hole just in case it has plans to devour us again.

Still wide-eyed and panting, he looks down at me, scanning my face. "How did you do that?"

I hold the acorn between us. "Lillian's magic. It granted one wish."

Wyshawn kisses my forehead, sweetly, too tender, and I can barely move. He's worth my one wish. Maybe the acorn knew I'd been waiting for him. The words, *'I might like you too much'* linger on the tip of my tongue. None of these thoughts make it to my mouth to tell him, but somehow, it's as if he knows anyway. The way he's looking at me now compares to the warmth of our suns shining after a stormy week, or the taste of the first piece of birthday cake, or bellowing a favorite lyric at the top of your lungs. He also likes me too much. We're screwed.

His lips trail down the side of my temple, sprinkling soft kisses along the way. "Thank you, Jade."

"Mhm," I reply, too overwhelmed by my revelation to manage anything else.

These feelings weren't supposed to happen. I'm not someone who has the luxury to get attached and the last thing I want to do is hurt Wyshawn. He's probably already planning a future for us, but how would that possibly work? I swear I'm not trying to trick him. I've been upfront and honest. All I can give him is me, now, right here.

He takes my hand in his and pulls me toward a path

between trees, dusted with water droplets from the recent rainfall. "Alright, lead me to the Falls."

During our hike on the uneven path, I point out vegetation and teach him about water lilies, rubber trees, Lobster Claws, and Cacao. I'm surprised that of everything I show him, Wyshawn's favorite is the Passion Flower. At first, he thought it was an orchid, so I pulled the periwinkle and white flower from the lush greens surrounding us and took a bite. This tangy superfruit always makes my nose scrunch in a twist. His laughter at my expression erases the worries infesting my heart. Maybe in every moment, I could somehow coerce this laugh from him. Maybe all it takes to build a relationship is living second by second. Maybe the concept of him and me is not totally impossible.

"What kind of bird is that?" He points to a branch, for the twentieth time.

"A Pharomachrus. They prefer ravines or cliffs covered in plants, so this area makes sense. They also like taking over spots that woodpeckers have abandoned."

The more I educate him, the higher his smile rises. I wonder if he's even aware of how long he has been wearing that joy during our walk. Holy Abyss, he is hot as Sols. The way his strong jawline clenches before he smiles boosts the temperature up a thousand degrees. Sometimes a girl just needs to stare at beauty at its finest.

As dusk approaches, I consider taking a wind-about-way to the Falls since they're so close, just to spend more time with Wyshawn without the distractions of Holland's threats or any other drama. This is a moment I can handle, comfortably walking hand in hand on the bumpy terrain where I'm familiar and at ease, sharing what I love with someone who cares.

"How about a story?" he asks.

I glance up, expecting his gaze on me already. Focused, Wyshawn studies the path, measuring each step before taking it, like he's calculating how strong the earth is, and the likelihood that one of us will fall into another sinkhole. What I'd give to see this man fully relaxed, without a care in the world.

"Okay, I had an idea for something new."

"I'm ready to be enchanted."

"Enchanted?" A legit pig snort explodes from my mouth, the most unattractive noise imaginable. "Okay, picture this, the land of Lodesa. Amidst the humans lives a secret population of magic wielders."

"Of course," he says, nodding along. "What is a story without a little magic?"

"Right!" I squeeze his hand. "So, the humans don't know that Mystiers exist until POOF, one day all males over the age of twelve disappear."

This time it's Wyshawn's turn to snort. "I'm gonna guess that you may have past trauma to unravel, Piper."

"No, I'm fine. Anyways, the main female character is the one who accidentally wishes away all males. Coincidentally, it's the same night she finds out she has fire magic. I think she's going to discover it later than others of her kind because she's the chosen one in a prophecy."

Wyshawn stays quiet, knowing I have more to share.

"Well, the catch will be that one male remains, let's call him Jadox. And he just so happened to save Kyra's life that night. Now, she's like, '*Who are you?*' and '*How are you still here?*' and '*How the Abyss do I have magic?*' and most importantly '*Why are you so damn hot?*'"

"Kyra?" His brows loosen the more I get his mind off the terrain. "Did you fabricate that name just now?"

"Yeah, and, oh, I know!" I hop in place. "She will be part of a fire tribe of sorts, and there are three other main tribes: wind, earth, and water. I can't wait to come up with more stories."

His glance lowers to me, as he says, "You're amazingly creative, babe. Always believe in that."

"That's what my dads used to say too."

Again, Wyshawn waits for me to elaborate. I love how patient he can be, knowing when to push and when to use the strength of silence.

"Do you think...no that would never happen." I rotate my shoulders in a circle, trying to roll off the thought, but it keeps nagging at me. "What if my dads die in prison and I never see them again?"

This time his silence is heavier and more meaningful. I know he's never met my dads, but he looks like he doesn't want to answer. Does he truly think I'll never see them again?

I avoid a prickly bush by nudging closer to Wyshawn's hip, brushing our bodies together.

He pretends not to notice, but I see his throat bob. "Um, how much further?"

"The Falls are right around the bend. Actually, I'm

surprised we can't hear it yet. Since Pixie is lighter in weight than water, these falls are quieter, but not silent."

I'm about to point out a cavity within a gaunt tree trunk that could possibly be a Pharomachrus' home when shadows emerge from the hole. I gasp and stop in my tracks. Wyshawn doesn't see it right away but still places himself as a shield in front of me.

"What is it?"

"RavenSoul," I whisper, pointing to where the gray fog curls in the air.

It spears ahead of us, infecting every plant the shadows touch. I can taste the diseased rot with every breath as evil pollutes the air. Flowers shrivel as RavenSoul sucks out their lives right in front of my eyes. Unable to tolerate this massacre, I dash forward.

"Wait, Piper, we need a plan," Wyshawn calls from behind me.

The distressed trees part like an iron gate opening to a haunted lair. A dark stone wall stands, dripping with... nothing. Gold Pixie dust is supposed to be falling into a stream below, which is empty. I feel like I can't breathe—like a rope is molesting my neck. The only thing left is cruel gray shadows that cling to the stone in feral desperation. The disturbing energy here sulks heavier than anything I've ever experienced.

If the Falls have run dry, there may not be any hope for Neveraj. Alarmed, I run to the troubled bank and fall to my knees. How has the raw Pixie vanished so quickly? An unsettling whistle harasses my ears. My hands dig into the soil before I can process what I'm doing. Nails full of dirt, with brown coating my skin, it's as if my dreams themselves have been assaulted, struck down, beaten to death. There's no Pixie buried. Where could it possibly have gone? How is the land deteriorating so drastically? A pounding sound bangs from above, stealing my attention. I find the source in a toucan fluttering wildly and acting deranged. Its wings batter against the branch. The image knocks me breathless—again. If it doesn't calm down, the poor thing will bash both wings into a pile of bones. That's when I see it. Shadows coil in and out of its feathers, slaying the innocent animal. It cries in agony, disrupting what's left of my reason.

I wave both arms and scream at RavenSoul, "Hey, you bitch! Leave him alone!"

"Piper, sshh!" Wyshawn says, trying to lower my arms.

I attempt to sidestep him, as I holler like a banshee. He wraps his arm around my waist and picks me up, carrying me like a mere sack against his side. Regardless, I flail and twist while the toucan's spirit wilts. He grows quieter and plummets to the ground with a thud.

"Damn you, stupid demon!" I wish that if I threw rocks at RavenSoul, it'd cause damage.

The shadow sweeps down, directly in front of Wyshawn.

"Put me down," I say, thrashing under his tight grip.

"Will you stop threatening it?"

"No," I say, trying to wiggle free again.

"Then, no way." Wyshawn repositions me so I'm not digging into his hip.

Could he outrun it? What does it want?

The shadow figure morphs into a human shape. At first, the details are vague, like a blob, then the angles of Father's chin become pronounced, followed by his large nose and bald head. His eyes are the only feature that doesn't resemble Davien Pan in the slightest. Cold, brutal pits take the place of the soft hazel eye I love. He was the caregiver, tucking me in at night and singing songs while we doodled together. Father was the one who gifted me my first set of binoculars and journals. He held me when I cried, listened with an attentive ear, and taught me how to braid my hair back when my blonde locks fell past my waist. He had convinced Dad that I didn't need to wear dresses if I didn't like how they felt on my body and donated all the frilly outfits hanging in my closet.

"The one who fights with a youthful charm will strengthen my shadow and bring them harm.'

I glare at the toxic thing that had killed the toucan. It repeats the phrase again and again which helps me notice the change in wording from when Lillian had told it to me first. I don't want anyone harmed, despite not knowing who it refers to.

"Okay, fine, I believe the stupid prophecy," I reply to RavenSoul, slapping at Wyshawn's wrist so he will release me, which has absolutely no effect on him. "But what does that mean?"

"You're the youthful charm. Who fights against you?"

Wyshawn says quietly while slowly backing away from the shadows.

"Lillian said it was *you*." I match his volume and tone, so as to not spook the thing into attacking us.

He grunts, possibly tired from lugging me around. "It can't be. I have no way of strengthening a mythical monster. You must have *one* enemy," Wyshawn whispers, keeping his eyes on RavenSoul towering above. "We'll find them and turn them over to the cops."

"There aren't cops here, and I doubt I have any enemy on the other side of The Window. I barely knew anyone over there, besides you, and well, all my dates."

His quick, fiery glance burns through my skin, and I wonder what he's picturing. A few seconds pass before he's able to snap out of whatever image he painted. I'm guessing he liked the forest green high heels I wore months ago to Walk the Plank, ones that had lifted me closer to his height. In hindsight, I wore them to get his attention that night but had left with Morgan.

His boot cracks a twig in half. We freeze. Did it hear us? The moon casts an eerie glow, warning us to run. It's too late. RavenSoul attacks us, in the shape of a lance. Impales a tree, chopping it in half, exiting through the other side. Closer. Bigger. Deadlier. Wyshawn staggers away, pulling me along. We trip over a rock. He drops me into the mud so fast that I roll away until a bush stops me. RavenSoul charges. And I scream, or it feels like I should be screaming, but no sound comes out. The shadows whirl into my open mouth, texturing my tongue like chunky gravy thick with mold. It lodges down my throat, coating my lungs. Need to spit it out. My stomach heaves, nauseous. Everything feels unclean, as if chemicals ooze in my blood. I try to grab at the shadow still forcing itself into my body. I cough on the muggy poison with such intensity that my whole body jerks.

Before I can fully panic, Wyshawn sweeps me in his arms and sprints. Cradled against his chest, I've never felt safer and so close to death simultaneously. Thud thud thud. His footsteps thunder faster than I've ever seen him move. The further we trek, the less the pull of the shadow. It weakens, streaming back out my mouth like I'm vomiting fire. It burns my throat and for a split second, I'm glad Wyshawn isn't the one in pain. The last of RavenSoul spills past my lips and I can finally breathe normally. In Wyshawn's rocky embrace, I clutch my throat, gagging. He doesn't slow a bit, not until the familiar scent surrounding my home hits me. The aromas of my favorite flowers welcome me like a hug, but they, like us, have no protection—yet.

"Put. Me. Down," I rasp, unwilling to be tucked into his safety any longer.

Finally, he does, his shirt clinging to his sweaty skin. I scramble to the button on the side of my front door. I've been waiting for years to use this contraption. From the highest point of the treehouse, a massive, lightweight barrier falls. It's crafted from thousands of intersecting pieces of paper I've stolen. Both Lillian and Tank helped me intricately fold the corners so there aren't any crevices or holes.

"Woah, that's...huge!" Wyshawn reaches out and skims his fingertip across the paper wall. "Uh, it can't be sturdy, though."

"Magic," is all I need to say while I pull him towards the spiral staircase. "Come on, we'll be safe for twenty-four hours. Nothing can get in or out."

"What about Sheila? We have a date tonight."

Halfway up the stairway, I turn, ready to smack whatever devilish grin he's trying to pull off. Yet, when I realize we're eye to eye, the same height, all I can do is push him against the wall and plant my lips on his.

CHAPTER
TWENTY-TWO

Wyshawn

Her kiss ignites my veins with fire, but there's too much at stake to become distracted. I go against everything I want and pull away gently, then swipe my finger over her pouty bottom lip.

"I definitely need a shower," I say to her.

Soft thunder rumbles and I glance at the massive paper shield bubbled around the treehouse. There must be wind on the other side if a storm is rolling in, yet the papers don't flap in the slightest. I'll never get used to the wondrous magic of this place.

"I could shower with you," Piper says, trailing one finger over my stomach.

I want to believe she will take the prospect of us as a couple seriously and that she meant what she said about trying to be together, even if it's just moment to moment.

"Tempting, but if I get you naked, I won't be able to stop."

"Then we won't stop." She bites her bottom lip, absolutely destroying me.

"No, babe. When I slide into you for the first time, it won't be rushed."

Her jaw drops and she slaps my arm playfully. "Wyshawn!"

I've never been the douchebag who winks, yet that's what I fuckin' do. I wink at my lady. "Wait here and we'll take turns washing off. I'll be quick."

Before I can change my mind, I descend the cramped spiral staircase to head straight to the outdoor shower. My hand skims over something scaly, scaring the living Sols out of me until I realize it's only Epoch. Little pitter-patter sounds ping as rain falls against our shield. I pass by all the plants Piper has taught me about, the best ones to use for cooking.

I kick off my damaged sneakers, the socks peeling off with them in a ball of muck. I try to lift off my shirt but a sharp pain jolts through my back. I hiss and freeze in place, my shirt halfway off, stuck over my face.

"You okay?" Piper slides between me and the outdoor

shower wall, then shimmies my shirt all the way off. Her gaze lasers through my bare skin.

How did she find time to also peel off her socks and shoes so quickly? The sight of her barefoot feels so natural, so intimate that it turns me on. I don't have a foot fetish, but apparently anything about Piper will arouse me. If I turn the faucet, water will glisten over her skin, making me so jealous I'd lick each droplet off her until I was the only thing touching her.

"Your face is all scrunched up," she half-laughs. "What's wrong?"

"I think I pulled a muscle trying to climb out of that sinkhole," I say, rotating my shoulder.

She places both hands on my chest and looks up at me through those long lashes. "Want a massage?"

"Do you know what you're doing to me?" I ask and focus on the increasing sounds of rain slapping above. If my mind is distracted enough, my body might not turn animalistic, raw, and carnal. "I want you so badly."

Her face flushes rosy as she lowers one hand to my crotch, feeling my hard length from tip to base. "Is this okay?"

I gulp and nod, then let my forehead rest on the stone wall and let out an exhale of tension. She strokes me through my pants, slow and steady. I had told her, yes, her touch was okay, but this is so fast. I want all of her, and that means knowing where she stands emotionally before I lose all control.

"Wait!" Reluctantly, I stop her hand and groan from the throbbing discomfort needing release. Then the solution hits me like bird crap on a hoverboard. Piper thrives on games, so I'll make her play to get what she wants. Once she had suggested strip truth-or-dare and I had refused.

Maybe I can evolve for her too, live a little, and enjoy the small things. The rain turns into a downpour, cocooning us in our safety net for one simple night of comfort. I may as well take advantage of my time with her, and prove to her how much we could work.

"Okay, I'll make a deal. For every question you answer truthfully, you get to remove a piece of clothing, yours or mine...but no touching yet."

Her green eyes shine with amusement, a challenge accepted. "First question?"

I could ask if RavenSoul has ever possessed her before, or what it had felt like, or why she thinks it attacked, or if she believes it'll happen again. Or ask what magic could possibly create an impenetrable wall of paper. Or if she thinks the Lost Souls are searching for us.

I think carefully. "How do you want to catch your enemy, the one in the prophecy?"

"Easy. When we go back to Kensington, I'll spread gossip of an offer Holland can't refuse, and she'll come to me."

I can point out multiple holes in the plan but lose my focus when Piper tears off her muddy tanktop. It's a physical fight not to drop my gaze to her perfect cleavage popping out of her sports bra.

Next, I could ask how much time she guesses that

Neveraj has left before RavenSoul overtakes the land. Or where she thinks Tank and Lillian have disappeared to.

"How was life growing up without a mom?" I ask. It's a bit insensitive, but I'm curious since I have two.

"Who said I'm grown up?"

"Don't change the subject."

"Well, I have nothing to compare my life to, so I'm not sure how different anything would be with a mom. Was I curious? Sure. But my dads took good care of me. They're opposites in every way. Balance each other out, ya know? Father was always more of a caregiver. He rewarmed my leftover pizza when I couldn't reach the microwave and took my temperature when I had a cough." She pauses. "He was always the one to warn me to be careful on my hoverboard and wear knee pads in case I fell off."

"He sounds great," I say softly, wanting to touch her, soothe her, erase her pain from losing time with them.

Her response is clearly finished since she wiggles out of her drenched yoga pants to reveal her curvy hips and toned thighs. Luna Above even her panties are green, these ones the shade of basil.

"Eyes up here, sir."

I snap my gaze to hers, guilt flooding my blood, boiling hot.

With only four pieces of clothing remaining between us, I have to be selective. I'd want to know if she'd be willing to let me talk to Mum again in the snow globe. Or who she thinks poisoned her with Baneberox.

Instead, I ask, "How will the Pixie Falls be restored?"

Her immediate cringe tells me she hates the question and has probably been avoiding that thought. Pixie was supposed to be falling in abundance, ready to fill our orb. How long has it been empty? Did someone steal it or did it dry naturally?

"I'll ask Tank, but I don't know. The sprites and nymphs have been here for centuries; surely it's happened before." She tries to sound casual but I hear the undertone of worry she doesn't want to admit. It's quite astounding how she trusts the world will work out in her favor.

Piper shimmies forward while reaching down to tug off my shorts. They fall into a puddle of fabric at our feet. I try to swallow, but my mouth is suddenly too dry. My erection presses against her belly through my boxers, and I have to count to ten to not eat her alive.

"You said no touching." She glances down briefly. Again, I'm the one to blame for breaking the rules.

"Sorry," I say, stepping back and grabbing her toothbrush and mint toothpaste from the natural shelf made of stone.

My next question could be if she'd ever share Pixie to heal my mom or if she'd consider staying in Kensington sometimes.

It's frustrating to constantly thirst for more knowledge, like a bucket that has a hole and drains with each new tidbit tossed in. There's one thing I need to know more than any other.

"What's the story of us—our future as you see it?"

"*Our* future?"

"If you wanna see my goods next," I say, nodding to my boxers, "then you need to answer."

Piper's eyes flutter shut as she leans her head against the stone wall. "Once upon a time, there was a sweet Starling who built his nest the same way each year, not a twig out of place. Females would flock to his home, hoping to catch his attention but he waited for one bird in particular, one that lived far away, in hopes she would be his mate." She pauses and her face tightens like she's uncomfortable. "An owl advised the Starling to settle on the neighboring female, but he refused, hoping for his heart to be claimed by another. A fox threatened his nest in the black of night, but our sweet Starling hid without becoming a meal. However, upon returning home, his nest had been ransacked by that fox, unlivable for any family or eggs. The Starling started over from the beginning, and his nest was ready again not a moment too soon. For off in the distance, a familiar song whispered on the breeze, the tune he'd been waiting for."

Piper's eyes open and her gaze drops immediately. "Now, drop those boxers."

"Wait? Did they become mates?"

She shrugs and points to the only clothing I'm wearing. Unsure if I'll win at a game against Piper, I forfeit and yank the hem down, letting my cock spring free. I savor her expression as a tiny gasp parts her lips. Shamelessly, she simply stares at my dick. With two clothing pieces still covering her, I want to know if she ever loved Kyle or Zheo or the other guy. But, since I'm a sucker for punishment, I ask the one thing I'm not sure I want to know.

"Where will you go if RavenSoul wins?"

"It won't win." Piper gestures to her domain. "Neveraj is where I have to stay. Okay, I answered, so I still get to remove clothing, rules are rules after all."

And off goes her bra. My heart hammers against my ribs at her breathtaking beauty. Under the passion of soft moonlight, with the glimmering lights flickering around The Hidden Gem, her breasts resemble damned eternal treasure. All the stories she's ever told me from dragons who live in mushrooms to mythical blankets and mermaids and slippery couples and the Land of Nothing and powerful birds and heists. All her charisma and whimsy rushes over me like a typhoon wave. I need to prove to her how much I'll cherish her body, mind, and spirit for as long as she'll let me. My mind is mush. There are probably other important things in this world, but all I care about is getting her underwear off her curvy, petite body.

"Wh-what's your favorite color?" I strain against the magnetizing pull to devour her entirely.

"Green, obviously." Reaching behind her she turns the faucet on, allowing the stream to flow over my back. "Wyshawn, I like you. Somehow, of all people, you straighten out the knots and tangles of my mind."

The panties slip down her legs. Gone. And all my rules vanish in an instant. I'm hers, no matter when she wants me or for how long. I'm hers.

CHAPTER
TWENTY-THREE

Piper

Wyshawn's eyes burn hotter than molten lava, studying my every curve as the water cascades over both of us. His gaze doesn't compare to the way greedy Partners have looked at me in other sexcapades. No, Wyshawn is a cake of sweet layers, starting with adoration, then respect, devotion, and commitment at his core. He's a delicious dessert that I'm afraid to taste.

What if I get a sugar high from him? What if I become a cake addict? What if he lets me devour him, icing and all, only to never be fulfilled, always wanting more? What if he's too scrumptious and I can't ever let him go? Maybe I want to save the last slice of Wyshawn-cake in my freezer to eat ten years in the future.

The future. The thought makes my heart beat harder than the idea of mind-blowing sex with this man.

We shower together, slowly, not kissing, not even touching. He sets the unspoken tone but we're both needlessly torturing each other. I watch his hands clean every inch of his skin, wishing it were me washing his shoulders, chest, stomach, lower. He lets me gape unashamed at his length. I know my body turns pink with arousal, but there's no use trying to hide how he affects me. I use the soap head to toe, the finale resulting in me bending over in front of him to scrub the dirt off my ankles. He sucks in a hissed breath as if I had just stabbed him. Careful not to let our bodies touch, I massage the soap over the back of my thighs to my ass. Without looking, I can feel the heat from his hands hover around my waist, desperately wanting to grab me, but still holding back.

Why is he waiting? Does he want me to make the first move? That must be it. He had told me not to start anything unless I was serious about him. I stand and stare into his dark brown eyes. They're loaded with questions, patience, and understanding. If I were to walk away, dry off, and clothe, I know he wouldn't push me for more. He'd accept the limits of what I can give. Just to make sure, I have to remind him once more.

"The stars are almost aligned for The Window to reopen. You know what that means, right?"

"Nothing is guaranteed, Piper. I'll take my chances and hope for the best. I want time with you, however long that is."

The thought of separating from him soon is a cutlass to my chest. Neveraj and I are both a disastrous mess, but ever since Wyshawn has been by my side, something has started to change. What if he's the key to conquering my fears? What if his support is what helps me past the hurdles to finally move on?

Refreshed and clean, I take Wyshawn's hand and lead him out of the shower, around the path, and up the spiral staircase. The journey is short but intimate, the sounds of rainfall slamming against the shield above and the intoxicating heat of his stare burning into my back. He knows what I'm about to give him. Which means he understands how vulnerable of a position this puts me in, what I'm telling him. I want to try to plan a life with him, make Epoch a comfortable place to sleep where we both agree to live, argue over whose book is better, plant seeds together in our garden, teach him more about birds, and learn his cooking techniques.

Upstairs, I lead him to the bed. I've had sex in crazy places—under waterfalls in the Mermaid Lagoon, in a tree, on a hoverboard back in Kensington, even on the rooftop of Walk the Plank, but I've never been with someone in a bed. Over time, I've denied myself basic human traditions because I wanted to share them with someone special. Wyshawn is that person.

He has barely complained about how I dragged him to this new world, he's saved my life multiple times, was brave enough to face the challenges, and showed maturity when he learned Kyle was my ex. Never once have I put my fake mask on in his presence or felt ridiculed or judged. Wyshawn is my safety zone, and I want to be that for him too. He's made me a better person, and for that, I know we work better together than apart. I think while I've been hiding, the thing I've been searching for this whole time has been right in front of me for years. It's time to let someone see all of me. Not someone—Wyshawn.

"You sure you want this?" he asks as I sit on the bed. "You want me? *All* of me?"

The insecurity of his tone is heart-wrenching. I don't ever want him to second guess how I feel, which means I need to tell him. But how do I even know for myself? It's not like I've ever been serious with anyone.

"Yes. Wyshawn, I want you, past, present, and...and future." My voice is small, mouse-like, but I mean every word.

I'm staring at the wooden plank floor below his large bare feet until he lifts my chin with one finger. "Piper, my beautiful Jade, whatever you're scared of, I won't let happen. I promise. If you let me, I'll gladly protect all of you, help you fight your fears and raise your hopes, conquer your nightmares, and live your dreams. I'm here for you, past, present, and"—he smiles, warming my heart—"and our future."

I want to bottle up the moment to savor for a lifetime. Everything feels safe with him, and I want to be his for as long as this lasts. I want to tangle our bodies and passions together in a mesh so nothing in this life can pry us apart.

He leans over and claims my lips for his. I'm a sucker for how his hand wraps around the back of my neck, possessing me completely. I moan into his soft mouth. Want to share his very breath. Want to feel consumed for the first time in my life by something other than fear. Want him. Wyshawn Darl. Want his hands. His entire heart. His soul.

"Piper," he whispers into my neck, his lips brushing my skin, "I think, wait...I know...I love you."

Now it's my turn to suck in a breath. The shapes of his words are round and smooth, full of curves and easy waves. They lack any sharp pain of corners. No Partner has ever said that to me. How does he know for sure? How is he confident enough to admit words with such weight?

He trails kisses down my arms as he slowly kneels on the floor, our eyes at the same level, then says, "It's okay, I'm not expecting the same thing. I just wanted you to know before we...well, I'm not rushing you but it's important to me that you know how I feel."

I nod, wordlessly, and capture his lips again. One of his dreads falling over his face tickles my skin. This is it. If we keep going, it'll be the first time someone makes love to me. Will sex be awkward if he has said the words without me returning the sentiment? What if I can't ever love someone? What if caging myself in Neveraj for so long has stunted my ability to feel emotions like normal people?

Those questions can wait until later because the way his fingertips are skimming over my collarbone, creating an invisible path around my breasts makes me lose all train of thought. I need him. No matter what.

Since he's still kneeling, cock out and ready, I reach out and take him in my hand. Slowly, palming him up and down. He groans and scoots closer, giving me easier access.

"Piper, are we doing this?" He growls, an almost fictional sound meant for book boyfriends, "I need a green or red light."

"Yes, definitely yes, but let me use that acorn Lillian gave you."

He pulls back, brows pinched, but a flicker of a smile teases the corner of his mouth. "You want to make a wish right now?"

"Yeah, hurry." I nod to the last place I saw him lay it, on the coffee table.

Quickly, he grabs it, mumbling something about '*my crazy Jade*' under his breath. When it's in my hands, I whisper my wish and trust the magic. He chuckles and is about to kneel in front of me again, but I stop him. This angle on my knees in front of him is too good to pass up. "Come here." With one hand on his ass, I bring him closer until the tip of his dick glides against my bottom lip.

So smooth.

"Mmmmm, babe."

"I haven't even done anything yet."

"Doesn't matter. Just the sight of you..."

I wrap my mouth fully around the tip, suck briefly, then pop him out with major suction. His legs spasm and jerk, knees buckling, and his hands fly to the back of my head. "What was that?"

"A little trick. Again?"

"Yes, Jade. Holy shit."

I oblige. Take him in shallow, lick him in circles, feel his vein pulsing under his shaft and then suck and pop him out again.

"Holy!" he cries out. His fingers dig into my skull. "Fuckin' Luna!"

I doubt he's even aware that he pushes his cock deeper into my mouth. Or how much I love that he's taking control.

"Again," he rasps. His hips thrust forward, his eyes locked on mine.

He's gorgeous, with such intensity in his dark eyes. I'd do this all day for him if it meant I'd see that fire last. I suck. Swirl. Pop out. His groans sound like a dying man in such agony that it makes my body shiver. Again, I suck...but then he thrusts into my mouth like an animal. Again and again, completely relentless. Three, four, five times. My jaw stretches open so wide since I barely have space with how much room he takes up.

"Damn it, Piper, I'm sorry," Wyshawn says, pulling away. "I think I blacked out."

That only makes me grab his ass cheeks with both hands and take him deeper.

"Oooohh!" His eyes squeeze shut. His neck cranes back. "Piper!"

I run my tongue over his length, soft, then slow, letting his sounds guide me for what he likes, and damn is he vocal. I've never been with someone so willing to express their satisfaction. It's fuckin' hot as shit.

The next time, he actually hits the back of my throat. "Holy!" he yells. "Stop! Woah!"

Before I know what's happening, my whole world is flipped upside down. He's no longer in my mouth. I'm lying flat on my back on the soft mattress. His long black hair falls over him, framing his face with the tips dangling along my nipples in soft feathery touches.

"Do you know how many times I've pictured you under me?" He kisses my forehead and lowers his body fully on top of me so I can feel his heavy weight. His cock twitches between my legs, driving me mad.

At first, his weight is overwhelming since I've never been flattened like a pancake by someone his size. There's probably a foot difference in height between us. I've wondered how our bodies would align but as he readjusts, I learn how natural he feels against me. I absolutely love that I'm anchored by him, at the complete mercy of his body and strength.

"For tonight, you're mine, Jade," he says, kisses peppering my neck. "Say it."

"I'm yours," I can barely manage to say as his fingers wedge between our bodies and find my center. "I'm... oooh, OOOH."

"That's right, babe."

He slips one finger inside me, and my nerves implode. An aching pleasure tightens right where I want him to make me come so hard he'd have to piece me back together. Goddess, I want release but not yet. This night needs savoring. He deserves something special.

As much as it tortures me, I focus on speaking, "Wyshawn," I'm basically panting, "I want..."

"I'll give you anything you want."

"I want to play a game."

His deep chuckle makes a shudder rake up my spine. "Of course, how do we play?"

"You can't move your finger until I tell you something I haven't told anyone."

His hand freezes, halfway inside me, halfway palming my soft curls. "I accept, but I can't stop kissing you. Don't ask that."

I moan as his lips glide over my chest, practically worshiping my boobs. I gulp, hyperaware of how my hips are arching into his hand, trying to gain friction. He holds me flat with his other arm. "You know I'm a stickler for following rules."

That infuriating smile. I want to zip his lips together and take back everything I just said.

"Tell me, Piper, tell me a secret."

Hating the fact that I invented this idea, I say the truest fact that comes to mind. "I think I'll be a terrible mother one day."

"I hear you. I see you, babe." His finger inside me curls. Twists. Sends me into a frenzy. "Give me more."

"I don't think I know how to love..." I say, somewhat choking on the admission.

His second finger slides into me gloriously. And I can

feel how wet I am. Goddess, I need more of him. This is too hard to wait. Every muscle in my body is clenched. The sight of him on top of me, treasuring how I feel around his fingers is too much.

"Keep going, Jade, you got this," he whispers between kisses. Kisses that are murdering every concept I had of what I thought kissing meant.

"I...I don't think I care about my friends as much as they care about me."

Wyshawn's third finger pushes inside and my hips buck against him. He's gentle, moving slowly, pressing against my inner walls like a massage gifted by a Goddess. "I've got you, babe, just breathe. You're doing a beautiful job."

"Ooooh!" My fingers grip the sheets, probably white-knuckled. I can't stand how amazing he feels, how he's moving inside me so perfectly.

"One more, babe. Good, girl, just one more."

"I...I've faked all my...oooh...all my orgasms until... ooooh, Wyshawn...until you."

He fits his fourth finger inside me, little by little until I'm seeing stars. Memories of the first and last time I came whip me like a whirlwind. Like that moment, my ass clenches. My legs tighten. My nails dig into the sheet. My body jerks, tight in unexplainable pressure. Then an explosion erupts. All consuming. Everywhere. A burst of energy so pure I can't breathe.

Gradually, everything softens, and I ride out this wave of ecstasy as his fingers slow. Bit by bit, my breathing returns but my legs still shake. I blink open my eyes, unaware of when I had closed them, and look up to a smiling Wyshawn. His eyes are still darker than midnight, full of desire. Without wasting a moment, I roll him onto his back and straddle him.

"I can't wait anymore," I say, staring at his thick cock, twitching.

"I didn't have a condom with me the night you brought me here."

"It doesn't matter. I made a wish. We'll both be safe without risks."

"I trust you." His eyes meet mine, then flicker down to where we're about to connect.

My first time with someone who loves me. Maybe I can love one day—sometime in the future.

Positioning over him, I lock onto Wyshawn's brown eyes. "Ready?"

"If you don't get on my cock right now, I'm going to—"

I lower myself onto him, little by little. My mouth drops into a silent 'oh.' Wyshawn groans immediately, loud and uninhibited. And his chest rises hard and heavy. I can't believe it. He's inside me. A Partner who loves me is inside me. This isn't a random stranger at a bar, a one-night fling, or a toy to play with. This isn't a teasing game or a dare or control-battle. This is Wyshawn, my Wyshawn. It's real. It's love. Fuck.

Something warm and wet slides down my cheeks and I sniffle.

"Piper?" His eyes widen. "Damn it. Are you okay?"

I wipe at my face, fingers coming away wet. I'm

crying. Holy Goddess, this is crazy. I've never cried during sex. I nod to him, then lean forward so our chests are touching, so I can kiss him.

"Are you hurt?" he whispers, uncertainty coating his tone, but his hips still push up into me gently, like he has absolutely no control over his body anymore.

"No, you'd never hurt me," I say, swallowing down a sob before I scare him away. "I'm yours."

"That's right, baby girl." His lips claim me confidently again, in control, and mine.

I can't imagine not doing this again with him.

"How do you want me, Jade?"

"Slow."

And with that, he grabs under my thighs and lifts me high, at the tip of his dick, then lowers me onto his cock. Again and again. A man with power behind his promises. *Thrust.* A Partner who I can depend on. *Thrust.* A dragon mate meant only for me. *Thrust.*

Each time he lowers me, I'm unsure if there's enough space for him. Yet, each time he fits, my personal puzzle piece. I must be dreaming because it feels like I'm soaring among the clouds. Every species of bird, flying by my side, sharing in the joy of freedom. I have no idea how long he's been sliding in and out at such a devastatingly, agonizingly slow perfect pace, but sweat glistens on his chest so he needs a break. And I'm dying to watch him lose control, from a front-row seat.

I move his hands from my body and purposefully fold them behind his head. I want to be fully responsible for his pleasure. His smirk only eggs me on as I start riding his cock. The angle is different and a few gasps slip past my lips as I find myself sitting deeper on him.

"Wow, look at you. *My* Jade. Mine," he whispers then thrusts up into me.

I squeal...an absurd indescribable noise. "No, don't move. It's my turn."

Leaning forward, I almost lay flat against his stomach, his chest my pillow, and rock my hips so fast and so hard that Wyshawn's hands fly out and smack my ass. Whether from pure shock or if it was intentional to control my movements, I don't know, but I'm too far gone to command him again. All I can think about is how good he feels. He slams into me from beneath and I roll my hips so fast it's a damn workout. He's so deep inside that I never want him to be done.

But his body tenses and I know he's about to shatter.

"Babe!" he croaks, neck strained, every muscle bulging, cock ramming harder and harder up into me.

"Yes, now!"

A low throaty grumble roars out of him as he shoves my hips downward. I scream out, feeling all of him at once, everywhere. A feverishly fierce orgasm bursts through me.

I know I love him.

And everything goes black.

I've never passed out from sex. Until today. When I woke, lying on my side, with Wyshawn's face inches from mine, he had kissed me senseless. Cuddling, with the raindrops thwopping overhead like a hypnotic lullaby, I'm unsure how long he wants to lay in this position. Surely his arm must be asleep from holding me in the crevice between his bicep and chest. If given the chance, I'd stay here forever. Forever? I guess I *have* changed.

Wyshawn clears his throat, his thumb gently rubbing a line up my side, giving me gooseflesh. "What are you thinking?" he asks.

"That I wanna do that again."

His chuckle makes my thighs clench. "I need a few more minutes. Thank you for your secrets," he says, kissing the top of my head. "They're safe with me."

I reverse the play-by-play reel of what I had told him. I've faked all my orgasms except for him. True. That Lillian and Tank care more for me than I deserve. True. For the past few weeks, I've barely spent any time with them. What else did I admit? I think I'll be an awful mother if given the opportunity. True. That I'm incapable of love. I'm not so sure that's correct anymore.

"What are you thinking?" I ask.

"That I'm the luckiest man alive." He continues to trail my skin in long, soothing strokes. "And I want to know more about you, eventually, no rush."

I want to give this to him. I make a list of the questions he had asked me earlier, the ones I had ignored or cast aside, and make sense of them in my mind.

"Okay, but you may not like all the answers." I shift so I can see his eyes.

"We don't have to agree on everything to be together."

"You asked me where I'll go if RavenSoul wins." Instead of burying my fear, I share the burden with him. "I have no clue because I have no other home, no family, no money, no job, and definitely no friends on the other side of The Window."

"You can always stay with me if you want," he says without skipping a beat. "No questions asked."

"Thank you, but before I commit to anything permanently, I need to help my friends here. I don't even know where Tank or Lillian are. What if Holland hurt one of them? Or what if RavenSoul attacked another sprite or nymph and I'm here selfishly relaxing under an invincible shelter? Even if I stayed with you, where would Tank and Lillian live? I can't just abandon them."

"Since we can't leave the shelter anyway, how about we focus on keeping you relaxed? We don't have to plan everything out right now."

I give him a look. "You're changing too, my Starling." I pause. "I want to talk about us. Another question you had asked about—"

"Our future."

"Yeah," I bite my bottom lip, unsure how to say this. "I want you to be happy. I'm scared that even though you have feelings for me, I'm not the person who can give you what you need long-term."

"You don't need to give me any*thing*, Jade, not gifts or

undivided attention or even sex, though that would be a nice bonus. I just need *you* in my life, your stories, your passion, your energy, and your spirit, for however long you're willing."

I snort, then cover my mouth, embarrassed. "You sound like a guy in a movie reading a script."

"Nah, he's not as smart as me."

"True, probably doesn't have as big of a dick either."

"Is that a five-star review? Can I have that in writing? Because Sheila never acted impressed."

"Hey! I'm starting to worry that Sheila is real."

"She's only a joke, but I do have a *real* secret you need to know about."

CHAPTER
TWENTY-FOUR

Wyshawn

Sex with Piper has changed me. There are two versions of myself, with a clear slice down the middle, 'before Piper' and 'after Piper.' A 'before last night' and 'after last night,' waking with her in my arms.

We had talked for hours, filling in the missing pieces of each other to create a whole picture. I wanted to tell her about Tank's secret, that her dads apparently broke out of prison months ago, but I'm not even sure if it was a dream or part of the challenge. If it's not true, there'd be no reason to worry her. Plus, Piper refused to let me tell her anything too serious because she didn't want to taint the magical space we were sharing. The Starlight I've been saving also comes to mind. I had forgotten all about the bribe—or should I consider it blackmail?

For now, it's time to live in the moment and not worry as much about external factors. I'm lucky to learn that Piper's favorite fruit is kiwi, she doesn't like books over 400 pages, and won't start a series if it's longer than a trilogy. She found Epoch when he was a baby, barely able to walk, either abandoned by his family or lost. Apparently he has a special skill of sniffing out Venetresses. I've heard of creatures with this talent, but never thought I'd meet one. My favorite new tidbit Piper told me is probably how she anticipated seeing me at Walk the Plank and would be on the lookout for me behind the bar.

Through the paper shield above the treetops, I'd guess the suns' locations would make it late morning. We slept in longer since she can't leave for her morning flight routine. Waking next to her in the same bed is the perfect way to start a day.

As Piper yawns, her tousled blonde hair points wildly in every direction, and her face, soft and angelic, glows from the faint light shining through the barricade. What I'd give to wake up every morning like this. It doesn't matter that I can't feel my arm or that I've had to piss for the last hour. She's here and she's mine. And I love her. I love Piper. This feeling is different than how I had previously defined love. There were a few women in the past I'd said 'I love you' to, but this doesn't feel comparable. An extra layer has been added in, whether it's the intense protectiveness I feel, or the fact that I'd sacrifice anything for her happiness, or my jealous thoughts going into overdrive when imagining her with someone else.

"Mmm, good morning, Starling," she mumbles groggily, voice still stuck on sleep.

I plant a kiss on her forehead and stretch, but she only curls closer into me like a little leech.

"No, let's not move. Just stay here."

"But I need to feed you before you get grumpy."

She wraps one leg and arm completely around me, reminding me of a sloth around a tree. "No. Stay. You smell so good."

"Are you sniffing my skin?"

"I'd never do such a thing."

Laughing, I try to peel her off one finger at a time, but she's glued to me. "Okay, then I guess you're coming with me."

"Sounds good to me."

As I stand, her body grips around my torso in the most awkward position, one leg hanging down. Slowly, she slips down my legs and plops on the ground. Piper crosses her arms. "Not fair."

I hadn't expected her to be a clinger but don't mind in the slightest. If she's even half as addicted to me as I am to her, I'll call that a win.

"I need to take a leak. When I get back there's something I need to tell you. No more procrastinating, babe."

From the floor, she sticks her tongue out at me, then runs a hand through her crazed hair.

Outside, the temperature is as hot as usual, but not as muggy as I had expected from the storm last night. Still barefoot, I keep an eye out for any ant hills and relieve myself behind a tree—just in case Piper's spying on me out the window. She doesn't need to see me pissing quite yet, maybe one day if we move in together.

The air feels abnormally still with the barricade blocking us from the rest of Neveraj. Has she had to use this shield for protection before?

Suddenly, there's a movement on the lowest row that touches the ground. Then a slight tear down the sheet. A little green, scaly paw pokes through, followed by a matching arm until all of Epoch appears. I glance at the domed shield, still intact, other than that one spot. When I reach out to touch it, a mild zap courses through my veins. It's still functional, so how did he get through? Does that mean others can too? Did the storm weaken its power?

Epoch ignores me and skitters quickly up the trunk and over tree limbs until he disappears inside. I'll have to ask Piper if that's normal. Her sudden high-pitched scream splits the air.

I slip and stumble to the stairs. "Hold on!"

It takes way too long to wind up the spiral stairs. I

can hear Piper rapidly talking to someone and her footsteps pace against the wooden floor creak by creak.

"I knew it was her," Piper yells to Epoch as I race higher and higher. "How could she take them? What am I supposed to do? She's a Venetress!"

At the top, I rush to her side and check Piper for injuries. "Where are you hurt?"

She shakes her head in a frenzy while shoving her legs into pants and a tanktop over her sports bra. "How could she!"

I take her shoulders too tightly and spin her to face me. "Who? Piper, tell me what's going on."

Finally, she meets my eyes. "It's Holland, look," she says pointing to Epoch on her table of stolen goods. Only he's no longer green, but crimson from head to toe. "He can turn red when he finds a Venetress. And he delivered this message, it says 'H. Jameson' on the side."

I flip the little rectangle over in my hand, knowing the device is one that stores videos.

Piper grabs a backpack, stuffs her wingsuit in it, and bottles of water. "I...I don't want to see what's on there. Can you watch it and tell me?" She gathers snacks and rams them into her bag, her back towards me. "Please, Wyshawn. I can't look. What if...what if it's bad."

"Okay, how do I turn it on?"

"Rub the top along a plant or leaf."

I do as she says and a silent video projects onto the plank floor. Holly appears first, but she looks years younger. She could be seventeen if I had to guess. When she moves out of the camera lens, I gasp.

"What?" Piper drops something and it clatters along the floor. "What is it? Is it Tank or Lil? Please..." she says, her voice layered in fear. "I should've found them sooner and forced them to stay in here with us."

"It's everyone." I'm unsure how to break the news to her. "She has all of them."

"Who?" Her voice shakes and her breath turns heavy. I can't bear to look up.

"They're all wrapped in a glittering rope around tree trunks."

"WHO! Wyshawn, tell me who!"

"Tank, Lillian, Kyle, and the other two Lost Souls."

"Damn it!"

I suck in a deep breath, then add, "And your dads."

"What?" She runs over and stares at the projection.

Without ever meeting them, I know I'm right. Piper had described them so specifically that I could point them out in a crowd. Both men, average height, one bald, one with glasses, squirming against the rope binding them to trees.

"Oh my Goddess." Her trembling hand hovers over their image. "How are they here? How did she get them from prison?"

It's now or never. I have to come clean about what I know. "Tank told me that your dads broke out of prison months ago."

She shakes her head and takes a step back. "No, Tank's lying. He's jealous of you being here and just wants to create problems. There's no way that's true. They would've tried to contact me."

I can't stand the pain in her eyes. Every part of me wants to hold her, but she keeps backing away while staring at the image of those she cares about tied up, struggling, waiting as bait. I don't know why, but Holland apparently wants to find Piper and will do anything to make that happen. I have to make her see reason. This must be a trap.

"I've been waiting in Neveraj for them like they told me to," she says louder, her body visibly tightening. "They gave me clues to find this place and told me to never leave...that they'd meet me here!" She's screaming, her veins pulsing in her neck. "I've put my life on hold while waiting for them. Tank is wrong!" Her fist slams onto her kitchen table, causing her stuff to clunk to the floor. "Tank is lying. He's lying!"

It's clear that she doesn't believe he's lying at all. When she breaks into a sob, there's no holding back anymore. Her tears are ripping my heart in two. I rush toward her and press her to my chest.

"We'll figure this out. We'll figure it out," I repeat until her episode settles and she's able to gather her breath again.

"We need a plan," she says, completely surprising me. "Venetresses can cast spells. I don't know her strengths, but I know what she wants."

"What?" I glance around The Hidden Gem for anything I can use as a weapon.

"Pixie. Venetresses are the only humans who can reverse aging instead of simply stopping aging. It's why I didn't recognize her. Of course, Holland doesn't have her prosthetic anymore; she turned back her own clock to an age before her injury."

A light-weight black t-shirt and athletic running shorts appear on the counter. As always, the island provides. After throwing the clothes on, I pick up a sharp chopping knife from her kitchen that I've used for cooking.

"But you don't have any Pixie to give her," I say.

"Holland doesn't know that." Piper shoves her feet into her boots, accidentally kicking the acorn we had used the wish on last night. She stares at it too, likely thinking the same thing, that we should've kept it saved. "I'll have to make something up," she whispers while grabbing the acorn and pocketing it. "Let's go."

"Don't you need your wingsuit to get there?"

"No, Holland has them tied right outside," she says as she goes downstairs. "I could identify the landmarks from the video. We can't hear or see each other because of the shield, but they're all out there."

I follow her until we reach the front yard, standing in front of the shielded wall. "Don't we have to wait until the time is up? You had said twenty-four hours."

"Epoch changed that. Don't ask me how, I don't know."

I put a hand out to stop her charge. "Wait, why don't I go out first and try to negotiate."

Finally, I get her full attention. Piper meets my gaze, fire blazing in her eyes. "If you want to even try to make us work, I'll never accept being shielded behind you. I'll always be by your side. If that's too much to ask, then this"—she points between our chests—"will never work."

I blow out a puff of air and nod. "Okay, side by side it is. Let me tie my hair back quick." I use it as an excuse to gather courage.

"I had pictured you as an action movie hero who can fight with long hair whipping in front of your face," Piper says, rising on her tiptoes to kiss my cheek.

"That's more of Sheila's thing." I bend to kiss her lips and memorize the taste of her...just in case I don't make it out of whatever battle we're about to start.

"Shut up and cut that open with your knife."

I glance at the dagger on her hip, realizing she could do it herself, but is relying on me to be her Partner through this, trusting me, having faith in us. My body feels jittery despite not drinking coffee yet, or eating any food for that matter. I already regret not waking early to cook breakfast since neither of us has any substance in our stomachs.

With a slash of the knife that severs the shield, the dome vanishes. I'm immediately confused by our surroundings. The clearing I've grown accustomed to, with the vegetables I've used for cooking, is now consumed by gray shadows slinking around, every plant withered. It's supposed to be around noon, yet the light resembles dusk. None of the familiar birds chirp. I can't see any trace of the monkey family that often sits near the shrubs to our left. It feels like time has been put on pause.

Heart quickening, knife raised, I don't dare say a

word. Piper's footsteps barely make a sound in the wet soil while mine slosh and sludge in the mud like stupid prey, moments from being attacked.

"Took you long enough," a youthful female voice calls out from the darkness. "I was beginning to wonder if you care for your friends at all."

Piper leads me around a bundle of trees that opens to a scene I wish I could erase. True to the video, Tank and Lillian are bound and gagged to one tree, writhing against the ropes. Red welts line their bodies where the rope digs in. The Lost Souls are trapped to another, heads hanging in defeat. I squint to make sure their chests still rise and fall. Yes, alive. For now.

The last tree holds Piper's dads. They don't wrestle the rope, as if they've accepted their fate. Piper takes a step in their direction, but I grab a corner of her tanktop and keep her by my side. There's no telling what Holland has planned, and any rash movements could get my Piper killed.

"Father?" Piper's voice cracks. "Dad?"

Neither looks her way, both staring at Holland. Rage boils through my blood. How could they ignore their daughter? She's been waiting for them for years. Then I notice how neither is blinking; maybe she has them under a hypnotic spell. That wouldn't be their fault.

"I need more Pixie," Holland says as she smooths her wrinkled, blood-red shirt with both hands, like she's practiced this conversation in a mirror, playing it cool. "The *real* powder. The *raw* Pixie. You know what I'm talking about."

What does Holland mean? But I keep my mouth shut. Piper shifts uneasily on her feet and cracks her knuckle at her side. She doesn't take her eyes off her parents, but also doesn't look my way.

"Since you're the Princess of Neveraj, I thought it'd be fun for *you* to pick who donates their Pixie to me."

"Donates?" I try to keep my attention on Holland but glance at Piper again. All I can see is her throat bobbing. She doesn't reply or make a move. For the first time, she seems frozen, unsure, or maybe contemplating a plan—all of which are new to her.

Holland starts at the first tree and flicks her wrist. The rope tightens. Lillian screams, the sounds muffled behind the cloth stuffed in her mouth.

"Stop!" Piper raises both hands out. "You're already so young, Holland. Maybe sixteen? You're absolutely gorgeous. Why do you need more?"

"I have sisters and cousins and aunts, don't I?" she hisses. "They deserve eternal youth too. All those years dealing with these two idiots were worth it," Holland says as she marches to the tree holding Brax and Davien Pan. "I heard they found a map to Neveraj when you were only five years old, so I befriended these morons, and conned with them, all to gain their trust. And it worked, didn't it, boys?"

Holland spins her wrist again but this time their binds fall loose to the jungle floor. No welts or red lines mark their skin. They both continue to stare at Holland like trained dogs, awaiting a command.

Piper's jaw drops, and I grasp the bottom of her tanktop to keep her close.

"I'd rather not drain Pixie from your poor daddies." Holland's tone is full of mockery as she pouts with her bottom lip. "So, which of these other five deserves to die?"

"Die?" I whisper, the word slipping out. What does she mean?

The Venetress points to the three unconscious humans. "Will you choose an ex-lover, perhaps?" Holland grazes a long nail under Kyle's chin to lift it higher. "Don't consider yourself special, Mr. Darl. Piper will cast you aside once she's done playing with you too."

"Shut up!" Piper shouts, but she sways where she stands, as if she can't get a grip on the reality blooming in front of us.

"Oooh, she's feisty today," Holland says, smiling. "You don't like being called out for your childish shenanigans? Haven't you been forced to deal with any grown-up responsibilities yet?"

"Let them go and I'll lead you to the Falls."

Holland laughs, sinful sounds dripping from each cackle. "The Falls? They're all dried up, dear. No, we're staying here. Hold this." Holland pulls an orb from thin air and places it in Brax's hand. He stands like a statue, accepting the command.

In one fell swoop, Holland lunges at Kyle. Something silver is conjured from the air. It slashes across his throat.

Gold blood spills out. Gold? His head dangles unnaturally.

"No!" Piper screams and falls to her knees beside me.

My fist clutches tighter on my weapon until I realize I'm no longer holding the kitchen knife. Somehow, Holland had taken it with her magic. The Venetress smears the gold blood over her forehead and she instantly shortens and loses a few pounds. There are fewer freckles on her cheeks and her hands are thinner and smaller.

I don't know where to look so I shield my eyes from the gore. A sudden feeling of cold stretches over my body and my muscles go numb. Dizziness takes over and there's a tightness in my chest. That didn't just happen. I didn't see someone murdered. We can turn around and go back inside and start the day over.

"Perfect!" Holland dances in a circle, her features turning more youthful with every spin. When she stops in place, she resembles a thirteen-year-old. She turns toward Tank and Lillian. "Who's next? I need to store some for my friends."

"Wait!" Piper's hands fall to the ground too so she's on all fours. "Take me instead."

"Piper! Noooo!" I yell and reach out but Piper is already scrambling ahead, halfway standing, halfway crawling toward her friends.

"Take me. You can have my Pixie."

"Stop!" I scream so loudly that Holland flinches.

The nasty Venetress cracks up. "Oh, you're going to sacrifice yourself in her place too? How sweet."

"Piper, give her *the wish*."

Holland jerks in place, all entertained pretense of the game erased from her expression. "You have a wish? Hand it over. Now!" Her hand outstretched, I wonder why she doesn't conjure it with her magic like she did with my knife. Maybe she needs to see it first.

Ahead, too far for me to reach, Piper sticks her hand in her pocket and pulls out the used acorn. Even between the swirling shadows, I can see her back flexed, ready to run or fight. Slowly, while handing it over, her neck swivels between where Tank and Lillian are tied, then to her dads on the opposite side of the clearing. Back and forth. She's trying to choose who to save.

Holland will learn within seconds that the acorn is a fake. If only Piper would point behind her back which way she plans to go, I'd know to sprint to the other group. As if she reads my mind, her foot barely rotates towards her dads. Which means I need to dart towards Tank and Lillian.

I hold my breath, unsure how I'll free them. The acorn shifts possession and lands in Holland's palm. "I wish for all the Pixie to be mine!" she shrieks, her voice clawing through the jungle.

Piper races to her dads.

I dash to Tank and Lillian. My hand touches the rope strapping them. The heat of the suns burns my skin. I wail in pain, jumping backward.

"It's not working!" Holland repeats her wish, shakes the acorn, then chucks it into the mud. "You, bitch!"

Holland points to Piper but I launch myself at her and tackle Holland to the ground. We collapse in a crumpled heap. She flails and thrashes against me. Sharp scratches maul my arms and face. Pain sears one eye. I can only see out of one—complete chaos.

A kick to my gut. Rolling in the mud.

Through RavenSoul's growing shadows, I make out Piper dressing into her wingsuit and latching her dads onto the handles. As I straddle Holland on the ground, she bares her teeth at me and her nostrils flare. A guttural string of curses fly from her wicked tongue and I'm flung off of her onto my back.

The world disappears and I have tunnel vision for Piper only. She glances over her shoulder, terrified. I hear a *thud* nearby then Piper's eyes widen even further. I follow her gaze back through the misty shadows. Lillian is dead. Chopped to pieces. Gold blood flows from her body. Piper screams and screams and screams, but I need her to leave.

I hurl myself at Holland again. She hits my side. Smashes my knee. Yanks my hair. I'm stronger, but she's faster and has magic. It's not an even fight. In my peripheral vision, Piper's airborne with both her dads. Wings outstretched, they float for a moment, then both wings flap and they fly away.

Only Tank, Zheo, and Felix remain. Two of us are conscious, one of which is bound. We're doomed. I manage to roll away from Holland and struggle to my feet. Coated in mud, unable to see out of one eye, I raise both fists. My breaths come heavy and labored. Muscles tired.

Holland flicks her wrist. A flash of sweltering pain like I've never felt wraps around my torso. I look down at the glittering, enchanted rope blistering my skin, then collapse into the mud.

CHAPTER
TWENTY-FIVE

Piper

The birds are silent as I land outside Cannibal's Cave, the last place I'd expected my wings to take me. My arms are strained from the flight and I don't remember a second of it. Usually, I savor the warm air flapping my hair, but everything's a blur. The murderous scene we had fled plays on repeat in my mind. Kyle's neck severed, his head unattached. I clutch my chest and pull at my wingsuit, too tight. It's suffocating me. Lillian chopped up like meat. Can't breathe.

Everything's too hot. I'm sweating all over and need

to escape this outfit. I tear at the zipper unsuccessfully, then drop to the ground. My knees slam into the mud. Extra weight crashes down with me, reminding me both my dads are in tow. I come to my senses and unhook them both from the wingsuit harness.

"Ssh, don't cry, sweetie," Father says while reaching over to wipe away a tear.

His eyes look clear and no longer entranced. When he wraps me in a hug, I breathe in his familiar, comforting scent of laundry detergent and pineapple lotion. Every ounce of tension my body has been holding for years detonates. Sobs rack me, body and soul, as I drop the mask I've worn that has hidden built-up rage, loneliness, guilt, bitterness, and fears. Father's large hand pets the back of my hair; his child needs soothing.

"I missed you." My voice hitches.

"It's okay, sssh," Father repeats again and again. "I'm here."

His specific use of the pronoun 'I' grabs my attention. My parents have always been the 'we' type, like, '*We* are looking for a new job,' or '*We* shaved a little crooked today, didn't *we*?' Never have I heard either refer to themselves as a single unit.

So, I glance across to Dad, who stares greedily at the dark entrance of the cave. The color in his eyes is pure venom and when he reaches towards the unknown, shadows unfurl dreamily from his bald head.

"Dad?"

Father grabs my elbow. He shakes his head slowly and retreats a few steps, dragging me with him. He keeps his eyes on his husband, my poor daddy, and whispers, "A shadow creature got to him. I've been trying to keep him lucid, but once Holland cast a mind-control spell, I couldn't help him anymore." He cringes when noticing how tightly his fingers dig into my skin. "Oh, sorry... Piper, listen, I'll figure it out. While I do, you go save your friends."

"What! Are you kidding me?"

"Ssh! Piper, anything could set Brax off."

"I don't want to go." I try to keep my voice quiet so as not to spook Dad, who is still entranced by the cave. "I'm not leaving either of you." But even as I say it, the words don't feel true, because Wyshawn whirls like a tornado in my thoughts.

Wyshawn—joining my scheme to trick Holland with the useless acorn. Wyshawn—determined to help my friends. My Starling—the man I can't abandon, no matter how much I've missed my parents.

My head spins with questions. Is Wyshawn injured? How do I fix Dad? What is Holland doing to the others? Did Lillian feel pain before she died?

That last thought is a wrecking ball crushing my ribs. I can't consider Lillian suffering. Maybe we could've prevented her death. Who will help me carve the rest of my journal entries into The Hidden Gem? Who will listen to my stories under the stars? Who will read my fortune? The absence of her spirit feels so wrong, like nothing will be right or whole again.

"...and I swear once you break into their lair and find Holland's secret Pixie spot then I'll never scam another mark again, you have my word. I'll have enough powder to last us lifetimes and more."

"What did you just say?" I drop my hands from my head, not realizing until that moment that I've been pressing my palms into my eyes to try and relieve this pounding headache.

"Hey, Pipe, you're still crying. I bet this is all overwhelming, but I need you to sharpen up. Follow the *plan*."

"The *plan*?" I straighten like a rod has been rammed down my spine and glare into the eyes that have fed lies to so many innocent people. Is he joking right now? This would be a terrible time to play a prank.

Father readjusts the glasses on his nose— his one and only tell. "Yes, I'll tie Brax to the tree and wait for you to return with Holland's stash."

"Wait, let me get this straight. We've been separated for years, we've been attacked, Dad is currently unstable, two of my friends just died, and my boyfriend is probably captured or injured and you're asking me to go steal Pixie for you?"

"Don't say it like that, Hun. There's no need to worry, things will work out and like I said, I have a plan."

There's that word again. *Plan*. Suddenly, my past rushes at me like a runaway train. I have tried to block out unforgiving memories, but they wash over me like a wave. I had begged my parents to stop their con work, to let us settle down in one spot so I could grow up with the same friends, in the same neighborhood. They always promised that after their next con, we'd buy a cottage at the edge of Lacordia, along the coast, and they'd retire from crime. Until the next morning, when I'd wake with a colorful chart highlighting the steps of their next mark, their next *plan*. Excitement would be drawn all over their faces, so being the spirited daughter I was, I played along, matching their endless enthusiasm.

A strange pull tugs at my heart. Are my parents the reason I resisted the magnetic draw to Wyshawn for so long? Do I have an underlying fear that he will disappoint me too, upend my life to serve *his* plans, *his* future, *his* goals, *his* needs?

The tears haven't stopped; in fact, they're rolling down faster, harder, making my eyes burn. "It all makes sense now," I say quietly as I collapse against a boulder's top. "You conned me too."

"Excuse me?" Dad shifts his glasses again.

"You both made me believe I couldn't survive without you, that I was too young and immature, too inexperienced, and that I had to find this place"—I stand again, throwing my hands in the air—"and stay frozen in time until you found me. Because Goddess forbid I find a life that didn't serve your games."

"Hey! Watch your tone!" With brows tight, his expression reminds me of the times I cried myself to sleep under the covers because of how similarly upset he'd become when their plans backfired, and their safety net had fallen apart. "I did no such thing. How could you be so selfish after all I've given you?"

I actually laugh out loud in his face, then cross my arms, creating a shield against the one person I had thought loved me unconditionally. "Given me? All you did was take take and take! And expect me to follow any whim, pack at a moment's notice, and crawl through tiny spaces to find locked safes hidden underground. Should I go on? I was your PAWN!" I begin to pace, keeping one eye on Dad, who starts to salivate as he crawls closer to the cave entrance, one hand and knee at a time.

"Piper, what in the Abyss has gotten into you? Is this because Holland told you I did one more mark with her first when I escaped last year? Obviously, I can't trust her, but the opportunity was too good to pass up."

The world jerks to a stop. The mud under my feet ceases to exist. Any air left in my lungs has been sucked out. I'm the only living being left in this universe. I must have heard him wrong. There's no possible way Father said they escaped last year. Last *year*? As in twelve months ago? They've been living free without my knowing for a *year*?

I have to consciously think about closing my dropped jaw. "Say that again?"

Father rubs a hand down his face. "Listen, I was going to give you a third of the treasure, I swear, but Captain Schmee made me a deal I couldn't resist, so when I sailed to Coendriel, I dropped a stash off there with an old friend. But you'll get your portion!"

Treasure. My parents went on a voyage to another country without telling me. "Let me get this straight." I march to him, blood boiling. "You scared me into thinking I needed to be tucked away in this magical dimension to control me, to know where I was in case I could serve a purpose later on. Is that correct?"

"Hun, I—"

"You *knew* I was waiting for you. You *knew* I was alone! You *knew* I was here!"

He raises both hands and backs into a tree. For the first time in my life, Father seems shorter than me, withered and frail.

A wicked breeze brushes past my cheeks, screaming my trauma as it hisses past. It doesn't feel natural. "I changed. No thanks to you. See here's the thing, Father, no one can stay still forever. You tried to use me as an innocent child to do your dirty work, but you failed. I've grown up, like it or not. And I see past all that bullshit now."

Slowly, Father lowers his hands, his shoulders sagging.

"My answer is no. I will not find Holland's stash of Pixie for you." I stoop to grab my wingsuit from the ground.

"It's all your fault," he says, deadpan.

"Wh—" I stumble, catching myself on my wrist at a bad angle. A bone snaps painfully but I refuse to show any weakness in front of him. I'm no longer a child needing comfort.

"I didn't want to tell you this, but the reason why Neveraj is dying is because of you. Because you've brought so many Partners here to mess around with. Honestly, Piper, I thought I taught you better than to spread yourself thin with possible liabilities."

With my good hand, I sweep my wingsuit against my side. "What are you trying to say? Don't sugar-coat it."

"Humans aren't meant to be here. I learned this when you were a young child in Kensington. I'd hop through The Window if the time was right, steal Pixie, and return before it closed. Only once did I get stuck here for a month by accident. I bet you don't remember my business trip to Ozaron when you were little. Well, I was here. It showed me all its secrets. Have you wondered why this land provides for you?"

My words are scraped away.

"Pixie is their life source, Piper. Think about it. It's in everything. The more humans that stay here, the more it is strained against its natural tendencies. Those you've brought here have weakened the land. You being here for so long has done enough damage, but then you enticed Holland? She's half-Venetress! She's using Pixie's energy at an unsustainable rate. And you caused that. The shadows grow stronger when the Pixie is weakened. This place grows weaker because you stayed."

"YOU TOLD ME TO COME HERE!" My throat burns from yelling so loudly. "YOU TOLD ME TO STAY!"

"I didn't tell you to invite everyone you've ever wanted to sleep with." His voice grows to match mine. "I didn't tell you to ask around about Holland, so she'd track you down and follow you. She's here because you were sloppy, you didn't cover your tracks. That nymph would still be alive if you would've only used common sense."

Lillian's prophecy clicks into place. '*The one who fights*

with a youthful charm will strengthen my shadow and bring them harm.' I had been wrong about 'the one' being my enemy. The prophecy needed a comma. *'The one who fights, with a youthful charm...'*

Ever since my dads' trial, I have fought against growing up and moving forward with my life. The prophecy was referring to *me*, someone who has been stuck, trying to remain youthful. I attempted the impossible, to stay young, to stay here, without responsibilities, blind to what my parents had done. I can't stay here with them. They're no longer my priority. Wyshawn needs me. But I can't swoop in there without power. A partial plan forms, which is better than nothing.

Quickly, I glance at the sky. Knowing the stars will align once it gets dark, I consider the timing. Even though I'm infuriated at my parents, I can't let them suffer.

"Can you take them to *The Window*?" I ask the camouflaged nymphs eavesdropping behind me. "Please don't hurt them."

To Father's utter shock, dozens of nymphs step into the clearing, limbs reaching out toward my parents as I walk into the cave's darkness.

CHAPTER
TWENTY-SIX

Piper

A distinct earthy smell covers me inside the cave. Thankfully little specks of golden Pixie dust light my way. Sheila wouldn't be scared. Sheila wouldn't be scared. My wrist scorches with sharp pain anytime it shifts the slightest. I swear I can feel my heartbeat thumping right where a bracelet would lie. It's creepy to possibly be the only living thing in a vast world of black. All I can hear is my breathing, the rustling of my clothes, and the light tread of my sneakers against the ground until a little skittering of claws scraping stone comes from ahead. I freeze.

Epoch's little snout emerges from around a bend, and he hops onto my shoe. How does this sweet demon always find me? He scurries up my pant leg, slightly scratching my skin through my pants, and flops himself into my pocket, barely fitting. His snout peeks out from the top, clearly in surveillance mode. I don't dare greet him out loud in case a monster lurks ahead, ready to grab me in its talons.

Now that I don't have to stay in Neveraj for my dads anymore, I have the impulsive need to leave this cursed land. For so long I've convinced myself that this is my home, my only option, but this whole time, it had caged me as a prisoner. I've been a victim, tricked by my parents with false promises. If I had known the truth I would've seized my life, taken risks, traveled, tried new experiences...right?

Keep moving. I pretend I'm a bird that likes to burrow in dark, cold, damp spots. The pathway already feels different than the last time I attempted this challenge. I don't dip lower in the same parts or have to climb or wedge through crevices. This route stays flat, long, and narrow. If I spread both hands out wide, I could probably reach both walls with my fingertips grazing along the rough surface. Keep going. Don't stop. My body feels at war with itself, half wanting to return to Wyshawn, half wanting to finally conquer my fears. Unexpected tears pool and warm my eyes again, threatening to fall, but I won't cry again. Dad and Father have crushed me so devastatingly that I can't process what I learned yet. Maybe later, after Wyshawn is safe, I can think about them. I must hold on to any chance at helping Wyshawn escape. While stepping one foot after the other, heart pounding as if it might explode, I continue the plan. My plan.

Holland wants Pixie more than anything else. She has enough for herself but is greedy for more for her coven. If I offer the strongest Pixie possible, it may give me enough leverage to trade for Wyshawn's freedom. Once she sees the orb I'm about to win, I'll cut my wrist with my dagger to fill it with my blood and free Wyshawn.

Is he the only one I'll be able to help? What about the other Lost Souls? Can I live with myself if I leave them with Holland? What Father said haunts me. Neveraj is dying because of the humans so the only choice is to bring everyone through The Window with us. Otherwise, Neveraj will be consumed by shadows. I can't allow that fate for the sprites and nymphs. It may be pointless if I can't drag all of them out too.

My energy seeps away, stealing my hopes with it. My legs feel too heavy to move. I should simply slump down to the ground and let myself rot here where no one can find me. This is it, the end of my days will be here, in this cave—the exact place I've feared to roam.

No, I can't give up. Not this time. Memories of the last time I attempted this challenge assail me; it ended with me curled in the fetal position.

Keep going. I'm brutally aware of my hurt wrist dangling at my side. Once in a while, my hip nudges against it, and pain fires through my forearm. Taking a deep breath, I try not to think of Wyshawn suffering from any similar pain. What if Holland has cast a sadistic torture spell on him? What if she's already letting him bleed out to collect his Pixie? Hopefully she'd realize his blood would be the least potent since he's been here the shortest time.

If only I could send him a telepathic message to relay that I'll be there, that I haven't forgotten him, and never will. I create an imaginary story of our future. He smiles wistfully on our first real date, at a library, of course. He runs a finger along my cheek while driving our shared hoverboard into town. I can hear his deep voice laughing as his face brightens when we visit his mothers. I can make plans—for Wyshawn—my love.

Love. Yes, I truly love him. We'd have weeks, months, and years to learn more about each other, his least favorite cereal, and what concerts he wants to attend, how fast he allows me to speed over the street limit before stepping on the hoverboard's emergency brake. I want a lifetime of cuddling on the couch, in pajamas. I want it all—but only with him.

Epoch wiggles in my pocket and turns in a circle for better comfort. I tap him softly while I walk into the unknown. How far away could this challenge be? Something doesn't feel right.

A thick, slow press of air rolls over my skin.

A strange, eerie chill scrapes up my spine.

"Hello?" I whisper, squinting ahead into the darkness.

I see a silhouetted shadow, shifting and morphing as

it approaches slowly. Leaning forward, I squint since the gold Pixie powder lining the cave walls seems to be moving too. Is the shadow creature eating the Pixie dust? The light is swallowed whole, bit by bit until RavenSoul towers directly in front of me.

A boom. I instantly cover my ears and duck down. Harsh bone-white light bursts through a split in the stone wall. I shield my eyes and tilt my head away. A strong heat, boiling hotter than a shooting star. My skin feels like it's been razored off with a thousand knives. I scream until the light softens and the pain subsides. Panting, I pat down my body, checking for burns. I'm fine. Even my clothes remain intact. I'm sweating profusely, but my wrist remains my sole injury.

"What the Abyss?" I shiver as a blast of frigid wind funnels from the darkness and smacks my face. My eyes water and I can barely stand as the wind tries to push me away. "What do you want!?"

The shadow, amid the chaos of light, heat, wind, and noise, forms the shape of a woman, curvy and petite. She walks forward with a familiar flick of her hip. Something about her gait reminds me of the impossible—of my mother, but I've never met the woman who gave birth to me. When I hold out my hand, she mirrors me.

I gasp and jump back. The shadow does the same. She's not my mother. She's me. I wipe my clammy hands on my pants and try to stop my lip from trembling. I want to get the Abyss out of here.

Little by little the shadow forms more realistic features. First, her tendons stand out in her neck, her vein beating a visible pulse beneath her skin. I've lost the ability to speak, rooted to the spot. Do I look as scared as her? Are my shoulders that tight and are my breaths bursting in and out too? Do I have the same beads of sweat on my forehead?

A shrill voice echoes from the darkness. I flinch at the sound. Need to get out of here. Everything's happening too fast. I could be trapped, forced to live with this fake version of myself until I lose all sense of reality. Has it been a minute or days since I entered? I want to jump into action, turn around, and dart away, but that's the wrong choice. It's what I've always done in the past. If I want to beat this challenge, I must think differently.

What would Wyshawn do? The comfort of his dark eyes focuses me. I need to resist every natural pattern I'd usually consider and do the opposite. Face the responsibility. Which means keep moving forward. I take a step towards the Shadow-Me. She hisses, fangs sharper than the stalagmites above.

"*You won't make it out alive.*" Shadow-Me snarls. "*Poor Wyshawn is trapped. It's no usssse trying to sssssave him.*"

I swipe my dagger out of my sheath and point it at her.

She cackles. "*You plan to ssssstab a shadow?*"

"You're not real," I say and step forward again. The temperature drops further, and I can't feel my toes.

"*Your parents are ssssearching for you, yet you desert them.*"

"Shut up." I step forward again, but she multiplies.

Three Shadow-Mes glare back, mimicking my every movement.

"Sssstay here with ussss."

"No, move out of my way," I say, continuing to step forward despite my ankles going numb.

"We're the ssssame, you and I," they say in unison, splitting off into five shadows, all imitations of my features.

"We're not the same. I've changed. I've grown."

"Don't tell liessss. We can be young and carefree together. With nothing to worry about."

"Stop! I want a real life, away from here. This place has only held me back."

"She's delusional," one says, but this time she turns to one of the others, independently.

It's sentient.

I try to run. Can't feel my legs. I slam to the ground. My palm lands on ice. I scream out when my bad wrist holds my weight. Heart thrashing in my chest. Sweat beads freezing on my temples. I have to get out of here. Have to finish the challenge. I crawl on my hands and knees, excruciating pings shooting through my wrist with every push off the ground. The Shadow-Mes chase. Half jog, feet silent against the ground. Half fly, no sounds or breeze moves through the cave.

I don't know what's on the other side, what awaits me, what tomorrow brings, but I will fight to get there. I must fight for Wyshawn—anything to protect him. And the only way to share a future with him is to defeat my demons.

One Shadow-Me clutches my thigh. I kick her away. Her pain radiates up my body as I feel the kick bruise on my body. Another's claws swipe at my arm. They slash a deep gash and I cry out but punch her face with my good hand. A hard whack smacks against my cheek at the same time. I crawl faster, harder.

The cold creeps up my thighs, numbing the rest of my legs. Must keep moving.

Another Shadow-Me from above swoops down and wraps an arm around my neck, choking me. I fling my head back, ramming my skull into her face. She releases as a whiplashing jolt hits me straight in the eye, making my vision fuzzy. Pain throbs under the skin. It must already be swelling shut because I can only see from one side.

Keep moving.

Keep going.

I don't know what's ahead, but I have to get there. Barely able to crawl, Epoch jumps out of my pocket and chomps at the air when any remaining Shadow-Mes attack. They stay back, following at a close distance but no longer touch me. The freezing, heart-stopping, piercing cold travels up my back. But ahead I finally see a circular light of day. The unknown beckons me. I'll gladly welcome what is to come, as long as it frees me from my shadows. Hand in front of knee in front of hand in front of knee. So close. Just a little further. Crawling at a snail's pace, I exit the cave. The moment my whole body leaves the cave, warmth returns to my limbs, and a small orb rises from the ground. The pain in my wrist continues to throb, but the rest of my body is intact.

"I did it!" I say to Epoch, exhausted and now sweltering from the drastic temperature change.

I pocket the orb, planning to fill it later with my golden blood. When I look up, I don't expect the scene above me. A gasp whisps from my lips.

CHAPTER TWENTY-SEVEN

Wyshawn

My body is wrapped in slippery silk, high in a massive spiderweb above The Hidden Gem. The thin strands are strong as fuck, holding my arms tight behind my back. I can't move an inch, no matter how much I've struggled against the binds. I can't even shout, since the gross threads cover my mouth. My nightmare turned reality.

Birds still chirp and the suns still shine through holes in the canopy, as if this were any other day. As if I hadn't made the biggest mistake of my life earlier. I should've grabbed Piper and ran. Then we never would've been separated. Who knows if I'll ever see her again? I have no idea what Holland plans to do with me. My whole body tenses.

Far below, a puff of smoke explodes in the mud. Something rolls out of it, coming to a stop. I see familiar broccoli-colored sneakers, then matching leggings on a body I've memorized.

"Piper!" It comes out as a muffled slush of nothing.

Below, she glances around, left, right, up to her home, but doesn't seem to see me. I writhe against the strands once more, hoping it won't signal Holland to come eat her prey. Of all the insects in this world, spiders are the absolute worst.

Below, Piper staggers to her feet, nursing an injured wrist in one hand. I try to call out her name again, but my voice is too muted, and I'm too far up. She has no reason to look this high. There's no point in trying to make eye contact. At least I've partially overcome my fear of heights from flying with her the past few weeks. That doesn't lessen the speed of my crazed heartbeat slamming against my chest though.

"Piper!" It's useless. She can't hear me. My bucket of hope has run dry. She disappears from view, and I let out a strangled groan.

I've let Piper and her friends down. The two surviving Lost Souls are somewhere in her treehouse, also bound and gagged while Holland left us here to search for something. Tank is the only one of us she hasn't caught; he had flown away, willing to leave us imprisoned. Piper should rescue her exes and get out of here while she has the chance.

I lower my chin to my chest and my hands go limp. All this insanity has stripped away what's left of my energy. I let my body sag further. Even if I weighed a little more, the spiderweb restraints would never snap. This is my new role—bug food—may as well accept it.

Piper needs to flee now while Holland is gone. Since the stars will align soon, she needs to fly to The Window and jump through with her dads. After all that time separated, she deserves a safe, loving life with them.

Creepy shadows appear, swirling around the trunk of the nearest tree, carrying the scent of disgrace and defeat. It'll devour me. My mind fogs into oblivion as it moves closer and closer.

The shadow seeps through the sticky web-rope and I watch it sink into my skin. I cough and gag on the taste of burnt licorice. My head spins. I haven't been successful in any goal. Unable to keep the women I love safe. I hate what I've let happen to Piper. Not to mention my parents. Mum and Mother will be better off without me.

I choke, panicked, as shadows scratch down my throat. With every breath I take, RavenSoul overtakes me. Gasping to control each inhale, I fight the urge to pass out. No, no, no, this isn't happening. The shadows smother me, and I can't get enough oxygen. My chest tightens and a tingling spreads throughout my fingers. Spots blur my vision and dizziness rocks me side to side.

Hyperventilating, I squeeze my eye shut and wish it away.

And then with one overwhelming zap through my nervous system, the shadows settle within. A strong, damp scent wafts near, one of death and floral—a lucid dream. I can smell the ingredients as if mixed into a candle—decay and dirt blended with aged dried boysenberries with a pinch of that dreadful feeling of something long forgotten.

My eyes dart open to a world smudged in gray. My sight feels altered, but my thoughts become as clear as the sky. There's no need to worry; Holland is on her way to help me out of this mess. I simply need to have faith in her, my best friend, my mentor.

Holland Jameson—my devilish master.

A new, light buzzing sound whizzes near my ear. Is it a fly? Delicious. I love their carcasses and enjoy chewing on their bodies long after they should be swallowed. Alas, a hilarious sprite flies in front of my face, gesturing with his hands. I try to laugh, then remember my mouth has been sealed shut by our nemesis, Piper Pan, the traitor who stole everything from us, our life's work. Rage and revenge, so intense, whip my form into a new shape. I slip out of the sticky substance and laugh. How was I ever trapped in the first place? My feet float above the web, morphing shapes like vapor.

The sprite's jaw falls open and he points a tiny, sharp sword at me.

"Aye, matey, you care for a duel," I raise my finger at him, noticing how it has no real shape. Strange.

His sword moves straight through my finger as if it passes through air. I laugh again. I could get used to this, but there's no time, Holland needs me. I reach out to clutch the sprite in my hands but my flesh goes straight through him.

He sticks his tongue out at me.

"How fun!" I try again but can't feel his body. Am I a ghost? Odd. Have I always been this way? No, surely something is different. I try to remember what came before, but nothing sparks in my mind.

The sprite flies down through a crack in the planks and zips out of view.

"Tank! I'm so glad you're okay. I'm so sorry, but I have to get them out of Neveraj!" a female voice says below, fire and passion darken her tone. "No, you can't come with. This is your home. Where's Wyshawn?"

After a beat of silence, a male responds. "We haven't seen him. Let's get the Sols out of here before she comes back!"

There's a clatter and flapping sound, so I flatten to peek through the slats of the patchy rooftop of this ramshackle treehouse. Below, three humans flitter about, shoving items into packs. One human in particular, the smallest with hair the color of the suns and clothes as green as the jungle, focuses on a table full of random knick-knacks, her eyes flickering between two objects. She looks fun. I'll play with her. Bouncing in place, I silence a giddy squeal begging to burst free.

"Did Holland say where she went?" the woman in all green asks.

"Something about a secret stash."

The green-girl chooses a globe from her table and buries it into her backpack. She grabs a black spandex outfit from a hook and starts to thread her leg through it. How strange clothes are, as well as bodies, shells to contain a spirit. I know what I'll do—I'll scare her so badly that her soul jerks out of her body. Yes, that will be entertaining. Excitement stirs within me like ants in a blender.

I dabble with the wind, daring it to play my game as I sweep my arms back and forth. An unsettling creaking sound makes the treehouse groan long and slowly. All three humans glance to the ceiling, waiting, only the sound of their breaths detectable. Hide and seek may be my new favorite.

"What was that?" the male says, his eyes dazed, dripping with terror.

Faster than possible, navy bruises splatter across the clouds.

"Hurry, we need to get out of here," the green-girl says, her voice trembling. "Where did that storm come from?"

The breeze crawls with soft voices, slithering in unison. "*Play with us, we can see you, plaaaay with ussss, we can ssssee you.*"

"What the fuck?" Green-girl's eyes widen.

Her fear fuels me, strengthens me. Power floods me. It's intoxicating. I decide I don't want to share this dramatic one with anyone else. She will be mine and

Holland will need to accept that. Never have I wanted something so badly.

The wind around me gains speed, soaring through me. Branches and wood tear through the treehouse, ripping the siding to shreds. Green-girl screams and runs down the staircase while yelling at the others. How satisfying.

"Go!" she hollers as the wind whips at her from all directions.

The humans scream again. Little pawns run and scream through the clearing. I whirl myself towards green-girl and tornado around her. Round and round. She's trapped. Mine.

To my absolute delight, flying branches join around us, forming a tight cage, unbreakable in every way. I stop my spinning and freeze still in front of her. There's something about her piercing emerald eyes that sends a chill through my soul. I stare into the depths of her glare but despise what lies within.

Flowers and journals. Birds and the sky. Laughter and kisses. Quick side-glances and flushing cheeks. Sprites and nymphs. Picnics and stories. They all roll in an endless loop, their details becoming more crisp around the edges each time it repeats. The sensation is draining me. I hate every second.

"Wyshawn!"

"He's gone!" I hiss, my voice strange and demented.

Her mouth falls open and she takes two steps back, ramming her back into the wall of brambles and branches. "Wyshawn?"

"Play with us. We can see you," I say, my words snake from my throat like delicious poison, both delectable and disgusting at the same time.

"It's okay, I'll bring you back." Green-girl fidgets with her bag.

Something's wrong. I inspect green-girl, moving closer, reaching out.

A sudden feeling of cold expands in my core. Do I have a body? Can I feel temperature? Why do I care? I glance down to see only gray shadows swirling in the air. I try to touch green-girl, but I fly straight through her, or maybe around her. The realization is infuriating. I want her to be mine! But I can't trap her for long.

She bangs at the walls of her cage with only one fist, snapping branches in two. Then she kicks at it, pounding, knocking, hammering. It breaks apart and falls to the dirt. With the momentum, she also staggers forward, landing on her knees and one hand. The other hangs limp, useless. Is she injured? Fury rips me to shreds. No one can torture her but me!

A boom of thunder crashes above and a flash of lightning brightens the sky.

"Lillian." Green-girl rubs her hand over something on the ground, as rain splashes to the soil with mourning teardrops. "Thank you," green-girl whispers, and then she gasps. She reveals a small acorn in her palm, then wraps her fingers around it tightly. After only a few moments, she stands and stares at me. "I know you're in there, Wyshawn. And I know you won't hurt me."

A growl wrenches my insides, splitting me apart. She doesn't know me. I don't even know me.

"We're going to The Window, and you need to come with us," she says, reaching out a hand, a hand I can't touch. "Do you understand?"

An edgy, twitchy, uncomfortable feeling courses through me. Sounds mash together, all a melody of her voice, but from another time, telling me stories, saying '*Starling*,' sweet and soft. What is happening to me? I want to barrel towards her and scream a war cry in her face. I want to grab a weapon and swing it in every direction. I want to cause pain, hurt, and destroy everyone who has done me wrong. I don't care what happens to me as long as ...

"Wyshawn, my Starling," green-girl says, her eyes watery and vulnerable, trained on me, "I didn't know before, but I do now. I love you more than the raven loves the sky. More than the pen loves an artist of words. More than the jungle loves rain."

Suddenly, I'm overheating. My mind races, searching for answers. I don't know what to do. I don't know who I am. Glancing around, I look for answers as the rain starts to splatter her hair flat. The warmth of the rain hits my forehead first. I raise a hand and feel my face. Wet skin. Reality comes into focus like a wave crashing into the shore, first smooth then an explosion of undercurrent that sweeps me off my feet. The pain glides away quickly and I can feel the moment the last bit of shadow exits my body and soul. Breathing hard, I clutch my chest with one hand and try to keep from falling over.

"Say it again, Jade," I beg.

Piper's smile could bring me back from my darkest of shadows. "I love you and all your pieces, the parts that drive me mad and the ones I savor. I love the smallest crumbs of who you are, the ones that you try to brush onto the floor. In fact, those messy parts of you are my favorite, Wyshawn Starling Darl."

Relief, gratitude, and every possible positive feeling meld into the perfect moment. I pull her in for a kiss and relish her minty scent and taste. I'd kiss her forever and a day if possible, but the storm is accelerating and Holland could be back any minute.

"Welcome back." Piper bites my bottom lip. "Please don't ever do that to me again."

"Deal, as long as you don't tell Sheila about that kiss."

"Oh my Goddess, you are terrible."

"I know, but we can fight later. You know I love you too, right?"

"Yes, yes, but we need to hurry."

I tug her waist toward the two Lost Souls, standing like statues, probably shocked by me emerging from the shadows. "Yeah, we need to leave. Now!"

Thunder rocks the world again.

"Can you carry us all in your wingsuit?"

"No, but I have another wish. Lillian was holding another acorn. I found it when I said goodbye." Piper gestures for the others to come over. "Tank?!" she yells into the storm. "I have to go, I'm sorry. I love you!"

I give her a reassuring squeeze. "Okay, should we all touch it at the same time?"

"Yeah, on the count of three, I'll say the wish." She blows out a breath. "One."

Lightning splits the word above.

"Two!"

A loud crack bends the air to our right. All three of us glance over as Holland appears out of nowhere, her shadowy smile is split into a curved grin with fangs of shining obsidian. "Let's play a game," she says, lunging towards our group, arm outstretched.

"I wish we would all be transported to The Window!"

CHAPTER
TWENTY-EIGHT

Piper

My feet slam into fresh mud where puddles are growing deeper. My knees buckle, but I land in Wyshawn's arms. Dipped in his embrace, The Window is visible straight above, framed by golden Pixie powder, though it's already fading.

"You okay?" He scans me quickly and then sets me upright.

There's no time to respond. Holland, barely recognizable as a young teenager, lands only feet away. She hisses in our direction, morphs into half a shadow, and then attacks, her mouth open wide. Cockroaches, beetles, and wasps fly out of her maw. Then a green vapor flows after them, warping the air with a scent of burning flesh and chemicals. I can't let RavenSoul or Holland or whatever this creature is possess Wyshawn again.

"Hurry! Climb!" I nod to The Window so Felix and Zheo understand where to go.

Tank zooms around my face, signing that he's going to Kensington. I don't even know how he got here. It scares me that he'll never see his sprite community again, but I'm also grateful to keep a friend. Life without Lillian will already be challenging enough.

Epoch slips out of my pocket. That sneaky little guy is going to get hurt one of these days. He skitters up the tree after the others. I guess there's no arguing with a mini-croc. I'll be glad to have him with me on the other side too. Rain splattering my face, I watch both Tank and Epoch pause at the top, then fling themselves off the branch. They both disappear through The Window and a moment of relief washes through me. Holland can't hurt them anymore.

"Piper, Hun, we're here!" Father and Dad jump out from behind a tree and run to greet me.

I'm split in half. Part of me wants to snuggle into their hugs yet the other part wants to cuss them out. I haven't even heard Dad's side of the story yet, but at least his eyes seem clear and no longer affected by a curse. I may never know how to fully trust my parents again. For now, I have to convince them to leave before it's too late. The only way to save the sprites and nymphs is to get every human out of Neveraj.

I can't believe I didn't notice the patterns before. Every time I brought someone here, RavenSoul grew stronger. I was too self-absorbed to pay attention. It's time to take responsibility for my choices and face the consequences. I already have a plan and will sacrifice myself, if necessary, to save the others. Since I've lived here the longest my Pixie blood is more potent than my friends' and therefore more valuable.

"Climb!" I yell at my parents, but neither listen.

Damn it. Heeding my sore wrist, I run to them.

"Piper? Where are you going? Get up here!" Wyshawn yells from above.

"I need to get my dads," I say, going faster. "Make sure the others go through, then jump after them. I'll be there soon." I know my request isn't fair since Wyshawn will have to face his fear of heights alone.

"I'm not leaving without you!" he yells but keeps climbing, hopefully to make sure the two Lost Souls leave Neveraj.

Wild thunder cracks across the sky and a strangled vein of lightning flashes bright. Am I imagining things or has the storm followed us? Each raindrop accelerates in speed, impeding my vision. I land back on the ground and use my arm to shield my face. The muck sludges around my boots with a mind of its own, in a raging current that sucks me downward.

"Dad!" I slush through the heavy mud, slower and slower with each step. "Father! Come on!"

Why am I not getting any closer to them? Adrenaline courses through my veins as I struggle for strength but when I look down, my feet are buried in mud to my knees. I shove forward with all my might, but my legs are glued in place. The mud starts hardening around my legs, forming a cast.

"Fuck!" I try to heave my leg forward. It's no use. "Dad!" I scream out and squint through the rain. Together, they're fighting against Holland. Half of her body is corporeal, throwing punches. Her other half swarms around them like a cloud of doom.

Shit. I can't help from here. There's no branch nearby to pull on to yank myself out. I bend at the waist and claw at the mud. The movement only makes me sink further. My pulse races and my heartbeat thrashes in my ears. I have to get out. Every muscle is tight and on high alert.

"Piper! They left..." Wyshawn yells something else, but I can barely hear him over the pounding rain. "I'm... back down!"

No, he needs to leave here too. I glance behind me. To the side. Everywhere, the mud is rising. It mixes with shadows, drowning the plants and sucking bushes under. I want to tell Wyshawn to leave, but I won't survive without him.

"I'm stuck!" Rain streams down my cheeks and saturates my clothes. "I'm here! Help!"

"What?" He still sounds so far away.

Suddenly, Dad appears at my side, but he's not submerged in the mud. He rides along a tree nymph's branch like a hoverboard. He wipes a hand over his soaked face, then reaches out to me.

"Come on, Hun!" Dad's eyes lock on mine, filled with terror. "I've almost got you!"

I can do this. Studying the scene, I prepare with a strategy. My life has a newfound purpose. Because of Wyshawn. I refuse to die here, in this sinkhole. If Dad can heave me onto the branch, it still might not be able to hold us both. Once I'm on there, I'll have to move across it fast to where it's sturdier. If it snaps, we'll both fall into the muck and breathe our last breaths.

This is my one chance. It's my responsibility to make this plan work.

"Ready?" Dad leans closer and our fingertips almost touch. "On the count of three!" My heart is in my throat. This has to work. The mud rises to my waist and the current underneath becomes stronger, determined to beat me in this battle.

"One!" Dad yells.

I want the chance to kiss Wyshawn again and have time to forgive my parents.

"Two!"

It must work so I can write another story and experience adulthood, the good and bad. I want to feel every part of life and not hide in a fairytale land any longer.

"Three!" Dad screams.

Right when our hands unite and he swings me onto the branch, there's a flash of an apology in his eye that I can't mistake. No, fuck no. No, no, no.

"Nooooooo!"

I land on the branch on my stomach as Dad jumps off simultaneously. I hold on tight and helplessly watch Dad sink into the mud. The tree lifts me away from danger. I can't take my eyes off where the top of Dad's bald head is the only part of his body breaching the surface. In the next second, he's completely submerged. Gone. Buried. My throat burns, and then I realize I'm screaming at the top of my lungs.

"Piper!" Wyshawn's muffled shouts come from somewhere nearby.

I glance around without seeing anything.

"Piper!?"

This can't be possible. I don't understand. We have to get Dad out. He was just here. Now he's not. There's a ringing in my ears. I lean over the branch and vomit into the air.

"Piper! Answer me!"

I've gone catatonic. All my thoughts go blank as if my brain has stopped working. Nothing makes sense. What am I doing?

"There you are." Wyshawn's voice breaks through the haze.

I feel a soft breeze against my skin then my feet gently hitting something solid. Strong warm arms wrap around me tightly.

"Are you hurt?"

"Dad ..."

"He's over there," Wyshawn says, pointing to Father and Holland balancing on a long branch over another sinkhole.

"No...Dad," I say, covering my mouth with my hand.

"I'll go help him. Stay here." Wyshawn kisses my forehead and eases me onto a boulder.

Instinctively, my eyes scan the ground around me, all solid, no famished soil ready to swallow me into its depths. I refuse to look at the spot where Dad was stolen from me. I want him to hold me in his arms and wipe away my tears.

Like an action movie, set in slow motion, I watch in confusion as three bodies fight in the distance. Two against one. They swing giant sticks like swords, trying to knock the shorter one into the pit of famished mud. My mind is in a daze, like I'm watching a movie. Suddenly, I desperately need Wyshawn.

Where's Wyshawn?!

I stand straight and focus on the figures shoving and striking. Pushing and smacking. I squint to see one dressed in all red—Holland. She's no longer wrapped in shadows. The Window is about to close. They don't have time to defeat Holland. She's not fully human, so maybe if we leave her here, Neveraj will still endure. I have to get Father and Wyshawn out of here. Now.

Reluctantly, I glance at The Window. Only a magical being from Neveraj has the ability to close The Window, so I need Tank unharmed to pull this off.

"Wyshawn!" I cup my mouth with a shaky hand. "We need to go!"

Somehow, he hears my weak trembling voice. Holland seizes his distraction. She thrashes her stick-sword at his gut. Father blocks her so hard that the clash rips through the jungle. Holland drops her stick. Both her arms flail in the air as she loses her footing. I gasp.

Holland falls over the side. Down. Down. Down. Splashes into the mud. She is immediately sucked under. A few bubbles pop at the surface, the only proof that she ever existed.

Dead and gone. Forever.

I flop back against the boulder and bow my head. So many deaths. I let my head fall back and rain streams over my face, trickling down my neck. They blend into my tears shed for Dad. My thoughts are so jumbled that it's hard to think straight. We need to climb. Need to leave. Only minutes remain. I won't lose Wyshawn too.

Across the clearing, Father and Wyshawn stare at each other for a moment before they quickly slide across the branch to the trunk. I wait, rocking back and forth as I keep checking The Window. Only ten golden specks remain.

"Hurry!" I yell.

When they reach my side, out of breath and covered in specks of mud, Father asks, "Where's Brax?"

I swallow the lump in my throat and lie, "He already went through, to make sure no pirates are waiting on the other side."

"You first," Father says.

"Wyshawn, can I ride on your back? My wrist is throbbing."

He scoops me up gently and positions me, so my legs are around his waist and my arms clasp in front of his throat. I cringe every time a movement sends a sharp stabbing through my wrist.

"Hold on tight," he says, then climbs steady and sure, as if heights have never been an issue.

I'm so proud of him for conquering his fear of heights.

At the top of the tree, he's out of breath, so he gestures for me to jump first.

"No, we go together," I say, holding out my good hand. Quickly, I glance back at Father. "See you in a minute. I love you."

Only eight golden dust flecks remain but I have to take a moment to say goodbye. Neveraj has been my home for years. It provided for me, fed me, protected me, and loved me. I'll never forget the gift this place gave me during the darkest years of my life. But more awaits me on the other side. I memorize the sharp greens, take a still-shot image in my mind, then turn back to Wyshawn.

"Ready?" he asks.

"Yeah. On the count of three again. We go together. Don't you dare stay here," my lip trembles as I speak. "One."

I thank the mermaids and nymphs and sprites.

"Two."

I thank The Hidden Gem and lagoon and peaks and valleys.

"Three."

Hand in hand, we leap. For a split second, my breath ceases to exist.

We tumble onto hard pavement and roll to a stop on our sides. Under a different set of constellations, we lay panting on the bar's rooftop, side by side. The air smells of campfire smoke and s'mores roasting, so different than a minute ago. I'll never smell jungle rain in the air in the same way again.

I stare at The Window, waiting for Father to appear. One speck flickers out.

"Come on," I whisper and brush the dust off my pants as I stand.

Any second now, he'll barrel through and roll to my feet. Another golden speck dims. I reach forward.

"No. Piper!" Wyshawn shouts, grabbing my waist and pulling me back. "He'll be here. Just wait."

A warm current blows against my face, then Father somersaults in the air, crashing at my feet in a ball. He's cursing under his breath. At the sight of him safe, I sag against Wyshawn's chest and let out a soft, shaky sigh. An unexpected release of tension oozes out of my wobbly legs. We're okay. We did it. No living humans remain in Neveraj so the land should heal itself. Everything should turn out alright for the sprites and nymphs. I let out a huge breath. The need to sit down and drink something overwhelms me, but a grip tightens on my waist.

Quickly, a calloused hand I've known since childhood shoves me behind his back.

"Father?" I glance around for pirates. "What is it?"

I peek around Father to see Wyshawn standing upright, hands out, commanding shadows at his fingertips.

CHAPTER TWENTY-NINE

Piper

The moonbeams cast a glow through Wyshawn's hands. Its soft light contrasts against the dark shadows spinning in a vortex. Each pine tree behind him resembles the bars of a cage, striking vertical lines of confinement.

With my dagger, I slice a cut through my palm. The sharp pain stings but I'm ready to bottle my golden Pixie blood into the orb. If I can get close enough to Wyshawn to spread it on his skin, it might heal his mind like my body was once healed. But when I look down my blood bleeds red again.

"No!" I gasp. Damn it. I hadn't considered that would happen once back in Kensington.

Wyshawn's shadow self frowns and then he rises a little off the rooftop, hovering a foot over the concrete.

"Jade, babe, let's go. We can do so much with this power. Think of all the trinkets you could steal under the mask of this." He gestures to his shifting form. "We won't need to work a day in our lives. No responsibility, no reason to worry. Everything will be fun and games, just you and me."

My heart clamps tight as I step in front of Father and confront the love of my life. "This isn't you. Come back."

At first, Wyshawn laughs. How do I save him again?

A scream rips from his throat as he throws both hands to the sky. It's louder than all the humming hoverboards in the alleyway below. Wyshawn bellows nonsense in an other-worldly voice, with eyes the color of blood narrowed into slits.

"Please stop. We can fix this. I'll take care of you," I cry. "We don't need the shadows."

"NOOO!" His nostrils flare and his lips pull back, baring teeth. "If I have to live out my greatest fear, then so do you!"

What is his greatest fear? What have the shadows shown him? We stare at each other for a lifetime. All the hairs prickle at the nape of my neck. What's he going to do?

Wyshawn's fingers curl in, gathering the shadows into a ball in his fist. He hurls the ball at me with all his might. Something strong shoves me to the side again. I stagger over my feet, falling to all fours.

A mass of snarling shadows smacks right into Father's chest and pierces straight through his body. He seizes in place and shakes while clutching his throat. I'm paralyzed, overcome with panic. Father collapses into a heap on the roof.

"Father!" I scream, crawling towards him.

Shadows attack, blocking my access to him. An explosion of grays and blacks stream like poisonous ink in the air. It smells of fumes and decay. I cough and squint. Lower my chin to protect my face. Still, I crawl towards Father. My fingers grope the rooftop. He should be right here. Blinded by the darkness, I brush my hands to the left and right. My pulse elevates.

Where'd he go?

"Welcome to your nightmare, little bird." A voice resembling Wyshawn's, but toxic around the edges, continues. "Good luck escaping."

Images swarm in the air. A *'final notice'* warning to pay the mortgage on a slip of mail. Dad packing our few belongings into boxes. A younger version of myself hiding in a closet, suffocating in fear. The sound of my parents arguing down the hall. I cover my ears and squeeze my eyes shut. I hate that they fight. I hate that we have to move again. I hate that they steal to survive. I hate that they keep conning. I hate that I can't rely on them to be mature grown-ups and take care of me. My breaths turn raspy, and I want to rush away from the threat. Strange blubbering sounds quiver from my lips as

I stay crumpled in a ball, clutching my favorite stuffed animal, a pink unicorn named Sprinkles.

In front of my eyes my childhood home burns to the ground. Flames lick at the sky, dancing in glee. The intense crackles are louder than the sound of my wild heartbeat. I moan and rock back and forth.

The scene disappears. Now Tank is tied to a tree by a cursed rope that scorches his wings when I push a button. It's so fun to torture someone. He writhes and flinches each time I push it. Again and again until his head sags and his chest stills.

I gasp, my skin turning clammy. "No!" I yell. I back away from his limp body, knowing it was my fault. My fault. If I never went to Neveraj, he would've lived.

I spin around, trying to spot a safe place to escape this nightmare. From the shadows, deep laughter booms, unnatural and terrifying. Lillian glares at me with all-red eyes, her body in pieces as she says, "Your fault. You didn't step up." A vague form of Kyle takes her place, his head unattached, sitting in his palm. "You were always such a child, only into your playthings."

I gulp at the grotesque sight of him. My eyes refuse to shut. Every vein and muscle from his neck sticks out of his flesh, on full display.

When he disappears, The Hidden Gem comes into view, being ransacked by pirates. They take all of my prized possessions, piss on my plants, and tear my journals full of stories.

I shake my head and cover my face, but whatever magic this is forces me to watch. Lightning strikes the treehouse, splitting it down the middle—my sanctuary destroyed.

My jaw clenches. This can't be real. I left Neveraj, didn't I? Where am I?

In a single breath, the shadows flicker away so I can see a figure lying unconscious in front of me, the moon slanted on his face. Father. I'm still on the rooftop, awake and alive.

"The nightmares aren't real," I whisper, then stand on shaky legs with clenched fists at my side and scream, "I'm not scared of you!"

"Oh, really?" Wyshawn's voice comes from a thousand places at once, but I stand my ground. He's not my villain. I will love him until the day I die. He doesn't know what he's doing. He'd never intentionally hurt me. How can I snap him out of this hypnosis?

I concentrate on forming a plan. Tank is somewhere near, he can help. I have my empty orb, my dagger, and my spirit. That's enough.

Suddenly the shadows create a realistic cave, surrounding me from all sides.

The darkness of midnight on the rooftop changes to pitch black. I can't see my hand in front of my face. Frozen in place, scratching sounds come closer, closer. I can't move. Can't run.

I don't want to run. It's time to face my fears. I lift both fists, ready to fight, and scream again, "I'm not afraid!"

A frustrated growl rips through the air, but I have no idea where it's coming from. Then the demonic snarls turn into moans of pleasure. My body pulsing with desire and need. Naked skin on skin. Wyshawn's dark eyes lock onto mine. His gaze pierces my soul, until he says, "I could never love you. Who could ever want a future with you?"

I stomp my boots hard, shaking me away from the illusion, and scream at the top of my lungs again and again. "I'm not scared of you! I'm not scared of you! I'm not afraid!"

But is it true? Because my biggest, most terrifying fears are coming to life right in front of me. Some of the characters in my stories come to mind, the brave heroic ones. They weren't strong because they were fearless. They were powerful because they faced their fears despite being scared.

I change my tactic and scream to the murderous shadows, "Fine! I'm terrified and that won't change. But I won't ever give up! I'll keep fighting until you release him! Even if it takes me a thousand failed attempts! I'll never stop planning ways to defeat you! I won't let you steal my entire future!"

The air stills for a moment and all I can hear is my rapid, heavy breathing. Across the way, the shadows hover over Wyshawn's head, unmoving. He tilts his head to the side in the familiar way I've memorized—the way he studies me, wondering what I'm thinking.

"What did I do?" Remorse covers his features.

A fluttering feeling patters in my chest. He's back. He's here and he's mine.

"Wyshawn!" I reach out to him. Take a leap.

RavenSoul rages towards me but I don't shield myself. I march straight through it. Unphased. Immediately, I feel a change of energy. It has weakened. As if knowing it's about to lose, RavenSoul flies toward The Window.

No! It can't destroy Neveraj.

"Tank! Close it!" I say and sign at the same time, knowing he's nearby. "Close The Window. Forever!"

I dash towards Wyshawn. Nothing can happen to him. I race faster, ready to fling him to the ground. My new fear is losing Wyshawn. I won't let anything happen to my love.

I catch sight of Tank buzzing to my left. He signs, **'The shadow will be trapped here with us!'**

"I can take care of it! Trust me!" I launch myself at Wyshawn, tackling him to the rooftop.

Tank hovers in front of the last two glowing specks of The Window. His arms move to the moon in a prayer posture. I hold my breath, but nothing happens.

Count to three in my head. Nothing.

"Wait!" Wyshawn digs in his pocket. "I have starlight. Lillian gave me this to close it. I can't believe I forgot." He holds out a vial of liquid gold.

Wyshawn opens the vial and pours it in the air close to the last remaining golden speck. A loud pop booms like a firework. Then a bright light shimmers in its place and floats to join the stars.

Is that it? Is it closed for good? The shadow turns towards us. A soft fingertip runs down my jaw. I startle from the touch and look down to Wyshawn's eyes on me.

"You're more than your shadows. Show it your light."

He's right.

"I'll be right back," I say, kissing his lips quickly, "Stay here, Starling."

Wrist throbbing, body bruised and tired, I stand. Unwilling to let RavenSoul break my spirit, I walk towards it with a long steady gait. With my shoulders back and my chin held high, I focus on the power the jungle had coursing through its veins. Each bird, each plant, and each drop of rain had shared their child-like whimsy with me for years. I may be ready to grow up, but that doesn't mean I have to let go of Neveraj's magic.

Lillian had gifted me magic by being my friend. The sparkling water in the lagoon shared its sorcery with me at each visit. Even the cotton-candy clouds shared their spellwork with me, an outsider. I still have the enchantments coursing through my veins, regardless of whether my blood is red or gold.

For the first time in years, there's a lightness in my chest. A sense of calm and ease washes over me in a wave. I can do this. The shadow hovers in the same spot, watching me with interest, not initiating the first move.

I hold out both hands and aim at the darkest center, where it holds my fears within. I can shape my future and restore what was broken.

My stories are my weapons. They mix into a maze of hope. My creativity is my strength. The characters become my soldiers; the fishermen providing for their daughters, travelers finding a secret entrance to a non-existent land, monsters creeping between cracks, buckets overfilling with wishes, unicorns, and tendrils of hair bound by starlight. Haunted mermaids and battling pirates. Weighted Weavens and mythical blankets.

And together we shine our light on the shadow.

It bursts into a thousand pieces. Just like that.

Tiny, black ashy pieces float slowly to the ground, covering the rooftop in a snowfall of magic.

I let out a huge breath and look at the twinkling stars. "Thank you," I whisper to Dad. There's a feeling of expansion in my lungs and everything is full, complete. Strangely, I can't stop crying from relief.

Wyshawn catapults into me, lifting me off my feet and swinging me around in a circle. I need to pause to rein in my emotions before speaking. Wyshawn sets me on the ground and kisses my forehead, my cheek, my lips. I want to sink into him fully but a low groan from the ground catches my attention.

"Wait, where's Father?" I grab Wyshawn's hand and rush across the roof. We both drop to our knees, side by side.

Father stirs, rubbing his temple with one hand and slowly sits up in a daze. "Piper?" He's squinting, and for the first time, I see all the wrinkles that hadn't been there before he was incarcerated. "Piper! Thank Luna, you're okay! My baby girl!" He pulls me into a hug and cries into my shirt.

Over his shoulder, I meet Wyshawn's eye, unsure what to say or how to respond.

"I'm here," I say softly. "What's the last thing you remember?"

Father looks confused. He looks around. "Where is he, hun? Where's your Dad?"

A happily ever after is never one hundred percent. I swallow, knowing it'll be a rough conversation. I haven't even told Wyshawn yet what happened in the mudslide, but his serious gaze means he has caught onto the truth. Father will need support in the next months and years, but we'll get through this together. I can't tell him that Dad died yet when the events are too raw and my body is too exhausted.

Miraculously, Wyshawn senses that too. He wraps an arm around my waist and extends a hand to Father.

"It's nice to meet you, sir, I'm Wyshawn Darl. Let's go downstairs so I can buy you a drink."

I nod, my body slowly going into shock as I lean into his strength. In the future, we will make it, as long as we rely on each other when needed. Real relationships aren't all gumdrops and lollipops and soaring through the sky. They're also full of muck and shadows that occasionally need extra light and a bit of magic to get through to the other side.

CHAPTER
THIRTY

Wyshawn

1 week later

We sit at a corner table in Walk the Plank, where the strong scent of oranges is a comforting smell. Since Ibrahim invited us during non-business hours for a free lunch, the dance floor is empty and the bare light bulbs hanging over repurposed furniture don't need to be turned on. It's brighter than I've ever seen it. Whimsical sunsshine dances through the windows, casting light throughout the open concept room while highlighting more stains on the walls than I'd care to notice. I grab a napkin from the table, dip it in my glass of water, and scrub at a dirty mark.

I had spent years as a zombie working as a bartender here, waiting for my life to wake up. I'm glad I had the good sense to volunteer to work the extra shifts to make sure I was here on the thirteenth of each month. Piper has convinced me to quit all my jobs and apply to culinary school.

"She's two minutes late," Piper says, then gives me a stern look to stop my obsessive scrubbing of the stain on the wall.

She pulls at her green tanktop, another one of her anxious tells. "Hey, there's nothing to worry about. Mother will adore you." I wrap an arm over the back of her chair.

Piper's wrist cast, extending up her forearm is already covered with *'get well'* and *'feel better'* notes and signatures. In only one week's time of living in Kensington, she's managed to accumulate more friends than I have over my combined thirty years. The nurses at the hospital had loved her and wanted to extend her stay before discharging us. Even my sisters had both given me winks behind Piper's back when they stopped by during visiting hours, after yelling at me for disappearing, of course. Now, the only people she has left to meet are my parents. Mother is coming alone, letting Mum rest at the senior center.

The clock above Piper's head ticks away as we wait

side by side. She taps her freshly lime-green manicured nails on the table and glances at the front door.

Piper sips her fruity cocktail and makes a little sour face with her nose scrunched tight.

"Doesn't taste good?"

"Your drinks are better." She slurps more anyway. "Hey look, all the posters of the '*WANTED*' pirates in the area have been taken down. I guess our town is also looking at a more positive future."

Our town. She used the word 'our'...as in a unit, a couple, a pair. I could get used to this.

After the craziness of escaping Neveraj, I'm eager to spend a few relaxing weeks lounging on the couch with Piper before classes begin. I won't have plans or expectations in mind; I'm simply ready to sink into her company. So much has happened, and I still have a few unanswered questions for her, especially since I blacked out during the time RavenSoul apparently possessed me. Quite a terrifying thought to be honest.

Her eyes dart to the door again, and her hand rubs against the exterior of her pocket where there's a bulge I hadn't noticed before.

"Babe, what's in your pocket?" I slip a hand across her leg.

"Nothing," she says, avoiding my eyes.

Oh, damn. That could mean anything. At least I can rule out the possibility of Epoch in her pocket since he is messing with the saltshaker, trying to swat it over with his tail.

"Did Sheila blackmail you?" I poke her side. "You're being so sneaky."

The corner of her lip quirks up, but her foot still jiggles under the table—nonstop.

I gently slide my hand over her body, knowing how much it soothes her. "Hey, tell me a story, Jade."

Finally, her piercing eyes meet mine. Goddess, I love her and her fierce heart. Pride can't even describe the feeling that consumes me whenever she looks my way. Not only for conquering her fears last week but also for trying to close The Window permanently and then for confronting her Father. She may want more of his full story later. Though, I completely agree with the boundaries she has placed with her Father about not visiting until she processes all the new information.

"You want a story, now?" Her gaze flitters towards the door again, but I grip her chin and turn her attention back on me.

"Your hands are clammy, and you won't stop fidgeting, babe. Either tell me a story or I'm going to give Ibrahim a show he won't forget to get you to relax." I move my hand under her shirt, trailing my fingertips against the lines of her ribcage.

She sighs, the sound intoxicating, then laughs softly. "Fine, don't you start anything you can't finish."

"Is that a challenge?" I ask, kissing her neck slowly.

Her good hand pushes against my chest so she can see my face. Her mouth drops mockingly. "Did Mr. Wyshawn Darl just joke about public sex? You wouldn't dare...think of the health codes."

I have my lips back on her addictive skin in less than a breath. "I'd kiss you in the dirtiest, most run-down bar in town..."

"Mmmm," her throat vibrates, "tell me more."

Even though I know she's teasing, the pleased tone in her voice can't be faked.

"I'd go through a door with a '*Do Not Enter*' sign and find a forbidden storage closet with shelves lined neat and orderly and I'd..." My tongue swipes against her neck. "I'd knock everything off the shelf to place you on the dust."

Piper moans, playing along, a smile hidden in the sound. "You'd make such a mess."

"Yeah, and guess what..." My fingers pinch her nipple. "I wouldn't even clean it up."

She gasps and I'm truly unsure if it's in a dramatic response or because of my hands on her body.

"Well, well, you two are a sight," a deep female voice says, one whose pitch has been imprinted on my mind since birth.

I leap away from Piper and sit straight in my chair. Quickly, I scoot it closer to the table, making the legs screech against the floor.

Mother shakes her head, amused, before pulling out her own chair. The charms on her bracelet jangle and clink together, reminding me of a similar one Piper wore on the night we were tied up by pirates. Maybe these two could hit it off by chatting about what charms they've collected over the years and what each means to them. Whatever happened to Piper's bracelet? She'll probably never again see all the little trinkets she had stolen. I bet she'd enjoy a little gift, perhaps another bracelet to start fresh. The first charm I'd buy her would be of a twisting tree, a token to celebrate her time at The Hidden Gem.

"Oh! Maram, it's so nice to meet you. I love your top, it's beautiful," Piper says.

I happen to agree. Any turquoise shade pops against Mother's dark skin.

"You poor thing. What happened to your hand?" Mother asks Piper, then lowers into the seat across from me.

"It's a good thing I'm left-handed; I can still write my stories until the doctor takes this thing off."

"You're a writer?" Mother's eyes whip to mine, sparkling with acceptance already. "What do you write?"

Piper's foot jiggle has evolved into an entire leg jiggle. If she doesn't calm down the table will start rattling. This time, my hand caresses deep pressure circles above her knee, which settles her temporarily.

"Um, mostly short stories that have whimsy to them."

Mother leans forward, clasping her hands together. "Can you tell me one you're writing now?"

This is going so much more smoothly than I had expected. But of course, I should've known my parents would accept Piper in all her magical ways.

"Sure, um," Piper glances at me, then bites her bottom lip. "Well, it's about a shadow monster who overtakes a land full of sprites and nymphs. There's a special dust called Pixie powder that keeps the land youthful, but a human invades their space, sucking out its energy which eventually leads to Neveraj's doom."

"Neveraj?" Mother reaches across the table and smooths out one of my eyebrows without my permission. "What happens next?"

Piper gulps and her hand drops to her pocket. "Well, it's a long story with challenges to overcome, fears to conquer, oh, and mermaids and con artists—"

"Don't forget the treehouse in the sky," I add and give her thigh a little squeeze.

"Tell me it's a love story too. My book club will beg you to add a little romance." Mom's smile eases any remaining concerns I had about introducing Piper to my family.

"Mhm," Piper says quietly.

I track her hand again. It's fidgeting around her pocket, dipping in and out and the wrinkle in her forehead becomes more pronounced as her frown deepens.

"There's love, but there's also loss," Piper whispers.

Mother meets my eye again, a knowing look that tells me a thousand things in a single heartbeat. We're losing Mum to dementia, and she must know Piper has suffered a tragedy too. It's too early to expect Piper to talk about her dad's death, but in time, she'll get there and I'll be waiting patiently by her side.

"So, I stole something for you," Piper continues, shocking me as a small, glass orb rests in her open palm on the table.

"Stole? Dear, if you're to be with my son, no more of that, you understand?"

"Yes, ma'am. This is special though. Pixie powder is real, and it might be able to help Georgia, or give her more time. I can't guarantee anything, but it's yours to do with as you wish. Use it to delay your wife's memory fading or give it to a team of researchers to study, I don't care. That's your choice."

My heart spasms in my chest. She brought Pixie here. Among all that fighting and rushing to escape, she still remembered Mum's diagnosis.

She's right, that we won't know if it'll make much difference, but it doesn't hurt to try. My love for her doubles as she places the orb in front of Mother.

I tuck Piper closer to my side. This woman is mine and I'll never let her get away. She has taught me to search for joy, the little moments with the potential for a wild adventure, especially if that journey leads to a lifetime of love.

EPILOGUE

Piper

Two Years Later

I sit on the beach, toes in the sand and sunlight kissing my skin. With my journal in hand, I jot down descriptive lines of the scenery for my next short story about talking dolphins. Behind me, the scent of the grill cooking meat from Wyshawn's food truck trickles through the air. I breathe in deeply and my stomach immediately rumbles.

Father splashes in the shallows with his new puppy, kicking water in its face. I laugh at the child-like joy he shows as water soaks his pants. Living in Kensington and finding a job hasn't been as scary and dreadful as I had previously thought. Sure, Wyshawn and I have had arguments, trouble paying for his cooking classes at first, and feelings about Dad's death will never fully go away, but every day has given me a different tiny treasure. Whether it's the artistic angle a pelican swoops low to catch fish, or the sound of the night owl outside our apartment when we fall asleep, cuddled in bed, I continually look forward to what the next day will bring with Wyshawn.

Fear will always stretch its sharp claws around a dark corner, but it won't stop me from living.

"Jade, you want chicken or beef tacos?" Wyshawn yells from behind.

I twist towards him, feeling a crack in my back, then groan aloud. "Holy Sols, I'm getting old."

"I'm gonna pretend I didn't hear that," Father says from the water.

"Surprise me," I say to Wyshawn and watch his smile burn brighter than the suns.

The smoke gathering from the grill makes him fade in and out of focus for a moment, reminding me of when once upon a time dark shadows had overtaken him completely.

Sometimes, I still have nightmares, waking in sweat and screams, reliving that exact moment. Every time, he's there to soothe me, kiss me, and comfort me. I'll never care for anyone as much as I love Wyshawn.

My sexy chef holds a towel in one hand and a spatula

in the other. He catches my gaze. Those dark brown eyes are constantly trained on me. I give him a little smile and he stops in place. And just stares. Goddess Above, I could devour him right now.

I place my baseball hat in the sand near my bare feet. Most people wouldn't wear a skirt and cap together, but most people also don't hang out with merfolk either. I rise to walk towards Wyshawn. A dozen palm trees with leafy canopies stand proudly, protecting my loved ones. The glaring suns each wink behind a cloud to give us relief from the heat so we have cooler weather to play our games. Tank and the Mermaid Club will be here at any moment for our tournaments. At least Wyshawn's food truck has air conditioning if it gets too stuffy out here.

When we visit this beach, I can feel Neveraj's unique breeze against my cheeks and the sounds of the parrots squawking in the trees. I was fortunate to live a life most people could never dream of, and then things got even better when I committed to Wyshawn.

I'm thankful he agreed to invest in a food truck. This way we can travel the world without being tied down to one spot. I may be ready to grow up, but I'll never relinquish my longing for adventure.

From the speaker system by the truck, delicious chords play from a guitar that match the beat of the drummer's hand.

With each step closer to Wyshawn, a rush of energy zaps through my veins. His studious expression has me on pins and needles. I can tell he's already picturing our bodies entangled under the stars tonight. He's a strange addiction and I hope it never fades.

Plus, I never knew that a side bonus of having a boyfriend is the family that comes along with the relationship. I may have lost my Dad two years ago, but I gained two sisters and two mothers. I can't even put into words what it feels like to have a motherly presence watching over me. Georgia's memory has faded drastically, so our exchanges are usually awkward, to say the least, but she is happily unaware. From the last update I heard, the medical research team has made advances with their trial drug based on Pixie powder's effects on aging and memory loss.

At Wyshawn's side, I say, "I need your help with something."

To this, his brows rise. "I'm listening."

I've found my purpose in life with him. Stories. Everyone craves stories, whether it's from poetry or lyrics or a book. They connect our pasts to our futures.

"I can't think of a good character arc."

He leans closer, resting his chin on my shoulder and peeking at what I've written. "Rynn? Is that her name?"

"Yeah, she's a witch who works at a shop in an all-human town. What's cute about her shop is that everything is purple. The soap, coasters, t-shirts, sunglasses, magnets, signs—they're all purple."

"That's unique. And there's a romantic interest I'm assuming?"

"Yeah, Elias has a pumpkin shop across the street. But anyways, Rynn has an under-the-table side gig that customers have to be referred to specifically." My fingertip skims the lines of my notes. "She can *'poison'*, or I guess *'curse'* any item purchased for an extra price. Don't worry, it's nothing fatal. The results are petty revenge things like the person it's intended for will never find a matching sock pair again or will always forget their password to log-ins, or gets a parking ticket weekly, that sort of thing."

"Ah, I see." Wyshawn smiles and starts to massage my shoulders. "So where are you stuck?"

"What should Rynn learn about herself?"

"Hmm...to let go of what she's trying to control?" Wyshawn shoots me a knowing look. "To dive in headfirst and let life work itself out instead of holding onto fear?"

I get a whiff of his cologne, a scent I could bathe in.

I lean up and kiss his scruffy stubble. "Maybe, I'll think about it. Hey, look. Eribelle is here."

I wave to Eribelle, a mermaid, who just breached the surface. As my wrist twists, my new charm bracelet jingles like a song. So far, Wyshawn has bought me a tree, acorn, mountain, and waterfall charm. They're all beautiful. The next one I want resembles a sprite. I haven't seen Tank in a while as we only recently returned from a trip to Ozaron.

Ahead, Tank flies fast, above the surface, gesturing wildly to me about his trip back to Neveraj with the mermaids. Apparently, they fed him the plant that helped him breathe underwater to go through the only other *Window* deep in the ocean. He rambles quickly about the reunion with his family and friends and how Neveraj is thriving, free of shadow. The news warms my heart and I let out a little sigh.

"You'll translate that for me later? I only got half of what he said," Wyshawn says, chuckling.

"Yes, my darling Starling. And that's not all I'll be doing for you later."

He kisses my forehead. "Is that so?"

I rise onto my tiptoes and pull his neck lower until our lips lock. We both moan at the same time, then a laugh escapes us as well. He's my everything, my future, my whole world sprinkled in magical moments.

I used to be fractured by fear, but now I am whole.

THE END

CHARACTER LIST

Aqua - Mermaid messenger
Brax - Piper's Dad
Cade - Piper's date at the bar
Davien - Piper's biological father
Epoch - pet reptile
Felix - Lost soul #1
Georgia - Wyshawn's Mum (with Alzheimer's)
Holland Jameson - con artist/villain
Ibrahim - Wyshawn's manager at the bar
Jeniqua - Wyshawn's sister
Kyle - Lost soul #2
Lillian - Piper's best friend/nymph
Maram - Wyshawn's biological mother
Mikali - Wyshawn's sister
Piper 'Jade' Pan - heroine/protagonist
RavenSoul - the shadows
Schmee - Pirate captain
Tank - Piper's sprite friend
Wyshawn S. Darl - hero
Zheo - Lost soul #3

THE WICKED BLUE PREQUEL

A SHORT STORY

By Cassie Swindon

CHAPTER ONE

How can I paint the taste of saltwater? I swipe more colors from my palate to stroke the beach I'm overlooking. How will the viewer experience the taste of the sea?

I've been raised to fear the waters and detest the merfolk who lurk Below. Yet I find myself licking my lips to savor a little flavor from the forbidden.

Standing on my balcony, gazing at the crimson horizon, wind whips my hair. Sometimes I have a strange compulsion to lean forward, slightly too far over the balcony's edge. Do the wind nymphs detect the confusing longing that teases me to test the boundaries and dip my toes in the waves just once? If I fall over this balcony, will those very nymphs catch me and carry me to the tides to please my soul?

I brush another curve on my canvas, then try to move a stray hair out of my face with my forearm. Otherwise, my hands would be responsible for a cluster of pinks and oranges smeared across my forehead.

Bending sideways, I survey the landscape from a different angle. What would it be like to sail on a ship to where the sky kisses the luminous blues? I may never have been aboard a boat, but I can still envision every shade the ocean would have to offer, from navy to cerulean to teal and cobalt.

I finish painting, I wait for Sampson's design in which he promised me the same colors for his latest fashion genius. I glance around my studio, past the other two easels and the mess across my bed to where my best friend sits at a desk. His back is turned towards me as he furiously scribbles his vision on paper.

"Done yet?" I set down my palate and try not to trip over the half-hazard books strewn around my rug.

"Don't rush me, Eribelle," Sampson mumbles, but I can hear the smile in his voice. That's good news. If he's smiling, he likes what he has created. "And don't brag that you finished first."

I have half a mind to throw a pillow at his back but wouldn't want to destroy his drawing. He groans, then flips the pencil over to erase something. In his frantic movements, he accidentally knocks eyeliner and eyeshadow onto the floor. Among my disastrous domain, they may be lost forever more.

"Done!" He twirls around fast in the spinny chair, holding his paper to his chest so I can't see. "Show me yours first."

"No way!" I block his view to the balcony where my painting is drying. "This was your idea, so you go first."

He huffs. A burst of air blows a long lock of brown hair puff up for a moment. "Fine. But it'll be better when its finished, I swear."

As he turns it towards me, I gasp, and walk towards the beautiful outfit he drew. "Sampson! It's perfect!"

"I hate that word. Nothing is supposed to be perfect. In fact, maybe I'll rip the seam a little once you put it on just to teach you a thing or two."

"You wouldn't dare!" I grab his notebook.

The intricate detail of the outfit for my upcoming twenty-first birthday is breathtaking. Sampson used shades belonging to the sea: indigo, denim and berry. Blues shift and slide against each other in both contrast and balance.

"If I wear this, Dad will arrest you." I choose to, in fact, throw the pillow in question to his head.

"Hey! The crop top isn't *that* tight. And it'll let you throw up your arms while dancing without any precious treasure falling out."

I agree. But it's the high-rise skirt that I can't take my eyes off of– a piece made from liquid heaven. The way the fabric glides mirrors the fluidity of the ocean. It's as if Sampson knows the one and only secret I've kept from him–my longing to explore the sea. Yet, he's also my only confidant who understands the harsh punishment Dad would lash out at me if I were to be caught in the waters.

I should have better sense than to wish to explore the Below. Apparently, my stupid genes have won in a battle against my survival instincts because I'm seriously considering changing my plans tonight and taking the risk.

"So...? You like it?" Sampson's biting his nail, while his knees are curled into his chest.

"No! I love it! Don't change a single thing." I point to the blue skirt. "What material do you have in mind? This looks like silk."

"I'll surprise you." He winks and takes his notebook back. "Well, Sugar Pants, what time are you leaving?"

I dramatically collapse on Sampson's lap. "Do I *have* to go?"

"Eribelle, Eribelle, Eribelle..." he starts with an outrageous fake accent, "you, m'lady are the most popular, most anticipated person at the ball tonight. Of course, you have to go, unless..." Sampson loops and twists my hair into an updo with mastery skill, despite my odd angle of hanging off his lap. "Unless you are planning any shenanigans. I think I can get on board with shenanigans, especially if they involve Kilka milkshakes."

Sampson taps the Taj99 device on his wrist and pushes buttons until a milkshake recipe is projected against my wall, with a very high level of alcohol mix required.

"Holy Abyss, Sampson, do you plan on killing me with that?" I topple off his lap onto the floor and begin cleaning the mess. "If I drink that much, I might even make out with *you* tonight."

He makes a gag face and rolls his eyes. "Fine, I'll go

easy on the Kilka this time." Sampson slaps my ass while he moves towards my bedroom door. "You need to get ready and I need to find a snack, which I won't be sharing."

"You have so much hatred."

"I said what I said." He glides out the door, humming a recent Talia Sanchez song that echoes down the hallway.

Alone, I groan and check the time on my Taj99. Only an hour until the guests expect my grand entrance. Maybe I can convince Dad to let me skip this event. Not even a second goes by until I laugh away at that possibility. Possible buyers from Khajit, Gonia and even Ozaron will be in attendance, and they all expect to see Finley Erickson's famous daughter– the only human known to have blue eyes. If Dad has any chance of selling more yachts than last year, I should play my part.

A strong cinnamon aroma wafts through my doorway and footsteps thud against the hardwood, growing louder with each step.

"Damn it," I quickly crawl to toss a blanket over my most recent painting and shove my paintbrushes under my bed.

"Eribelle?" Dad's voice booms like a giant. "What are you doing spread out on the floor like that?"

I bend into a yoga pose, one foot and one hand off the ground, then take a centering breath.

"Ah, that's my girl. It's always good to brag about your flexibility."

I almost puke. Maybe I should. Then perhaps I can get out of this party if I fake an illness.

"I brought your favorite snack," Dad says, offering a cinnamon bun mid-air.

There's no point in correcting him with my intense chocolate obsession since he'd forget by tomorrow anyway. Dad starts talking business and his expectations for my behavior tonight, but I tune him out and listen to the waves crashing into the pier outside. Seagulls squawk and the familiar shouts of fishermen greeting each other all blend into a painting in my mind. If I close my eyes, I can see the white foam making shapes on the seashells and footprints pushed into the sand. The textures, shapes, and colors all form an image of freedom.

"... Eribelle? What do you think?" Dad checks his Taj as an incoming message alert him with a beep. "Can I count on you to do that, tonight?"

"Uh, yeah. Definitely."

"That's my good girl. I'm so lucky. You'll always be my biggest prize." Dad turns away, his shoulder width barely fitting through the doorway. "Oh, and if the mayor of Runlose cozies up to you, just play along. We wouldn't want a repeat of last year, now do we?"

My insides turn to mush. Of course, I'm a prize. Of course, he backhandedly threatens me. Of course, I'm forced to attend another boring event with a silent competition of whose wallet is bigger than whose. Of course, I'll be used by Dad to make sales.

As his footsteps fade away, I shove a bit of a delicious

cinnamon roll in my mouth. Sugar probably coats my lips, but it's not as if I'll be putting on lipstick anymore. There's no way in Abyss I'm going tonight. I leave the rest of the dessert for Sampson to finish off when he returns. But by then, I'll be gone. I can't send him a Taj message because if there's one thing Sampson sucks at, it's lying.

Quickly. I tug on the straps of a backpack. It's buckle sticks on something under my bed. I yank and pull until it comes flying at me and I somersault backwards. As I shove essentials inside the bag, our three suns setting change the shape of the shadows within my room. I follow their rays to the open doors leading to my balcony. Running out the front door of Dad's estate isn't an option. Too many of his employees will ask why I haven't yet changed into a ballgown. Or they'd take the opportunity to politely congratulate me on my appearance on the new billboard downtown. I'd have to flash another fake smile and gently bob my head until they'd eventually mosey away.

I carefully move my still-wet painting inside in case this fierce wind is followed by a storm later. My balcony doors lock from the inside once closed so if close them, there's no turning back. I suck in a deep breath and shut them softly.

Warmth caresses my cheeks when I step out of the shade. Carefully, I peek over the edge. Heights haven't ever scared me, but I've also never considered scaling the side of a four-story mansion before. Voices holler and laugh far below. If I fall, there aren't really any wind nymphs to save me. This could be the most moronic choice I've ever made.

Heart pounding, I straddle the railing and wipe my sweaty hands on my t-shirt. Hoverboards rush by below but thankfully no rider has noticed me yet. I say a useless prayer to whatever Goddess might be watching over me and swing my legs over. The stone exterior creates many divets for someone experienced to latch their fingertips and toes on, but I'm no professional.

My shoe slides off its spot.

"Fuck!"

The muscles in my arms scream in protest. I manage to balance and gather my breath. *I can't fall. Keep going. Don't fall.* At a torturous speed, I scale down one stone at a time and somehow stay alive. Left foot. Right foot. Left arm. Right arm. Sweat drips down my temple. My pulse races.

Finally, my sneakers hit the pavement and my knees buckle. Shaking, my trembling hands hover over the street. I gulp and give myself three moments of panic. One. *I can't believe I just did that.* Two. *If Dad finds out...* Three. *Sampson will think I'm a rockstar.*

Pressing off the ground, I straighten, walking taller, more confident than ever before. With each step, the waves pounding against the boulders roar louder. I'm almost there. A couple holding hands passes by me without a glance in my direction. They both seem captivated by the cheery song blasting from their Taj. I start walking to the beat with a bounce in my step, believing for the first time that I'll swim in the ocean that has called me my entire life.

Why have I been such a coward? I should've tried this long ago. A bird swoops low, white wings outstretched, then lands to my right. Some of my classmates at university have rambled on when drunk or high about wanting to be a bird to soar through the open skies. I've never understood that desire. If given the chance, I'd be any sea creature besides a merfolk– perhaps a dolphin. I'd glide in the murky depths to experience a new life, where no one could tell me how to act or what to say or wear.

At last, the sounds from the bars down the street dissolve into distant hums and thumping beats. Ahead, the suns dip lower, ready to skim the horizon. My gaze locks onto a sail and I wonder if they're headed to Ozaron, the city famous for its art and deep forests. Slipping my shoes off, I wiggle my toes in the sand. Do I dare enter? I scan for any signs of creepy merfolk spying on me. No one.

I toss my backpack where it'll remain dry then slowly wade in the water. Ankles deep. I hold my breath. Water reaches my knees. Nothing catastrophic has happened yet. Maybe all the years of fears being carved into my mind were pointless.

I cringe. If Dad ever knew my thoughts, he'd ...well, he wouldn't listen to my pleas for the finances necessary to attend art school.

The water reaches my hips and I bask in the sensation of being halfway submerged. As corrupted as the merfolk are, I still wonder what it'd be like to live like them– under the sea. Do they have any form of art that could survive the elements of the wicked deep?

"ERIBELLE!" The familiar voice skids like scissors sliding against metal. "ERIBELLE! Get out of the water!" Sampson yells again and again, his calls growing louder and closer.

I should've explained to him, but this may be my only chance. Headfirst, I dive under. The icy cold doesn't hit me as harshly as I expected. Instead, it's soothing, like I've always been meant to swim. But it's not where I belong since I can't paint here.

Sampson's muffled demands come from Above and I almost turn around. Unfortunately, I can't hold my breath forever, so I swim as far as possible then breech to suck in a lungful of air. The waves rock me and water splashes my cheeks. I smile. Perfection. I don't care if Sampson hates that word. This moment, right here, during the last moments of the setting suns, drenched from head to toe in the ocean is my perfect paradise.

Another scream comes from further out. In a small canoe, a woman bends over the side grabbing at the water like a lunatic. What is she doing? Did her hand get caught in her fishing net? I swim closer, faster, ready to help.

"Nate!" She peers over the side with wide eyes. "Nate!"

Immediately, I freeze. A high pitched sound rings in my ears. Shit. Someone has fallen overboard. I dip under but don't see a sinking body nearby.

"Hey!" I yell but the lady doesn't seem to hear me. "Hey!"

"Nate! No, no, they took him."

My heart stops. They? I glance back to the shore. Sampson is jumping up and down, waving both hands in the air and wildly pointing behind me.

I spin. Bright scales shimmer. Merfolk. Many of them. Terror clenches my gut. I don't stand a chance of outswimming them. If I can pull myself into the canoe, maybe the two of us can paddle back faster.

"Hey! Help me up!"

In a daze, the woman stands, paying me no attention and stares at the sky. I guess I'm alone. Struggling, I heave myself into the boat despite it rocking back and forth.

"Nate," she sits on a crate and mumbles the name again and again, "Nate, my Nate."

Regret floods me before I act but I slap the stranger's face. She whirls at me, noticing me for the first time.

"Take an oar!" I say, while paddling myself. "Come on!"

We move in a circle, the waves rocking us. What the Abyss was I thinking coming out here?

"Hey! I place my hands on either side of her face and stare into her brown eyes. "You need to row. We're going to land. And you need to row now, understand?"

Slowly, she nods, tears running down her face. As she picks up an oar, slippery pale arms slide over the side of the canoe. Arms made of nightmares wrap tightly around my boatmate's waist.

Screaming. Someone's screaming. It might be me.

I clutch the oar and smack the merman's arms until he let's go.

A loud horn blares and bright headlights blind me. The merfolk all instantly swim away. We're safe–for now. Shielding my eyes, I catch the name of the yacht drifting towards us, '*The Eribelle*.' Dad's boat. Double triple fucking shit.

To read all of Eribelle's story, read '*The Wicked Blue***,' a gender reversal spin of Little Mermaid. This adult fantasy romance has two points of view, so prepare yourself for Axton, the merman warrior and protector of the Queen of Nerida. **

ABOUT CASSIE SWINDON

Cassie Swindon loathes wet socks, leaf blower machines, tight hugs, and rickety fans. Things she might murder for: a free massage, cuddles from a kitten, chocolate milkshakes, and long naps. Some of her favorite activities include decorating for the holidays, playing board games, and avoiding phone calls. She has four more ideas for upcoming books so sign up for her newsletter below.

Check out free short stories as prequels to my upcoming works in progress and also sign up for my newsletter here: https://cassieswindon.com/

- facebook.com/cassie.swindon.3
- twitter.com/CassieSwindon
- instagram.com/cassie_swindon_author
- bookbub.com/profile/cassie-swindon
- amazon.com/stores/author/B091N72414
- goodreads.com/cassieswindonauthor
- tiktok.com/@cassieswindon

www.ingramcontent.com/pod-product-compliance
Lightning Source LLC
LaVergne TN
LVHW010306070526
838199LV00065B/5460